Bethany Adams

Abyss
Return of the Elves
by Bethany Adams

Copyright © 2018 Bethany Adams
All rights reserved
ISBN: 978-0-9975320-8-1

First Edition

Edited by Jody Wallace at www.jodywallace.com
Cover art by Eve Milady
Interior design by Gaynor Smith of Indie Books Gone Wild

Published in the United States of America

Acknowledgments

As always, there are so many people I'd like to thank. Forgive me if I miss anyone!

First of all, my family. Thank you to my husband and children for their patience and support. My husband had to bring home a lot of dinners that last week. Thanks, love! And a big thank you to Mom, not only for your love and encouragement but also for the quick read-through. I'm glad you enjoyed it.

Massive thanks to my editor, Jody, and to my critique partners, Shiloh and Catherine. This book would be only a shadow of itself without all of your help. You even listened to my editing angst. Thanks for dealing with my spazziness and for being my friend!

Thank you to Eve Milady for my beautiful covers. Your art is phenomenal. Keep creating! And speaking of beautiful, thank you to Gaynor Smith for such lovely interior formatting. Between you two ladies, my print books are works of art.

A huge thank you to all of my readers! Every message warms my heart. And extra thanks to everyone in my Facebook reader group, The Worlds of Bethany Adams. I appreciate you letting me bounce ideas around and just being there in general. Thank you to Roxana for providing Aris's name and Buffie for helping with Kezari's name. Sorry I had to change the spellings a bit to make the names fit with the rest.

Books by Bethany Adams:

Soulbound
Return of the Elves Book 1

Sundered
Return of the Elves Book 2

Exiled
A Return of the Elves Novella

Seared
Return of the Elves Book 3

To Jason:

I wish you could've read the rest

Prologue

Shudders wracked Aris's body as the blade sliced across his outer thigh. He hissed at the sting, but the pain numbed quickly in the frigid cave. The longer Aris dangled against the icy stone, his arms bound above his head, the more the burn of exposed skin faded. But the cold was not an oversight, nor was it mercy.

Frostbitten skin would be agony to regenerate.

"You have the power to end this."

He squeezed his eyes tight against the sweet, cajoling voice. "No," he managed to gasp through his raw throat.

"Just bond with me," she said, slashing her knife along his side. "That's all it would take. Our souls were made to be together, but your stubbornness keeps us apart."

He didn't bother to answer. If he didn't goad her, she might leave him alone for a while, possibly even lengthen his chains so he wasn't bound so closely to the wall. Sometimes weeks would pass between her torture sessions. She could give him a measure of freedom, even a few small kindnesses. Water to bathe. A walk to the mouth of the cave. If she interpreted his silence as weakening resolve, she would go easier on him.

Maybe.

She removed the blade from his flesh, but he didn't move. "You're no fun today, Aris," she said, a pout to her voice.

Finally, he opened his eyes and glanced at the beautiful woman. Lips pursed, his captor stared at the blood dripping down his body before her gaze captured his. A tremble shook him at the coldness of her eyes, the window to her wicked mind. Her expression never changed. Her soul might be a match to his, but she was twisted inside.

What did that say about him?

She tucked her hair behind her ear, leaving a smear of his blood on the pale strand. "Start the bond, and I will treat you as the king you should be."

Aris held back a snort. She led a small band of outcasts who'd made their home with the dragons, but she certainly wasn't a queen. "Not this day."

Her green eyes narrowed. "Then I'll leave you to the cold."

His captor spun away, and anger rang through her footsteps as she marched from the cave. He slumped against his bonds, a soft groan slipping free despite his resolve. Void take her, he shouldn't have spoken. There would be no small kindnesses now. She would leave him hanging for days, and that was the best-case scenario.

At least she hadn't lowered him into the crevice.

The light that streamed from a hole far above faded until the cave darkened into night. The unrelenting cold numbed the newest cuts but barely slowed the blood flowing from the wounds, and Aris could no longer contain the shivering of his body as he weakened. Maybe he would die this time.

Gods willing.

Then something shifted in the shadows. Had his captor returned? His heart leaped in alarm even as he peered into the darkness. An illusion meant to torture him further? She never arrived in the dark herself— the night was purely for the dragons, and any fae who wandered free risked death. That was their pact. Who would risk coming here?

A small flame sparked to life, and Aris cried out at the unexpected pain that speared his eyes. But he didn't dare to blink. Someone had come, and he wouldn't be caught unawares. As the light moved closer, his vision began to adjust.

He wasn't reassured.

The flame hovering above the woman's palm cast a soft glow across the sharp features of her face. Her golden eyes sparkled vividly as they stared into him, seeming to weigh his soul. Long brown-gold hair flowed around her otherwise naked body. His blood chilled at the blank, unnatural expression of her face. Then her head tilted in an almost birdlike gesture, and clarity hit.

A dragon in the guise of a woman.

"I refuse to wait any longer," she said, her voice resounding oddly through the cave.

His brows wrinkled together. "What?"

"Your mate has delayed me for years, but—"

"I have no mate," he snapped. He couldn't stand the thought of anyone associating him so intimately with his captor. "Certainly not the *drec* who has held me here."

The dragon's uncanny gaze lifted to his wrists, manacled to the stone by thick iron shackles. "Perim said you were training."

Rage heated his insides and caused his muscles to tense. "Is that her name? The blond woman who torments me?"

The dragon tilted her head again. "You've been with your mate for years, and you must ask me this?"

"She. Is. Not. My. Mate."

The flame hovering over the dragon's hand grew brighter. "I see. You are here unwillingly."

"Very," Aris answered, though her words hadn't sounded like a question.

"Then Perim must pay." Her other hand lifted toward his manacles. Power built in the air until every hair on his body stood on end. With a sharp crack, the metal split and fell away, freeing him. "You'll be coming with me."

Aris dropped hard to his knees as feeling roared back into his limbs. Heat washed through him, banishing the earlier cold, and he bit back a yell at the harsh pain. His muscles quaked, but he braced his hand against the floor and shoved himself to his feet. Though he had to lean against the cave wall, he faced the dragon standing.

"Who are you?" he demanded.

"I am Kezari," she answered. "Your dragon."

He shook his head, certain he hadn't heard correctly. "My what?"

"Have your kind forgotten the bond we once shared?"

His stomach lurched at the mention of a bond. "Like a soulbond?"

"Not typically," she answered in a flat tone. "But it has happened. No, I speak of a synthesis of elements. Magic most compatible. I am earth. You are earth."

Aris frowned as he tried to understand her words. He had the feeling that she hadn't been around many people—her grasp of the language was off. "You are here because our elements are compatible?"

"There are more links than soul to soul." Her head tilted again. "You understand this?"

4

Unbidden, Selia's laughing face flickered to life in his memory. Then an image of his son, Iren. His heart twisted at the memory of his family. Gods knew where they were now. "Yes."

"Let us go, then."

Before he had time to consider her words, Kezari stepped back, and the fire winked out. Fear sliced through him like his captor's blade. Had this been some strange trick? A new method to torment him? Power built in the air once more, stronger than before. Aris shrank back against the wall as his head throbbed with the force of the rising energy.

A rough slithering filled the cave. Then a gust of air rushed over him, tossing his sweat-slicked hair around his face. Another flame sprang to life, but it was too far away to hurt his eyes. It glimmered near the far ceiling of the cave—beside the massive golden head of a dragon.

Aris froze like prey at the sight of the huge talons only an arms-length away. As the dragon lifted her claw and rested the tip of a single talon against his chest, Aris forced himself to remain still. If this was how he died, he would greet the moment with courage.

Power roared through him without warning. Thank the gods he'd braced himself against the wall. A slight pain flared across his skin, but the sensation was swept away by the glorious energy filling his depleted body. His muscles strengthened and his mind cleared. For the first time in years, he could detect the life in the cave around him as clearly as his own breath.

Then it was done.

The flame above Kezari's head brightened, and he felt the surge of power in his own blood. She'd linked them. Bile rose up the back of his throat. Aris dug his fingers into his palms and breathed through his nose before he vomited. Linked against his will. The dragon was as bad as his captor.

"Leave me alone," he rasped.

Kezari's wedge-shaped head lowered until all he could see was her golden eyes. *"You are distressed,"* she said into his mind.

"You stole my choice."

"I offer freedom." Her heated breath warmed the rock behind him. *"You were too weak to choose. Once a cycle of the moons has passed, you may sever the link. If you wish."*

Aris studied the dragon's face, but he couldn't tell if she was lying. Her slit pupils focused, unwavering, on him. In fact, the only movement came from her nostrils as she breathed. Then she tilted her head, much as she had in her elven form, and he caught a hint of uncertainty.

"The war between our peoples was millennia ago. Do you still hold animosity?"

Aris frowned. *"Of course not."*

"Only elves who link with a dragon may ride one." Her long neck arched upward as she pulled her head back. *"Do you want to live? I can take you from this place."*

He swallowed at the thought. Freedom. He'd believed he would die here once his captor grew tired of trying to force their soulbond. How many years had passed? Four? Six? He'd tried to keep count of the days, but he'd lost more than a few to unconsciousness. His people probably thought he was dead. Selia would have moved on, and his own son would barely remember him.

Worse, he was damaged. Broken.

"Do not cast aside the millennia of life you could have because of your torment." Smoke puffed from between Kezari's lips. *"Perim is not worth it. And we can do great things, you and I."*

Aris held the dragon's steady gaze. He didn't trust her, but he no longer trusted anyone. What did he have to lose? Better if Kezari

killed him than his wicked potential soulbonded. Dragons were typically straightforward creatures, so the former would be a quicker death than the latter. And if his soul was twisted like Perim's, Kezari would know. She could end him before he caused harm.

He took a deep breath and nodded. "Then let's go."

Kezari circled the village stretched out along the coast below, descending gently to avoid upsetting Aris as he clung to her back. Though it was night, she could identify each stone dwelling with ease. More buildings had fallen into disrepair since she'd last flown by, though it had only been a year. The once-proud population of fae, descendants of the dragons' riders during the war with the elves almost forty thousand years prior, continued to dwindle.

No wonder Perim wanted to gain her freedom from the island.

But the fae woman had gone too far. It was one thing to interrupt council meetings to demand redress from the queen—that had earned Perim a month's imprisonment a few decades ago—but something else entirely to torture a dragon's *skizik* under the guise of training. Of course, Kezari had allowed herself to be fooled. She swallowed down the acrid taste of flame rising up the back of her throat at that reminder.

Perim would pay.

Kezari glided lower, though she wanted to dive as though catching prey. Even at this slow pace, Aris's arms tightened around the base of her neck, and his legs dug his saddle into her shoulders. She couldn't risk tipping him into madness by hasty actions.

But finally, she hovered near the house she sought. Her wingbeats resounded around them, echoing off walls and rattling

glass windowpanes. Kezari cried out, a shriek of challenge, and blasted a stream of flame just above the tile roof. It was a traditional summons, though one never given at night when the fae remained indoors.

"I smell Perim," Kezari said into Aris's mind. *"Is it a remnant, or do you sense her presence?"*

Aris trembled against her, and his mental voice was a faint whisper. *"I feel her near."*

She hadn't wanted to risk the reminder, but she had to be certain. She shrieked again, more loudly now that her target was certain. They ignored her at their peril.

One of the windows lifted, and a man gaped at her through the opening. "My lady?"

"Send forth Perim," she sent into his mind.

His expression shuttered. "She is not here."

He dared to lie? Kezari shot a stream of flame high into the sky. *"Then she breaks the law by wandering in the night?"*

"No. I didn't mean…" the man stuttered.

"I will have justice." Kezari lowered her head until the smoke from her nostrils curled through the open window. *"Send her out, or I will melt this rock into a puddle of lava."*

A deep, harsh scream echoed from the other side of the village as another dragon plunged from the sky. Tebzn. What was she doing here? Kezari whipped her head around and hissed as her cousin hovered a neck's length away, her forearms lifted in challenge.

"This is beyond the bounds of law," Tebzn snarled in their tongue, too high-pitched for the fae to easily discern.

"Perim tortured my *skizik*." Kezari gnashed her teeth. "She will pay."

Her cousin's claws lowered. "If that is the case, then justice will be delivered. But not now. The fae are to remain undisturbed in their homes at night."

"Tebzn—"

A cry from the window interrupted her cousin's words. "What have you done to my bonded?"

Perim. Steam poured from Kezari's nostrils as she focused on the wretched woman. *"I have saved him from you. Come out and face me."*

Tears leaked from Perim's eyes as she peered out the window, the man no longer in sight. Her guileless expression might have fooled Kezari under different circumstances, but not after finding Aris chained and bleeding. Not after connecting to him and examining his memories.

"You must return my bonded to my care," Perim said, her voice shaky.

A clever ploy, but a wasted effort.

Unfortunately, Perim's demand proved too much for Aris. Though only a shadow in Aris's mind, Kezari felt the exact moment his hold on reality shattered. His unending mental scream filled her own head until she sent him hurtling into sleep with a quick spell. Another flex of power ensured he would not topple from the saddle, but she could only hold this spell for so long. She had to get him away from here.

Kezari pinned Tebzn with her gaze. "She lies."

"Regardless, we do have laws."

Without warning, Kezari sent a single memory of Aris's torture into her cousin's mind. Tebzn reared back, her wingbeats faltering before she recovered control. "As you can see, I speak the truth."

"In the morning, we can haul Perim before the queen," Tebzn answered.

"I must get my *skizik* out of here now." Kezari's nostrils flared. "Now. His mental health is fragile."

Below, Perim let out a sob. "You cannot take my soulbonded."

Neither dragon answered her.

"Go," Tebzn said to Kezari. "I will ensure that justice is served."

Through her connection to Aris, Kezari detected his thoughts beginning to stir. She had to get him somewhere alone. "See that you do," she conceded. "I will check with you soon."

Perim's shriek sounded below as Kezari propelled herself into the sky, faster than she would dare with Aris awake. There was a small, abandoned island a short flight away. She could take her *skizik* there. And she would do her best to help him heal.

1

Selia opened the door to her son's room and sighed to see him awake, still curled up in his favorite reading chair. Iren startled, slamming his book closed and jumping to his feet with a guilty expression pinching his face. But his contrition faded quickly. As he placed the book on a side table, he tried for an innocent grin.

"I just wanted to get to a stopping point."

"Bed," Selia said with an impatient gesture. "Now."

Huffing, he trudged across the floor. "*You* stay up late reading sometimes."

She couldn't help but smile at that truth. "And I usually pay for it. You're sharing a magic lesson with Arlyn tomorrow, and I want to be certain you are rested and focused."

Iren paused beside his bed. "I thought she was traveling with Kai."

"They leave again tomorrow evening."

Her son crawled beneath the covers, and Selia resisted the urge to tuck them up around his shoulders and smooth his hair. At eleven, he had become resistant to such shows of affection. All too soon, he would be a man grown, and even these moments would end. A point she reminded herself of when he was being particularly difficult.

"I guess you and my father weren't soulbonded like Kai and Arlyn," Iren said sleepily. "The bonded couples here seem to travel together all the time, but you and *Onaial* didn't."

Selia froze at the unexpected comment. Even after seven years, the loss of her beloved cut deeply. "Our lack of bond had nothing to do with that. Your father traveled to wild places, and I had students to train besides."

Iren twisted the blanket between his fingers. "Do you think you have a soulbonded out there somewhere? I hate to think you're lonely. I thought about asking Eri, but it didn't seem right."

"Do not bother your friend about such things," Selia said, a bit more sharply than she'd intended. She didn't like to think about her possible soulbonded. "She might be a seer, but she's still younger than you are. If you want to be her friend, you'll not ask about the future."

Iren nodded. "I kind of thought that, too."

"About the possibility of a soulbond..." Selia took a deep breath. "I don't think about it. I loved your father dearly, bond or no. I'm not certain when I'll be ready for another relationship."

"I understand," Iren said.

Unable to resist, she pushed a strand of his light brown hair out of his eyes. "What has you thinking about this, beloved?"

Iren nibbled at his lip. "I don't want you to be unhappy."

"I'm not," Selia said firmly, although she wasn't certain it was true. An uneasiness had been growing inside her, a feeling closer to glum loneliness than she wanted to admit. But overall, she was content. Wasn't she? "Moving to Braelyn was an adjustment, but I enjoy my work. Are you homesick?"

She and Iren had lived at her father's estate, Fiorn, until she had accepted the role of teacher for Lord Lyr's newfound adult daughter, Arlyn. Iren had struggled at first, but Selia had thought her son was happy here, especially once he'd befriended young Eri. Maybe she was mistaken? Worried, she studied her son's frowning face.

"Why would I be?" Iren asked. "I don't get lectured here."

Selia laughed at that. "I know your grandfather is gruff, but surely you miss your Aunt Niasen."

"Sure," he said. Then he shrugged. "But she's the heir. I could visit through the portal and see her just as often." Iren tugged the blanket close to his chin, his eyes growing heavy. "I like it here. I want you to like it, too. You find a soulbonded, maybe we can stay."

His words trailed off as his eyelids slid closed. Smiling softly, Selia waited until his breathing slowed and his body went lax before she dropped a kiss on his forehead. So he wanted to stay here at Braelyn, did he? As she slipped out of his room and down the stairs curling around a broad tree trunk, she could understand why. The plains of Fiorn were beautiful, but the forests and mountains of Braelyn held their own unique power.

At the bottom of the stairs, Selia glanced across the entryway at the massive side of Eradisel, one of the nine sacred trees. Perhaps it was the tree's influence. Fiorn did not house one of the nine, but Braelyn was built around the very trunk. Lord Lyr, Myern of the Callian branch, guarded the sacred tree and the priests who tended her. Her power permeated everything.

Selia found herself stepping closer to the tree as though she were being pulled. Did Eradisel wish to communicate? Only once, when she and Iren had first arrived, had the tree spoken to her. Well, sent feelings of joy and welcome more than words, but it was communication nonetheless.

When Selia was close enough, she extended her hand, palm outward, until she could almost touch the bark. Then she waited. A sense of peace filled her a moment before the tree's thoughts flowed in, more concept than true words. *Prepare yourself. They come.*

Selia jerked back, stumbling slightly with the motion. The image had been vague and blurred, but she'd discerned the form of a dragon and rider gliding across the mountains to the east. That couldn't be good. Dragons had originally shared territory with the elves after their migration from Earth to Moranaia, but after a long, brutal war, the dragons had retreated to an island on the other side of the world, too far away for the mostly land-locked elves to reach. They'd only taken a few of their fae allies with them.

Why would they return after millennia of peace? The elves hadn't had contact with the dragons for so long that few if any people had even seen one. She hoped war wasn't brewing, but Eradisel's warning to prepare didn't bode well. Still, it didn't make sense. Lyr was lord of this estate. If there was danger of war, wouldn't the tree have told him instead?

Selia spun away and strode across the entryway, sending her mind out in a sweep to try to locate Lyr. She found his energy in his study, as she'd expected, and headed that way even as she gave him a gentle mental nudge. Her steps rang out on the wooden floor as she waited for him to connect.

He completed the mental link almost immediately. *"Good day to you, Selia."*

"Good day. Please forgive me for interrupting your work," she sent back. *"I hope I have not caused undue disturbance."*

"Of course not," Lyr answered. Not that he would be so impolite as to say otherwise. *"Is all well?"*

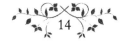

14

"I believe so." She took a deep breath. *"Eradisel provided me a vision. I am near your study and would like to discuss it, but I thought it best to ensure you were available."*

"I am. Come straight in."

When Selia pushed through the door and stepped into the long oval room, Lyr already waited, leaning against the edge of his desk. She glanced around, but aside from a pair of people beyond the large windows, she saw no one else near. Not even his soulbonded, Meli, who often read in one of the chairs situated in the center of the room.

Good. She had a feeling her vision didn't need to be general knowledge.

"Thank you for seeing me so quickly," Selia said.

"It is truly no trouble." A slight smile crossed Lyr's face though he stood with crossed arms. "You needn't have been so formal, you know. I'm getting used to disruptions. *Clechtan,* but Ralan has practically made it a hobby."

Her cheeks warmed. "He's the prince. The king's own heir."

"He's something," Lyr muttered, though affection colored his tone. "Please, sit."

Selia hesitated only the briefest moment before settling into one of the center seats. Maybe someday she could be as casual as Lyr, but the informality here had been a difficult adjustment after Fiorn. She had never enjoyed her father's stern, cold household, but she still struggled to slip free from the hold of her early training.

Lyr sat across from her, brow furrowing as he focused on her face. "Am I to assume the vision was a bad one?"

"I'm not certain," Selia admitted. "Eradisel said only to prepare myself. They come. I caught a vague image of a dragon and rider flying over the mountains. I'd guess from the look of the area that it's the eastern side of this mountain range."

"A fair distance if we weren't talking about a dragon." Lyr's fingers whitened around the chair's armrests. "This doesn't bode well."

Selia shook her head. "No. But why did Eradisel warn me? She said 'Prepare yourself' not your*selves*. There must be something I'm supposed to do."

"Do you have spells for dragon containment?"

Selia considered her options. She knew a fair number of pre-set spells, enchantments prepared in advance for easy use, but none of those had been designed with dragons in mind. However, she was adept enough at magical containment. Given a bit of time, she should be able to devise something suitable.

"I can come up with something." She glanced at the water clock on the wall and sighed. "Even if I must sacrifice sleep. But do you think containment is wise? If the dragon comes in peace, using magic against them could cause more harm than good."

Lyr nodded. "I wouldn't do so unless necessary. But after all that has happened over the last few months, I automatically prepare for trouble."

Selia winced in commiseration. When she and Iren had first arrived, one of the lords under Lyr's command had been trying to kill him. No sooner had that threat been ended than exiled prince Kien had attempted to send more assassins through the portal between Moranaia and Earth. Prince Ralan had finally defeated his evil brother a couple of weeks ago, and none of them had settled into the apparent peace.

Perhaps that was a good thing.

"I understand," Selia said. "I hope we're concerned for nothing. Eradisel might have wanted to keep us from acting rashly when the dragon arrives. After all, neither Ralan nor Eri have warned us of danger. Surely one of them would've had a vision."

Lyr's gaze flicked to the door. "I suppose we'll know it's bad if Ralan bursts into my study without knocking."

Selia half-expected him to do so, but after a few moments of silence, she chuckled. "Guess we're on our own."

"It appears so," Lyr answered with a grin. "I'll have the *Taysonal* standing guard in the trees pay close attention to the skies, and I'll contact some of the estates to the east for news. My House was the diplomatic liaison with the queen during the dragons' time here. If they seek to contact the current monarch, it makes sense that they would come here first."

Selia stood, smoothing the fabric of her long gown. "I'll work on a containment spell just in case. Do you think we should be concerned about the harvest festival? I could contact my sister and see if she would send extra mages so that you don't have to ask my father. As his heir, she has the authority."

"That's a good possibility." Lyr pushed to his feet and started toward his desk. "We have four days until the festival. I'll see what Lady Imai to the east has to report. As the duchess just above me, she has a good portion of the eastern coast under her command. If the dragon and rider have made it that far, she will know. It's possible your vision hasn't happened yet."

"That is true," Selia said, considering. "I didn't get a strong sense of time beyond *soon*. Perhaps you'll learn more details on this situation from Lady Imai. And I'll report back once I've completed my own work."

After a quick detour to her room to grab her cloak, Selia headed out the back door and into the chilly gardens. It was almost the end of the month of Eln, which marked the middle point of autumn, and the promise of winter blew in with the nighttime breeze. She tucked the warm cloak tightly around herself and marched along the

path toward the magic workroom at the bottom of one of the outside towers. Fiorn rarely grew colder than this at any time of year, and she'd first arrived at Braelyn during the summer. None of her other teaching assignments had been in places with deep winters, either.

Walking to lessons would be much more unpleasant in the snow, but such was life.

As soon as she entered the workroom, she adjusted the cooling spell to warmth. Some days, like this one, were still hot when the sun was out, so the room needed cooling during the afternoon. Fortunately, it only took moments for the magic to work. By the time she hung up her cloak and seated herself on one of the cushions in the center of the room, the temperature had grown comfortable. Thank the gods for the long-dead elf who had first designed the enchantment.

Now it was time to design one of her own.

In the sky, Aris could almost forget the fractured mess of his life. The wind tugged at his hair, pulling strands across his eyes, but the power of it was more relief than annoyance after being confined for so long inside a cave. Far below, the mountains rolled by, the peaks growing gentler the farther west they traveled. His life was nothing compared to this ancient range. A single drop in the endless measure of time.

Thousands of heartbeats thrummed in his own blood as his magic connected with the creatures below. Stone held no interest for Aris, but animals and plants were altogether different. He could sense living things and even link with them to varying degrees. If he wanted to, he could manipulate and change them—or snuff out their spirit if they proved to be a threat. During his capture, the spells somehow worked into the iron shackles had cut him off from the life he'd always felt around him. Isolation of the worst sort.

"How much longer?" he sent to Kezari.

"We should arrive by the sun's zenith."

Aris studied the golden scales on her long neck. The light struck them, making them glow amber in the sun. With each wingbeat echoing through the air, her shoulder muscles shifted beneath him, but she peered ahead with no sign of effort or concern. As far as he could tell, in any case. Every once in a while, she turned her head enough to check on him, but he had no idea how to gauge a dragon's facial expressions.

Perhaps he would learn during the next month—if he made it that long. How simple would it be to shove himself free of the dragon's back? No healer would be able to save him from such a fall, and his torment would be over. They'd already lost a week to his madness. Kezari had taken him to a small isolated island, working with him until he'd returned to himself. Or as close to himself as he would ever be again.

Before they'd left the island, Kezari had told him that she had to travel to Braelyn to speak to the lord or lady currently in charge there. She claimed to need Aris's aid. Was she worried that the elves would hurt her? Although their peoples had remained separate for millennia, there was a peace treaty. She didn't need Aris to make it through. In his current state, he could only be a liability.

His gaze flicked to the ground so far below. A tempting release, but no. He was unlikely to hold onto his sanity for a month, but he could ensure that his rescuer reached her destination. She might not be harmed, but a guide would make the journey easier. He owed the dragon a few more days at the least.

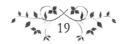

Then he could end his torment for good.

He gave Kezari's neck a pat to catch her attention. *"What message is so urgent that you rush to Braelyn?"*

"Can you not feel it?"

"Feel what?" Aris asked with a frown.

"The Earth weeps. The energy seeps."

He glanced past the dragon's shoulder at the ground. All seemed well to both his eyes and his magic. *"I don't understand."*

"Not Moranaia," she said. *"You do not explore our link. Join with me and know the Earth as I know your animals and plants. This will tell you."*

His muscles seized at the suggestion, and he tightened his legs reflexively on the small saddle Kezari had conjured. Explore their link? This wasn't the first time she'd implored him to do so, but each time the thought of being bound to another made him want to vomit. He shoved the knowledge of their connection to the back of his mind as he had when she'd mentioned it before. No way he could access a link. No.

"It is not a soulbond. I am not Perim."

Bile scalded his throat at the name. *"It doesn't matter."*

"We will need to link," Kezari said, her tone implacable. *"But you have time yet."*

"You should have found someone else," he muttered aloud.

Although the wind whipped his words away, she still heard. *"That is not how this works,* skizik. *Your kind has forgotten the closeness we once shared."*

"I was taught that the dragons began the war when we would not yield the portal to their control. And they wanted too much land."

Kezari huffed, and smoke whirled from her mouth and nose. *"Convenient. There was wrong on both sides, I will allow. However, keeping the portal from our control was foolish. We are still bound to the Earth. The elves are not."*

Aris smiled at the indignation in her tone. *"The Veil leads to more places than Earth."*

"Irrelevant." Her wings beat harder. *"This is a useless discussion."*

"I don't think so, but if you want to drop it, I'll grant you the same grace you do me," Aris said. *"I take it your link with Earth has revealed something dire?"*

"Yes." A pause. *"We are essential. I can alter stone and mud. You can help the life of Earth. Together, we may fix. A mage would help, but Baza refused to leave the island. Useless reptile."*

Aris shook his head. Even in her dragon form, Kezari's body emitted warmth. He wouldn't classify dragons as mammals, but they were warm-blooded, more like birds that had scales instead of feathers. The best he could tell, dragons used the association with reptiles as an insult. The gleaming blue dragon he'd seen in her thoughts had earned Kezari's rancor. If they'd been friends, they weren't any longer.

"Perhaps an elven mage would help. My wife…" The mental image of Selia's face sent a wave of pain through him until he clenched his fingers around the saddle. His weak left arm protested the strength of his grip, but the ache was an effective distraction. *"You'll be able to find help, I'm certain."*

Kezari turned her head, her gaze fastening on his face for a moment before returning to the skies. *"I thought you were unmated."*

"I was married before my capture." Aris closed his eyes and let the wind wash around him. *"I have no doubt she has chosen another after so much time."*

"I am sorry, skizik," Kezari said. *"I will rend Perim myself. There are ways to prolong the pain so that—"*

"If you manage to find her, kill her quickly." Aris shuddered. *"I'll have no part in torture. Neither of us should be like her."*

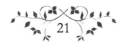

"If you insist," Kezari answered placidly.

Aris wasn't certain he believed her easy acquiescence, but he didn't want to dwell on it. He didn't want to dwell on anything, really. As the mountains rolled by, he tried not to imagine what would happen when they reached Braelyn—and not because of the dragon. He'd learned from Kezari that seven years had passed since he'd left home. Seven years without seeing any of his own people. But he didn't want to be around any of them now.

He could only hope that no one would try to confine him. Losing control around Kezari was bad enough, but doing so in front of some of the most important people in Moranaia would certainly lead to disaster. Especially after arriving on a dragon. Then again, it might be a quick way to die. The *Taysonal* guarding Braelyn would be skilled and efficient archers. An arrow to the eye and—

Kezari's voice cut sharply across his mind. *"No. Die and I go with you. We are linked this cycle of the moons. Longer, if we should decide such."*

"A soulbonded often survives the death of his or her mate unless the bond is incomplete," Aris argued. *"Why couldn't you?"*

"As I've said before, this is not a soulbond." The dragon's wings snapped sharply with each beat. *"Live out this cycle or kill us both."*

His body shook with the helpless anger her words brought. Days. He'd planned to give her a few days. *"Why not break the link now?"*

"I cannot," she said. *"Only the moons' full turning brings the time of choice."*

"Choice," he snarled aloud.

She'd taken away his final and best escape from this hell. Consigned him to suffer through this nightmare of a life for another twenty days when he hadn't been certain he could even make it to Braelyn. His fingers quivered around the edge of the saddle as

darkness teased the edges of his vision. *Control yourself. Control this.* He'd survived years of torment. He could last a month to save Kezari.

"We'd better be camping in the woods," Aris sent. *"I am uncertain how much I can handle."*

Her lack of response was no reassurance.

2

Selia spun the glowing ball with a quick thought, examining each side of the enchantment. She'd started with a spell she'd learned for subduing the wild plains cats, but that was far from strong enough to contain a being as powerful as a dragon. She'd added enchantments designed to nullify magical talents and immobilize powerful prisoners. What else might the spell need?

After searching through her mental catalogue of prepared spells, Selia grasped a sleep spell and cobbled it carefully onto the ball. On a creature with the size and strength of a dragon, it was unlikely to work as intended, but it might provide drowsiness or dulled senses. If she had to use this spell, they'd need all the help they could get.

Another mark passed before she was satisfied with her work. Swiping away the sheen of sweat from her forehead, Selia settled the enchantment into a neat mental compartment. She would only need to trigger the symbols of power to release the spell when necessary. Whether it would work on a dragon was anyone's guess. She had been well-trained, but not even the most conscientious teacher had thought to prepare for something like this.

They'd been at peace with the dragons for almost forty thousand years, after all.

Selia slumped, glancing at the water clock with a frown. After all of her fussing at Iren, here she was, awake at the twenty-fifth mark. In five more marks, it would be dawn. Well, at least her lesson with Arlyn and Iren didn't begin right at dawn. If she went to bed immediately, she could get the rest needed to handle two inexperienced students.

She shoved to her feet and grabbed her cloak from its hook before heading back out into the gardens. The second moon was near to setting, so the forest had gone dark. Only a few dim mage lights illuminated the trails as she returned to the main part of the estate. Cold rushed around her, and she huddled more deeply into her cloak.

With the hour so late, a guard stood sentry at the back door. Ah, Febith. He smiled and nodded, a gleam of attraction in his eyes, but Selia only gave a polite smile and nod in return as she hurried inside. She didn't know him well, and she hadn't been able to summon any interest during their few exchanges. She might never be ready for a relationship, at least not for a few more decades, and she didn't want to give a false hope.

She wouldn't risk hurting someone the way she'd hurt Aris.

Selia tried to bury that thought the way she had for the last couple of years, but Iren's earlier words haunted her. Her son would never say so, but she could tell that he missed having a father. Some day he would want to know more about what had happened with Aris, and she would have to confess the truth.

Iren's father might still be alive if not for her.

Her beloved had had a wild, free spirit, perhaps because of his link with nature. He'd been an explorer before they'd met

and remained an explorer after. Selia hadn't begrudged him his expeditions, even when they'd lasted months at a time. Those trips were essential for his soul, and she'd had her own work as a magic teacher. She'd missed him, of course, and she had worried, since there was a fair bit of danger in the unexplored parts of Moranaia, but few had the talent and desire to uncover the secrets of their world the way Aris had. Over the centuries, he'd discovered and catalogued several species of plants and animals. Some of the maps their people used bore his signature.

Then Iren had been born. Aris had been happy to stay close during the early years, but around their son's fourth birthday, the first of the great ocean ships had been completed. He'd been invited to go on the initial voyage, a month-long journey to test the ship, and for days, they'd debated what he should do. Her beloved had wanted to remain behind with his family, but Selia had seen the tension radiating through him, that drive to explore that often came upon him.

And she understood it. Despite tens of thousands of years on this planet, her people had still barely explored a quarter of the world. They reproduced so slowly that it had taken millennia before the Moranaians had settled throughout the more habitable regions of the continent where they'd emerged. Only then had they looked toward the oceans and given real effort toward crossing. But they were not natural sailors, and the sea was too rough for fishing boats. Their new ships were revolutionary. Of course Aris had wanted to go.

So she'd talked him into the journey he'd decided against.

When a storm blew up unexpectedly, the vessel had been dashed on one of the western islands, leaving only two survivors. Aris hadn't been one of them. How could she tell Iren that his father wouldn't

have been on that voyage if not for her? The accident itself had been out of her control, it was true, but she couldn't help feeling responsible. Even after all this time.

Drooping with weariness, Selia pushed into her room and flung her cloak across a chair. She would pick it up in the morning—hopefully before Iren noticed her carelessness and used it as an excuse to clutter his own room. Right now, she needed rest. Maybe sleep would give her the strength to rebury the past.

There was nowhere to go but forward.

"If you insist on coming with me, then you'll have to wear clothes," Aris said.

Kezari's head tilted. "Elves are not ashamed of their bodies. Or they once were not."

"It isn't shame." Or for most, it wasn't. If he considered the question for himself, his mind might fracture. Again. "In this weather, a naked woman would cause as much comment as a dragon. And as much as I appreciate the care you have given me, I would like to eat something not roasted by your breath. I'll go alone if you don't create yourself some clothes."

Her hair rippled as she shifted her shoulders in a motion almost like a shrug. "Very well."

Aris glanced away as power glowed around her, then checked her appearance once the light settled. A thin sleeveless dress flowed around her, beautiful but insufficient for the weather. "Kezari…"

"I cannot bear much in the way of bindings," she said. "I produce too much heat."

He winced at her choice of words but forced his mind away from the images that *bindings* had evoked. Not now. *Not now.* "It'll do," he answered. Better to get on with their tasks than to think. "No stranger than I look, I imagine."

The long-sleeved tunic and cloak Kezari had made for him didn't match the pants he'd found in the cave, and they no doubt resembled nothing in current Moranaian fashion. His ancestors might have worn something in this cut and fabric—if a dragon had designed it. Severe, almost scale-like... Between his clothes and her dress, he and Kezari were certain to draw notice.

Well, nothing for it.

They'd landed a fair distance from the village huddled in a small valley, so it was a long, chilly walk to find the tavern likely to be in the center. Though the cold increased the ache in his already sore muscles, Aris didn't pull his cloak tight. Nothing tight. He'd experienced worse conditions over the years, before and after capture. Kezari appeared unbothered by the weather, but he'd come to realize that she didn't always show what she felt. She might be able to shapeshift, but she hadn't yet learned the non-verbal expressions that he took for granted.

The late time meant few people wandered the trails even in the center of town. Those who did invariably stopped to stare, but Aris ignored their rudeness. Their opinions meant nothing. So long as he and Kezari didn't draw enough attention to get the local lord or lady involved, he didn't care. The dragon had her own goals, but for himself? He wanted a solid meal and a set of clothes created by elven hands. It was the least he deserved for agreeing to this mad journey to Braelyn.

Only two of the ten tables were occupied in the tavern Aris found. Four pairs of eyes turned his way as the door swung shut

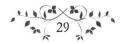

behind him, and he scanned each face for signs of hostility or danger. He found only surprise and curiosity. After a few heartbeats and a sound from the barkeeper at the back, the four returned their attention to their drinks.

Aris skirted around them, careful to remain out of reach, and settled at a table in the far corner. Though he was able to sit with his back to the wall with the door in sight, a sheen of sweat broke out on his forehead at being enclosed, even in a building. He'd hoped an elven-made structure would be different. But no. He swallowed down the rising bile and took steady breaths until the feeling passed.

Then the woman appeared.

He barely heard Kezari settle into the chair beside him. The scrape of wood against floor was drowned out by his heartbeat as the pale-haired female approached from an archway in the other corner. Nothing about her was threatening. Her face held a friendly smile, and she weaved her way jauntily through the tables. The energy flowing from her was open and kind. But that white-blond hair...

As his vision began to gray around the edges, Kezari's warm fingers wrapped around his wrist. "It is not Perim."

"I know," he whispered. "But she's still free. Maybe tracking me. What if—"

"I would detect her, *skizik*." Heat surged from Kezari's hand, shocking him abruptly from his panic. "My cousin hunts her while we seek the leader of Braelyn. Justice will be served by claw or tooth."

She'd said so before, but her assertion did nothing to ease his fear.

Shame flooded him until he averted his face from the dragon's astute regard. He would never be whole again. If he couldn't even go into a blasted tavern, how could he survive for another month? It was impossible.

What did any of it matter, anyway? It wasn't like he could return to his family if he did prevail over his inner turmoil. Selia had surely remarried. So many had died in the shipwreck that had sent him drifting on the sea that he would have been counted in their number, especially after his long absence. It was better not to bring chaos and conflict to her current life or that of his son.

Better for Aris to *be* dead than that.

"Good day to you," a cheerful female voice said, but Aris didn't glance up. He couldn't. "What may I get for you?"

"I will have only roasted meat," Kezari said. "He will have a variety of other elven foodstuffs."

Unexpectedly, Aris found himself stifling a laugh. A laugh, of all things. They'd better eat and go, for there was no way the local authorities wouldn't be contacted at this rate. When the silence began to stretch, he risked a look up at the woman. Her befuddled stare shifted between Kezari and him.

"Elven foodstuffs?" she asked slowly.

Aris focused on her eyes—brown, not green—and tried to ignore her pale hair. "Please forgive my friend. She is not from Moranaia. I'll take whatever warm meal you have available. She meant to say that I'm not picky."

The woman relaxed, and her smile returned. "It's getting late, but there's still plenty of stew. I'll need to see about the roasted meat."

As the serving woman headed back toward the kitchen, Aris slumped in his seat. This had been a terrible idea. He'd considered camping in the forest beyond the village for the rest of the night, but after the disaster of this trip, it would be better if they moved on at once. In such a small village, their oddness would not go unremarked for long. And it was a small step from being noticed to being challenged by the guards.

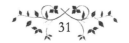

Perhaps he and Kezari could camp on a distant mountain. A *very* distant mountain.

Thankfully, the tavern keeper had a portion of roasted *daeri* left over from the evening meal, so both Aris and Kezari were able to eat. Aris kept his head down, trying to savor the stew but ultimately shoveling it in as though he'd just returned from a long mission to the southern desert. A simple stew had never tasted so divine.

As they stood, Kezari dropped two valuable gems, sought after for their rainbow hues and durability, on the tabletop. He lifted a brow. "Food does not cost that much."

She frowned. "One should always pay well for excellent nourishment."

With a shake of his head, Aris pressed one of the gems back into her palm. Even one was excessive, but he had a feeling she wouldn't take both. "Fine. Let's go."

Because once the serving lady found the treasure, the rumors about him and Kezari would grow exponentially.

They reached the exit before the woman hailed them. "Milord. Milady. This is too—"

"Please keep it," Aris interrupted before she could mention the value of the jewel. Best if the other patrons didn't overhear the woman's good fortune. "Your kindness is well appreciated."

He urged Kezari out the door before he received an answer.

A few marks later, Kezari circled a remote portion of the mountains and then landed in a large clearing. Tiny flakes of snow drifted around them, tossed from the clouds by the cold air, but the ground wasn't yet cool enough even at this elevation for the flakes to stick. Miserable regardless, but he'd faced worse.

"I'll gather wood for a fire," he said.

"No need." Kezari nodded her wedge-shaped head toward the nearby line of trees. *"Let's settle by the forest. If you sleep against me, you'll be more than warm enough."*

The ground vibrated beneath his feet from the weight of her steps as Aris followed the dragon to the tree line. She curled up beneath a large tree, the branches still holding enough leaves to block some of the snow. After a brief hesitation, he settled in the space between her foreleg and chest, and sure enough, blessed warmth suffused him, easing the ever-present ache in his body. She curved her wing in front of him, enough to block the wind but not confine.

He couldn't quite relax, but he wasn't panicking, either.

Aris tipped his head back against her chest. There was much he didn't understand and even more he wasn't sure he wanted to know. But if he closed his eyes, he would be back in the cave, tormented once more. He gripped his knees until his hands stopped shaking. Asking Kezari questions could prove painful, but it was also a needed distraction.

"Tell me about the mark on my chest. About being a *skizik*. I'm not even sure what the word means."

"Ah, yes." Kezari turned her face toward the forest, though her mental voice sounded thoughtful more than upset. *"Long ago, dragons recruited helpers. We are elemental, more so than your kind, but our elements are frequently…incomplete. A* skizik *is the other portion of the element, one you've joined magics with. It requires no mating or soulbond, but you do have to merge minds and powers."*

He frowned at her explanation. "It makes no sense for your kind to be reliant on elves for complete powers."

Kezari's eye pinned him again. *"I did not say we were. A* skizik *can be another dragon. However, around the time of the war, no small number were*

elves or fae. We began to mark our non-dragon allies lest they be confused in battle. The tradition remains."

"This is madness, Kezari. You know that, right?" Aris heaved a sigh. "I almost lost control ordering food in a tavern, and you want to merge minds with me. There must be another who could become your *skizik*."

Her answer was a few moments in coming, and her voice was thoughtful when it did. *"Compatibility is not always so easy. But even if we didn't have to wait for the moons to be full to break the link, I would not. I like you."*

He snorted. He wasn't particularly fond of himself right now, but a dragon had decided she liked him? Nonsensical. "Perhaps you are as crazy as I am."

"You are not crazy." A puff of smoke escaped her nostrils. *"There is greatness in you, Aris, but you'll have to forgive yourself before you find it. Give yourself a chance to heal."*

"Sure."

He fell silent, considering her words. She believed he'd recover, but she couldn't know the extent of his wounds. He could give her what she wanted and fully link—his memories would disillusion her quickly. But he refused to inflict that on Kezari, especially after all she'd done to help.

That kind of pain should die with him.

Aris closed his eyes and shifted against her smooth scales. "Help me sleep? I need rest if we're to reach Braelyn tomorrow, but the dreams…"

"Of course, skizik,*"* she answered, her voice echoing in his mind as he drifted toward oblivion.

3

Selia noticed the exact moment Arlyn faltered. Unfortunately, so did Iren. As Arlyn lost her grip on the group shield they'd all been holding, Iren sent his own energy forward to try to fill in the lack. But he overestimated, unbalancing the half-globe of power shimmering around them. Selia steadied the spell and then dispersed it safely. The hazy room beyond the shield came back into focus as the magic disappeared from around them.

"I was just trying to help," Iren said in a rush.

Selia nodded. "I know. It was a good instinct, but this type of work takes a light, steady touch. It was a shield of illusion only."

"I'm sorry," Arlyn said, her face almost as red as her hair. "I'm not feeling myself this morning."

Selia peered at her student. Before embarrassment had blushed her skin, Arlyn had looked a bit wan. Selia had assumed she was nervous about training with Iren. Although Arlyn was grown, she had lived most of her life on Earth and hadn't reached Moranaia until a few months ago. She'd barely started her magical training.

Iren had a great deal more experience despite the gap in years. But she hadn't mentioned that. Perhaps she was ill.

"Do you need to go see the healer?"

One corner of Arlyn's mouth tipped up. "No. I've seen him about this. There's not much for him to do about my condition."

Arlyn's expression had Selia lifting her brows. Her condition, hmm? "You're pregnant!"

Iren's mouth fell open, but Arlyn chuckled as Selia lifted her hands to her own burning cheeks. "And now I am embarrassed," Selia said. "Please forgive my lack of courtesy. I should not have blurted such a supposition, especially since we are not alone."

Arlyn grinned. "You know I'm not formal, and I'd like to think we're friends."

"Of course," Selia answered. "Still…"

"Don't worry about it. Seriously." Arlyn glanced at Iren's stunned face. "I should have mentioned it outright, but I wasn't certain if I should with a child present."

Iren rolled his eyes at that. "I'm eleven years old. Why wouldn't I know all about babies?"

"Customs vary," Arlyn answered with a shrug. "Just please don't tell my father. I…maybe haven't mentioned it to him yet."

Oh, that couldn't be good. Were Arlyn and Lyr fighting? They hadn't seemed to be at odds, but one never knew. "Might I ask why not?" Selia ventured.

"I'm a chicken."

Selia blinked, not certain she'd heard correctly. "A…what?"

Arlyn laughed again. "Sorry. A chicken is a kind of bird."

"You're a bird?" Iren cried.

"No," Arlyn said, chuckling. "There's an Earth phrase. If someone is being chicken, it means they are acting cowardly."

Iren's expression grew thoughtful. "I'm a chicken," he whispered, probably putting the phrase back for future use.

Selia's lips twitched, but she stifled the laugh. "So why are you being a chicken about this?"

"He was upset that Kai and I bonded so quickly. I don't know how he'll react to this news," Arlyn said. "Besides, Kai is being annoying enough. I'd rather not have two people worrying about every little thing. Please tell me *you* won't do that."

Selia shook her head. "Of course not. I know well enough how frustrating that can be. We'll need to go back to meditating and connecting with your energy, though."

Arlyn groaned. "I thought I'd finally mastered that."

"Sure." Selia remembered her own struggles with magic when she'd been carrying Iren and winced in sympathy. "But as your baby grows, their magic will develop along with their physical body. It'll mess with your energy in the process. You'll need to re-center yourself periodically or your power might do strange things in the middle of a working. Like today."

Arlyn's shoulders drooped. "Figures."

"Before we try the shield again, we should—"

Selia's words cut off as the protections around Braelyn shrieked a warning into her mind. She wasn't fully linked to the estate's magic, but she'd helped reinforce the spells that detected intruders—such as the one sounding the alarm now. She sent her power into the spell and found what she'd already suspected. The threat came from the sky.

Arlyn shot to her feet, her brow creased in alarm. "That's not the portal."

"The dragon is here." Selia stood at the same time as Iren, though without the whoop of excitement her son released.

"A dragon?" Arlyn's eyes widened.

"Didn't your father mention it?"

"No, he absolutely didn't mention a dragon. You're kidding, right?"

Selia brushed at her pants in case she'd picked up any stray dust and then headed for her cloak. "Eradisel warned me last night. I assumed you would know."

"I haven't seen my father since yesterday afternoon. Guess that's what I get for avoiding him," Arlyn muttered as she retrieved her own cloak.

"Sounds like it." Selia gestured for Iren to hurry. "I want you to stay inside the main building, Iren. Watch from a window if you can't contain your curiosity, but don't come out. And don't dawdle. The only place clear enough for the dragon to land is the ridge above the valley, so we should be safe crossing the garden. But I'd rather get into the shelter of the main house even though we should be fine under the trees."

Her son nodded and rushed out the door behind her. She wasn't happy with the gleam of excitement in his eyes, but there wasn't much to be done for it. Iren had an adventurous spirit, much like his father, and little beyond tying him up would do much good if he was interested enough. But he was also smart, and he'd grown more cautious about danger after having to use his magic against an assassin to save Kai and Arlyn a few months prior. He would at least wait to analyze the danger.

She hoped.

By the time they arrived in the entryway, Lyr and Kai already waited. Iren rushed immediately to the window despite Selia's sharp warning, but she relaxed slightly at the calm expression on Lyr's face. Kai didn't appear nearly as collected. Frowning, he placed his hand on Arlyn's shoulder.

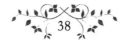

"You should stay in here with Iren."

Arlyn's mouth pinched. "You'd better rethink that."

"We don't know what the dragon wants. There's a chance—"

"How many *Taysonal* will have arrows trained on the dragon?" Arlyn demanded. "If you thought it was here to attack, none of you would be going out. I am my father's heir. Unless you have evidence of danger, I'm going, too."

Kai scowled. "I don't like this."

"She's right," Lyr said. "I've spent the night thinking about this. There's no way a single dragon would come here intending to attack. They are powerful, but they are neither invulnerable nor foolish. And in Selia's vision, the dragon had a rider. According to lore, only a dragon's linked *skizik* would be allowed astride except in an emergency."

"So?" Kai asked.

"If they were hostile to non-dragons, there would be no rider." Lyr spun toward the window beside the double doors as the throb of wingbeats began to drum against the walls. "This is almost certainly an act of diplomacy."

In the end, even Kai shifted close to the glass to watch the dragon land. Selia's breath caught at the gold shimmering from the massive body. Branches swayed in the tempest as the dragon alighted on the ridge outside the door. When it stilled, pulling its wings against its body and waiting with wedge-shaped head held high, its beautiful scales gleamed like a thousand tiny flames. They were so blinding in the midday sun that she could barely make out the shadowed form of the rider.

"You have your spell prepared, Selia?" Lyr asked.

"Yes, but I cannot guarantee how well or how long it might hold." Selia tore her gaze away from the mesmerizing sight of the

dragon and made sure the spell she'd created was ready. "I can also put up a fire-resisting shield. It seems like a reasonable action even during a diplomatic mission."

Lyr nodded. "Please do. Meli and my mother are in the library searching the archives for information about the initial peace treaty with the dragons and anything else pertinent. I've studied it, but my memory is hazy. Meli will relay word of anything they find."

"Arlyn should help them," Kai said.

Lyr shot his friend a quizzical look. "*Clechtan*, Kai, what is your problem? Do you not have faith in your bonded?"

"Of course I do, but—" Kai's words cut off when Arlyn grabbed his arm and glared at him. "Forget it. Let's just get this over with."

"If there wasn't a massive dragon outside that door, we'd be discussing this now," Lyr grumbled. Then he shook his head and started for the entrance. "Well, come on. Except for you, Iren. Do not put yourself into danger."

Selia pinned Iren with a glance as she followed the others. "If you don't listen to me, you'd better listen to the Myern."

"Okay," Iren said.

It wasn't precisely agreement, but it was the best Selia would get in such a short amount of time. *"Don't make me give you extra lessons. Or ban you from watching the warriors train,"* she sent to her son.

"I'm smart enough to understand real danger, Onaiala."

Selia snorted at the indignant frustration in his tone. *"I love you, Iren. Stay safe."*

"I love you, too," he answered.

As the group passed through the double doors and out into the clearing in front of the estate, Selia squinted against the flashes of light reflecting from countless scales. The autumn sun hung a bit lower, the perfect angle to strike against the dragon's body in a

blinding display. She fought the urge to shield her face and stiffened her spine instead, not wanting to show weakness.

Thankfully, her eyes adjusted by the time Lyr halted, Arlyn and Kai to his left and Selia to his right. They stood just out of reach of the dragon's long neck and massive head. Selia hoped. Despite the nerves that danced in her stomach, she gathered energy and cast the flame-resisting spell in an arc in front of their group. The dragon's warm breath hissed over them, but it made no complaint about the use of magic.

"I bid you good day, honored visitors from the Isle," Lyr announced, no hint of worry in his tone or expression. "It has been millennia since one of the fabled dragons has graced us with their presence. I hope this is an occasion of peace and not of strife."

The dragon's voice—a female-sounding voice—poured into Selia's head despite not establishing a link. *"I have come to demand passage through the portal for myself and my* skizik.*"*

Lyr didn't so much as blink. "Such passage was forbidden as part of the treaty."

"Forge a new treaty," the dragon sent. *"We must pass through."*

At the implacable tone and the puff of smoke from the dragon's mouth, Selia drew the containment spell into her mental hand. The dragon didn't appear ready to budge, but Lyr didn't, either. "Does your council know of your presence?" Lyr asked.

Selia barely managed to contain a shiver when the dragon snapped her mouth in annoyance. *"I will go through,"* she insisted.

"Calm down, Kezari," another voice said. A male voice, and one that sounded oddly familiar.

Selia narrowed her eyes against the sun and peered at the dragon's rider, but he bent down, obscuring his face. He threw his leg over and slid off. When his feet hit the ground awkwardly, he stumbled and leaned against the dragon's massive leg. A chill passed

through Selia at the sight of his long braid. Light brown hair striped through with dark green. Just like…

He settled himself and spun to face them.

Aris. He looked like Aris. But that was impossible. Selia's head reeled and her knees grew weak. She darted out a hand, gripping Lyr's shoulder for balance. Seven years. Aris would not have stayed away from her if he was alive. He'd loved her and Iren. Perhaps this man was a relative.

Had to be.

Shock lined Lyr's face as he turned her to face him, taking her wrists and squeezing gently. "Selia?"

"It's impossible," she said aloud.

"Are you unwell?"

"That man looks like my husband," Selia whispered. "Iren's father. But he's dead. I…"

Lyr's expression softened. "You can go inside if you need to. We can manage."

For a moment, the temptation was almost too strong. But no. Selia had promised to use her magic to aid Lyr, so that was what she would do. She forced strength into her legs and shoved her shoulders back. "I can stay."

Lyr let her go, though he gave her a sidelong glance before returning his attention to the dragon's rider. "Please state your name and purpose here."

But if the man heard Lyr's words, he gave no indication. He stared at Selia, his eyes so shadowed with pain she could almost feel it across the distance between them. His mouth thinned into a line, and he turned his face away, resting his weight against the dragon's leg. In the shadow of the dragon, she could examine him more easily, but it didn't make her feel better.

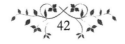

Oh, Gods. It *was* Aris. With every breath, suspicion grew into certainty. She'd caressed those sharp cheekbones. Kissed that generous mouth. Tapped her finger playfully against the small cleft in his chin. Her fingers had twisted in those long locks as she'd marveled at the green, a gift from his dryad grandmother.

She still dreamed about the shifting hazel of those eyes.

At the surge of hurt, Selia clenched her fists and locked her knees. She wanted to run into the house or crumple into a ball beneath the weight of her pain. But she would not do that. She had a duty to protect the rest of the group. Even as her heart shattered into dust.

For one long moment, Aris considered throwing himself over the edge of the ridge behind him. Only Kezari's warm bulk at his side grounded him. Supported him. Of all the things he'd expected to happen when they reached Braelyn, seeing Selia hadn't been one of them. His love. His light.

She had moved on.

"Your impoliteness does you no favors," their leader said, an edge of annoyance entering his voice. "What is your name, and why have you come here?"

It was gravely rude not to answer, but Aris couldn't force a single sound through his aching throat. Selia must have married or bonded to the lord here. As soon as she'd recognized Aris, she'd reached for the other man. Who had held her arms gently, whispering to her out of the range of hearing.

He hadn't been ready for this. Theory was one thing, but the reality... His stomach roiled as he struggled to think of what to do.

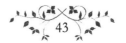

Kezari wasn't going to give up on her mission. Maybe she would fly him to another location until she received approval to use the portal. She could return for him, and he'd help her solve her Earth problem.

Then he could be free.

He cleared his throat. "Forgive me, I…"

His throat seized, and his lungs burned with the shallow breaths he tried to force through. Each pair of eyes trained on him was a weight strangling away his very air. Wooziness blended with nausea until Aris had to settle his face against Kezari's leg to regain his equilibrium.

"I wish to shift, skizik.*"*

That shocked him out of his daze. *"What? Now?"*

"They cannot relate to me in my natural form. Perhaps an elven body would provide reassurance."

"Maybe," Aris answered. *"But by Arneen, wear some damn clothes."*

"Warn them. I do not wish to have an arrow to the wing."

Aris made himself look at the small group, but he couldn't meet anyone's eyes. "Kezari is about to shift into a smaller form. Please do not be alarmed by the surge in energy. I give my oath she intends no harm."

He could have sworn he heard a soft snort from Selia's direction, but her expression was blank when he ventured a glance. But then, she'd always been good at hiding her emotions. Her father had demanded his children master the art, and she'd excelled at that task as expertly as every other. Of course, the more impassive she appeared, the more emotion she was typically containing. Unless she had changed. A lot could change in seven years—he shot a glance at her new lover—obviously.

Lyr nodded. "Very well."

Power expanded around them as Kezari's form began to blur and shrink. Aris shielded his eyes against the flash, but it only lasted

a moment. Then she stood beside him in her elven form, her body barely covered by a thin, short dress. Without her larger body, the space between their two groups grew into a chasm. An abyss he wasn't certain he could cross.

Kezari said nothing, only wrapped her hot fingers around his wrist and tugged as she started forward. Instinctively, he balked, his feet digging in when she pulled. He couldn't do this. Even in the open sky, he couldn't. His chest tightened with each reluctant step, and his vision grew blurry at the edges. He needed to stop. He didn't want to break again, not here.

But Kezari's unrelenting grip dragged him forward.

"I am Kezari," the dragon said when they drew to a halt. "I wish to seek shelter for myself and my *skizik* while we resolve this matter. He needs a healer's aid."

Aris's muscles seized with the shock of her words. His throat closed around his denial.

"And I am Callian Myern i Lyrnis Dianore nai Braelyn," the lord answered. "I am willing to offer shelter so long as you vow to maintain peace and to not attempt to go through the portal without my permission."

"I vow such," Kezari answered.

Lord Lyrnis inclined his head. "Very well. In what way has your *skizik* been injured?"

Kezari peered at the trees ringing the clearing and then at the small group before them. "He would not wish to say at this moment. I would not. There are many ears."

"Perhaps we should continue this discussion in my study," the lord said. "Provided you are able to maintain your current form for that long."

Her nose wrinkled. "I can stay this strange shape for the needed time."

The door to the estate opened, and a woman with light blond hair exited. She held a book, not a knife, but her resemblance to Perim had Aris's chest constricting with the force of a great jungle snake. He gasped, a strangled sound of pain slipping free, and his vision wavered. With barely a glance his way, she rushed over to Lord Lyrnis, but her lack of attention wasn't comforting.

Kezari's fingers tightened on his wrist. *"It is not Perim."*

"I know." The woman stopped beside the Myern, the corners of her mouth curving as she leaned close to whisper. *"But they could be sisters. Even her energy is similar. What if she… A trap. This may be…"*

The clearing faded from his vision, replaced by memories of the cave. His captor's wicked smirk as her cajoling hands ran along his body. The sudden surge of pain as her knife sliced into his flesh. Aris attempted to dispel the images, but he couldn't seem to find his grip on the present. She was here, and he would suffer for these weeks of freedom.

Something squeezed his wrist and shook, causing a twinge of pain, and he tried to tug his arm away. Too strong. The chains had always been too strong. Aris gasped for breath, but his chest hurt too much to take in air. Chills wracked his body as his mind splintered.

"Aris," a female voice snapped. "Stop, *skizik*."

"Told you…couldn't…"

Power flashed painlessly through his mind, and he fell into blessed dark.

4

Before Selia had quite processed what was happening, power surged and Aris crumpled. The dragon woman caught him in her arms and lowered his slack body to the ground. Beside Selia, Meli's words cut off, and Lyr hissed out a low curse. For a drip of time, they stood unmoving, the very air taut with tension.

That had been a spell of incapacitation—not something typically cast by a friend.

Selia rushed across the space between them. The dragon, Kezari, glanced up from where she crouched at his side, and power built around her. Selia readied her own magic, but she didn't stop. Not until she dropped down next to her husband and placed her hand on his cheek.

"What kind of dragon attacks her rider?" Selia demanded.

"Guard your words, elf." Kezari's head drew back as if she were about to breathe fire or consume prey, but on the shorter neck of this body, the motion threw her off balance and she had to catch herself on her hands. "Cursed useless form."

Aris let out a groan, and Selia studied his face. His eyes fluttered, but they didn't open. "What did you do to him?"

The dragon leaned closer, her voice dropping to a bare whisper. "The memories held him in their grip. I am uncertain how to heal him."

Memories? Selia recalled how the birds and other forest creatures had begun to make sounds of distress. Then the blind panic in Aris's eyes moments before the dragon had used her power. Selia's own heart had pounded with the frenzied rhythm of his, a sure sign that something was dreadfully wrong with her husband. He only lost control during times of extreme duress or pleasure, and his reaction hadn't been the latter.

Something terrible must have happened to him.

"You know the cause," Selia accused flatly.

Kezari gave a sharp nod. "But I do not know you."

Selia's hands shook as she brushed a strand of dark green hair from Aris's forehead. "I am his wife. Unless he rescinded his vow. I...I don't understand. He's dead. Was."

"He was on our isle for some years," the dragon said. "But not voluntarily, I discovered."

Aris had been held against his will? A frown creased Selia's brow as she stared down at her beloved's face. The survivors of the shipwreck had claimed to see Aris sink beneath the wreckage and never emerge. He must have been swept away by the currents and somehow ended up on the dragons' island. But who would have kept him captive for seven years—and why?

Why hadn't he run to her when he'd recognized her?

His eyelids flicked open, and his hazel eyes collided with hers. For a heartbeat, joy surged in his gaze, only to morph into pain. "Selia," he said, his voice rough.

"I can't believe it's you," she whispered. She wanted to throw herself across him and hold him close. She wanted to shake him and demand to know what had happened. Neither option seemed like

the best plan considering his earlier breakdown. "I don't know what to ask first."

Aris winced. "Perhaps you should return to your husband."

"What are you talking about?" Selia blinked in confusion. Had he lost part of his memory? "You are my husband."

Aris shifted restlessly. "Lord Lyrnis."

That startled a short laugh out of her. "I am not married to Lyr. He's bonded to the blond lady who just joined us."

"Bonded to the…" Aris stiffened, his eyes going wide. "Who is she? What is her name?"

"Meli," Selia said quickly, hoping to stem the panic building on his face. How odd that Meli's presence caused him such distress. "She is one of the Ljósálfar, but I don't understand why that would upset you. I've never known her to be anything but kind."

Aris let out a breath. "She looks like—"

"Perim," Kezari hissed. "I will rend that reptile limb from limb. But I will not consume her. Oh, no. Her wicked body would give sickness, not nourishment."

Selia sat back on her heels. A reptile who looked like Meli? It made no sense. She started to ask for more information, but Aris distracted her by sitting upright. His cheeks reddened as he caught sight of the group watching them from a few paces away. Shame tinged his expression before all emotion left his face.

Aris had always loved people. To have reacted like this to such a small crowd… Whatever had happened to him must have been horrific.

Selia made quick contact with Lyr. *"Meli's appearance caused him distress. Literally."*

"Meli? You must be joking."

"I don't know the full story," Selia sent. *"But it seems he was captured at some point by someone who looks like her."*

Lyr gave a slight nod. *"I'll ask her to go back inside."*

After a moment, Meli's mouth fell open. Then she grimaced, and without a word, she spun and darted back inside. Once the door had closed behind her, Aris relaxed slightly before shoving himself to his feet. But as Selia studied his harsh profile, she had a feeling the man she'd known was gone.

Would she get the chance to learn who he'd become?

Aris forced his emotions to blank as he stared at the lord of Braelyn. Despite the humiliation of falling prey to panic in front of the Myern, focusing on him was a better alternative than Selia's stunned, hurt gaze. Once, he'd yearned with all of his heart to be with her again, but that longing had been severed at Perim's hand. Selia deserved far better than this broken shell.

"As Kezari stated earlier, I am…unwell," Aris said carefully. "Please forgive my lapse."

Lord Lyrnis's expression remained placid. "It is of no consequence. However, I must insist you accompany me to the healer's tower before negotiations continue. Once you have properly introduced yourself, of course."

Aris hesitated. Who was he, really? He could no longer define his place, but one's title described that very thing. Selia called him husband. Could he step back into that role? He had no idea, but it was the closest thing he had to give. "Taian ia'Kelore ai'Flerin ay'mornia Ayern Aris Baran ne Selia nai Fiorn."

Lyrnis inclined his head. From the Myern's lack of surprise, Aris assumed Selia had somehow told him. "Follow me, Aris Baran. I have a feeling we need you well."

With that cryptic statement, the Myern strode back toward the building. The other two who had been with him, a red-haired woman and a black-haired man, stared after him for a moment before following. Then Lord Lyrnis cut left down a side path and paused, glancing over his shoulder with a raised brow.

"Kezari?" Aris asked softly, knowing she would understand.

"You will see this healer." She reached for his wrist again, but he shook his head in denial. He would move forward on his own this time. "I can shift into an elven form, but I do not know how to fix one. Your body may be unwell. I cannot tell."

Avoiding Selia's gaze, Aris made himself take a step. Then another. Although his heart pounded in his chest, he managed to shuffle toward the others without another breakdown. Kezari and Selia kept pace with him, one on each side, but he couldn't think about them. He had to concentrate on advancing.

How pathetic was this? He'd spent years traversing deserts and hacking through jungles. He'd helped blaze trails and establish settlements in the remote areas of their continent. Now, he could barely stand to cross a simple clearing in the heart of his homeland. He had nothing to fear here—he'd never heard an ill word against Lord Lyrnis or his father before him, and Aris sensed no hostility.

Too bad fear wasn't logical.

Or perhaps it *was* logical. The other half of his soul had been willing to torture him for years. How could he trust strangers to treat him any better? His heart knew Selia, at least, wouldn't hurt him, but he had no faith in anyone else. And being around Selia brought its own agony.

Just as he reached the others, the estate door opened again, and another, smaller form slipped out. Aris halted, his muscles locking at the sight of the boy frozen in the doorway. Light brown hair flopped

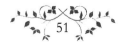

around his young face, a few strands shading his wide hazel eyes. Aris didn't need Selia's strangled groan to know who it was.

His son.

In a flurry of movement, Iren dashed across the distance between them and threw his arms around Aris. "*Onaial!*"

Aris's heart twisted and then pounded hard at the constraint. Even as joy surged through him, a thousand knives pricked at his nerves until his whole body thrummed with the need to push Iren away—but also to pull him close. Memories swelled of the last time he'd seen his son. Iren had curled his small body around Aris's leg and begged him not to go. Now his son's arms spanned his waist. *Miaran.* He would not let his sickness ruin this moment.

Even as Aris shuddered, he wrapped his arms around Iren and hugged him back.

Aris would never under any torture reveal the relief he felt when Iren finally pulled away. "You have grown too much," Aris whispered through a throat gone raw.

Iren swiped tears from his cheeks. "I thought you were dead."

"I did, too, but it seems I must live." Aris sighed at the frown the comment inspired. There was no way he could explain to his innocent son all of the horrors he'd been through or the times he'd longed for death. "I was a prisoner, Iren. I did not abandon you."

Trust gleamed in Iren's eyes as he smiled. "Now you're home."

What could he say to that? He hadn't thought to live beyond the next month. But seeing his family—perhaps he could find a way. Somehow. "I…"

"Your father was just rescued," Selia said softly. "He needs to see the healer."

Iren nodded. "Let's go."

Before Aris could think of a way to discourage him, Selia solved the problem. "You have studies to focus on, and I am certain your father would like privacy for his examination."

"But everyone else is going," Iren cried.

The red-haired woman stepped toward the estate, dragging the other male with her. "Kai and I will wait in the study. Come on, Iren. We can work on our history together."

Though he protested, his son was finally nudged back through the door by the unknown woman. Aris peered after her for a moment. She wore the medallion of the one named Kai, so she was clearly bonded. Why would she still be studying basic history at her age? With a shake of his head, he shoved the question aside. The mystery would have to wait.

"If you are ready?" Lord Lyrnis asked with a polite motion toward the trail.

Aris wanted to groan. They watched him like an invalid, and he couldn't even argue the point. Not when he could fall into madness at any moment. "Yes."

As he followed the Myern, Kezari gave him a pointed glance. "You did not mention that you have spawn."

Selia made a choked sound, and he winced. She had to think the worst of him despite his capture. If she even believed that part. "Speaking of my lost family brought me pain, and I did not want to spark another breakdown."

"I do not know what to do," Kezari said. "I would not put one with young into danger, but I must have your help. You are important."

His lips twisted. "I'm not an asset to anyone."

Kezari squeezed his shoulder. Though her fingers closed like talons, the gesture brought an odd sort of comfort. "Give yourself a chance, and you will be."

Once they reached the tower standing alone in the trees, the Myern stopped. The door was open, but Aris didn't see the healer. "I will stay outside," Lyrnis said.

Aris gave a small grateful smile. "Thank you, Lord Lyrnis."

"Please, call me Lyr." The impassivity faded from the Myern's face, replaced with lines of concern. "The sacred tree Eradisel Herself warned us that you would be arriving. Considering that and your connection to Selia, I suspect we'll attain more than a passing acquaintance."

The sacred tree? Aris blinked. He'd assumed the gods and their emissaries, the trees, had long forgotten him. "Very well."

"I will go into this place with you," Kezari said.

Aris stared at the gaping hole that was the door. It was too bright outside to see into the interior darkness of the tower. "I'm not sure I can go inside, regardless," he admitted.

"I could…" Selia began, but her words trailed off uncertainly when he met her eyes. Gods knew what she saw there. "Perhaps my presence would no longer bring comfort."

He lifted his hand to brush his fingers across her cheek, longing to smooth away her pained frown, but he let his arm drop. His fingers curled into his palm. Aris could never touch her again, not with hands as dirty as his. She wasn't some pure and perfect creature—no one was—but she deserved better than him. Once she learned the extent of his torture, she would surely agree.

"If I am to attempt to enter, it must be alone," Aris said. "Not even you can come, Kezari."

Her nostrils flared. "That is unwise."

His laugh held little humor. He had no idea if he could bring himself to go through the door, but if he couldn't perform that simple task under his own power, he had little hope of making it in this world. "Perhaps, but it is my choice."

Aris focused on his goal and took a resolute step forward. Then another. He had to do this. Now that he'd found Selia and Iren, Aris couldn't simply give up. It was one thing for his family to have never known he still lived. If Aris had killed himself, well…they'd already thought he was dead. But returning to his family only to leave them forever was a cruelty he couldn't inflict. The trust, joy, and love in Iren's eyes haunted him, but they also propelled him. If nothing else, Aris had to discover if there was any hope of fixing his broken mind.

And maybe the healer would be able to tell if Aris's soul was as twisted as Perim's.

Selia stared after Aris and tried to shove down the pain that threatened to choke her. For the briefest moment, he'd almost touched her. Love and concern had flickered across his face, and he'd reached out to comfort her the way he'd always done. Then he'd shut down and pulled back.

Aris had told the dragon that thinking of his family caused pain. He hadn't mentioned Iren. Had he even intended to return to them? Perhaps he had decided to start a new life on Earth with the dragon. Selia eyed Kezari. She was certainly beautiful in her elven form. Selia would never have thought it of Aris, but anything was possible.

Kezari leaned close. "The female who tortured him claimed to be his mate."

Selia went cold as she processed the dragon's words. The implications of that whispered statement tore into her heart. "Tortured by his mate?"

"He rejected the claim," Kezari said. "I do not know more."

Selia had no idea how dragons used the word, but mate implied a soulbond. Gods, that couldn't be true. No one would do that to the other half of their soul. Bonding wasn't always as perfect as the idealized view so many held, but *torture?* It made no sense.

As Aris paused in the doorway of the tower, Selia had to hold herself back from running after him. If he believed she would reject him because of the torment he'd gone through, he was mistaken. And if he had bonded, she needed to know. Either way, one thing was perfectly clear—she would never stop loving him.

5

Aris reached the entrance before his resolve gave out. He dug his fingers into the wooden door frame and peered into the dim interior of the tower. But it wasn't dark now that he'd moved out of the sunlight. High windows allowed natural light to stream in, giving the room a soft glow. There was a long workbench along the left wall, a stone table at the back, and a bed near a staircase to the right. No healer, though.

As soon as he'd had the thought, someone started down the spiral stairs. Aris froze, hoping the healer wasn't another woman with Perim's coloring, but it soon became obvious that the healer was neither female nor blond. A stern-faced, auburn-haired male came to a halt a few paces from the door, his brow raised in question.

"Are you coming in?" the healer asked.

"I cannot tolerate being enclosed in the dark," Aris found himself admitting beneath the healer's steady regard. "I was kept in a cave for over six years."

"I am Lial," the other man said. At a quick gesture, the mage lights dangling from sconces brightened until the room was filled with light. "Lyr gave warning of your arrival, but he was unable to tell me much about your condition beyond what happened outside."

Aris snorted. "I think it was fairly obvious that I had a breakdown."

"Panic attack," Lial corrected softly. "I am not a mind-healer, but I have seen the results of trauma. How long has it been since your escape?"

Aris's grip loosened on the door frame. "One week."

"Five days of freedom would hardly be sufficient for your mind to recover." Lial took a cautious step closer. "Do you have physical injuries? Would you allow me to examine you?"

Suddenly, a helpless rage surged through Aris, stealing his breath. The healer, the others in the clearing—they looked at him like he was a wild animal, ready to snap at any moment. Next, the healer would hold out a treat and try to coax him. Was he really that messed up? Aris lifted his chin and shoved away from the door, striding toward a wooden stool beside the workbench. The bed was too far from the exit, but he would sit down and be examined, iron blast it.

"If this causes you discomfort—"

"Everything causes me discomfort," Aris snapped.

"Fair enough." The healer chuckled. "No need to be angry at me. At least not yet. I'll annoy you legitimately if you stay around long enough, or so I'm told."

"Healers often have that effect."

"Ah, but I have a talent for it." If the confession bothered Lial, his wry smile gave nothing away. Shrugging, he moved closer. "No more evading. May I scan you with my magic? I assure you that it causes no pain."

"I know that." Aris lifted a brow. "I have been healed before. I'm not a child."

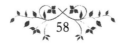

"I've had patients from beyond Moranaia of late," Lial said. "I've learned not to assume."

Interesting but irrelevant. Aris braced himself, fighting the anxiety of being in contact with another person's energy. "Just get it over with."

Despite his initially tentative approach, Lial didn't hesitate. Aris squeezed his eyes closed against the blue glow and gripped the bottom of the stool as the light settled around his body. Peace rushed in with it, easing his clenched muscles. His mind floated, much as his body did when Kezari carried him across the sky. He let go and drifted.

Lial had grown adept at stifling anger while working, but for the first time in centuries, he struggled to maintain control. Aris's body was riddled with signs of abuse, from a just-healed gash across his thigh and side to bones that had been broken and improperly set. Typically, elven bodies healed from even serious injuries with a modicum of care. For Aris's bones to be misaligned, his tormentor would have had to warp his limbs out of alignment and leave them there while they healed. Probably stretched out while chained.

Stifling another surge of fury, Lial proceeded to Aris's mind. The maelstrom there would need a mind-healer to fix, preferably with a mage present to guard against Aris's power overflowing. Lial had a small amount of mind-healing talent, but not enough to touch this. So many pathways created by torment and fear. Aris must have a strong will to be so lucid. With a sigh, Lial did what little he could to ease the panic. If there hadn't been a dragon outside, waiting impatiently, he would have rendered his patient unconscious until a

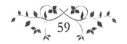

mind-healer arrived. It went against his every instinct to allow Aris to suffer more, but in this, he had no choice.

Lial gathered more energy and healed the cuts and strained muscles he'd found on his first pass. Then he did what he could for the misaligned bones. Most would cause no active trouble, only leave a weakness that would make future breaks easier, and a few others he was able to smooth out. But the large bone in the right thigh and one in the left forearm would need to be rebroken and set again.

Not today. With his patient's permission, Lial would undertake that after the mind-healer arrived—and while Aris was sedated. Lial had had plenty of recent practice restructuring bone after fixing Lynia's spine, so the task itself would be more draining than difficult. Hopefully, Aris would agree before the damaged bones caused him trouble.

After a quick pass to ensure that any injury to the organs had healed, Lial pulled his consciousness fully back to his own body. But he didn't remove his healing magic while he opened his eyes. How could he reawaken his patient to the torment of existing with such scars? The tension and stifled fear had smoothed from Aris's face, and his half-slitted gaze was clear of stress. It would be a difficult return to awareness, but neither of them had a choice.

Muttering a curse, Lial lowered his spell as slowly as he could. It was always his nature to heal, no matter his joking threats to the contrary, but for the first time in a long time, he wanted to hurt someone. As each line of anxiety returned to his patient's face, the urge to annihilate Aris's tormentor grew. Too bad Lial would never have the chance.

As the light faded, so did Aris's moment of peace. He tumbled back into his body in a slow fall, and though he could tell that the healer tried to give him time to adapt, there was no stopping reality. He felt…different, and his heart gave a hard leap until he realized that it was a good different. He'd grown accustomed to a constant ache, varying degrees of pain that shifted rather than disappeared. Almost all of that was gone. Even his emotions seemed a bit steadier.

Emphasis on *a bit*.

Aris focused on the healer's angry face. "That bad?"

"I was able to fix everything but two misaligned bones." Lial's lips thinned. "And the bulk of the damage to your mind. That will require a specialist."

Aris frowned. "Bones?"

"Do you not remember having them broken?"

"I do." Aris shuddered as he tried to concentrate on the knowledge of the events rather than the actual memories. "I thought such injuries heal quickly."

Lial gave a sharp nod. "They do, but it was not a boon in this case. You must have been held in a position where they couldn't realign correctly."

His very bones. Aris's shoulders slumped as despair rather than anger filled him. If the healer couldn't fix them, he would carry those remnants of her always. "Will it cause me future trouble?"

"Not if you let me correct the problem." Aris glanced up at those words. "Your mind is damaged enough that I must bring a mind-healer here. Once you've undergone that treatment, I'll render you unconscious, rebreak the bones, and heal them properly. I will not do that in your current state. Even unaware, it resembles torture too closely. It's bad enough that you must remain awake and aware until a mind-healer can be found."

Aris winced at the blunt truth, but it was preferable to the alternative. "I appreciate your candor. I did not expect it after your initial caution."

Lial's brows rose. "Did you expect me to be rough with a patient suffering such severe anxiety?"

"I did not give it much rational thought," Aris admitted.

"Do so in future." Despite the gruffness of his tone, Lial's eyes pinched with concern. "And do not give up. I sense the risk of that in you, and I will warn your dragon as such. Were she not insistent on your presence, you would be in a deep sleep instead of speaking with me. Do anything rash, and I will be dealing with a dragon's wrath over your unconscious body."

Kezari's voice popped into his mind as though summoned. *"The wrath will be at you,* skizik, *if you attempt to harm yourself."*

It seemed she hadn't quite left his mind after all.

Aris rubbed the back of his neck. "I will do my best. But I must know this. Was there…other damage? I worry that this darkness has spread to my soul."

Lial's eyes narrowed. "I am no priest, but I detected nothing like that in you. Being abused does not make you an abuser."

But having an evil soulbonded might. Aris opened his mouth to voice that concern, but his throat closed around the words. He couldn't confess that. Everyone already regarded him warily. If they knew the other half of his soul was a twisted, torturous woman, they would watch him with fear, too. He couldn't bear it.

"Thank you," Aris finally managed.

"Send for me at any hour." Lial gestured at the door. "Now, I suggest you rejoin your dragon before she storms my tower. I will search for a suitable mind-healer."

Aris shoved himself off the stool. "There are things… I would prefer another male."

With a grimace, Lial nodded. "I will see that it is so."

The benefit of the healing became obvious when Aris strode for the door. Now, only a slight ache in his right thigh remained, and his muscles flexed easily with each step. Some pain wasn't obvious until it was gone, he supposed. Although anxiety still threaded its claws into his heart, his physical body felt so much better that his mental burden grew lighter, too.

Perhaps he could make it. Perhaps there was hope.

Selia tapped her fingers along her crossed arm and watched the dragon pace. The longer she was in Kezari's presence, the more obvious the dragon's otherness became. She bore an elven form, but she lacked typical facial expressions and physical motions. Although pacing, it seemed, was universal. Kezari's feet slammed down with a force that would have razed buildings in her dragon form. Wordlessly, she'd circled the clearing in front of the healer's tower countless times in less than a mark's time.

"Did Meli find something useful?" Selia asked Lyr softly. "She was quite intent on bringing you that book."

Lyr nodded. "A record of the treaty, complete with commentary."

Well, that was curious. A forty-thousand-year-old record in their library? "I did not expect that to be housed here."

"It is not the original," Lyr said. "That is at the palace under preservation. But my ancestors deemed it prudent to keep a full copy close to the portal. My mother found the passage I thought I remembered from my studies, and Meli rushed it over. I suppose she could have taken her time."

"Poor Aris." A lump formed in her throat. "The way he reacted to Meli. To all of us, really. I don't know what's going to happen next."

Kezari drew to a halt, her head whipping around. "He's going to come with me through the portal."

Lyr frowned. "We will have this discussion later."

"You are a mage?" Kezari asked Selia, not acknowledging Lyr's words. "We will need you, too. This will be easier. Faster. You will come. But perhaps we must bring your young to guard."

Selia stared at the dragon's closed expression. "Do dragons jest?"

"Not in this manner." Kezari startled her with a toothy grin. "We need a mage, but young must be guarded."

"Enough, Kezari."

Aris strode from the doorway of the healer's tower with more confidence than he had entered, and although his face was still lined with tension, something about him was more…himself. She wanted to ask how much the healer had been able to help, but he avoided her gaze when he drew near.

Perhaps she no longer had the right.

"We need to explain the situation rationally to the Myern," Aris said. "And to Selia. She is a powerful mage."

Kezari stared at him. "I will go into the dwelling if it is required, but I do not like it. I do not feel safe under so many trees."

"I am not fond of the concept, myself," Aris said.

"It is the most private option," Lyr interjected smoothly. "Which I believe you both desire. This is a large estate with many guards, not to mention residents. My study is secure."

"Very well," Kezari said, and without another word, she started down the path toward the main estate.

Lyr turned to follow, and suddenly, Selia was alone with Aris. She flicked a look through lowered lashes, but he barely glanced

her way as he started walking. She hurried to keep pace, her jaw clenching in annoyance. Was he going to pretend she didn't exist? If he'd bonded or otherwise decided to end their marriage, he could at least have the grace to tell her. There was no need to treat her like the ghost he'd been.

"You cannot avoid me forever," she murmured.

A hitch marred his stride. "I don't know what you mean."

"By the Great God Meyanen—" Selia began, cutting off her words before she could threaten bodily harm. That would be the worst thing she could say. "I understand that you are not ready to speak of what happened, but after three centuries of being together, I would have expected the common courtesy of looking at me and acknowledging my presence."

Selia had his attention then, but the dark annoyance lining his face was far from what she'd wanted. "If you understood, you would not say such things," Aris said.

"Maybe." Selia drew her shoulders back, bracing herself. "But I want you to know that if you have decided to end our relationship, you may simply say so."

Mouth pinched tight, Aris ran his fingers through his hair. "I have not. When I am able to tell you what happened, however, you will cast me aside. I am not whole, Selia. I have no idea how effective mind-healers are, but I doubt they can fix this."

"Aris, you know I—"

"Would not hold my capture against me." His hand lifted as though he would touch her, but once again, he lowered it without making contact. "I want to be here for Iren until he reaches manhood, but I don't know if I can. Each moment is agony. The endless stretch of years before me breaks me inside. I refuse, *refuse*, to drag you into this madness."

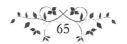

Selia wanted to scream, but she had no idea at whom. Him, in part, but shame filled her at the impulse. It wasn't his fault he'd been traumatized, and it would be wrong of her to push him. If she ever encountered this Perim, Selia would blast the *drec* with a spell so violent that ballads would chronicle the event for millennia. Then the dragon could chew up the remains.

As the front doors came into view, Selia leaned close to Aris but was careful not to touch him. "Speak to me as a friend, if you must, and we will resolve the rest when you are able. You know you will always have my love and support. Just treat me as though I exist."

"I did not intend to upset you," Aris said. "But it hurts. It hurts to see you and to know all that was lost. If I seem to ignore you, it is only to avoid a breakdown."

Tears burned in her eyes, for him and for herself. She'd believed his disappearance and death had been the worst thing that could ever happen to her and Iren, but she'd been wrong. Oh, that had been horrible. But nothing compared to the joy of finding him alive intertwined so painfully with the knowledge of his broken state. He was as dead to her as he'd been that morning even though he walked beside her.

Far too close to be so out of reach.

6

Aris had expected to feel trapped by the estate, but entering the large double doors filled him with a curious sense of comfort. Perhaps it was the fact that the massive house had been constructed quite literally around the largest of the trees. Just ahead, a staircase spiraled up a broad tree trunk in the middle of the room. Then he glanced to the left, and his breath caught. On the far end of the entryway, the wall had been cut away to reveal the most massive trunk he had ever seen, its energy unmistakable.

Eradisel, one of the nine sacred trees.

The reason behind the steady flow of comfort solidified in his mind. Because of his gift, he'd always resonated with the Great Trees. In fact, he'd considered becoming one of the priests that tended the sacred nine, but he hadn't felt a true calling for that path. The gods were a distant concept, worthy of reverence but not as immediate as the life his magic detected. Why be bound to one place, meditating on divine favor, when he could be discovering the gods' creations? Or so he'd once thought. Roaming the world had lost its appeal after his latest adventure.

Aris sensed the soft brush of Eradisel's energy against his mind. Lyr had said that the sacred tree had warned them of Aris's arrival. But why? His feet wanted to carry him to Her to ask, but the task at hand kept him from following his desire. The Myern certainly would have allowed time, Aris knew, but Kezari was low on patience. If the sacred tree affected her, she didn't give any sign of it. She slunk after Lyr with hunched shoulders, her uneasy gaze darting everywhere.

Why was she so bothered by Braelyn? Kezari hadn't been this uneasy in the tavern or the clothing shop. Concerned, he connected to her mind. *"What is it? Do you sense danger?"*

"This place curves in little tunnels. You will see."

He found his brow lifting. Tunnels? Then Lyr pivoted down a corridor that did curve here and there to accommodate trees, though the hallway was hardly a tunnel. *"Don't dragons live in caves?"* he asked, trying to hide his amusement. *"With narrow passages, too, I'd wager."*

Kezari let out a small but pointed snort. *"Those are inside* mountains. *What if one of these trees crashes on this puny structure? There is no bulk. The other structures we entered might have been flimsy, but they weren't so ill-placed."*

Aris chuckled at that, earning a questioning glance from Selia. "How many spells would you say fortify this place?" he asked aloud.

Selia's brow furrowed for a moment before she answered. "There are seven types upholding the walls themselves, mostly preservation against natural degradation but some for fortification. A solid twenty-two maintain the roofs, and approximately fifty are layered carefully to prevent damage to and from the trees. Why do you ask?"

"Dragon taming," Aris answered as Kezari lifted her chin and pretended not to hear. "Kezari was concerned about the possibility of collapse with so many trees."

"*Reasonably so,*" the dragon sent to him alone. "*This form squishes easily.*"

As Aris choked back another laugh, Lyr peered at Kezari. "Braelyn has stood on this spot for thousands of years. In fact, the main entry and the rooms above were built just after the war with your kind."

"After we burned the original, I suppose," Kezari said stiffly.

"There was no ill-intent behind my comment." Lyr paused in front of a door and caught the dragon's eye. "We are not our ancestors. Even had our own parents warred, I would not hold you in poor regard because of it. I meant only to highlight the security of the building."

Kezari inclined her head. "I thank you, then."

Lyr opened the door and gestured for them to precede him. Aris followed Kezari through a short hallway that opened into a large oval room. Bookcases and tall windows lined the longer sides of the oval, with a short dais and large desk on the farthest end. The couple from earlier rose from two of the chairs in the center as the group entered. From their tense body language, he had a feeling the pair had been arguing, but he was hardly one to judge.

Quickly, Lyr made the introductions. Aris processed the formal titles with a smile, although the information prompted more questions he wouldn't ask out loud. The tall red-haired woman with green eyes was Lyr's daughter and was soulbonded to the frowning male with black hair. Arlyn and Kai. Seven years ago, before Aris had left on the expedition, the Myern hadn't had children. At least he didn't think so. Either Aris hadn't been paying attention, or something strange had happened in the last seven years.

"It is an honor to meet you," Aris said, keeping his curiosity to himself. "I appreciate your assistance with Iren. I hope he didn't give you too much trouble."

Arlyn grinned. "I had him go study with Lady Lynia. My grandmother will keep him in line."

He knew nothing about the lady in question, but from Selia's low laugh, he assumed it had been a good decision. "Thank you," he said.

Aris studied Lyr's tense posture as he strode across the room and opened a book on his desk, frowning down at the pages. Something was obviously bothering him. Were the terms of the Moranaian treaty with the dragons so dire? Kezari's request hadn't sounded like a problem to Aris, but his knowledge of the war didn't go beyond the basics every child learned. It seemed that hadn't been the case for Lyr, who flipped through the tome like he knew what he was looking for.

"It is as I thought," Lyr said. "No dragon can pass through the portal without the permission of both rulers. Even then, there are very specific conditions listed."

Aris took a step closer to Kezari, who had stopped her pacing to glare at Lyr. "Our queen could not feel the scope of this danger. She did not believe. You must be wiser."

Lyr placed his hands on his desk and leaned forward. "Perhaps you should explain what is going on."

"*Skizik?*" the dragon demanded.

"Oh no," Aris answered, shaking his head. "I barely understand this myself."

Kezari shifted on her feet. "I am of the Earth and the earth. I can work with the rocks and soil here, but my connection to our original world remains strong. Something is wrong there. It is terrible."

Lyr's lips turned down. "I have guides who travel there regularly. Although there was trouble with poisoned energy, that was resolved about a month ago. Is this feeling recent?"

"It is now," Kezari insisted. "It grows. It seeps into the ground. The plants and living creatures must be affected. Aris and I, we can heal it, especially with his mage."

Beside him, Selia let out a soft sound, a sure sign of her annoyance to any who knew her. "I have not agreed to such a thing."

Kezari turned her golden eyes their way. "You will. You must."

"This requires more investigation," Lyr said as he straightened. "I will not send any of you through with so little information. I do not mean offense, but it is difficult to believe that none of my guides would have noticed this kind of danger."

"It can't be too bad if Ralan isn't here giving orders," the one named Kai muttered.

"Prince Ralan?" Aris stared at the other man, uncertain he had heard correctly. The prince had left Moranaia centuries ago. "Why would he be?"

Lyr grimaced. "I'm sorry, Aris. You wouldn't have heard of his return during your...absence. The prince has been back for a couple of months now. Ralan, his daughter Eri, and his bonded Cora are currently staying in my home while a secondary palace is being built to the south of my lands. They are at the site consulting with the builders today."

"Eri isn't," Selia said, giving the door an uneasy glance as though someone would rush through at any moment. "She asked to stay and play with Iren after lessons."

"She was with my grandmother," Arlyn said.

Silence fell, and Aris pursed his lips at the oddness of it. He could deduce that Eri was a child, but why would that make a room full of adults nervous? Suddenly, he felt like an outsider in the land where he'd been born. Important events had obviously occurred, things the others knew well. As an adventurer, he'd always tried to

keep up with the news from the larger estates—it was how he'd found some of his best missions. Now he was a tree with no roots.

"I do not care who is here," Kezari said, her voice rising in annoyance. "Something must be done. Contact your ruler. Work out a new treaty."

Lyr's expression turned sympathetic. "I understand your concern. I do. There has been much to handle here, so I have grown accustomed to crisis. A rogue Moranaian caused the initial energy poisoning, and it affected quite a few fae realms as well as Earth. That foe has been defeated and a counter-spell activated. In truth, I have experienced enough chaos lately to know better than to dismiss your words."

"But?" Aris demanded.

"I must obey the law." Lyr gestured at the book still open on his desk. "This treaty is older than any of us, save perhaps Kezari. Ralan could negotiate on his father's behalf with the king's permission, but unless you are dragon royalty, Kezari, there is nothing to be done."

"I am not a princess." Kezari sniffed. "Nor am I so old. That happened in my grandparents' time, thank you."

Aris smiled slightly at the dragon's vanity, but he didn't want to hurt her feelings by calling her on it. "What would you suggest, Myern?"

"I'll send Kai and Arlyn through the portal to see if they can detect any hint of trouble. Arlyn destroyed the other spell, so she might be more sensitive to new problems."

"No," Kai said at once.

"If we weren't bonded, I'd shove you off the top of the brooding tower." Arlyn poked her finger against Kai's side. "Stop it."

Brooding tower? Bemused, Aris glanced between them. The group's arrival had definitely interrupted an argument, one that

appeared ready to erupt again. Arlyn glared at her bonded, who stood with crossed arms and set jaw. If the Myern thought she was skilled enough to take on such a mission, why would her bonded protest? How unusual.

"This is not the time for such a disagreement," Lyr snapped. "We can discuss this in greater detail once I have found our guests shelter."

Kai clenched his jaw tighter, but Arlyn's face reddened. "Of course," she said.

Though Lyr's eyebrows were lowered in frustration, he strode easily around his desk, and the emotion had smoothed away by the time he stopped in front of Kezari. "I assume you will want a place where you can shift back to your natural form?"

"Oh, yes," Kezari said emphatically. "This skin itches after a time. Far too small."

Aris frowned. His mind had been too muddled to consider this problem. There'd been fewer trees on their other stops, but the area around Braelyn was largely ancient forest. They'd learned to build their houses in, around, or on those trees, but Kezari's dragon form wouldn't fit in any of those structures. The few clear places along the ridges weren't particularly secure.

"The stone beneath Braelyn is fairly solid, but there is a small cave system on the north end of the ridge," Lyr said. "If it does not cause offense to be so removed from the bulk of my home, I would suggest you stay there. You are more than welcome to make subtle changes to the caves if they are not large enough."

Kezari's head tilted back. "You would trust me to make modifications?"

"Dragons are renowned for such work," Lyr answered. "And it would not be in your best interests to destabilize the land above you."

Cave...land above... Aris's shoulders jerked in an involuntary shudder. At Selia's concerned glance, he shook his head. He did not want to reveal yet another weakness, but he had no choice. Kezari was certain to be upset by his refusal. Still, what else could he do? Not even under the prompting of the Nine Gods of Arneen would he go into a cave voluntarily. "I will have to beg a different kind of shelter."

Kezari spun, her nostrils flaring. "I will not leave you unguarded. We should be close."

"I cannot." Aris let out a shaky sigh. "A cave would be living torment. Perhaps I could camp on the ridge just above? Anything out in the open."

"You are not considering the season. The nights are turning chilly, and the cold rains are almost upon us. Late autumn is an unpleasant time to camp," Lyr said.

Fiorn, where Aris had lived most of his life, didn't suffer through autumn rains—at least not in the same way. The plains did flood off and on through autumn and winter, but it was warm throughout both seasons. However, he'd been on several expeditions to climes like Braelyn's, and those had been sheer misery. Too bad he wouldn't be able to abide a tent. Fabric close to his face, blocking any view... No.

Selia stepped forward, catching his attention. "What about the brooding—I mean, the observation tower?"

Shame and frustration curled through his insides and sharpened his tone. "What, you think I need space to mope?"

"No." Selia lifted a hand in conciliation. "It's a nickname that has nothing to do with you. I wasn't trying to insinuate anything."

Lyr chuckled even as his daughter winced. "Arlyn has caught both myself and Kai atop the tower in times of distress, so she dubbed it the brooding tower. The name stuck."

Aris rubbed the back of his neck. He'd grown too sensitive during his capture, and he had a feeling it would cause him more than a little embarrassment. Selia wouldn't have been so rude. She, unlike his so-called bonded, had never insulted him like that. Well, besides a few well-placed barbs during arguments, but he'd never held that against her. He'd said his own share of foolish things.

"Forgive me," he said.

"Of course," Selia answered softly, but the tense set of her shoulders told him she was still upset. Nothing to be done about it now. "I suggested the tower because the walls of the top floor are largely glass. You can see from any angle but still be inside. And Kezari could perch on the top when she wished to be close to you. The roof is flat."

Lyr nodded. "Excellent suggestion. Would you mind showing Aris and Kezari the tower while I speak with Kai and Arlyn?"

"It would be my pleasure," Selia said.

Oh, he just bet it would. She was probably eager to reprimand him for thinking ill of her. "We would greatly appreciate it," Aris said.

Selia gestured toward the door. "Then let us go."

Hoping she wouldn't be too hard on him, Aris nodded and then followed.

As soon as the door closed, Lyr rounded on Kai. "That's it. What is wrong with you? Don't try to tell me everything is normal, either. Clearly, it is not."

Kai's nostrils flared. "I don't want Arlyn put in danger again. Last time was bad enough."

"You're joking." Lyr stared at his friend, aghast. Kai had never reacted this way before. He was treating Arlyn the way he'd seen some human males act toward their women, possessive and overprotective. "Would you say the same for Kera or any of our other female warriors?"

Kai gaped at him for a moment before shaking his head. "You think it is because Arlyn is a female? That's not it at all. Well, I suppose it's related, but—"

"I'm pregnant," Arlyn blurted, her words ringing into a sudden silence.

It didn't hit Lyr immediately. Then the full import trickled through, along with a shock so profound it rattled him to the core. His daughter was expecting a child? But she'd only been here for three months, had only been bonded with Kai the same length of time. Few elves conceived so quickly.

Joy sparked inside him as the news settled in.

"I should have waited a few more weeks to tell you," Arlyn mumbled.

Lyr's gaze shot to his daughter, his rising happiness stifled a little by her statement. "How long have you known?"

She nibbled at her lower lip. "Since just before Ralan went to Earth to find Cora."

Hurt pinched Lyr's heart, warring with joy. She'd kept something this important from him? It explained Kai's growing protectiveness and reluctance to travel to the Sidhe realm of his own father. Had they told Naomh? Anyone else?

Such amazing news—and only Kai's snit had revealed it to him.

"Why didn't you say anything?" Lyr forced himself to ask.

"Because of this. Your reaction." Arlyn sighed. "I knew you wouldn't take it well."

Comprehension dawned as Lyr stared at her worried face. "You think I'm upset that you're pregnant? No. I'm thrilled beyond telling about my first grandchild. But I am hurt that you didn't trust me enough to tell me sooner."

Frowning, Kai crossed his arms. "You were furious when we bonded."

Lyr made a sharp, impatient gesture. "Not at the bond itself. Only your haste in starting the bond. I thought we resolved that two months ago."

"I'm sorry," Arlyn whispered.

At the sight of his daughter's upset face, Lyr's hurt, and his heart, melted. He wrapped his arms around her in a gentle hug. "Ah, *tieln*, I'm the one who is sorry. This shouldn't be about me. Let's not mar such wonderful news with worry."

"I should have told you," she said with a sniffle. "Only Lial knows. I had to see him to check, of course. Well, Selia guessed this morning when my energy went awry during a lesson. I don't know why I was so worried. Hormones, maybe."

Smiling, Lyr gave Arlyn's shoulders a reassuring squeeze. "Don't stress this. Are you well? Is Kai so protective because there's a problem?"

Arlyn took a step back and glared at Kai. "No. We're perfectly fine."

"If she and the child are healthy, why would she not continue her duties?" Lyr peered at his friend curiously. Color had leeched from his face along with any hint of anger. "What is this really about?"

For a moment, Kai didn't answer, his expression twisting with an odd sort of pain. "I didn't know my own mother beyond my first few days of life. I can't abide risk to either you or our child, Arlyn. My family is so fucked up, but this…I want better for us. The fear isn't rational, but I can't silence it."

"I never said I wanted to go on this mission," Arlyn said with a shrug. "Unless there is truly no one else, I'd rather not. I don't think it's a good idea to expose our child to poisoned energy."

Kai scowled. "Then why—"

"I didn't want you speaking for me, either," Arlyn interrupted, giving her bonded a pointed look.

Lyr couldn't help but laugh at Kai's chastised expression. "You deserved that, my friend. As to our current crisis, I'll see if Inona is ready to resume her duties. If so, she and Delbin can travel to Earth. Delbin can seek out Fen and see if he knows what is going on. Hopefully, he isn't involved."

"I don't think he is," Kai said. "But our acquaintance was admittedly short."

"I suppose we'll see. Now…I won't tell you to rest, Arlyn. I'm sure Kai does that countless times already." Lyr grinned at his friend's disgruntled frown. "I'm sure you'd rather take Kai to task a bit more in private. Or have my mother work with him on his manners."

Kai groaned. "Can I just grovel?"

Lyr made a shooing motion. "Not here. I have work to do."

As soon as Kai and Arlyn closed the door behind them, Lyr sank into his chair and rubbed his hand across his eyes. Dragons had been denied access to the portal for a reason. The few dragons who had opted to stay on Earth instead of migrating to Moranaia had lingered for millenia and had caused a great deal of trouble. And during the war, some of the Moranaian dragons had raided Earth with impunity to bolster their resources. The humans had their dragon myths for a reason—dragons did not live well with other species.

But Lyr had a bad feeling that the dragon would have to go to Earth, and navigating the situation was a mess he'd rather not handle. Too bad it was his job. With a resigned sigh, he prepared to contact Inona.

7

By the time they neared the tower, Selia was ready to scream. Eradisel had told her to prepare herself, but there was no way to get ready for this. Her beloved husband walked beside her like a near-stranger, asking polite questions about the scenery. Who cared how many different kinds of blasted flowers were in the gardens or how long it had been since the last rain? No one in this situation.

"How long have you been here?" Aris asked.

"About three months." Gritting her teeth, she shoved the words she wanted to say to the back of her mind. "Lyr's daughter arrived unexpectedly from Earth. Her gift was strong but untrained, so he sought a teacher for her. Iren and I came to live here then."

Aris frowned. "How did Iren take the move?"

"He has loved being away from Fiorn," she answered. "We've had a few rough days, but he's thrived away from my father's strict rules."

"I imagine so." Aris grimaced. He'd never gotten along with her father, either. "There is so much I want to know about Iren. So many years… I'm not sure how I can ever make up for that."

Her heart pinched. She'd wanted him to talk about something more serious, but now that he'd broached the topic of his missing years, she wasn't sure how to continue. "It wasn't by your doing," she ventured.

Aris shook his head. "It doesn't matter. The result was the same."

She twisted her fingers together. "I don't know what to say."

"Selia," Aris said softly. "Don't get upset on my account."

She snorted at that. "Sure."

As they stopped at the door in the base of the tower, he surprised her by taking her hand. His hold was light, but it was there. Voluntarily. "I mean it. I don't know if the mind-healer can help. I don't know if anything can. But I will do my best to keep from hurting you more. That would never be my intention."

Her shoulders drooped. "I know."

"*Skizik*, this tower is broad," Kezari said from a few paces away, seemingly oblivious to their conversation. "I could maybe sleep on top."

The wide stone tower stretched up high in the middle of the clearing. But though the top was at the same height as the branches of the nearby trees, it didn't appear big enough for a dragon to sleep on. At least not to her eyes. "Let's go up. It's a bit of a climb, though, and the staircase is enclosed."

His hand jerked in hers before he abruptly let go. As he peered at the stone, Aris shivered. "With few windows."

"Were you…" How could she ask about his captivity without throwing his mind into chaos? She didn't want to, but it was difficult to suggest suitable shelter if she didn't know how he'd been held. "Do such structures bring back bad memories?"

His lips thinned. "Anything enclosed, which is nonsensical. The cave was large enough to hold Kezari in dragon form. But I was rarely free to explore it."

Although his words were even, Aris's pupils had begun to dilate, and his breathing was growing shallower. Her instinct was to reach out to him, but she held back. "Perhaps I can help," she offered softly.

"Selia—"

"Not with mind healing. I have an idea, if you'll indulge me."

His nod was sharp, but he gave it. Quickly, Selia sent a mental request to Lyr and stood with bated breath until he gave his assent. She hadn't been sure he would approve such a major modification, but he was eager to see Aris settled. All she needed now was energy. As she stepped through the doorway into the small landing at the bottom of the stairs, Selia reached out with her senses and connected to the power of the world around them.

Magic streamed through, burning in her blood like purest sunlight. Selia smiled with the joy of it, but she didn't take the time to bask. Instead, she funneled the power through the proper channel in her mind and stretched out her hand. She started up the steps, letting her hand rest on the wall, and forced the image in her mind outward.

Her body jolted as the magic poured free, bringing her inner vision to life. Beneath her fingers, the stone heated, and the slight resistance of rock gave way to the smooth glide of crystal. Although her body shook with the force of it, Selia took another step up. Then another. Trembling, she climbed and transmuted until her chest ached and her fingers stung from the constant heat.

Once she reached the upper landing, Selia slumped against the inside wall and stared at the shimmering crystal that now bordered the stairwell. It wasn't as clear as a window, but light poured through with hints of the outside world beyond. Would it be enough? Her transmutation abilities weren't strong enough to change rock to

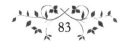

glass, only one kind of stone to another. She swiped the sweat from her forehead. It had been challenging enough to manage so much of that.

Selia drew in energy to replace some of what she'd used, but only sleep would fully rejuvenate her. It would be more than worthwhile if it gave Aris some relief. What else could she offer him? She wasn't a healer, and he didn't want her touch or even to talk. But this she could do.

Once her energy settled, Selia pushed away from the wall and started down the stairs. Only to halt halfway down at the sight of Aris climbing up, his hand—and gaze—on the hazy crystal. Surprised wonder filled his face instead of the fear he'd shown earlier. A few steps below, Kezari came into view, a toothy smile widening her mouth she stared at the crystal.

"Do you like it?" Selia asked softly.

Aris paused on the step beneath hers. "I am in awe of it. And you."

"No need of that," Selia said, smiling. "I hope it helps."

His hand rubbed absently at the crystal. "It does. I cannot tolerate the thought of being cut off from nature again. I was denied even the sight of it for so long."

Oh, how that must have hurt him! Selia's heart pinched, and she was glad to have eased that burden for him, if only a little. "Let's go see the top."

As Selia climbed again, she felt his presence behind her with each step. His energy was as familiar to her as her own, so she could sense his tumult without much effort. The alteration might have eased his panic, but his struggle was still evident. And why wouldn't it be? With Aris's connection to living things, it must have been pure agony to be cut off. Not just because of his magic, either. He might

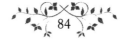

have scaled back his expeditions after Iren had been born, but he'd never wanted to stay indoors for long periods of time. He'd spent hours outside each day.

Selia paused when she reached the top landing again, an alcove that opened into the circular tower room. Sitting on one of the padded benches built into the base of the windows, Iren and Eri waited for Selia and the others. How in the world had they known…? She gave a soft snort at her own thoughts. Eri was there, so of course they'd known the right time to be in the tower.

She expected Iren to run up to Aris, who'd frozen at Selia's side, but their son stayed still. "Eri suggested we help set up the room," he said.

Selia huffed. "You were supposed to be studying with Lady Lynia."

"Our help eased things," Eri said, not a hint of chagrin in her tone.

After a glance around the bare room, Selia lifted a brow. "What did you do?"

Iren did jump up then. Excitement lit his face as he pointed at the ceiling. "We added a door."

"Irenel Baran," Selia breathed when she caught sight of the wooden rectangle angled awkwardly overhead. "Please tell me you did not modify Lord Lyr's property without express permission. I must be mistaken since you have very little of the artisan's gift and surely would not have tried such a thing."

Of course, Selia knew very well he would have done it, especially with Eri's encouragement. He might be the older by five years, but he wasn't a mature influence. Sure enough, a guilty flush stained his cheeks as he studied his feet. Selia took the opportunity to pull in a few deep breaths. He would admit it fairly quickly if she let him stew. He might be mischievous, but he was honest.

"Answer your mother, Iren," Aris said.

Although he didn't raise his voice, Selia and Iren both startled at the sound. Annoyance at his interference flashed through her, followed promptly by guilt. She might have grown accustomed to disciplining Iren herself, but Aris still had that right. It certainly motivated their son, who snapped to full attention.

"I did do it," Iren said, lifting his chin and squaring his shoulders. "I didn't think about asking, but I guess I should have. Eri said that if there wasn't a way for the dragon to get up there, they'd move to the cave area, and—"

"And they don't need to know that," Eri interrupted cheerfully. "Trust that it would be bad."

The brush of Aris's mind against hers was so light, Selia almost missed the request for communication. *"What's wrong?"* she asked.

"Is this the child everyone seemed worried about earlier?"

As the smooth timbre of his mental voice filled her mind for the first time in years, heat slammed into her, low and hard. Gods, she'd missed him. But she was careful to keep her reaction from crossing through their faint connection. *"Yes. Eri is Prince Ralan's daughter. She is a seer, same as he, but I wouldn't be surprised to find she's stronger."*

"Wonderful," Aris answered wryly before ending the link.

That loss hurt, but she didn't have time to dwell on it. "How in the world did you two manage this, Iren?"

"Well, Eri showed me an image of what we needed and where we could find it," Iren said. "I did a dual transport spell to switch the stone of the ceiling with a hatch from another tower. Eri said it wasn't being used."

"A hatch from…" Selia counted to ten. Then twenty. She choked down a bubble of laughter as she wondered what Lyr's reaction was

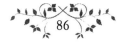

going to be. "Did it not occur to you both that this might cause a problem?"

Eri shook her head. "I checked. No one is going to need that tower for three months and nineteen days, and that's not even the most likely strand."

"Perhaps Lord Lyr does not want a ladder to the roof in this location," Selia said, struggling to control her tone. Shouting would not solve the problem. "Did you consider that?"

"He only yells in one strand." Eri shrugged. "In three, he is frustrated, and in two, he's amused. In all of them, he'll assign artisans to fix both towers. No big deal."

"*Miaran*," Aris muttered softly beside her.

Selia had to concur with the use of an expletive in this case. Eri was a force all her own. "I hope your assessment is correct. However, I fail to see why you couldn't wait if you knew the Myern could solve the dilemma himself."

"They are clever younglings," Kezari said before either child could answer. "There are too many trees nearby for me to land on the ground. I would not be able to check on Aris without this hole. How does it work?"

Iren pointed at an indention in the wood. "Direct a bit of magic there, and it'll slip down to release a ladder."

The dragon hurried forward, her curious gaze on the spot. Energy trembled through the room, raising little bumps across Selia's arms, a moment before a click sounded. As Iren had said, the wood angled down, and a ladder slid free. A breeze wafted through the hatch, bringing the sound of birdsong and the sharp scent of forest with it.

"Well," Selia said.

Part of her wanted to punish Iren for his actions, but an equal part was proud. He'd only been studying magic for a couple of years,

yet he'd managed a complicated set of spells on his own. He was innovative and quick-thinking, traits that would serve him well in the centuries of training to come. But he also had to learn not to act rashly.

"I wanted *Onaial* to be close," Iren said.

Aris crossed the room to kneel in front of their son. "I appreciate your effort. I have missed you more than I can say, Iren, and it lightens my heart to know you want me near. But I must be honest and tell you that I am not well. Inside my mind, where you cannot see. If there are times when I am distant, know that it is not your fault."

"I'm eleven now." The solemn expression on Iren's face made Selia want to weep. "I've learned enough about war to guess the kinds of things that happen to prisoners."

"I may not always be able to fight back the darkness," Aris said. "I am not the father you deserve. Not anymore."

Iren averted his gaze. "I haven't exactly been great myself."

Selia shivered as a cool tendril streamed through the open hatch. What was he talking about? Iren might have a bit of a wild streak, but he was an excellent son.

"I can't imagine you've done anything too bad," Aris said.

Iren bit his lower lip. Then he met his father's gaze, and his next words came in a rush. "I think I killed someone a couple of months ago. He was shooting arrows at Arlyn and Kai, so I used fire magic to stop him. I'd never used that kind of fireball, though. It was only supposed to burn the bow, but I lost control. Sometimes I wake up hearing his scream."

Selia gaped at her son, disquiet sliding through her at his words. He'd saved Kai and Arlyn, it was true, and she'd known he struggled with it. But why hadn't he told her he was still having nightmares?

Tears filled her eyes. She should have insisted on a mind-healer, at least for a quick check. Some mother she was.

"Did you eat him, too?" Kezari asked, missing the undertones of the conversation. "That is not always best. There are some beings it is better not to ingest."

Iren's eyes widened, and Aris gave the dragon an exasperated look. "Kezari."

If the dragon noticed the warning in his tone, she ignored it. "Fire is an excellent first attack. Your young one is strong, *skizik*."

Aris sighed. "Thank you, Kezari."

"I…I didn't eat him," Iren said.

Smiling slightly, Aris laid a hand on his son's shoulder, and Selia's heart squeezed at the sight. "I am proud of you, Iren," he said. "You acted to save others. How could you think I would be upset at you for that?"

Iren's lips turned down. "Because *I* am, I guess."

"Understandable," Aris said. "Killing should never be easy, but sometimes it's necessary. I'm certain your mother would have told you that."

"Sure. But I worried… I thought your spirit was maybe watching. Disapproving," Iren blurted.

Selia crossed her arms over her stomach, an inadequate wall for the pain churning inside. "I didn't know that," she whispered.

Iren scuffed his foot against the floor. "I wasn't sure if I should say."

"Well, you should've said something to me," Eri said suddenly, giving Iren a quick nudge. "I could have told you that you didn't kill anyone."

Selia's brows lifted, and her son spun back to face his friend. "What do you mean?" Iren asked. "You weren't here."

"I Saw stuff about Moranaia before we came here from Earth." Eri shrugged. "In the vision, the man you attacked ended up at a bad guy's house. The bad guy killed him."

Aris's forehead furrowed. "I fear I have missed a great deal these seven years."

"Nah, it was pretty boring until the last three months," Eri said with a chuckle.

Relief etched Iren's expression as he threw his arms around his father, laughing, but he pulled away when Aris stiffened. "Sorry. I just can't believe it. It wasn't me."

A little pale, Aris stood. But he didn't run away. "I am glad to hear it for your sake. And please don't be afraid to show affection. Even if...even if it is a struggle for me. It is not your fault."

"I know. Eri told me—" Iren's words cut off at another shove from his friend. "Never mind. I understand."

Suddenly, Eri tugged at his hand. "Let's go play."

"But I want to see my father," Iren argued.

"You'll see him more later." Though half his size, she dragged him toward the stairs. Her voice echoed behind their retreating backs. "Lord Lyr will be here in a quarter mark, and now he's yelling in two strands instead of one. Those odds aren't good."

Selia couldn't help but laugh. She probably ought to make them face Lyr's disapproval, but Iren needed some relief after the burden he'd carried for so long. She could give him his punishment later. Besides, Lyr would no doubt lecture both children, as would Ralan and Cora upon their return. Selia's gaze landed on Aris. A hint of a smile curved his lips as he stared after Iren. She had a feeling they'd both go easy on their son.

Just this once.

8

After a solid mark spent staring out the window, Aris could understand why they'd named this place the brooding tower. He could watch the limbs of the surrounding trees as they swayed in a gentle breeze and let his mind roam where it would. Here, he was apart from the world. Even the occasional person walking through the garden below didn't mar the feeling, for no one even glanced at the windows at the top of the tall tower. He could have been invisible.

The room had grown chilled with the open hatch, but Aris welcomed the coolness. The breeze carried the scent of fallen leaves and damp moss, the essence of autumn. A reminder that he was alive and free—and for the moment, alone. Kezari had flown in search of a stray *daeri* for her dinner after an exasperated Lyr had left with Selia to discuss the estate shielding. Thank the gods the Myern was a steady soul. Instead of shouting, he'd peered at the ladder, shaken his head, and said he'd find a proper artisan to situate the hatch correctly and replace the one now missing from the other tower.

He smiled at the memory of his son's guilty but proud expression. When Aris had left for his last expedition, Iren had only begun to show the promise of future power. Now he was using complicated transportation and alteration spells with a skill beyond his years. Aris's smile dropped. Iren had also been forced by circumstance to seriously injure another.

Would it have happened if Aris had been here?

Foolish thought. If assassins had shot at the Myern's daughter in the heart of Braelyn, then the danger must have been extreme, not to mention unusual. But he couldn't dismiss the notion. Nor could he shake the sinking feeling that he'd failed his son in more ways than he could ever know.

Aris spun away from the window and frowned at the round, empty room. Could he tolerate sleeping here? With so much glass, he didn't feel trapped, and if he kept the ladder down, he could see the canopy of trees and the gleam of moonlight after dark. But would the place trigger nightmares once the sun set?

He would have to hope not. The girl had said something bad would happen if he camped near Kezari's cave, and atop the tower it was too cold. Though he wouldn't usually give credence to the words of a child he'd never met, there was something uncanny about her. He'd never met Prince Ralan, either, but Aris had heard enough tales about his skill as a seer. If Eri was more powerful than her father, as Selia seemed to believe, then Aris would do well to take her seriously.

Whether he wanted to or not.

Selia stared at her reflection in the softly glowing mirror with barely restrained impatience. Why wasn't her sister answering? Selia's

time was limited. Lyr had asked her to add more nuanced dragon detection to the estate's existing shield and to expand its range in case any followed Kezari. That would take several marks and a lot of energy, something she was short on as it was. She also wanted to check on Aris, and she needed to have a long talk with Iren about today's actions.

All before bed.

Abruptly, the light from the mirror flared and then settled into her sister's image. They could have been twins, despite the couple of centuries separating them in age, except that Niasen's hair was closer to brown than gold. But their dispositions differed greatly. Her sister was more bold and assertive, but she lacked Selia's patience.

"Selia!" Niasen called. "I did not expect to hear from you today. I hope all is well."

Selia studied her sister's harried expression with a frown. "I could say the same for you. You look frustrated."

"Father chose a poor time to take one of his little trips." Niasen grimaced. "Erek and Temeth ran off together before Erek could formally dissolve his marriage bond to Bothen, and Bothen is understandably furious. And Erek and Temeth each had three students who have to be reassigned. Nothing that I can't handle, but the drama is monumental. Odes will be written about this mess, I've no doubt."

Selia barely heard most of what her sister said. She was stuck on the first part. "Father took another trip? Where?"

Niasen drew back in surprise. "Earth, of course. I thought you knew."

"No," Selia said through gritted teeth. More hurt to layer on the day's pain. "He must have decided not to visit me before he traveled through the portal."

Regret and sympathy crossed Niasen's face. Braelyn guarded Moranaia's only portal to Earth, so her father would have passed through here to take one of his jaunts. On one of his previous trips, he'd conceived and then abandoned a son with a human woman, but neither Niasen or Selia had known. They'd only discovered the truth after Selia had tested Lyr's newfound daughter, Arlyn. That abandoned child had been Arlyn's grandfather. No doubt her father had feared Selia's anger, which still hadn't cooled after his long deception.

Even knowing that, his lack of contact hurt.

"I hope he behaves himself this time," Selia simply said.

Niasen's lips thinned. "He swears he will take more care."

"We shall see."

"Is everything fine otherwise?" Niasen asked. "You do not tend to connect in the middle of the day."

"You aren't going to believe the news I have to share." Selia took a deep breath as her sister stared in confusion. "It's about Aris. He's...he's alive."

Niasen's mouth dropped open. "What?"

"Aris is alive," Selia repeated. "He just arrived."

"That *drec*," Niasen said with a snarl. "He abandoned you?"

Selia hurried to explain before her sister became truly angered. "No. He'd been captured and held against his will."

"Sure."

"He's with the dragon who saved him," Selia said. "She confirmed it."

Her sister's brows shot upward. "A dragon? If you are jesting with me—"

"No, I'm not," Selia interrupted. But she hesitated, uncertain of how much to say. "If you'd seen them, you would believe. Aris... He

is severely traumatized. I don't know the entire story, but I'll tell you what I can when I do. Just…don't tell Father if he returns without stopping here. He never liked Aris, and I don't want to deal with him in the midst of everything else."

Niasen peered at her for a moment before finally nodding. "If you believe Aris, I'll take your word. The dragon, of course, would be tough to fabricate. And you may be assured that I will not tell Father when he contacts me tomorrow to check on estate business. I am still angry at him, myself."

"Thank you."

They chatted a little longer, Selia offering advice on finding teachers for Niasen's abandoned students, before her sister had to rush off to solve another problem. Once the connection ended, Selia leaned back against her seat and rubbed her eyes. The discussion could have gone worse. Niasen was fiercely loyal, and Selia had half-feared that she'd storm Braelyn to take Aris to task. One crisis averted, at least.

Blowing out a long breath, Selia pushed to her feet. Transmuting the stone tower had taken a good half of her reserves, but she had enough left to tackle the estate shielding. Barely. If Arlyn's magic wasn't going awry, Selia would have asked for her help, but her student would need to practice attuning her power while pregnant before taking on such delicate work. And Iren didn't have enough experience, tower adventures notwithstanding.

Of course, if Aris were well, he could have shared his life energy with her. His rare talent provided one of the few types of power that didn't require transmuting, and they'd once worked together often when she had need of more magic. Her heart squeezed at the memories. They might never be able to work together like that again.

After a moment's hesitation, Selia opened a small chest on her desk and grabbed an energy crystal. Pulling in natural energy and converting it to something she could use took a good bit of her inner reserves, but the crystal held her stored power. She hated to use one, but it seemed prudent. If more dragons arrived or Kezari wasn't as friendly as she appeared, Selia might need her magic to stop them. She couldn't afford to drain herself completely.

Perhaps a thought she should have had before transmuting a tower, but Selia didn't regret it. She would never regret helping Aris.

She hurried from her room and down the staircase to the lower floor. She'd just turned the corner to the hall leading to the library when she spotted Ralan striding her way. He must have returned from the building site. Had he spoken to Eri yet? Judging by the crease between his eyebrows, Selia had a feeling he'd either heard or Seen something.

"Ah, Selia," he said, coming to a halt at the same time she did. "I am glad you took the most likely path. I wanted to offer my apologies for my daughter's behavior as well as my own absence this day."

Selia smiled. "Eri hardly acted alone. And you can't be everywhere."

"I had intended to be here for this had the strands not shifted," Ralan muttered. "I should have been paying more heed."

"Is the situation that serious?" she asked.

His lips twisted wryly. "Is it ever otherwise? I can't say much, but I suggest you speak with Arlyn about Earth. And have Inona find you suitable clothes. A future visit is a high probability."

Excitement and fear streamed through her in equal measure. "So the dragon is correct?"

"More correct than she knows." Ralan sighed. "You'll likely go, as will Aris when he is able. Possibly Iren. And *that* is all I will say."

Absently, Selia bid the prince good day as he departed. Her mind was on the news he had delivered. Her, go to Earth? Some of her kind, like her father, traveled there to explore the human world without the humans' knowledge, but she'd never really considered it. Still, Arlyn's descriptions of the Earth realm had piqued Selia's curiosity. The elves had magic, but they didn't have moving vehicles, computers, or space stations circling the planet.

Because of magic, her people had never needed to create the type of physical devices the humans had. Why burn natural resources fueling vehicles when one could step through a transportation portal? Moranaians rarely even rode horses for long distances, though they were more common outside the mountainous regions.

Lost in thought, Selia slipped out the back door and headed for the training room, the best place to perform detailed magic undisturbed. Was it any wonder they hadn't created ships capable of sailing the rough eastern ocean until the last decade? Travel had become easy once magical transportation was established, and the population grew too slowly to make expansion to new continents necessary.

From what she'd heard, Earth was teeming with people. Humans everywhere. Did she have it in her to take this journey? She'd moved around over the centuries to teach, but she'd never been particularly adventurous otherwise. Frowning, she entered the training room and hung up her cloak. No, she hadn't been adventurous, but the idea held an odd appeal.

Selia settled on a cushion in the center of the room and placed the energy crystal in her lap. There was a lot to consider, but she would have to do it later. She wanted to complete the shielding quickly so she could check on Aris and get his thoughts on Ralan's words. They would have to think very carefully about what to do with Iren.

But first, work.

By dinner, Selia wanted nothing more than to curl up in bed and sleep, preferably wrapped around Aris, but she'd long ago learned that wants often went unrealized in reality's domain. Instead, she sat at the table with the others as they discussed the day's events over the evening meal. She'd come to enjoy spending time with her new friends each day, but today was different. Today, she felt alone.

Lyr sat at the head of the table, Meli at his right and Arlyn at his left with Kai next to her. Ralan and then Cora were beside Meli. That left Selia on her own at Kai's left. The only other person at the table without a mate was Lynia, who'd settled beside Selia instead of her usual place at the other end from Lyr.

Selia hadn't given much thought to all the couples until Aris had refused to attend the meal, too concerned about another breakdown. Now she felt the lack most acutely. What would it be like to share a secret glance with him over some point of discussion? To have his hand brush hers and linger? She could lean into him as she told an amusing tale or simply smile into his eyes, secure in the knowledge of his love.

If he hadn't gone on that expedition, everything would be different. Selia curled her hands in her lap and stared down at the food on her plate, her appetite stifled by the turn of her thoughts. Aris never would have been tortured if she hadn't insisted he go. He acted concerned that he would hurt her, but she'd caused the most harm of all. How could he not be angry at her for that?

"Are you unwell, Selia?" Lynia asked softly. "It has been a difficult day."

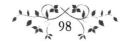

"I am not certain what to think of it all," Selia admitted.

Cora leaned forward, a sympathetic smile on her lips. "It wasn't helped by our children."

Selia chuckled at the reminder. She'd ended up making Iren eat dinner in his room and do two marks' extra studying, though she really wanted to let his actions pass. Judging by Eri's absence, she'd been given a similar punishment.

"Indeed not."

"I like the changes," Kai said, surprising her. "I didn't go up, but I've long thought it would be nice to have a ladder to the top. I did see the crystal walls, though. I hope you don't transmute them back."

Meli nodded. "Oh, yes. It reminds me of Alfheim."

Selia lifted a piece of bread and took a half-hearted bite. She was glad that Meli found comfort in the tower, but the knot in Selia's stomach hadn't disappeared. "I am happy to hear it."

"There are no interior rooms besides the one at the top, so the new walls won't interfere with anyone's privacy," Lyr said. "I imagine we will keep it."

An awkward silence descended as they all avoided broaching the most serious topic. Finally, Prince Ralan cast a serious look around the table. "I know you are all wondering, and the answer is no. I do not know all that is to come. At least not as well as I would like. There are quite a few future threads, all with different outcomes."

"At least your Sight has returned now that your brother is dead," Cora said.

Ralan shrugged. "Sometimes there are too many options for it to be useful. But you know I will help as I can."

"Delbin and Inona left two marks ago," Lyr said. "I'm not certain what, if anything, they'll be able to find. They are going to check with Cora's half-Sidhe friend, Maddy, and then see if they

can track down Fen or Vek. With Fen's earth magic, he might have already detected the same thing Kezari has."

Selia shifted in her seat. "But what then? Finding a problem won't negate the law forbidding Kezari from going through."

"It is my hope that if we gather enough evidence, the dragons' queen will reconsider her refusal," Lyr answered. "Provided I can find a suitable way to communicate with her. It hasn't been attempted in some time."

Ralan leaned forward. "My father can. You may be the liaison between Moranaia, Earth, and those fae we speak with through the Veil, but our ruler is ultimately in charge of negotiations with the dragons. The king has the only communication mirror to them, so far as I am aware."

"I will contact him as soon as possible," Lyr said.

Selia took a long drink of her wine, a wasted effort since it wasn't the type to easily intoxicate. "I hope Lial will be able to find someone to help Aris. I don't think either of us should travel to Earth until then."

"Lial will succeed, likely by tomorrow." Ralan smiled. "But I would have guessed that without my Sight. Mind-healers are accustomed to traveling quickly."

The conversation drifted to other topics, as did Selia's thoughts. Would this day never end? She still needed to speak to Aris about their possible trip to Earth and what to do about Iren. Would it be better to try tonight or to wait until the healer arrived? Maybe there would never be a good time. There was a chasm between them that their love once filled.

Selia had no clue if that hole could ever be healed.

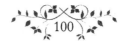

9

Delbin skidded to a stop at the door to The Magic Touch, Inona close behind. He sighed with relief at the sight of the Open sign hanging at a tilt against the glass. The Veil had been unexpectedly turbulent, or so Inona had said, and he believed it. He hadn't experienced the strain of trying to grasp the strands and pull them through, but the journey had taken longer than usual, and he'd been sick to his stomach by the end. Then he'd had to charge his phone with a bit of magic before they could call for a ride into town.

"Looks like we made it," Inona said.

His insides clenched at the strain in her voice. On their last trip to Earth, Inona's throat had been slit in a confrontation with Kien, and only Cora's quick healing had saved her. Inona was cleared by the healers to resume duty, but Delbin still worried. She'd been remote and contained since her near-death. Understandably, of course, but he couldn't help but fear that she blamed him in some way. Maybe this return trip reminded her of the trauma—and her anger at him.

"Well?" Inona's head cocked, a question in her eyes, before she shrugged and opened the door. "No need to stand here staring at the entrance."

Delbin shoved his concerns to the back of his mind and followed her inside. They passed several racks of clothes on their way to a long counter in the back, where the red-haired, half-Sidhe Maddy perched on a stool.

"Inona! Delbin!" With abroad smile, she jumped down and rushed around the counter. Delbin halted beside a display of shirts, just in time for Maddy to launch herself at him for a hug. Surprisingly, she did the same for Inona, although they hadn't had much time to get to know one another during the previous trip.

"What are you two doing here?" Maddy asked as she pulled away. "Please tell me this is a friendly visit and not some other disaster?"

Delbin grimaced. "I wouldn't call it a disaster, but I'm afraid we *are* here for more than just a visit. I don't suppose you know where Fen is?"

"His Uncle Vek's house, I think," Maddy said, her nose wrinkling. "He just bought it."

Delbin's brow quirked. Vek had a house? He'd only arrived a couple of weeks before, hadn't he? "He must've used magic to get a sale through that fast."

"Probably. An Unseelie like him wouldn't have any qualms."

He almost reminded her of how Fen had been willing to sacrifice himself to save her from Kien, but she'd scowled enough at his name that Delbin decided not to. Whatever was going on between them was none of his business. Unless, of course, either of the Unseelie males hurt Maddy or Jase, the other full-time employee here.

"They haven't caused you trouble, have they?" Delbin asked. "Or bothered Jase?"

Maddy waved her hand. "No, nothing like that. But I'm Seelie. I don't trust how nice they've been."

"They've given us plenty of cause to doubt their intentions," Inona interjected. "Especially Fen, since he worked with Kien for a time, but we may need their aid. Have you noticed anything odd in the last couple of weeks?"

"Odd how?"

"Wait," Delbin said as a hint of unfamiliar magic drifted across his senses. A chill went through him. He peered around the room and out the front windows, but he didn't see an obvious source. "How long until you close?"

Maddy tugged her phone out of her back pocket. "Fifteen minutes. Would you mind doing a quick check of the floor to make sure the displays look okay? Doesn't have to be perfect. I'll start closing out the register, at least as much as I can while we're still open."

Delbin almost laughed as a hint of panic pinched Inona's face. Maddy might as well have asked her to give a report on the current state of human fashion. "Why don't you scan for any threat, love?" he asked Inona. "I'll work on the shelves."

"Yes. Thank you," she said under her breath.

It wasn't a difficult task, not after all the jobs he'd done during his hundred-year exile on Earth. Really, straightening purses and shoes was more natural than practicing magic or learning Moranaian history. He was finished with the task before Maddy locked the door and headed back to the counter.

"Come on," Maddy said, grabbing the till from the cash register. "We can talk in the back."

Delbin and Inona followed her through the door behind the counter and into the small office beyond. Past the desk and the small

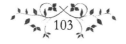

safe, the space became a stock room, with tall shelves full of shoes and other merchandise. Maddy pulled a couple of extra chairs up to the desk and then sat at her own. As she sorted through the money, she flicked a glance at Delbin.

"Okay, why'd you tell us to wait?"

He lifted his brows. "You didn't sense that strange energy moving through the room?"

"I did, but I didn't give it much thought." Maddy shrugged as she copied numbers into a book and put some of the bills into a bank bag. "Those have been happening lately. The first time was maybe a few days after you left? Jase and I wondered if someone was spying, but then other fae mentioned the same thing. It's like a pulse. A wave that flows through and then is gone. No one knows what's up."

Inona straightened in her seat. "Has anything else unusual happened?"

"Well." Maddy's hands stilled. "Jase thinks it's my imagination, but I could swear there are more brownouts. Anna said the power went out at our house twice while I was working yesterday. I mean, it happens, but when I looked at the outage map online, the affected area seemed pretty large. The website said they are doing maintenance, but I still think something isn't right."

Random waves of magic and possible interference in the electrical grid? Delbin's lips pursed. It could indicate a problem, but neither sounded serious enough to have a dragon from Moranaia ready to storm the portal. They definitely needed to speak with Fen and Vek. Especially Fen, since he'd helped Kien poison the local energy fields not that long ago.

"What do you mean by outage map?" Inona asked, reminding Delbin that although she traveled to Earth as a guide, she wasn't familiar with human technology.

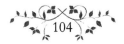

"Here, I'll show you." Maddy turned to the computer and wiggled the mouse, waking the monitor. After a bit of typing, a website popped up with a map of Chattanooga. "See all those reddish dots? That shows where the electricity is out."

Frowning, Inona leaned closer. "How does this map know?"

"I have no idea," Maddy said. "I guess the electric company has sensors. But look how many dots there are on the west side of town. The neighborhoods and businesses near Prentice Cooper State Forest keep losing power, especially near the mountain where Fen set up that spell for Kien."

Delbin studied the screen for a moment. "I don't suppose you'll show us where Fen and his uncle live? If you know the exact place."

Maddy's cheeks reddened. "I might have driven by after Vek mentioned it. Once. Or twice."

He let out a low chuckle. "I hope Anna's not too mad about that."

"I'm trying to build up the nerve to really thank Fen for saving me," Maddy muttered.

"Whatever you say," Delbin said, but as his friend squirmed uncomfortably in her seat, he dropped the teasing. "You can just give us the address. I'll blame Ralan, so Vek won't know who did it."

Inona shoved his arm. "You're going to cause a multi-dimensional incident if you make the princes annoyed at each other."

Delbin smirked. "Couldn't be too bad or Ralan would've told me not to do it."

"What if Prince Ralan wasn't checking for these future strands?"

"Then he'll have a fun surprise," Delbin quipped. Then he sobered. "Seriously, I'm not going to cause trouble. After all that has happened lately, I don't think Prince Vek will be upset at our arrival, especially not after we explain."

Maddy gestured at the desk. "Let me finish this, and I'll drive you there myself. I really do want to tell Fen thanks. Maybe having you two there will give me the courage."

"Sounds good," Delbin said. "Anything we can do to help?"

"Make sure the front door is warded with magic and turn off the lights." Maddy picked up another stack of money. "I'll add the final count to the books and prepare the deposit. Then we can go."

As Delbin returned to the front room to finish closing up, Maddy's words circled in his mind. *I still think something isn't right.* Maddy was a healer, although a barely trained one, so if her intuition hinted at a problem, it was worth investigating. Could the energy poisoning be seeping back in, too slowly for non-healers like him and Inona to notice? Did Maddy's power have some connection with Earth? The dragon might be mistaken—or lying.

But Delbin would trust Maddy with his life.

The wind bit into the skin of Aris's face, but it made a welcome contrast to the heat of Kezari at his back. The dragon had curled up on the top of the tower after her hunt, leaving just enough space for him to climb up through the hatch. She wasn't at her full size, but she didn't complain as much about this as she did her elven form.

Not that he could blame her.

Aris hugged his knees closer and snuggled deeper into the space between the dragon's front leg and her chest. What would it be like to completely change size and body structure? She must have practiced before their first meeting, for she hadn't struggled to walk. If he managed to turn into a dragon somehow, he'd probably fall flat on his snout in less than a moment.

"I have faith in you, skizik," Kezari sent.

His sigh puffed into a cloud of frost. *"Do you read my mind constantly?"*

"Almost." She tilted her head enough for one eye to focus on his face. *"I worry about what you might do."*

"You should have chosen someone less broken."

Kezari hesitated before answering. *"What makes you think I am so whole?"*

Aris stared at the side of her wedge-shaped head, but her unblinking eye gave no indication of her mood. Only the rustle of her wings betrayed any agitation. *"I'm admittedly no judge of dragon behavior, having met only you, but you seem well enough. You have the confidence to cross half the world, and I can barely go into a room without panicking."*

"There's more than one type of scar." Kezari lifted her head, breaking eye contact. *"I do not have the support of the dragon queen for a reason."*

His fingers dug into his legs at her words. *"You led the Myern to believe that it was the queen's error."*

"It is." A tiny flame slipped from Kezari's mouth before she continued. *"Most do not believe me, but what I sense is the truth. You see, we are born with the call of Earth in our veins. No one is certain why after all these years, but it is so. But as we grow, it fades. Most choose to have the connection severed or stifled since it no longer serves a purpose. I did neither, and instead of fading, my link grew stronger."*

"Ah." The tension eased from his shoulders. *"You believe you are broken because you are different."*

Kezari's chest heaved beneath his back with her sigh. *"It is true."*

"It is not." Aris lowered his hand to her leg and gave a gentle squeeze. *"Sometimes the very thing that seems a hindrance is our salvation. I believe it will be so with you."*

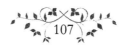

"I hope you are correct. I am uncertain we can convince the queen, but I cannot deny the Earth's cry for help."

"We'll figure something out," he reassured, though he had no clue how they would.

They both went silent as the frigid wind swirled around them, bringing the scent of rain. The cold approached from the north, and the yearly autumn battle between seasons would begin. Would he be here when the rain turned to ice and snow? At this rate, he wasn't certain he could make it to the equinox in a few days' time.

Before his thoughts could drift too far along that line, a shiver of awareness traced his skin as the protections he'd placed on the tower alerted him to another's presence. It was poor form to add his own shielding to the building, but he hadn't been able to stand the thought of anyone approaching him without his knowledge. He connected fully to the spell, seeking the information it held, and followed the warmth of Selia's energy as she ascended the steps. She'd taught him this spell and could have unraveled it easily, but instead, her presence halted at the top of the inner stairs.

Aris shoved to his feet but hesitated to move toward the hatch. That clawing fear that had been eased by the healer's magic itched at the back of his mind, waiting to engulf him. Anytime he entered an enclosed space, he risked releasing it. Love, guilt, regret—they converged on him each time he saw Selia. But she'd said before dinner that she would return to speak to him about Iren and their possible trip to Earth. He couldn't hide up here and avoid that discussion.

No matter how much he wanted to.

"Should I transform?" Kezari sent.

"No," he answered. *"Some things I must do myself."*

In truth, he wanted to be alone with Selia as much as he feared it. He'd been able to speak with her before dinner, even survived

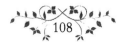

rejecting her invitation. He could do this. Resolved, he edged around the dragon's arm, lifted the hatch in the floor, and descended the ladder. Cold air followed him down, but he didn't close it. At least not until he peered through the dim light at Selia to see her shivering. He shoved aside the thought of being trapped and pulled the hatch closed. He could shatter a window or rush down the stairs. Kezari could break through the top with a single claw. It was fine. He would be fine.

"I can go back down and get my cloak," Selia said softly. "I left it on the hook without thinking. Or I could ask permission to alter the spell so you can leave the hatch open without freezing."

His heart warmed at her concern, but he pulled his shoulders back and shook his head. "I must learn to be inside. The windows help."

Selia shifted a step closer, into the glow of the single mage light he'd activated. "If you say so. But the offer stands."

He stared at her beloved face as uncertainty flooded him. What could he say to her? Seven terrible years filled the chasm between them. Did he deserve to have a say in Iren's life anymore? He hadn't been there for the two of them, and it didn't matter that his absence hadn't been by choice. He didn't know anything about his son's life in the interim. How could he say whether Iren was capable of traveling to Earth?

"If you are not ready, we can have this discussion tomorrow," she said.

"Why do you want my input?" he found himself asking. "Am I even really Iren's father?"

Oh, clechtan. He hadn't meant that the way it had sounded, but it was too late to recall the words now. Selia flicked her fingers, and the mage lights ringing the room leapt to life. Her tan skin had gone

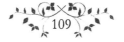

ashen, but her lips had thinned until they were white. Nostrils flaring, she stomped across the space between them.

As she came to a halt, the color rushed back into her cheeks. "I may not know what happened to you, but I can't believe you would—"

"I'm sorry," Aris said. "That came out wrong. Truly. I was wondering if I had the right to call myself his father, not questioning that he is mine. I would never do that."

Her eyes narrowed, and her chest heaved. "I don't know if I can believe you."

He couldn't stop staring at her flushed cheeks and parted lips, not even to defend himself. Except for the anger in her gaze, she had always looked much the same after he'd kissed her. Well, there had been a few arguments where he'd pulled her into his arms and… Groaning, Aris spun away and shoved his hands into his hair. Waves of memories both good and bad beat at his mind, but he built his mental wall ruthlessly higher. He *would* make it through a single discussion.

"Aris?"

"I give my word that I meant no offense," he answered, though he wasn't ready to look at her. Not yet. "But how can I call myself a father? I don't know what Iren is capable of. I haven't been here to see his character form. There is no way I could decide this."

Selia stepped close enough for her energy to brush his. "I wouldn't expect you to make the decision, but you deserve to give input. You will always be his father. It's up to you to earn the name *Onaial.*"

A smile ghosted across his lips at the word. *Onaial,* a blend of the words 'heart' and 'father.' Iren already called him that, but Selia was correct. There was much Aris could, and should, do to earn

it. He'd missed too much time with Iren already. If there was any chance of healing, of moving forward, Aris had to take it.

He took a deep breath and turned around to face Selia once more. Their bodies nearly brushed, she was so close, but he forced himself to hold his ground. "If you want my opinion, well... I believe we should bring him with us."

Her brows rose. "You do? But with your dragon so upset, I can only imagine what we'll find. You want to bring him into danger?"

"I don't think we'll have a choice."

"He has barely started his training." Selia crossed her arms beneath her breasts, and he forced his gaze away. "Iren is very powerful, but he has no discipline. Just today, he modified the tower without a thought to the consequences."

Aris let out a soft laugh. "Didn't you, too?"

"I asked permission first," she said with a huff, but he could tell by the twitch of her lips that he'd made a point.

He gestured at the hatch. "What he did today? That's why we need to take him."

"I don't understand," Selia said, frowning.

"He has your confidence and strength, but he has my personality." Aris smiled. "If we tell him he has to remain behind, he'll find some way to follow. His best friend's a seer, so he might even succeed. I don't want to have to worry about that. Do you?"

"By Arneen," she muttered. "You might be right. But the danger... I'll have to think about this."

At the worry pinching her face, the urge to hold her rose like fire within him. Once, he wouldn't have hesitated to offer comfort. Now, his hand shook as he lifted it to cup her cheek. Her soft skin warmed his chilled fingers until her heat seeped into his blood. He'd never experienced this kind of connection to another, not even—

No. He wouldn't think about her.

"Ah, Selia," he whispered, "If only…"

Her breathing grew ragged, and her arms tightened around her ribcage, pushing her breasts higher. Gods. He needed to hold her. He had to. In this moment, the darkness was locked away. He could be normal, right? Her gaze, full of longing, met his, and he was lost.

His hand slid from her cheek into her hair, and his other hand dropped to her waist. Aris took a deep breath and pulled her against him. Her head settled in the hollow between his shoulder and neck, just as it always had, and she wrapped her own arms around him. Home. He'd finally made it home.

For a few heartbeats, he savored the feel of her body against his. Then her hold tightened. Softly, but as her breasts pressed into his chest, her hips came into alignment with his. He went hard, painfully so, and the wall he'd tried to build crumbled into dust. Memories rushed over him, but not of Selia. His vision went black.

Perim's hands squeezing. Caressing. Demanding. The rock beneath his back as he was shoved down to the cave floor. Chained.

Bile scalded his throat, and he jerked back from the female wrapped around him. A cry sounded, then a soft thud. Maybe he'd hurt her this time. She'd thought using his body for her pleasure would force the bond, but she'd been wrong. Maybe he'd hurt her too badly for her to try again. Please, gods.

Please.

Rock bit into his knees as he dropped, shoving his hands against his eyes. Why couldn't he see? Had she hit him again? He hadn't refused her demands, had he? His body would cooperate even if his heart and mind screamed in denial. But she only hit him hard enough to blind him when he'd said no.

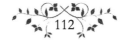

A thud resounded from overhead, and the female let out a sound of pain. Good.

Then the world went dark.

10

As her spell hit Aris, Selia shoved herself to her knees from where she'd fallen and shuffled over to catch her husband as he toppled. She let out a soft *oomph* as his dead weight hit her, knocking her over. As her body crumpled backward, her lower legs became trapped beneath her, her heels digging painfully into her bottom. Her upper thighs stung from being stretched into an unnatural position, and her breathing shallowed beneath his weight.

What had just happened?

Aris had stunned her by drawing her close, after he'd avoided touching her as much as possible since his return. Then, just as abruptly, he'd tensed and shoved her away with enough force that she'd lost her balance. He'd gone insensible. As a thud resounded from the hatch above, Selia had acted on instinct and cast a spell of unconsciousness at him.

A sob slipped from her lips. Once he learned that she'd used her magic against him, he would never forgive her. Not after he'd suffered at the hands of that other woman. Why had she done such a thing? She should have tried to reason with him first. Maybe. She'd never seen such panic before. His eyes had lost focus, and he'd clawed his hands across his chest as though trying to scour his flesh.

But that was nothing to the low, tortured moan ringing in her memory.

Selia tried to wiggle out from underneath him, but he was too heavy. Drat. She needed to get out from under him before he came to and lost control again. She had to think of something… Her lips twisted as she pulled in energy for a levitation spell. Too bad she hadn't considered doing that instead of shoving her body beneath him like a blasted cushion. She sucked in a breath as his weight lifted off of her and then shifted him to the side while she still had the strength.

Before she could get up, the hatch crashed open, and the bottom of the ladder hit the stone floor with a crack. Kezari rushed down, completely naked in her elven form, and knelt beside Aris. "What did you do to him?" the dragon snarled.

"Me?" Selia blinked up at the dragon. "He went from pulling me close to shoving me away. With force. I didn't hurt him."

"Why is he not awake?" Kezari leaned over Aris to glare down at Selia. "I had to shift and learn the way of opening the hatch. Your magic hit him, and he fell."

Selia uncurled her legs and groaned as she straightened them along the cool floor. The dragon leaned back, and Selia sat up. Pain shot through her thighs and up her back from the awkward strain of her previous position. Wincing, she twisted in a slow, tentative stretch to ease the twinge in her back.

Kezari's brow furrowed. "You move like a decrepit *daeri*. Were you injured, too?"

"I caught him when he toppled over." Selia rubbed her hands across her thighs. "I'm not injured, just sore."

"I know your magic was to blame for Aris's current state."

Selia sighed, her shoulders slumping. "It was instinct. He was so lost, and I...I didn't know what else to do. You can see for yourself that he's only unconscious."

The dragon lowered her hand to Aris's forehead, and the solid, earthy thrum of her power vibrated against Selia's shields. But Selia detected no threat, no hint of attack magic. It was a probing spell, though not one that she had ever used. Like a tune a few notes off, the enchantment was just familiar enough to be disconcerting without causing true alarm.

Kezari drew back, her posture easing as her magic winked out. "A different version of my own spell. Forgive my assumption."

She couldn't blame the dragon. She would have been suspicious, too, under similar circumstances. "Of course. Were you connected when he lost control? What happened?"

Kezari's lips turned down as she glanced at Aris. "You should not have pulled yourself so close."

"*He* hugged *me*," Selia insisted.

"Lightly," the dragon said. "Then you curled together like lovers entwining necks."

Bemused, Selia stared at Kezari. "What?"

"Your bodies wrapped together."

Ah. Perhaps dragons hugged with their necks? Despite the situation, Selia smiled. "It was an innocent embrace, not uncommon among our kind."

"There is no innocent hold for Aris," Kezari said sadly. "I will not tell his tale, but consider everything the woman might have done to him as part of his capture."

Selia's stomach lurched as she studied Aris's sleeping face. She could think of one thing in particular that would have caused her

touch to break him, and it wasn't pretty. Anathema. Punishments for rape varied, but they were always harsh. If she had Aris's tormentor in front of her now, Selia would cast a spell of pain so convoluted a healer would spend a solid week unraveling it.

Not that Lial would. In truth, he would probably help her devise the proper punishment.

"Aris must believe I'll blame him. Reject him," Selia whispered, caressing him with her gaze. The only touch she dared offer right now. "That's why he can barely look at me."

Kezari's expression gave nothing away. "I cannot say."

Selia peered at the dragon. The history books she'd read had contained very little about the bond between dragon and rider. Was the dragon usually so protective, or had Kezari and Aris formed a true friendship? "Thank you for guarding him so well. And for saving him. You couldn't have known you were returning him to me, but I appreciate it regardless."

Kezari gave a toothy smile. "I would have made sure he found you despite his fears."

A voice echoed up the stairwell, and Selia scanned with her magic to find Lial approaching, an unknown presence behind him. "It's the healer. I suspect he found another to help."

"I smelled him," Kezari said. "The tinge of herbs and frustration. The other carries the scent of flowers and smoke."

Selia raised a brow. "Your nose is so keen in this form?"

"Some benefits I will not relinquish. It would be a quick shift if the prey smelled tasty." The dragon's shoulders lifted. "And scent reveals much."

If the prey smelled tasty? Selia focused on the top of the stairs and tried not to wonder what qualified as prey. She'd read a few tales about the war. None of them mentioned the dragons eating

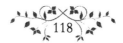

Moranaians. Of course, she'd not paid a great deal of attention to the finer details, being more concerned with more modern events.

A scowl already marred Lial's face as he appeared at the top of the stairs. He barely glanced at Kezari, naked though she was, and his stride didn't break as he crossed the floor. Another man trailed behind, his short white hair bouncing with each step. The flower-embroidered robes of a priest of Bera, Goddess of Protection and Healing, flowed around his body like the peaceful energy that surrounded him.

"What happened?" Lial snapped.

Selia's cheeks heated as she described the events leading to Aris's current state. She should have known better—should have seen the signs. The way he'd drawn back from her. His shame and avoidance. If she'd considered the extent of his abuse, she might not have held him as tightly when he did reach out. Maybe she wouldn't have let him hug her at all.

"Do not follow that river," the stranger said softly. "You'll be swept into the rapids."

Her gaze jerked to his as Lial made an exasperated sound. "Dispensing wisdom before I've introduced you, Tynan?" he asked.

The priest smiled. "Please forgive my lapse in manners."

"So long as you don't have a method of reading minds without breaching shields," Selia answered.

"I needed no such skill to guess where your thoughts were headed." Selia scooted back as Tynan knelt beside Aris. "Only experience."

Lial dropped to his knees on Aris's other side. "I do not believe we should move him to my tower while he's unconscious."

"No. An abrupt change in environment—"

Aris groaned, and his head rocked gently against the floor. Too bad her spell hadn't lasted longer, but it was only designed to give the caster a chance to escape—or a head start on preparing an attack. Prolonging such a state was too dangerous for a non-healer. As Aris's motions became stronger, Selia stood and backed away until her calves brushed against one of the long benches circling the room.

He wouldn't want to see *her* when he woke.

The deep murmur of voices—male voices—broke through the haze, one of them familiar. Aris struggled to catch hold of any words, some clue as to what had happened. Where was he? Smooth stone pressed against his back, but he was warm and dry. No…no chains. What had he been doing? He searched his memory, but his mind was slow to provide the answer.

He'd been talking to Selia. Hadn't he?

Aris pulled upon the magic welling fitfully in his chest, feeding him information about the life around him. The healer he'd seen this afternoon perched beside him, Kezari leaning over his shoulder. A stranger knelt at Aris's right, and the man's life-force pulsed with the comforting steadiness of a priest. And yes—Selia was present, but she was at the far end of the room.

Why had she moved away? They'd discussed Iren, and although he'd unintentionally offended her, she'd accepted his explanation and apology. Then…what? He had touched her cheek. Drawn her into a tentative embrace. She hadn't been upset by that. She'd curled close, and…

His eyes flew wide, and his breath hissed out as memory returned. He'd lost his senses entirely. A female had yelped in pain—

twice. Gods, he must have hurt her in his madness. He cried out as grief and shame burned in his blood, and red tinged his vision once more.

No wonder she was on the other side of the tower room.

"Do not," the stranger said, pressing a finger to Aris's forehead. Power flowed into him until his vision began to clear and his heartbeat to steady.

"Selia," Aris forced out through parched lips.

The healer, Lial, stared down at him. "She's fine."

Lial might be correct that she was physically unharmed, but mentally? His mouth went even drier as a new thought hit. "Gods, I'm like Perim. I pushed Selia. I can't believe I—"

"No," the priest interrupted, the flow of his magic increasing.

"I can't believe she didn't flee entirely," Aris whispered. "I am tainted."

The scuff of her shoes sounded across the stone a moment before her face appeared alongside the others. "Is that what you think? I...didn't think you'd want to see me. After what I did."

He lifted his shaking hand to swipe a hair from his damp cheek, and the priest shifted back. "What *you* did?" Aris asked.

"You don't remember? I used my magic to put you under." She nibbled on her lower lip. "I'm sorry."

"I'm not." He shuddered. "I thought you were Perim in that moment, ready to...ready for more torment. I don't know what else I might have done."

"You didn't hurt me," she said.

His brow furrowed. "I heard you cry out."

"I stumbled and fell on my bottom when you pushed me away, but I was more surprised than injured." Selia glanced at Kezari. "And a bit frightened when a dragon started slamming on the hatch."

"You were in distress, *skizik*."

A choked laugh escaped Aris at her tone, a blend of contrite and chiding. "Sorry."

"You must stay at the top of the tower," the dragon said. "You will be warm on me."

The priest coughed into his hand. "That type of comfort is not wise right now."

"You think that…" Shaking his head, Aris pushed himself upright. "Kezari was not offering sex. Did you miss the part about her being a dragon?"

Tynan flushed. "Lial mentioned the dragon's presence, not a naked woman's."

Aris ran his hand through his tangled hair. "This is not her natural form."

"Forgive me for my earlier assumption," the priest said. "Perhaps you should formally introduce us so that I might begin to repair the others' impression of me."

Aris lowered his trembling arms to his knees. Though shaky from his attack, he had to agree with the newcomer. Once the introductions were complete, Aris could request treatment, as this evening's disaster proved how much he needed it. He would not risk harming Selia again. He might never be whole or healed, but the priest would know better than anyone if he could ever be trusted around others.

"The sooner the better," Aris said.

Fen paced in front of the bank of windows overlooking the city of Chattanooga, but he'd stopped being fascinated with the view

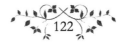

days ago when the odd waves of energy had begun. How much longer was his uncle going to keep him here behind this blood-magic shield? Fucking ridiculous. So he'd helped that bastard Kien escape to Moranaia in order to save Maddy. The prince of Moranaia had ordered him to do it.

Sure, Fen had once been part of Kien's crew. Fen's Unseelie mother had abandoned him as a baby, leaving him to fend for himself with little guidance. Sticking it to the fae had sounded like a great idea at the time. How could he have known that Kien was a sick fuck? As they'd traveled the world setting up nodes for the energy poisoning web, the guy had been normal enough. At first.

Then Kien had started dismembering the people in the group who displeased him.

Fen had tried to ease himself from the gang then. But escaping a guy who decorated the camp with body parts was easier said than done. Safer, he'd thought, to pretend to go along with the poison web, send Kien back to Moranaia, and then dismantle the bastard's work. Too bad Fen sucked at planning.

"Don't you enjoy my new home?" Vek asked smoothly.

Fen swiveled to face his uncle where he leaned against the broad archway leading to the kitchen. "If you're going to kill me for my part in the energy poisoning, just do it."

Vek laughed. "You know very well that I'm not going to kill you. You would've been dead days ago if that were my intent. I don't play with my prey."

"That's all I am to you?" Fen couldn't stop himself from asking, the old hurt surging within him. "I should've expected no better treatment from my *family*, I suppose. You've never paid me any heed."

Eyes narrowing, Vek shoved himself to his full height and strode closer. "I admit I should have done more for you after my sister's coldness, but I dared not approach you too often lest my father notice. The king's attention would not have been the boon you believe."

Fen snorted. "Sure. Must be a hardship growing up in a palace. Hell, you bought this house from a fairy with a handful of diamonds. You probably have a chest full of the damned things."

"Material wealth is nothing." Vek waved his hand dismissively. "You're barely twenty. Were you not wasting your time on revenge, you could have acquired some of your own."

"Spoken like someone born with money."

"Enough, Fen," Vek said. "This argument wastes time."

Fen lifted a brow. "You started it."

"How did I—" Vek's eyes closed for a moment before he glared at Fen. "Never mind. I have my reasons for holding you here. Get used to it."

"You are such a bastard," Fen muttered.

"Technically," Vek countered, shrugging. "But it isn't a point of importance to our kind."

Vek was a child of one of the king's many affairs? Fascinating. Fen didn't know a great deal about the Unseelie Court, but by all accounts, it was a cutthroat place, full of people vying to be named heir. The queen's two children from her marriage to the king had little advantage in the contest, as strength and purity of magic counted more than being born from a wedding alliance.

"I don't suppose your reasons have something to do with gaining the crown?" Fen asked. "You were supposed to take me back to face the king's judgement. Or kill me yourself."

Vek's cheek muscles flexed. "I don't give a fuck about the crown, no matter what my father… No, it isn't that."

"You owe me an explanation." Fen speared his fingers into his hair. "None of this 'I have my reasons' bullshit. You may think of me as a child, but I'm an adult in this world."

"Not a well-trained one," Vek said. "Or you could break free from your confinement."

That was *it*. Fen darted across the space between them and shoved his uncle's chest. He would probably die, but whatever. "Dammit, Vek. Don't you feel the storm building? The energy is warping, changing, and I'm stuck in here like a toddler in a playpen. The energy poisoning spell should have been destroyed, and Ralan sent word that Kien is dead. But I have to get back to the cave to make sure."

"Well, well," Vek drawled, a mocking smile crossing his face. "Maybe you'll figure it out after all."

What the hell was that supposed to mean? Fen took a step back, studying his uncle. Only one explanation made sense—Vek wanted to keep him from the cave. But why? If something was wrong with Earth's energy, Fen was well-suited to find and fix the problem. He'd worked with those energy fields extensively when he'd helped create the initial spell.

But perhaps his uncle didn't want the potential crisis solved.

"What game are you playing?" Fen demanded.

Vek's lips pinched. "Not the one you're thinking."

A series of chimes rang out, interrupting the question Fen was about to ask. Vek cursed, eyeing the front door with a scowl. "Visitors," he said. "That Seelie girl and her friends."

Fen's brows rose. "Maddy?"

"Yes." Grumbling beneath his breath, Vek headed for the door. "And from the feel of their energy, I have a feeling this visit isn't for pleasure."

Would it ever be? Maddy was taken, he reminded himself as he braced to see her once more. And she'd shown no interest in him even if she hadn't been. It didn't matter that he'd been drawn to her from the moment he'd seen her huddled in that cave, held captive by Kien. Fen had tried to help her as much as he could without blowing his cover, but so what? She would never see him as anything but the asshole who'd helped start this whole mess in the first place.

Seeking absolution would be an epic waste of time.

11

Maddy wiped her damp palms against her pants as she waited for the door to open. Night had fallen hours ago, and the porch light wasn't on. Only the bare glow of a single street light at the end of the driveway illuminated the area. The house's windows were mostly dark, a single a line of dim yellow gleaming between the nearest curtains. Figured that the Unseelie would prefer the shadows.

Delbin's sigh sounded from behind her left shoulder, and beside her, Anna shuffled her feet. Poor Anna. When Maddy had called to tell her where they were going, her love had insisted on joining them. She wanted to thank Fen, too, she'd said, but her eyes had been shaded with fear as they drove toward Vek's house. Thanks to Maddy and her friendship with Cora, Anna knew a few non-humans, but she'd never met any of the Unseelie before.

"Perhaps they are not home," Inona said from behind Maddy's other shoulder.

Wouldn't that just figure? But before she could worry too much about that, the door jerked open. The pale light from within barely illuminated the person blocking the opening, but the man's dark energy was unmistakable—Vek. Maddy squinted until she could make out the scowl on the prince's face.

"Well met, Maddy," Vek said, though his expression indicated otherwise. "I trust you are not abusing the knowledge I gave you of my home."

She hid a wince and pulled her shoulders back. "Not intentionally. We need to see Fen."

"I gave you his phone number," Vek said with a smirk.

Her cheeks heated, and anger surged as she felt Anna's questioning gaze. Now she would think Maddy had been hiding something. "Some thanks should be delivered in person. Anna wants to thank Fen, too."

"At…" Vek glanced down at an expensive gold watch. "Eleven o'clock at night?"

"Stop giving her trouble," Fen said as he nudged his uncle aside and took his place.

The shadow of an arm lifted beside the door before light flared from the porch light. Muttering a curse, Maddy covered her eyes until they adjusted and glared at a laughing Fen. "Warning would've been nice."

He grinned. "Probably."

"Blasted Unseelie," Inona muttered from behind her.

Fen's smile faded as he took in the others. "This really isn't a pleasure visit, is it?"

Delbin stepped up to Maddy's left side. "Nope."

"Come in, then," Fen said with a resigned sigh.

The line between Vek's brows deepened as he glared at them over his nephew's shoulder. "You cannot simply invite people into my home without permission."

"So you're going to lower the weird-ass blood shield you put up?" Fen demanded. "Because I have a feeling that this isn't business that should be discussed on the doorstep."

Wait, Vek was keeping Fen captive? The last time she'd seen Vek at the shop, he'd made it sound like his nephew was staying voluntarily. Something was definitely up. "Delbin told us about why he's here on the ride over," Maddy said. "You really don't want to talk about it out here."

"Fine," Vek said. "But do not attempt to leave the main room. I was not prepared for visitors, and I cannot be bothered to adjust the protective shielding on the more private areas. You will find unpleasant surprises if you venture far."

Well, that sounded charming.

"We'll stay in the living room" Maddy answered. "We're not here to cause trouble."

Fen's eyes crinkled with his smile. "Too bad."

He stepped back, gesturing for them to enter, and the light from inside caught against his fangs. She probably should've been afraid to enter a home with two Unseelie blood elves, but if either had wanted to hurt her, they'd had ample opportunity. So they required a sip of blood every so often to replenish their magic. They didn't have to hurt anyone in the process.

Of course, once they sampled your blood, it allowed them to drain your energy reserves using the connection, but she chose not to think about that.

Maddy entered the large main room. The right wall was almost entirely windows, and across from her, a blank flat screen television hung on the wall in front of a massive sectional couch. To the left, a broad arch led into a sleek modern kitchen. Only a few lamps brightened the space, giving it an almost empty feel.

Delbin whistled. "How did you score a place like this so fast?"

"Connections," Vek said smoothly.

Anna followed Maddy to the center of the room, sticking close. The amazing view beckoned, but Maddy refused to turn her back on Vek and Fen. Delbin stopped at Maddy's left and Inona at Anna's right as the Unseelie neared. Vek's scowl had faded, but his jaw was still clenched. Fen just looked bemused.

"Why did you bring Anna?" Vek's eyes narrowed. "Your mostly human girlfriend has no seeming place in this discussion."

"How do you know her name?" Maddy demanded as Anna squeaked out, "*Mostly* human?"

Vek's smile held little humor. "You didn't think I'd investigate you after your experience with my nephew? I assure you he has become my utmost concern. And yes, I said mostly. Something stirs in you, girl. Don't you feel it?"

Maddy glanced at Anna's pale, beautiful face. She'd expected instant denial, but there was a knowledge there that twisted Maddy's heart. "Anna?"

"I…" Anna shoved a strand of her blond hair behind her ear. "I didn't want to mention it. Then you'd have used your healing magic to check me, and I know you hate doing that. It's just a bit of odd tingling. It happens when I get near the river."

How could she have missed something so important about her love? Tears stung the corners of Maddy's eyes, but she blinked them back. "How long has this been going on?"

"Only a week or two." Anna grabbed her hand. "I didn't want to upset you after the kidnapping. I was going to tell you if it didn't go away soon."

"It's okay," Maddy said softly.

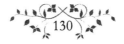

"Your non-human blood is stirring, what little there is." Vek crossed his arms. "But your Gwraig Annwn ancestor is a discussion for another day."

Her what? Maddy's forehead wrinkled as she tried to remember anything about the Gwraig Annwn. She'd heard of Gwragedd Annwn, Welsh fae. Maybe they were similar. Her father had mentioned the fae maidens who lived in the lakes and streams of Wales, sometimes emerging to marry human men. It made sense if Anna was being drawn to water.

"This is intriguing," Inona said, breaking the silence. "This tingling rises in her blood at the same time Earth is experiencing unusual energy surges and…what was it? Brownouts? We also have a dragon showing up at Braelyn claiming something is wrong on Earth."

"A dragon?" Vek's arms tightened across his chest. "Explain."

Maddy let Delbin and Inona handle that, since her knowledge was secondhand anyway. Instead, she closed her eyes and reached for her healing magic. It stuttered and shifted, as unpredictable as always, but she finally grasped it well enough to send her senses around Anna. Maddy couldn't heal anyone without risking harm, but if she strained, she could detect things about their health.

Sure enough, Anna's energy had shifted. A silver thread ran through her normally placid blue aura, and it throbbed periodically to Maddy's inner sight. What the hell? Magical blood didn't just… awaken, not without some major exposure to energy, which was rare and generally traumatic. But nothing had happened to Anna. Her beloved might not have wanted to bother her, but she would have mentioned something like that.

"Maddy?"

At the sound of Fen's voice, Maddy opened her eyes, and her magic flared. Color swirled around him. Not red, as one might expect

from a blood elf, but the deepest greens and browns. Except...there. Right above his heart, a thorn of reddish-black speared, unmoving.

"You're sick," she said without thinking.

"Fuck," Vek muttered.

"Sick?" Fen asked, an eyebrow lifting in surprise. "I feel fine. Well, except for low energy since my uncle hasn't deigned to feed me."

"You'd better keep your energy low, or you will make yourself sicker." Maddy shivered as she examined the magical thorn. If she was a true healer, she might be able to help, but she had no idea where to begin. "Your low power must be why you don't sense the sickness in yourself. That poisoned energy in the outer world? There's...there's a bit of it in your heart."

Selia slumped in her seat, rubbing her hand across her eyes. She'd helped teleport a bed to Aris's tower room while he spoke with the healers, and then she'd stood by as Tynan had nudged her husband into a deep sleep so he could recover from his panic attack. After that, she'd had to force an excited Iren to go to bed. She hadn't been this drained in years.

She ought to go to bed, but her mind was too restless. So many worries swirled through her that she felt tossed by the rapids Tynan had warned her about. He was right, but that didn't exactly help. By Arneen, she needed to get herself under control if she hoped to help Aris. But could she ever help? Maybe he would never be able to bear another person's touch. And though she would still choose him regardless, he might feel resentment that she'd told him to go on the journey that had cost him so much. He might...

And around the rocks she spun.

Selia shoved her palms against her brows and groaned. So much for control.

When the mirror on her desk chimed, she lowered her arms with a frown. Who would be contacting her at this hour? Sighing, Selia reached out and activated the link with a tendril of power. Her sister's worried face swam into immediate view.

This couldn't be good.

"Good evening," Selia said. "Is everything well?"

"I don't know." Niasen winced. "I'm sorry for the late hour, but I wondered if… Has Father shown up there?"

Selia sat back in her seat. "Father? No. I thought you said he was on Earth."

"He's supposed to be. I am growing concerned, however. It is two marks past when he was planning to contact me to catch up on estate business."

"That doesn't seem very long," Selia said.

Niasen shook her head. "He's not usually more than a few moments off our usual time. He calculates the time differences very carefully to make our weekly meetings."

"As far as I know, he has not traveled through here." Selia glanced at the water clock. Several marks had passed since dinner, but it wasn't unusual for Lyr to be in his study at this hour. "I'll check with the Myern. If he is unavailable tonight, I will ask him in the morning. Unless you think there is an imminent threat?"

"I do not yet have reason to believe there is," her sister answered. "This did happen once before, a few centuries ago, when he decided to return to Moranaia ahead of schedule. But with you so near the portal…"

Selia shrugged. "We both know he's avoiding me. Still, I will check."

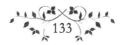

"Thank you." Some of the tension drained from Niasen's face. "Then I will bid you goodnight."

"Goodnight," Selia answered before the connection winked out.

She dropped her head against the back of the seat for a few precious breaths, but she couldn't afford to relax. Her father was very…exact. Proper. He would not abandon his meeting with Niasen without cause. It was possible that he'd miscalculated the time shift between the worlds, but it was worth checking with Lyr to see if he'd heard of any trouble. Just in case. With so many unusual events happening lately, anything outside the norm deserved attention.

Groaning, Selia scooted the chair back gently from the desk, not wanting to scrape the floor and wake Iren next door. A quick scan revealed that Lyr was in his study, as she'd hoped, so she started in that direction as rapidly as her tired feet would allow. For politeness's sake, she should send a mental request for a meeting, but she didn't want to waste more energy. Unlike her father, Lyr wouldn't hold such a lapse against her.

But to her surprise, she was halfway down the stairs when his energy brushed hers in a request for contact. *"Good evening, Lyr. Is everything well?"*

"Debatably," he answered. *"I need to speak to you if you are available."*

The coincidence wasn't promising. Had something bad happened to her father? Lyr certainly wouldn't deliver that kind of news across a telepathic connection. *"I'm already on my way to your study. I will be there in a moment."*

"Thank you," he said, cutting off the link.

Her heart pounded as she hurried, ignoring the ache in her feet and the leaden weight of her muscles. She might have a complicated relationship with her father, but she didn't want anything to happen

to him. Far from it. With trembling hands, she pushed open the door to Lyr's study and strode into the large, oval room.

Lyr slumped against the back of his seat, his face lined with exhaustion. His eyes opened as she neared, and he straightened. "You look the way I feel," he grumbled.

Selia smiled, far from offended. If he spoke so plainly, he must truly consider her a friend. "Either you feel terrible, or I look better than I expect."

He shoved his braid of dark brown hair over his shoulder. "It has been a long day, and the night promises to be longer yet. Dare I ask why you were on the way here?"

"It's about my father," Selia said as she stopped in front of the small dais holding the desk. "He's on one of his trips to Earth, and he failed to check in with my sister at their arranged time. I told her I would ask you if he'd returned, since he is avoiding me."

Lyr frowned. "He passed through the area quietly, then, for I have heard nothing. I will check the scouts' records for the details of his travel."

The lump in her stomach uncurled. "Then you weren't contacting me about news of him?"

"No," Lyr said. "But I wouldn't recommend relaxing. I spoke to the king."

Her forehead wrinkled. Wouldn't he have summoned Ralan about that? "I'm afraid I don't understand what that has to do with me."

"Nothing and everything." He leaned forward. "The dragon queen contacted him, and the news is not good. Kezari is on her way, as is Ralan, but Lial forbid me to wake Aris under threat of pain most dire. You know Aris best, so I thought you might give input on his behalf."

Just like that, the knot in her stomach squeezed tight once more. "I am not certain that is a good idea. I don't feel comfortable speaking for him."

"I would not ask you to do that," Lyr said. "Only give your opinion."

The door opened, and Ralan strode in. "Stay, Selia," he said.

She held back a groan. From the sharp command in his tone, his words obviously hadn't been a request. "Of course."

Before Ralan was halfway across the room, Lyr's third in command, Kera, entered with Kezari. The dragon appeared paler than before, apparently no more eager to be indoors than she had been before. She gripped her hands into the thin dress she'd donned, and she scanned the walls like they were hiding enemies within. Was it Aris's absence that had the dragon nervous or something else?

"Thank you for joining me," Lyr said as Kera left. "Let us recline in the center chairs as we discuss the matter at hand."

Kezari's arms drew in close to her body before she darted to the nearest chair and perched on the edge. Selia took the seat to the dragon's right. Ralan sat across from the dragon with Lyr beside him. The steady drip of the water clock filled the silence as they stared at the agitated dragon.

"I cannot abide this enclosed space," she said. "Not without my *skizik*. Why have you called me here?"

"I am afraid we have a problem." Lyr sat up straighter. "Your queen contacted our king. She declared you a renegade and refused any possibility of negotiation on the matter of returning to Earth. Something the other dragons apparently do not want after so much time."

A wave of power thrummed through the room, shaking the chair and floor before cutting off abruptly. Selia's heartbeat pounded in her ears as she observed the raw fury on Kezari's face. "Our queen has grown too soft. She neglects the needs of the young ones, those not old enough to sever their connection to Earth. She blames their agitation on boredom, but I know the truth. This must be stopped for the dragons' sake."

"That may be," Lyr said in a quiet, even tone. "However, the result of breaking the treaty would be war. The queen has decreed it. At this point, the only option left is to send Aris and Selia through without you."

Kezari hissed. "No. I must not be left behind."

"I'm not sure Aris will agree to it, either," Selia said. "Have you heard from Inona and Delbin yet?"

Lyr shook his head. "I expect them to return soon. Perhaps we will understand more then."

Heat trembled on the air, fighting against the cooling spell imbued into the room. Kezari's fingers dug into her legs as her piercing gaze moved to Ralan. "Who is this one? You have brought a stranger here to witness my shame. I do not like it."

Selia stretched out her hand, but the dragon's angry look had pulling back. "Please be at ease, Kezari. This is Prince Ralan, heir to the throne. I am certain he will help if possible."

Despite the dragon's anger, Ralan's expression remained relaxed. "Forgive my intrusion. As a prince, I spent more time studying the treaty than the others. I believe we may have one other option, one neglected by our ancestors and current monarchs alike."

Kezari leaned so far forward that Selia feared the dragon would fall from her chair. "Yes?"

"In declaring you renegade, am I correct in assuming that the queen has cast you out?" Ralan asked.

Kezari nodded. "That is correct. If I return without causing harm, I could petition to be reinstated. My cousin Tebzn will care

for my hoard until my banishment is certain. If I am not reinstated, all but a small percentage of my collection will be hers."

"Then you have a choice to make." A sly smile crossed Ralan's face. "The treaty gives no guidance on dragons who wish to join Moranaian society."

Lyr huffed out a breath. "You're certain? I do not recall the treaty sufficiently to say."

Frowning, Selia tried to remember her own school days, but she hadn't read the document since her early studies. "Nor do I."

"You believe I should become one of you?" Horror rang in the dragon's voice. "I cannot tolerate this form for so long. No, never."

"That would not be a requirement," Lyr said. "We have a variety of fae who have journeyed here over the centuries, like Kera, whose family is Dökkálfar. None have been required to change forms for any reason. One must only request entry into our society and swear allegiance to our king and laws. If your queen has disavowed you, there would be no reason not to accept."

Kezari sucked in a breath. "But my hoard…my cave…"

"Think on it tonight while we wait for my people to return," Lyr said.

Poor Kezari. The dragon gave a sharp nod and jerked to her feet, marching from the room without another word. Selia exchanged a tired glance with the other two before she, too, stood. "If you don't need anything else from me, I will rest. I have a feeling I'm going to require all of my energy."

"Of course," Lyr said. "Good eve, Selia."

With a parting smile, Selia hurried toward the door. If she was lucky, she could get a complete night's sleep before another disaster struck. She sent up a quick prayer and sped up her steps.

12

I *can't be poisoned. No way.*

Once again, Fen paced. Along the wall of windows and then around, circling the large sofa where the others sat. Even Vek was surprisingly quiet. But then, he'd been hiding a big fucking bombshell, hadn't he? It would explain why Fen's uncle hadn't wanted him to consume much blood or leave the house. If it was true, taking in more energy would increase the size of the sickness affecting him.

If.

"I feel fine," Fen said for probably the twentieth time. "Those waves of energy make me lightheaded sometimes, but that doesn't mean anything."

"Nephew…"

Fen rounded on Vek. "Oh, don't give me that regretful tone. If you thought I was ill, why wouldn't you want me to solve it? Maybe Kien left something in that cave. I can unravel it."

"There's nothing there to find. At least nothing you can fix." Vek drummed his fingers on his knee. "I went to the cave. It's… there's nothing poisoned there."

"I can tell the waves of magic originate in the cave where we fought Kien," Fen argued.

"They do." Vek's gaze encompased everyone. "There's a crack there. Not one you can see, of course, but a crack in the wall restraining the bulk of Earth's magical energy."

Delbin, who'd been exiled to Earth for much of his life, shook his head. Like Fen, there was a lot of magical lore he didn't know. "What are you talking about?"

"I do not understand, either," Inona said, appearing just as confused.

Maddy and Anna exchanged equally blank looks.

Vek let out a low chuckle. "Ah, how the so-called greater races have fallen behind. You didn't know we saved you so many millennia ago, did you? According to legend, the fae races began to abandon Earth because the magic started to fade. They slipped into different dimensions or journeyed through the portal to new lands. Even humans talk about the magic disappearing, but they attribute it to belief. Or the lack thereof. We Unseelie have been happy to have the stories say so, but it's time for that misapprehension to change."

"You make no sense," Inona said, her brows drawing together. "Our historians would have recorded the cause of decreased energy."

One corner of Vek's mouth tipped up. "They didn't know. We Unseelie have always been masters of shadow, you see. We understand better than others what happens when power goes unrestrained. Earth's energy was growing, not leveling off, enough that humans learned to use it. With magic so easily accessible, small wars broke out constantly. The fighting never would have stopped. So we bound and sealed much of the magic in a parallel dimension without the other races' knowledge."

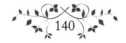

Fen dropped heavily onto one side of the sectional. Was Vek serious? "Why? Your kind crave conflict."

"*My* kind, hmm?" Vek asked with a smirk. "We don't shy from a fight, but a cataclysm makes even the shadows unpleasant. To lessen the chance of a catastrophic war, we bound the energy with blood. Now something has cracked it. You drew blood from Kien, did you not?"

Fen nodded.

Any hint of humor left Vek's face. "He must have done something to the barrier when he died. He was linked to Earth's energy…and to you. The power trapped behind that wall chips away at that crack with every moment, releasing magic with each fragment that shatters. Those with latent fae blood, like young Anna here, will awaken, and gods know what else will happen. Provided we aren't all killed by the force when the dam breaks. I'm no Earth mage, and you're weakened by the poison even if you were trained. In short, we're all fucked."

What in the hell were they going to do? The others' faces echoed the worry that slammed Fen's heart. Then Delbin cursed beneath his breath, and Inona pinned Vek with a glare. Anna gripped Maddy's hand, making Fen's insides twist in unexpected but acute longing. As the desire to wrap a comforting arm around both of them swamped him, Fen averted his gaze.

One hopeless situation at a time.

"I hope you have some evidence of this story," Inona said.

"I suppose you can create your own myth for it if you need to." Vek shrugged. "You are welcome to explore the cave yourselves to feel the crack, but good luck sealing it without a dragon."

Pain replaced the anger in her eyes. "I am uncertain I am prepared to return to the cave."

"That was not a taunt," Vek said evenly. "By my own blood, I swear that I have spoken only truth in this matter."

Fen's lips twitched. If the others didn't know how many shades of the truth there might be, he wasn't going to tell them. He had more important things to consider. Number one? Find a way to heal himself. Then he could see about averting the coming disaster. Vek might think a dragon was required, but Fen had his doubts. He'd inserted poison into Earth's energy field, manipulating it in the process. How different could some magical barrier be?

Maybe stopping an apocalypse would impress Maddy and Anna, provided he didn't die. Ah, well. He could deal with either outcome.

Panic and fear clawed through the layers of quicksand clouding Aris's mind. Why? Through the morass he dug, seeking something to hold, until he gripped the fear itself to pull his way out. Why did he feel this terror? Why did he follow it? The sand gripped him, but he fought through each layer until finally he was free.

A frenzied tapping met his ears as he opened his eyes against the dim light. For a moment, Aris processed his surroundings. The bed beneath him. The glow from the globe near his headboard. His sleep-stiffened muscles. Footsteps—the source of the tapping. He stretched each leg and then his arms before carefully sitting up.

Across the room, Kezari paced. Her form appeared different somehow, and he squinted against the dim light to try to discern why. Was her body larger? Taller? Her fingers extended farther than an elf's should, her nails curved into dragonesque claws. Her skin gleamed with the dark golden hue of her natural form, and he thought he caught a hint of scales along one arm.

Did he want to know what had led to her current state?

Really, he didn't have a choice. Her panic curled through him, threatening to trigger his own. Gods help them all if they both lost it. "Kezari?"

She stopped, her chest heaving as she stared at him. "You are no longer at rest."

"How could I be when you are so upset?" Aris pushed his hair from his face and stifled a yawn. "What happened?"

"The queen banished me," Kezari answered, her voice emerging in a deep rumble. A puff of smoke curled from her nose. "I must abandon this quest and petition to return, or I will be cast from my home. Your leaders say I could live here. Here, with the elves? Our kind did not cohabit well before. I do not know what to do. The Earth screams. Violation. Explosion."

"Slow down," he said. "When did you hear from your queen?"

Kezari hissed. "She did not contact me. She gave her decree to your king. But I could become Moranaian. I do not know if I want this thing. Where would I live? I would lose most of my hoard. This is a possibility most distressing."

It took a moment for his groggy mind the comprehend the import of her words. "My leaders? Do you mean Lyr or Ralan?"

"Both," she answered.

"They offered you citizenship? A new home?"

"But I will have no home. No place. No cave. No hoard," Kezari moaned.

Aris grimaced in sympathy, but at least he could help in this regard. "All Moranaians are provided with the basics for survival so long as they contribute to our society. We can work together to rebuild your hoard. I've gained enough wealth exploring over the centuries to contribute. Besides, wouldn't being a Moranaian citizen

free you to fly anywhere you want to seek treasure? You'd no longer be restricted to the dragons' isle."

Her head tilted in thought. "That is so."

"More importantly, it would allow you to go through the portal." He smiled. "Moranaians may do so, provided they follow the rules."

"It is much to consider," she said.

"Yes." Had the scales faded from her skin? Her coloring appeared a little less gold, he was fairly certain. "Is the threat you sense from Earth severe enough that you must give up everything?"

Kezari pressed her palms against her temples and let out a low groan. A wave of magic pulsed around her, rumbling through the floor and up the walls. Aris scrambled from the bed as her eyes went blank and her flesh changed color once more. Instinctively, he connected through their bond in an attempt to calm her as she had so often done for him.

Only to be swamped in sensation.

If he'd been in quicksand before, now it was a mudslide. A mountain's worth of screaming darkness tinged with the slow thrum of the Earth's heart. But something wasn't right. *Beat, beat, groan. Beat, beat, crack.* The burn of raw energy seeped into his core, shifting. Changing. Insects cried. Birds screeched a warning.

Something is coming.

Something is coming.

Something is coming.

Cold fingers brushed against his forehead, and the sensations cut off like a broken mage globe. He became aware of his frantic breathing and the heat of his own skin. As the haze left Aris's vision, Tynan's face solidified in his view. Aris blinked rapidly as the healer's magic flooded him with serenity. He stood in the same place, his legs shaky but holding his weight, yet his outlook had changed.

"Gods," Aris said under his breath.

But Kezari heard. "I am sorry, *skizik*. I did not know you would do that. But now you see?"

Aris nodded. The dragon still paced, but the healer's presence seemed to have given her some comfort since she'd returned fully to her elven form. After experiencing what she felt, he couldn't imagine how. And she'd been living with this for over a week? She was far stronger than he was.

"I'll help rebuild your hoard and find you a cave. Anything. We need to get to Earth before whatever that is erupts," Aris said.

"Yes," Kezari said sadly. "There is no choice. There never was."

Perim tugged herself through the narrow passage, ignoring the scrape of rough rock. She would heal quickly, as always, and the day's pain had been well worth the effort. The air vents hewn through the queen's own mountain were rarely considered by anyone, least of all the useless fae content to die off waiting for some dragon to claim them. Fools. The dragons rarely chose partners anymore, the bonds not happening as they once had.

Well, Perim wasn't waiting.

She'd almost had a way off the cursed island with Aris, but now that chance was gone. Why had the dragon claimed him now? Time passed so slowly for the dragons that Kezari hadn't even noticed how long Aris was "training." Hah. The wyrm knew so little about the fae that she hadn't questioned the little tradition Perim had made up. But as soon as she'd fished Aris from the sea and heard the dragon's roar at a *skizik*'s presence, she'd known what to do—hide him until she could use him.

If only he'd bonded with her. Why had he refused? Perim had tried pleasure and pain. Incentive and deprivation. Anything. Everything. She'd broken his bones, carved at his flesh, and claimed his body. Still, their souls remained separate. Curse him and his stubbornness. Why didn't he understand that she needed that bond? None of the dragons would link with her so she could escape this terrible place, but she could have used her soulbond with Aris to coerce Kezari.

She would've let him go after that. Probably.

Perim hissed as a protruding rock bit into her side, drawing blood, but she pulled herself forward without pausing. She had a solution now, and it was all thanks to Kezari. Based on the council meeting she'd overheard, the stupid dragon had enemies. What good fortune that Baza and Tebzn had paused near the air vent to discuss the…disposition of Kezari's hoard if she decided not to return.

Baza was a mage. If any dragon knew a way off this useless island, he would. And Perim could give him plenty of incentive. She could locate Aris, and thus Kezari, through their potential bond. They would never expect her to find a way off the island to track them down, so Baza's aid and a well-placed blade would solve everyone's problems. Maybe she would kill Aris, too.

No need to leave loose ends.

By the time Inona pulled Delbin through the portal onto Moranaian soil, she was ready to drop. She might not believe all that Prince Vek had claimed, but there was no doubt something important was happening. As with their previous journey, the strands in the Veil had twisted and turned, sometimes snapping back on

themselves, until her head had ached with the strain. But finally they were through.

At least now she knew the cause of the Veil's increasing tumult.

She leaned against Delbin's steady form and ignored the stares of the portal guards as she regained her strength. A shiver went through her with each bit of energy she gathered. Nothing could compare to the power of their home world, especially not Earth. Although if Prince Vek could be believed, Earth had once been far richer. Could that magic truly be breaking free?

"Are you okay?" Delbin asked softly.

Inona straightened and then curled her fingers around his. "I'm only tired. Let's go report in."

He frowned. "It's the middle of the night."

"The Myern will want to know what we learned immediately, even if we must wake him." Inona gave a gentle tug as she started down the trail. "He urged me to do so before we left."

Delbin fell silent as they walked, and her heart twisted at the hesitant way he held her hand. He claimed that the scar seared into her throat didn't bother him, but he hadn't acted the same toward her since she'd awakened in the healer's tower three weeks ago. They needed to talk about it, of course. Once she gathered the courage to ask.

"Was it bad?" Delbin asked. "Being back on Earth?"

A cold gust of wind blew around them, and a frigid drop of rain plopped on Inona's arm. Shivering again, she huddled closer to Delbin as they walked. "Yes and no."

Delbin released her hand, only to curl his arm around her waist and tug her close. "I wish you'd talk to me."

She halted in the middle of the trail to peer up at his face, barely visible in the dim moonlight. "What?"

"I'm sorry that I failed you in the cave." His jaw clenched. "I tried to take control of Kien, but I wasn't strong enough."

A low laugh burst from her lips before she could contain it. "Surely you don't think I blame you. I am a warrior, Delbin. I should never have put myself into a position where Kien could grab me, and I paid for that lapse. It had nothing to do with you."

"You're so quiet and withdrawn," Delbin said. "I thought you were upset at me."

She brushed the backs of her fingers against his cheek. "No. You've been different, too, and I thought…my scar…"

With a chuckle, he lowered his forehead to hers. "We've been reacting to each other's reactions. I don't care about scars. I love you regardless of the appearance of your neck."

Her heart warmed even as relief made her shaky. "As I love you."

Delbin lowered his mouth for a quick kiss. When he pulled away, he was smiling. "Let's go give that report. I'd like to finish this discussion in our room."

Though more rain began to fall, the chill couldn't cool the heat pooling within her. She had a feeling she was about to give the fastest report of her life.

13

When the knock sounded on her door again, Selia considered burying her head beneath the pillow. The room was too dark to see the water clock, so the sun couldn't be up yet. Could she ignore the disturbance? Just as she began to give the matter serious debate, she detected Arlyn's energy brushing against her privacy shield. If her student was being this persistent, there must be something wrong.

"Fine," Selia grumbled, shoving the covers aside and lowering her legs over the side of the bed.

She rubbed her eyes and opened a mental connection with Arlyn. *"What time is it?"*

"Not long before dawn," Arlyn answered, her inner voice just as sluggish. *"Sorry to wake you. Onaial sent Kai to consult with his father less than a mark ago. Now he wants us to meet him downstairs."*

"Now?"

"Delbin and Inona returned from Earth not long ago," Arlyn sent. *"The dragon's suspicions were correct."*

Selia rubbed her fingers across her nose. *"I'll be down in a moment."*

As Arlyn's presence faded, Selia jerked to her feet and rushed into the dressing chamber. Thank goodness she'd decided to have a soak last night before sleeping, since she wouldn't have time for a bath this morning. Instead, she brushed her long hair and braided it. Then she shucked her nightdress and tugged on a thick pair of pants and a long-sleeved tunic with practical boots. She grabbed her cloak on the way out the door in case she had to go outside in search of Aris. From the sound of the rain plopping against the windows, the weather would be wet, cold, and generally unpleasant.

Fortunately, Aris and Kezari had already joined Arlyn and Lyr in the study by the time Selia hurried in and hung her cloak on a hook. Her steps hitched when she focused on her beloved's face. There was an intensity there that she hadn't seen since he'd left on his last fateful journey. That unusual blend of curiosity and adventurousness that had so often propelled him to places unseen, far different from the shattered pain of the night before.

Selia took the only free seat in the center of the room, Aris to her left and Arlyn across from her. Lyr leaned forward in his chair next to Arlyn as Kezari shifted restlessly by the window. "Thank you for joining us, Selia," Lyr said.

Wordlessly, Arlyn grabbed a mug of tea and handed it over. Selia took a tentative sniff and then smiled. An energetic blend, perfect for morning. "I surmise that the news is not good," she said after taking a quick sip.

"No," Lyr said. "According to Inona's report, Prince Vek of the Unseelie claims that a crack has formed in the wall blocking much of Earth's magical energy. He told them that his people set up the block millennia ago to stop the fighting between the fae and humans, but I've never heard of any such thing."

Kezari snorted. "Leave it to one of *them* to claim such."

Lyr glanced over his shoulder. "What do you mean?"

"It was a joint effort," the dragon replied. "The power grew unchecked. Many frail humans hurt themselves trying to learn to harness it. The human use of magic required action."

Selia stiffened. Surely, they hadn't meddled with an entire world's energy to prevent a single race from accessing it? Humans struggled to connect with natural magic and thus required a stronger flow. Walling off enough would leave them fairly powerless.

Arlyn's eyes narrowed as she seemed to come to the same conclusion. "So the Unseelie and the dragons decided that humans were unworthy?"

Kezari shook her head. "Oh, no. I do not believe so. Humans live such short lives, and their magical channels are terribly small. And they do not require magic to live, as we do. We did not want them to die out."

"I suppose it didn't occur to you," Arlyn ground out, "that the human race might have evolved, shaped by the magic?"

"Evolved?" Kezari asked.

"Been changed by their environment, as all living creatures are."

The dragon stared at Arlyn for a long moment. "I do not believe dragons do this thing."

Arlyn's lips pinched. "It takes generations. Perhaps you live too long to notice much of a difference."

Varying degrees of horror filled the others' expressions, and Selia imagined hers was no exception. The Unseelie and the dragons had cut the humans off from any chance of evolving to be more like the magical races. Would they have changed to survive partially off of energy, as did many fae, and begun to live longer lives? According to myth, their natural lifespan had once been greater.

Walling off the magic might have harmed the human race.

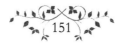

"We didn't mean…" Kezari whispered.

"Good intentions often go astray," Lyr said. "In any case, if Vek is to be believed, the human race may be getting another chance. Provided the release of that much magic at once doesn't flatten them all."

"We must go now," Aris said, his voice low and urgent.

Selia peered at her husband. "Why now? You were unsure before, but suddenly, you're ready to go?"

His hands clenched in his lap, but he nodded. "I connected to Earth through Kezari's link. Smaller lifeforms are already crying out for help, and I cannot neglect them. The Earth's heartbeat stutters."

Selia set her cup down on the side table with a decisive click. She had no idea what she was supposed to do—Repair the wall? Mitigate the damage?—but she was willing to try. "I'll help."

"Not so fast," Lyr said. "For one thing, there's still the matter of Kezari's citizenship. I'm afraid she can't go through without it."

The dragon marched over from the window and halted between Aris and Lyr. Lifting her chin, she stared down at the Myern. "I ask for a place among your kind. A home. I will make no war and will consume no sentient creatures. If there are areas where I may not hunt, I will abide by that law. All laws I will heed. I do not know if we can live in peace, unlike our ancestors, but I will put forth effort to do so."

Lyr smiled. "House Dianore welcomes you to Braelyn as one of us, although I recommend being confirmed by Ralan in this sensitive situation. He should—"

The door opened, and Selia almost snorted as the prince sauntered through. "Done," Ralan said. "I bid you welcome to Moranaia. Would you like to keep your clan's name, or do you wish a rebirth?"

Kezari's gaze flicked to Aris. "If I might be counted among my *skizik*'s people, I would be pleased. He is now my clan."

"Then you will be known to all as Callian iy'dianore tenah i Kezari Baran nai Braelyn." Ralan winked. "For now. If you return to Fiorn with Aris and Selia once Arlyn's training is complete, you'll have to petition Selia's father for entry to their branch, but your family name is the same. And you might yet earn a title besides *tenah*—dragon friend."

Kezari's body shuddered, though her expression was too closed for Selia to determine why. "I must fly," the dragon said. "My feelings ride close, and I must fly."

Aris frowned. "Should I—"

"Stay, *skizik*," Kezari interrupted. "I am not distressed like last night, but this form is difficult to maintain in my current state."

"So long as you remember your vow not to eat anyone, I see no issue," Lyr quipped.

Selia gaped at him and Arlyn's eyes went wide, but Kezari surprised them by laughing. "Not unless you have a citizen *daeri*."

The Myern chuckled. "No, we do not. And hunting is not restricted on my land if care is taken to avoid domesticated herds."

Kezari nodded once and spun away, rushing toward the outer door. Selia caught a hint of golden scale on the dragon's arm as she darted out the side entrance. A moment later, a sharp snap sounded, and the tree branches swayed with the dragon's wingbeats. Well, at least she hadn't changed forms in the middle of the study. That would have been unfortunate, indeed.

Before anyone spoke, Ralan plopped down on the floor where Kezari had stood and crossed his legs. Selia's brows lifted at the sight of the heir to the throne in such a humble position, but the prince appeared at ease. Would she ever be comfortable with his unusual blend of informality and authority?

"We do have more chairs," Lyr said wryly. "Kezari might have refused, but there's no reason for you to sit on the floor."

Ralan shrugged. "It is no hardship. Now, about this journey to Earth. You need to—"

"Don't start," Lyr said with a wave of his hand. "Unless you've Seen a highly probable future strand. You promised to stop interfering without being certain of the course. After last time…"

"Fine." Ralan's lips turned down. "I'll give you the chance to choose the least messed up option."

When Lyr made another gesture, this one much less polite, Selia had to cough to hide her surprised gasp. No, she might never get over the bizarre informality here. Her own father would have lost his mind at such a show of disrespect, but the prince only laughed and returned the gesture. Changes would almost certainly come to the kingdom when Ralan ascended the throne.

Lyr focused on Aris, ignoring the prince. "As I was about to say next, there is another matter of importance before you travel through the portal. Your health, Aris. Tynan reported that he had to interrupt another episode in the middle of the night."

A flush crept up her husband's neck. "Not the way you think. I connected to Kezari, and the combination of her distress and the Earth's pain almost pulled me under."

"You don't think that kind of vulnerability might be a problem during a crisis?" Lyr asked. "I mean no offense, nor do I minimize your trauma. I know a bit about such things myself. But you need a few sessions with the mind-healer before you leave for another world."

Aris's nostrils flared. "We do not have that kind of time."

"What do you think might happen if you have a breakdown while connected to the Earth?" Lyr asked softly, though his fingers

tightened around the arms of his chair. "Consider that. Also, Lial has reported that your body still needs repair."

"A few poorly healed bones—"

"Aris." Selia dared to lower her hand to his arm, and despite a slight flinch, he didn't remove it as he glanced at her. "You have said many times that undertaking an expedition in a poor state of mind or body, and without proper preparation, is a certain path to disaster. I know it is difficult for you not to follow your magic's call, but it will not serve you well to make everything worse."

His jaw clenched, and for a moment, she thought he would argue. But then his shoulders slumped as he let out a breath. "Thank you, Selia. Hard to argue with you *and* myself."

"You'll work with Tynan and Lial for the couple of days until the autumn festival," Lyr said. "I've sent Kai to check with his father, Lord Naomh of the Sidhe, a powerful earth mage. Depending on his advice, I may send Selia, Kai, and possibly Arlyn through for an initial analysis while you heal."

"Me?" Arlyn asked.

Lyr gave a sharp nod. "Consult with Lial on the possible repercussions to the baby. If he believes this may cause harm, then no. But being part human, you might be able to detect something the others miss. We'll have to see."

"Oh. Okay." Arlyn stood and ran her hands nervously down her tunic. "I'll go find Lial now. The sooner we know, the better."

As Arlyn hurried from the room, another thought occurred to Selia. "What about Meli? She draws upon magic when she's divining, but she doesn't carry a large store of internal energy. That could be a boon if the energy fluctuates. Plus, she could use her runes to guide us to the best location."

Lyr's lips pinched until they whitened. Selia could sympathize with his plight. He'd lost his soulbonded, Arlyn's mother, before they'd been able to join many years before. He'd found her reincarnated in Meli less than two months ago, and his fear of losing her again had to be intense. Finding Aris after believing him dead sparked a similar reaction in Selia's heart.

"As much as I hate it, you are right," Lyr finally said. "I'll ask her what she wants to do. She has grown more confident with the runes as she has worked with my mother, so I imagine she will agree."

"Kezari will not be happy," Aris grumbled.

"Then pose to her the same question I did you," Lyr snapped. "About losing control while connected to the Earth. Cooperate with the healers, and it will all go faster. Trust me."

Ralan stood in a single fluid motion. "I didn't have to interfere. Good job. Now let's get to it."

Laughter edged with worry echoed through the room, but no one argued. Even Aris headed for the door without another word, although he'd tensed up again. Selia gripped her fingers in her tunic to keep from running her hand down his back in an attempt to soothe. He wouldn't welcome her touch, not now.

But maybe someday. Maybe.

"So," Naomh drawled. "You come to me for help now?"

Kai bit back the words he wanted to say and kept his gaze locked on his father's. "If you have sensed a problem with Earth's energy, just say so."

Naomh leaned back in his seat with a slow smile. "If only you'd been more eager to return for your studies, hmm?"

Fuck it all, he didn't have time for this. Lyr was waiting on him to make a final decision on the coming mission. There was too much at stake. "Arlyn's pregnant," Kai snapped without meaning to. *Miaran.* "It has hindered our travel."

His father's expression went blank, his sly humor gone. "Another of our blood already?"

"Yes," Kai said sharply. "And I'm afraid Lyr might be thinking about sending Arlyn on this mission. It's her choice, but we need to know more about what's going on with the energy. Right now, we have only a dragon's concern and an Unseelie prince's word on the problem."

Naomh merely stared. "You would trust me in this?"

"Stop stalling," Caolte, Kai's uncle, said as he strode into the massive dining room. "When *you* consider breaking the ancient covenant, it's time to drop pretense."

Kai's head reared back at that. Thousands of years before, the Sidhe had agreed to remain in the underhill dimensions and leave the surface to the humans. Naomh had been so adamant that the deal be honored that he'd worked briefly with Kien to try to keep his brethren underground. Only something major would make him consider breaking that law.

"Your dragon friend is right. There is a schism in the wall regulating Earth's energy. Though the Unseelie think we don't know, we are not fools," Naomh said softly. "We've let the barrier stand because it serves our purposes, too. But this fissure…it's tinged with poison, same as the kind Kien tried to use. This has his mark all over it."

Kai went cold at those words. "Kien? He's dead. Beheaded by the king himself."

"He must have found some way to inject his poison before he died," Naomh said, his gaze never wavering. "Others might not have

detected it building, but I know this sickness all too well. More is released with each surge of Earth's heart. Do not send Arlyn there. In fact, I recommend evacuating any vulnerable fae—pregnant women, children, elderly."

"I thought the greatest risk was the wall breaking, releasing the energy," Kai said.

Caolte settled his fists on the table and leaned forward. "Oh, that'll definitely be bad."

"Now imagine the greater catastrophe of poisoned energy flooding Earth." Naomh sat up straight, and for once, true worry lined his face. "Forgive me for giving you grief. I've been considering what I could do for days now, but perhaps my thinking was incomplete. Maybe we need to work together."

For once, Kai fully agreed with his father.

Clechtan, he thought. *Didn't see that coming.*

14

Aris made no effort to block the rain that dripped onto the hood of his cloak, penetrating the fabric until a few chilly runnels made their way down his neck. The door to the training room beckoned, but it also repulsed. Aris had circled the tower twice as he searched for his courage, but no matter how many times he perused the walls, the current two windows were the only ones. Small windows, too, barely enough to let in light.

It might be the best shielded room on the estate, but it looked like a prison.

The mind-healer had insisted on meeting here in case Aris lost control of his magic during the session. Reasonable—if he could manage to go in. His fingernails dug into his palms, and he recoiled, the ill-timed pain tipping his mind toward darkness. Aris took a deep breath. It was a room, not a cave.

The door opened, and Tynan stepped beneath the doorframe. Beyond him, light from several mage globes filled the mostly empty stone room. The priest eased back and gestured silently toward a pair of cushions situated in the center of the floor. Though Aris's shoulders ached with tension, he forced his feet to carry him through the door and into the room. Creatures needed saving, and cowering outside wouldn't do it.

"Thank you," Aris said as he hung his sodden cloak on a hook and shook the rain from his hair. Then he shuffled toward the cushion and sat. "I appreciate your quick action on my behalf."

"Opening the door?" Tynan asked wryly before taking the other cushion.

If the question was designed to lighten the tense mood, Aris had to admit it worked. A little. "Your arrival. And helping last night. I don't know what would have happened if I'd broken while Kezari was so upset."

The priest smiled. "As a mind-healer, I am accustomed to quick action. Mental injuries can be dangerous for all involved."

"I never…" Heat crept into Aris's cheeks. "I never thought I might need this type of aid."

"Who does?" Tynan asked, his eyes crinkling with his grin. "Trust me, I am accustomed to such a reaction. Our thoughts form the base of our existence, and no one wants to contemplate a weak foundation. But it is the part of us most in need of care, lest everything else crumble."

"I would think the base would be the soul."

"No." The priest's smile faded. "The soul *is* existence. The structure and base change with each incarnation, but our spirits flow on, retaining only an echo of the shape before."

Aris averted his gaze. He must have done terrible things in his past lives to shape his soul into its current form. "I met my potential soulbonded," he whispered.

"Did you, now?"

At the calm curiosity in the priest's tone, Aris glanced at him. Tynan sat cross-legged, his palms upturned on his knees. For the

first time, Aris detected the steady flow of cool, calming energy emanating from the other man. It didn't stop the nausea creeping up his throat or the tension in his muscles, but the admission wasn't threatening to suck him into madness.

"My captor," Aris said. "She tortured me." He gripped his hands together until his fingers stung. "And violated my body. All to try to force me to complete the potential bond. What does it say about me that my soul is a match for hers?"

Despite Aris's words, the priest's expression remained neutral. "Absolutely nothing. It isn't the shape of the soul that makes the bond, it is the flavor. Her actions must stem from a broken mind, for I can tell that your spirit is whole and untarnished by that kind of evil. If her soul was evil, it would not be a match for yours. The bond would not be possible."

Relief flooded Aris's body until his head spun with it. Only when he'd steadied did the full import of Tynan's words hit. "How could she torture me for almost seven years and not blacken her soul?"

The priest's brow lowered in thought. "It is difficult to say without examining her. However…we all have darkness within us. Echoes of poor choices in this life or the ones before. It doesn't prevent bonding. But a soul is not turned to evil easily. Perhaps it is her mind that is broken but not her very core. Insanity sometimes leaves its mark for the next life."

Aris shoved his fingers through his hair as he tried to process the priest's words. Could Perim be redeemed? His stomach lurched as the image of her cruel face flickered into his thoughts. If so, it would not be done by him. She'd forfeited any right to his aid. She could be responsible for her own poor choices.

And she never would have gained his love in any case.

"I don't understand soulbonds," Aris finally said. "I would swear Selia is the other half of me, but some cosmic force decreed otherwise. The gods? Fate? I don't know."

"It is true that some souls are able to join, but plenty of others are perfect complements." Tynan let out a long sigh. "I would be well pleased to find either."

Aris peered at the healer, and the reason for the longing he'd noticed on Tynan's face when he'd been near Kezari came clear. He wanted a relationship, and for some reason, he was drawn to the dragon. If they were friends, Aris might have asked if that were true, but it was too intrusive of a question for a near stranger. Even one who would soon know his darkest secrets.

"So what do we have to do to heal the damage to my mind?"

Tynan grimaced. "The process is unpleasant, and I must warn you that the mind doesn't heal without scars. There is no cure for the type of trauma you've experienced. I can help you reroute the worst of the mental connections, but doing so will trigger terrible memories. It is more painful than physical healing."

"Will I be able to…" Aris swallowed against the lump in his throat. "I couldn't even hug Selia without losing myself. I worry that sexual intimacy will not be possible."

"I'll help as much as I can," the priest answered. "However, much of your ultimate recovery will rely on establishing positive patterns to replace the trauma, and that includes sexual experiences. Some mind-healers offer that kind of aid, but I'm afraid I can't help with that. I'm afraid I do not favor men. No offense intended."

Aris summoned a slight smile. "None taken."

"Good." Tynan gestured toward the floor. "I recommend you lie down during the healing. You might collapse from the intensity of the memories."

Lie prone on the stone floor, vulnerable to another? Fear erupted through his blood and reddened his vision. Was there another choice? Not the wall. He'd been chained there all too often. Leaning against it…no. A chair. Why were there no chairs? Perim had never granted him one.

A touch against Aris's forehead followed by the cool, soothing rush of magic sent the panic skittering away. He cursed as clarity returned, shifting quickly to lie on the smooth floor before the sense of peace disappeared. He rested his head on the cushion, a luxury he'd never enjoyed in the cave, and stared up at one of the mage globes overhead.

He hadn't been allowed much light in the cave, either. The small variations made such a big difference. He could remain here in this time and space instead of being sucked into madness—barely.

Just barely.

Tynan moved his own cushion so that he could sit at Aris's head. As the healer settled his hands on each side of his temple, Aris pressed his palms against the cool stone and fought the urge to run. But even if he flew away with Kezari, he couldn't escape his own mind. Instead, he panted against his fear and tried not to be sick.

At first, the healing magic soothed his dread. The tension in his muscles eased, and the nausea faded. His eyes drifted closed when he sensed the healer's presence at the edge of his consciousness. Aris's breath puffed out on a sigh as he established the connection. For endless time, Tynan examined the countless channels in his mind, an unusual ruffling sensation but hardly painful.

Then it hit.

The sea roiled above the side of the ship in a solid wall. Unnatural. Deadly. How had they sailed so far from shore? Miaran, it shouldn't be like this. Tessen should've known better. But Tessen had been swept overboard with the last wave.

Aris knotted the rope around his waist and leaned his weight against the wheel in a desperate attempt to turn the ship.

The wall of water crashed over them before he had a chance. Snapping. Screams. Aris gripped the wheel as the world turned to liquid, dark and cold. The rope bit into his waist, snapping him back when the sea tried to tug him away. His head cracked against something hard, and water rushed into his lungs as he cried out.

Darkness.

Aris thrashed, gasping for breath. The faces of the lost flashed through his mind, and he moaned. All dead. He should have monitored Tessen. What three-hundred-year-old was ready to captain a vessel? All Aris's fault, every death, but he'd survived. Ice seeped into his body until his teeth chattered with it.

"What have we here?"

The smooth female voice crawled inside him, waking him from his doze. Where was he? The board, his endless home, buoyed him. His arms dangled over the side, trailing in the water. He must have fallen asleep. His fingers brushed against something solid, and he cracked his gritty eyes open. His vision filled with the sight of the woman, pale hair falling across her beautiful face as she bent toward him.

His soulbonded?

Aris recoiled at the thought. He'd never wanted to bond. He had Selia and Iren. Perhaps the woman hadn't noticed the connection. Gods, he hoped not. As soon as he figured out where he'd landed, he'd be on his way back. Selia would be worried sick. Still, he didn't want to hurt the woman now gripping his arm to pull him onto land. Rejecting her would be poor thanks for the rescue. But there was nothing for it.

In the distance, a roar sounded, and the woman jerked. Her fingernails dug into his flesh, drawing blood.

Aris's arm twitched, and pain crept from the remembered spot along his skin, arrowing toward his heart. Power surged, and he cried

out at the ache blooming in his head. What had he been dreaming? He reached for the memory, but another took its place.

His captor grabbed his left arm in both hands, lifting it high. Aris gurgled out a scream, his throat sore from begging, as his raw, bloody back slid along the rough floor. Red coated her naked body as she glared down at him. She hadn't been sated. She never was. No matter how often she forced him, the bond wouldn't form.

He wouldn't let it. Please, Gods, never let it.

"Say the bonding words, Aris," she demanded. "Say them now."

He turned his face away and thought of the cool stream outside the mouth of the cave. The ocean where he'd drifted. But a sea of water wouldn't wash him clean. His tormentor screamed, the shrill sound echoing through the cavern, and air rushed around his arm.

Crack.

The pain.

He bit his lip to hold back the cry, but a strangled moan slipped free. He barely felt the bite of the chain around his wrist. It was drowned by the agony crashing through him when she tugged, drawing his battered body along the stone until his arms were pulled wide.

"Bond with me, or I'll let it heal like this. It's a simple thing, really."

Every nerve in his body screamed at him to accept, but his spirit held firm. It was all he had left. "Eat iron."

She laughed. "Enjoy being misshapen."

He barely knew when she left. He screamed into the darkness then. Agony. Fury. Prayer.

Gods, let me go. If you are there, let me die.

Pain was his only answer.

Aris convulsed against the tower floor as the pain echoed through muscle and bone. And the shame. How could he have let her take his body, even knowing she would torture him afterward?

She shouldn't have been able to arouse him, but he hadn't been able to stop it. Maybe some part of him had wanted her. Could he be that sick inside?

Sweat prickled his skin as he fought to keep hold on sanity. The foundations of his being shook until the wall holding in his power crumbled. His shout sounded through the room as raw life magic streamed from him in a flood, cracking against the shield and tormenting him anew.

It would never end.

Never.

"You should carry your walking stick," Lial said, knowing it would bring a delightful flush of anger to Lynia's cheeks.

The ploy didn't disappoint. "I've been walking in the garden without trouble for several weeks now. Although it might come in handy for whacking annoying healers."

He hid his humor in a wicked smirk. "Then—"

Pain crushed into Lial's skull, temporarily blinding him. He sucked in a breath, then expelled it on a yelp when his knees crashed into the stone. Aris. Ah, *miaran*, why hadn't Tynan warned him? Didn't he know that Lial kept a link with all of his patients? His head drooped, and his hands sank into the grass beside the path.

How could anyone bear this?

Fingers gripped his shoulders. Delicate. Tentative. "What happened?" she asked, panic edging her voice. "What do I do?"

"Rebound. Aris." He gasped against the pain and struggled to pull back from the link enough to form solid thoughts. "Workroom."

Lynia pressed against him, linking an arm around his waist as she tried to haul him to his feet. He jerked away, almost falling into the grass in the process. "No, Lynia. Your back. No."

"Can you stand? I'll brace you while you walk."

"A moment."

Lial let his mind sink into the cool earth beneath him, grounding himself as best he could. Distancing himself from the link had done little. *Miaran*, but the images pouring through alone… His muscles spasmed in sympathy.

Nothing for it. For the first time in years, he severed a healing link completely. The crushing agony ceased, but the echo never would. Shaking, Lial pulled in lungful after lungful of fresh air. The chilly mist was a welcome relief on his skin.

Then he stumbled to his feet, wavering there while the world solidified around him. Lynia stared at him, her beautiful face almost as pale as her white-blond hair, and he reached out a trembling hand to brush his fingers against her cheek. A weakness for a weak moment.

"I need to lie down," he whispered through lips gone dry.

Her brows furrowed. "You mentioned Aris."

"Tynan is with him."

He should stumble to his tower as quickly as possible before he cracked beneath the weight of all he'd seen, scaring Lynia away for good. But when she kept pace beside his careful steps, he didn't have the heart to tell her to leave. Not even when a few rogue tears escaped from his eyes and crept down his cheeks.

Why did the world hold such pain? Why couldn't he bear it as he usually did?

Lynia followed him into his workroom, closing the door softly behind her. He studied her beloved face, now filled with sadness, and

took a step back. This pain was a healer's burden, not hers, and one he usually guarded well. He should have known that Tynan would work quickly and stayed close to his workroom.

"Tell me," she whispered.

"Tynan is working with Aris." Lial swallowed. "You do not want to know, Lynia. Trust me on this."

She stepped closer. "I don't have to."

Then she held him in her arms as he wept.

"You dare a great deal to step foot in my cave," Baza announced before Perim had even cleared the entrance.

Perim froze at the harsh bite to the dragon's mental voice. His red-and-gold scales glinted in the light from countless globes suspended from the ceiling, highlighting Baza's hoard of crystals, more types than she could ever count. She shifted her gaze quickly away from the treasure, though, lest the dragon believe her intent was to steal.

Nothing so simple as that.

"Please forgive me," Perim said. "I have heard rumors that suggest we might have a mutual enemy."

They both knew that there weren't any rumors. Dragons guarded secrets as securely as any other hoard, but that very quality meant that Baza was unlikely to ask how Perim had gained her information. Not unless the source became relevant.

"Elaborate."

Perim braved another step forward. "Kezari. She stole my potential soulbonded."

Baza lowered his wedge-shaped head, the spines around his eyes tilting at an ominous angle. *"That is not what I have heard."*

"Her claims about me are lies." They weren't, of course, but she was counting on the dragon not to care. "But they hardly matter. Help me escape this island, and I will ensure Kezari's death."

Baza snorted. *"The barrier around our isle is mere formality to any decent fae mage. You should not need my aid."*

Impotent fury surged through her, but Perim shoved it down. "I don't know why my ancestors journeyed here with you when you care so little for us. Yes, we could get through the barrier. But none of us can construct boats. Even if we could, our population lessens every year. I want out before we are nothing but a memory, easily forgotten by dragonkind. I'll do anything."

"I suppose that includes torturing your own soulbonded," Baza answered, baring his teeth in a grin.

Perim snapped her mouth closed. She would admit nothing.

"Where will you go if you succeed?"

"Far from here." Her nostrils flared. "The other fae won't leave, but I hope to seek asylum with my distant ancestors, the Ljósálfar. My line traveled from Alfheim to Earth, departing for Moranaia with the dragons. Perhaps our family will be remembered."

The slow hiss of Baza's breath filled the chamber as he seemed to consider her words. She fought the urge to fidget. He couldn't know how much this meant. This island was death, and she would not go down without a fight. She hadn't been lying about doing anything—torturing Aris was proof enough of that.

Her patience was rewarded by Baza's nod. *"Very well. But you will have to journey farther than you imagine. Are you willing?"*

Perim smiled. "More than willing."

15

Selia pinched the strange, thick fabric between her thumb and forefinger and gave a tentative tug. The stuff felt coarse and restrictive around her legs, and the metal closure sat uncomfortably against her waist, pinching oddly. Her nose wrinkled in distaste as her skin itched beneath the uncomfortable cloth.

A few paces away, Meli wore a similar expression. She'd braided her light hair back in a simple plait before she'd donned the dark blue pants and thin, stretchy tunic. Selia glanced down at her own similar top. What had Arlyn called it? A tee shirt? These had been made on Moranaia by an elven artisan based on samples the scouts had brought back from Earth, but the clothes still felt foreign.

At least the metal button was made with *peresten* instead of steel. It wouldn't interfere with magic or cause any allergic reactions. Selia could deal with a little iron, thankfully, but it could sometimes make things go awry.

Arlyn glanced between her and Meli and laughed. "Don't look so thrilled."

"Why do humans enjoy being uncomfortable?" Selia asked.

"You need Earth jeans," Arlyn said. "Modern styles are stretchier. If there wasn't the chance you'd be going into a cave, I'd say just wear a sundress."

Meli picked at the sleeve of her shirt. "We're going to be cold."

"I put a light sweater in your backpack." Arlyn gestured toward the bags on the bed. "Inona said it's still summer on Earth, so you'll just need cloaks to get to the portal. The sweater is for the cave."

"Are you upset that you're staying behind?" Selia asked.

Arlyn smiled. "Nope. Lial didn't think there would be any issues, but when Kai reported what Naomh had said, I decided on my own to stay. I'll help my father manage estate business and coordinate the efforts here. Such things are just as important."

Selia hadn't spoken to Lyr since earlier that morning, so perhaps Kai's news wasn't relevant to her part of the task. Still. "What Naomh said?"

"I believe *Onaial* was going to mention it at lunch," Arlyn explained. "According to Kai's father, there's poisoned energy in the fissure, and it's starting to seep out. I'm not exposing my unborn child to that."

Well, that was unfortunate news. "Blast it," Selia said. "Iren will have to stay here for both missions. Aris was worried that he would try to follow and get into trouble. We'll have to hope he's wrong."

"Maybe I'll make Iren help me sort through the latest reports on the final harvest." Arlyn grinned. "If you don't mind."

Meli let out a long groan. "Oh, that's cruel. I offered my aid last week and regretted it sorely."

"You'd better keep my father in good health," Arlyn joked. "Not gonna lie. I'm not looking forward to being charge of all this. I'd rather wait a few thousand years."

The sound of Meli's open laughter warmed Selia's heart. The young Ljósálfar woman had been too afraid of mages after her experiences in Alfheim to be comfortable around Selia at first, but that was slowly changing. In time, they might even become friends.

"I'll only gently scar him after our next argument," Meli said, still chuckling.

"Good enough for me." Arlyn's smile held a wicked glint. "Now. Do you want to wear these clothes until time to leave?"

Selia rubbed her hands along her pants, hoping to stop the tingling itch spreading up her torso. Even her scalp had started to prickle. She examined her forearm, but there was no physical rash. "I…I don't know. Something doesn't feel right."

Arlyn's eyes narrowed on her face. "What do you mean?"

Pulling the fabric away from her waist, Selia glanced at her stomach, but it was clear, too. A tremble built in her limbs, spreading until she sank down on the side of her bed. What in Arneen? She focused her attention inward. Her personal shields were undisturbed, but a faint reverberation echoed along the link to the training room. Iren was studying next door, and Arlyn was here with her. Who else could it be?

"Someone's in the training tower," Selia whispered.

She reached for the shield that kept rogue magic safely within the tower. The disturbance there shrieked along her senses until the itching threatened to drive her mad. But she shoved the physical sensations away and focused on merging her consciousness into the spell. If someone was causing trouble, she needed to know. Especially after all that had happened over the last few months.

Without warning, pain slammed into her mind, raw and elemental. A strangled sound choked in her throat as Aris's energy filled her with the speed and heat of a plains fire. Selia doubled over,

trying to contain the surge within her own body before it seeped out to the others. The screech of birds, the drone of insects, the cry of animals—all filled her head under the grip of the powerful life energy.

But that was nothing compared to the memories.

Her stomach lurched, and Selia surged to her feet. She struggled to disconnect from the tower's shield as she stumbled toward the refreshing room, barely managing to reach the closest basin. Footsteps rushed behind her, and someone reached out to pull the plug and let water into the bowl to wash the vomit away.

As her insides settled, Selia lowered her hands into the cool stream and gathered a small pool into her palms. She took a drink to rinse out her mouth before splashing the rest across her face. Then she leaned against the basin as her legs shook beneath her. Gods above. Why hadn't anyone warned her that Tynan would be treating Aris in the training tower? She was responsible for upholding the shields there and could have reinforced them. The current protections would never hold against such an onslaught.

A hand settled between her shoulder blades. "Is there anything I can do to help?" Meli asked.

"No, thank you. That was…" Selia swallowed against another wave of bile. "I need to get to the training room."

Arlyn's voice came from somewhere behind her. "Please don't tell me there's another intruder."

"There isn't." Tucking a strand of hair behind her ear, Selia straightened. "Aris was being healed, and I inadvertently intruded. He probably won't want me there. But I have to help."

"Go on," Arlyn said. "I have a feeling you won't be in the mood for lunch, anyway. My father can share his plans later."

Selia gave a grateful nod and hurried to gather her cloak along with a pouch of empty energy crystals. The twisting hallways seemed

eternal, but she finally burst out the back door and rushed down the garden path. Overhead, the snap of wings sounded, and Selia glanced through the few remaining leaves to see the dragon circling overhead. Did the workroom block Aris's distress from Kezari? Selia would have expected her to be with him.

Some of the birds began to shriek warning cries, and the branches swayed as others launched themselves into the sky. Aris's power hadn't technically escaped containment, but his connection with life was strong. Soon, the people preparing the gardens for the coming festival would be overcome with the same fear and pain swamping the birds.

"Is the dragon causing this tumult?" a male cried, dropping his side of the table he carried to stare up at the canopy. "The birds are not usually this restless."

His partner bit her lip. "Maybe we should go in. The table can wait."

Selia paused long enough to offer reassurance. Mass panic would help no one. "It isn't the dragon. Please, continue your tasks. I'll take care of the source of discord."

She didn't stay long enough to see if they believed her, but she did send a quick warning to Lyr about the current crisis.

When Selia reached the tower, she braced herself and sent her senses delicately toward the shields. Prepared this time, she let her magic settle in just enough to integrate without engaging Aris's power. Now she needed to bolster her own defenses. Layer by layer, she built the counter shield around herself until the bubble shimmered around her form.

Only then did she dare open the door.

Tynan's gaze snapped to her, panic filling his expression as she closed the door behind her. She waved toward Aris where he lay

convulsing on the ground. "Don't stop. I need to channel this power or the shields will shatter. I wish you'd warned me."

"This is not safe to be around," he said, his own shield glowing like water glinting in the sun.

Her trained eye caught a hint of weakness in his defenses. "You'll be the first to find that out if you don't hush and get to work. I am a mage and teacher. You do your job, and I'll do mine."

Without another word, Tynan nodded, his eyes closing as he returned to the maelstrom of Aris's mind. Selia tried not to look at her husband's thrashing form. When he screamed, his leg jerking violently, she averted her gaze and settled just out of reach. Then she grabbed her pouch of crystals and emptied them into her lap.

She gripped the first in her palm and opened herself slowly to his magic as it swirled through the room. She did her best to blunt the memories, but the occasional image slipped through as she channeled the raw life energy into herself. Only instinct born of training let her push those aside to be examined later. Converting another's power to one's own use generally took more effort than it was worth—unless the other person was like Aris. They'd done this very thing before when she had a lot of work to do, but he'd been in control then. This…this was like trying to pull a waterfall into a tea cup.

Well, she'd just have to go one scoop at a time. If she failed, his magic would escape containment and upset everything living within a half-day's radius of the tower.

Endless moments passed as Selia funneled the energy whirling around them, purified and converted it, and transferred it to a waiting crystal until it hummed with fullness. The warm stone nearly slid out of her sweaty palms before she set it aside and gathered another. Then another. Even as a headache built at the base of her skull, she continued.

Suddenly, it was over.

Aris's magic stuttered, then flickered out. She peered at him as she converted the remnants of power, and her heart twisted at the sight of him huddled on his side like a child. His shoulders heaved as he wept silently, his knees curled up close to his body. The mind-healer better have been successful after making Aris relive that nightmare. She lowered her forehead to her own knees as shadows of his memories paraded through her mind. How was her husband even close to sane?

"Thank you, Selia," Tynan said, his voice rough as though he'd been the one screaming.

She pinned him with her gaze as anger flooded her. "Did you have to do everything at once?"

The priest rubbed both hands across his face. "Not by preference. I was told the situation is urgent, and this particular method only works when all of the memories are confronted at the same time."

"You should have warned me." Selia scooted until she sat at Aris's back, but she didn't try to touch him. "Even if he told you not to. You should know better than to work on someone like him without a mage's aid."

Tynan's jaw firmed. "I was *also* told that this room was well-protected."

"For most things." She glared at him. "Are you a novice to act so rashly? I cannot believe Lial would request your presence. And speaking of Lial, I'm surprised he hasn't rushed in himself. He keeps a connection with those under his care, you know."

"Iron blast it," Tynan muttered. "I should have thought... It's that dragon. I wanted to complete the healing before she returned."

Selia lifted a brow. "You muddled this because of Kezari? Do dragons frighten you that much?"

The priest's cheeks reddened. "Fright has not been my experience with her. But she wouldn't…" He sighed and rubbed the back of his neck. "Forget it. I will endeavor to keep my thoughts in order in the future."

Before she formulated a reply, Aris groaned and rolled onto his back. His eyes crept open, and his empty gaze scanned the room. Then he blinked a few times before focusing on her. "Selia?"

"Forgive my intrusion," she whispered. "There was too much power for the shields to contain."

A slight smile crossed his lips. "You are never an intrusion."

"How do you feel?" she asked.

"Raw," he answered honestly. "But…different."

Tynan leaned forward to catch his attention. "I repaired what I could, but you'll have to build positive experiences on your own. The mind is complex and ever changing."

Aris nodded, though his attention seemed focused on her rather than the priest. "Selia, I want…" His voice trailed off, uncertainty entering his gaze. "I'd like to hold you. I can think of nothing more positive than that."

She sucked in a breath. "You're sure? Before…"

"I need to try," he said softly. "I need you."

Though she trembled, Selia stretched out beside him and let him gather her close. Shudders still rippled through his muscles as she rested her cheek against his chest, but he didn't go tense and his breathing remained even. Slowly, she wrapped her arm around his waist and tucked her body nearer. His heartbeat sped up beneath her ear, but it settled back to a steady pace after only a moment.

She barely noticed when the healer stood and let himself quietly out.

"You gave me more strength than you know," Aris whispered.

Selia stiffened. "Me?"

"You gave me a reason to keep going, even when I didn't realize it. It didn't matter that I wouldn't see you again. Knowing you existed in the world was enough." His lips brushed her hair. "You will always be my heart."

A lump formed in her throat. "You should've hated me."

"What?" he asked, his arm tightening around her back.

Now might not be the best time, but it felt right. Selia's hand gripped the fabric of his tunic as her greatest regret poured free. "If not for me, you wouldn't have been on that ship in the first place. It's all my fault."

Her whispered words dug into his heart, turning it over. Aris caressed her soft cheek with shaky fingers. "No, love. No."

"You were going to stay, but I convinced you it would be fine."

He cursed the weakness that kept him from sitting up and lifting her into his arms where he could look into her eyes. But his nerves groaned with the echoes of pain, and his muscles refused to do more than shift her a little closer. "You knew my heart's dream and encouraged me to seek it. I've always wanted to be among the first to successfully sail the seas. Do you know how much your support means to me?"

Her head moved against his chest. "You wouldn't have landed in such torment if—"

Aris placed his finger against her lips. "Stop. You aren't a seer. I hope you haven't carried this for seven years."

"Of course I have." Selia snorted softly. "How could I not?"

He smiled at that. Yes, she would have. Selia had always taken responsibility for more than she ought. "Well, drop that burden. It isn't yours."

She fell silent, but he didn't mistake that for agreement. He wouldn't argue the point, not now. Not when he could savor the feel of her against him for the first time in years. Although spasms still shot through his muscles and his body felt as heavy as a mountain, the priest's work held.

Mostly.

As Tynan had said, the healing wasn't perfect. A thread of unease wound through him as Selia shifted higher, closer to being on top of him than beside. He knew by the tension winding into his shoulders that he might never be able to bear her completely above him, but having her this close so soon after reliving his past was enough of a miracle.

If he'd learned anything, it was that miracles should be cherished.

"How did you end up in here?" he asked.

"I prepared the bulk of the shields on this room, and after I caught Iren experimenting with lightning one day, I set it to alert me to excessive power," Selia said, her tone dry. "The whole thing would've shattered if I hadn't brought crystals to fill."

Aris trailed his fingers through her hair and smiled again to remember the times they'd worked together in the past, loading energy crystals so she'd have extra power when she needed it. "At least my suffering will serve some good."

She gasped. "I wasn't thinking of it that way. You may have the crystals if you like."

"No," he said quickly. "No, they are yours. We would have had to fill them anyway in case we need them on Earth. I imagine this was faster."

"I would not have them in exchange for your pain," she whispered.

"My pain was inevitable." He kissed the top of her head even as he gave her hair a slight tug. "Anyway, I like the thought of creating something out of this. Stop overthinking it."

Her sigh caressed his neck. "Fine."

There was so much they needed to discuss, so much still between them, but for the moment, he didn't care. He wanted to ignore the last seven years and just be. Tomorrow, he could begin to tell her bits of his torment—and that Perim had been his soulbonded. But not now. One day's torture was enough.

16

Selia breathed in Aris's wild, woodsy scent as she twisted a lock of his brown-and-green hair around her finger. There was a tension to his muscles despite the peace of the moment that told her there were things unsaid—things beyond the terrible images she'd already seen. She wouldn't ask now, though. He'd gone through more than anyone should suffer in this day alone.

The door clicked open, and Lial's and Tynan's energies flowed in before their footsteps sounded on the stone. Selia nuzzled into Aris for another moment before she reluctantly pushed herself up with one arm. She glanced up, hiding her surprise at Lial's red-rimmed, solemn eyes. Oh, yes, he'd been linked. She'd never seen such a haunted look on the cranky but self-assured healer's face.

"How is he?" Lial asked.

"I'm alive," Aris murmured. Selia blinked at the hint of humor in her husband's voice. His lips curved up as he stared at her for a moment. Then he winked. "Can't complain about being able to hold my wife without going insane."

Lial's expression barely lightened as he crouched on Aris's other side. "For so much trauma, you deserved a complete healing. I am sorry you had to suffer."

Aris sighed. "You'd have to wipe my mind for a complete healing. I have a feeling you know that well enough now."

"Unfortunately," Lial said, flinching before he could smooth out the reaction. "Tynan's haste prevented me from severing our link as quickly as privacy would demand."

Tynan huffed. "I feared the dragon would try to—"

"So you said." Lial's voice could have frozen the sweltering plains in the height of summer. "I was assured of your skill despite your being out of your apprenticeship for such a short time. You may have treated many in those seven years, but you were obviously not ready for a task of this magnitude. Were any others available, I would call on them before attempting to fix Aris's poorly healed bones."

Selia lifted her brows at that. Training and apprenticeship for a healer lasted hundreds of years, but even after that, they often worked alongside someone with more experience for the first quarter century. She peered at Tynan's ashen face as he stood a few paces away, his eyes averted. He should have known better, but he was young. Despite his lapse, she found herself hoping Lial didn't go too hard on him.

"Torture isn't something our people often see," Aris said suddenly, his soft voice carrying across the silence. "Those inclined to that kind of cruelty are brought to justice before they reach that level of depravity. The shock of my trauma couldn't have helped."

His first assertion was certainly true—or at least she'd always believed so. But the whispers she'd heard of Kien's depravity trickled through her mind. He'd tortured Ralan's beloved for weeks before being discovered, and he had been a prince committing his foul acts near the palace at the very heart of their kingdom. Then there had been Allafon, a lord under Lyr's command. He'd hidden a great deal of damage before he'd been caught.

Perhaps there was more darkness in their society than any of them wanted to believe.

"One might think so," Tynan said softly, reinforcing Selia's own thoughts. "But I have seen my share of terrible things. Lial is correct to berate me."

"It remains to be seen if I will report this matter to your superior," Lial said. "I am strongly considering it."

The door opened again, and Kezari in her elven form slipped through. She glared at Lial as she strode toward Aris. "Do not threaten Tynan."

Selia's mouth dropped open at the dragon's angry demeanor. Kezari wasn't breathing fire, at least, but it might not be far off based on her expression. Aris groaned and shifted, and when Selia glanced at him, worry lined his forehead. He shoved his hand against the floor, trying to push himself up, but he dropped back down without making much progress.

Lial cursed. "Don't move. Your body is weak, and it would be best to let me heal the strain to your muscles before you hurt yourself worse."

"Kezari…" Aris began.

"Will certainly know what her *skizik* needs," Lial finished, his eyes narrowing as the dragon halted.

"Do not berate Tynan," Kezari said.

"I can't…" The priest shook his head. "I shouldn't have…"

Kezari thrust her shoulders back and glared at Tynan, too. "Your actions were necessary. Elves waste too much time, and a quick, hot flame cauterizes best. You were correct."

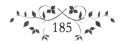

Lial's lips pinched. "There is more to consider than his methods."

Aris lifted a hand and then let it drop heavily on his chest. "I would appreciate it if you'd heal me enough so I can get up instead of arguing? Please?"

"Yes, heal him," Kezari said. As she sank to her knees behind Aris's head, her thin dress bunched around her legs, and she almost toppled before she caught herself. "His body must be in good health for our mission."

After a few muttered expletives, Lial got to work, and Selia glanced away from the bright blue light surrounding Aris. Her gaze landed on Tynan, who stared at Kezari's back with unmasked longing—until he noticed Selia's regard. Then he spun away to pace a circle around the room.

Was there something between the two? Selia tried to remember if dragons and elves could bond, but she didn't think any of the histories she'd read had mentioned it. She'd heard a ballad about such a pairing once, but then, she'd also listened to a song extolling the virtues of running naked outside in the season of ice. One never knew what the *omree* would put into verse.

As soon as the healer finished, Aris shoved himself up to a sitting position, drawing Selia's attention. His long hair shifted around him, more than a little tangled. He braided it as best he could in a few quick motions and let his hands drop into his lap as he studied her. His gaze trailed down her body before returning to her face.

"What…what are you wearing?"

Oh. Selia found herself chuckling despite the situation. "Earth clothes."

"They look good on you, of course." He flicked a glance at her breasts. "But definitely different."

Selia smiled. "You'll have to admire them later. I have a mission to do now that the crisis has passed."

"I should go with you," Kezari said. "I am Moranaian now. That solves the problem."

Aris frowned at the dragon. "Not without me. You said our magic would work best together. We're a team."

An unexpected sliver of pain sliced Selia's heart. He didn't protest her departure, but he didn't want Kezari to go without him. There were plenty of good reasons for that, of course. Selia knew that. Just preventing the dragon from behaving rashly was difficult enough in Morania where dragons were known to exist. But on Earth, without Aris there to guide Kezari? Visions of humans running in panic from a flame-breathing wyvern flickered through her mind.

But feelings weren't rational.

"I do not like this delay, *skizik*," Kezari muttered. "The crack widens with each day."

Aris rested his arms on his knees. "Lial. While Selia and the others are on this first mission, I would like for you to repair my bones."

"No," Selia said before the healer could respond. "What if that sets off bad memories and your magic leaks out again?"

Lial's nostrils flared. "That will not be a concern. Aris will be placed into a deep sleep, his nerves deadened during the procedure. Tynan will ensure that memories are not triggered while I work."

Selia frowned. "Why didn't Tynan block the pain today?"

The priest's pacing cut off abruptly as he spun to face her. "I could not. Mental pathways formed by pain cannot be rerouted while sensation is blocked. Please do not think I am cruel in addition to inept."

"I meant no offense," Selia said.

Tynan nodded, but doubt shadowed his expression. Unfortunately, she didn't have time to deal with his insecurities. Meli and the others would be waiting on her to journey to Earth. Selia glanced at one of the small windows and frowned at how dim the light appeared. It was well past the midday meal. Why hadn't anyone come looking for her?

Aris stood, still wavering on his feet despite his healing session. Kezari shifted beneath his shoulder to help support his weight. "We can discuss my bones later. I want rest," Aris said.

"I'll see you to your room," Lial said. "If necessary, I can put you into a light sleep."

Selia stared at her husband's back as he limped across the room with Kezari. He wouldn't leave without saying anything to her, would he? Surely not, especially with her impending mission. Her throat tightened. She wasn't jealous of the dragon, exactly—not in a romantic sense—but she did envy their closeness. He'd formed this connection alone, a symbol of the new life they didn't quite share.

Then Aris looked over his shoulder, his brows lowering. "Aren't you coming with us, Selia? I want to see your face as I fall asleep."

A bit of the heaviness left her chest at the pleading in his eyes. The mission would have to wait. Aris needed her.

Water sucked at Perim's body as the waves surged in frenzied eddies around her waist. Salt stung the healing cuts from her crawl through the tunnels, but it was a small discomfort. *Twenty. Twenty-one. Twenty-two.* She stopped at the proper number and studied the sea around her. Baza had claimed there was an outcropping twenty-two steps from the shore. A quick swim from there, and she was supposed to find a fissure of energy that connected to the Veil.

What a delicious secret that had been. All this time, Kezari had sought a way to convince the queen to petition the Moranaians for use of the portal while Baza had quietly been expanding a newly developing fissure. Like the other dragons, he had no desire to leave the island—or so he claimed—but gathering control of a valuable resource like a new portal would give him a great deal of power.

If he didn't want Kezari's hoard of earth-magic gems so badly, he never would have revealed the truth to Perim. He'd even shared that Kezari was likely to head to Earth with Aris to solve a problem with the energy there. Perim grinned. The dragon wasn't likely to get anything useful out of Aris after he'd been so thoroughly broken.

Perim shoved her hand over her eyes and squinted against the sunlight striking the sea. The only outcropping she could see was at least another thirty paces away, maybe more. Had Baza lied about the whole thing? This was far more than twenty-two. Although… She groaned. How did dragons count steps? Not the way elves did, it seemed.

She straightened her spine and started walking again, ignoring the pull of the water. She'd swim if she had to—anything to escape the living death of the island.

As she exited the brooding tower, Selia gathered the edges of her cloak in her hands, blocking the sight of the strange Earth clothes from others' view. With the dragon gone and the birds settled, the workers had resumed their preparations for the autumn festival.

Only two days away now. Soon, crowds would gather to hear the *omree* practice their songs.

Warriors from surrounding areas would also arrive to compete in the tournaments the day after the main festival. There would be archery and swordplay for certain, but Selia wasn't sure what else they did here. At home, the mages held contests for the most innovative spells, but that probably wouldn't happen at Braelyn.

She'd been looking forward to experiencing the festival, and now she might not see it at all.

Selia ducked into the door near the library and hurried toward the study. Once she'd checked in with Lyr, she could talk with Iren. It would be just like him to try to follow the group to Earth, especially considering his fascination with Arlyn's stories. He'd already considered and discarded several ideas on how Moranaians could use magic to create a space station circling the planet like Earth had. She smiled. Elves in space—what a thought.

To her surprise, Iren was already in the study, bent over a stack of papers in the seat next to Arlyn. She'd certainly wasted no time in recruiting his aid with those reports. When Arlyn cast a sheepish look her way, Selia grinned and inclined her head. She had no problem with other adults giving him tasks, within reason. It was good for him.

Lyr stood with Meli beside his desk. His hand rested at her waist, and his face was pinched with worry. But as soon as he caught sight of Selia, resignation replaced it. His hand lingered for another moment before he sighed and straightened. Meli leaned up to give him a quick kiss on the lips before walking over to Selia.

"Ready for our grand adventure?" Meli asked.

"Now?" Selia's brows drew together. "I thought we'd need to do more preparation."

Meli shook her head. "We're only waiting on you. Kai, Inona, and Delbin are already at the portal with our packs."

Her cheeks heated. "Forgive me for holding everything up."

"It was necessary," Lyr said, striding over. "Lial reported to me already. But now that Aris is settled, it seems best to proceed quickly. I didn't want to say this in front of Kezari, but I would like to have a better idea of the situation before sending a dragon to Earth. Although I don't doubt her honesty…"

Arlyn glanced up from the report she held. "I wouldn't send her without good reason, that's for sure. There are lots of ways to explain pointy ears on Earth, but a dragon is sort of hard to pass off as something else."

"Just so," Lyr grumbled.

"Perhaps it will be unnecessary," Selia said. "If I am capable of correcting the problem, would you like me to do so, or should I stick with gathering information?"

Lyr's lips pursed. "If you are certain you can fix it, please do. I would be happy to avert another crisis."

"Me, too." Selia smiled at Meli. "Well, then. I'm ready when you are."

The younger woman nodded, turning to give her bonded another kiss. Selia walked over to Iren's chair and knelt to look into his eyes. He grinned at her, no hint of the nerves twisting her stomach in his eyes. "I'll be good, *Onaiula*. I want to go to Earth, but I don't want to be poisoned. Then I'd have to see the healer."

Selia chuckled at the dismay in his tone at the last word. In this case, it wasn't just because of Lial's grumpy nature. Iren balked at any healer. "Remember that, love. Perhaps you could check in on your father later?"

"I will," Iren said, his humor fading. "I promise."

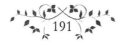

"Good." Despite the others in the room, Selia leaned forward to kiss Iren on the cheek. He groaned at the display, but his arms wrapped around her neck for a hug. "I love you."

"I love you, too," he answered as she stood.

Then Selia joined Meli by the door. Selia gripped her cloak together with shaky hands, took a deep breath, and stepped out into the hall.

Toward her first real adventure.

17

They emerged into darkness.

Selia squinted against the sudden night, her eyes taking a moment to adjust after the dim glow of the Veil. After a few heartbeats, the thin trickle of moonlight resolved the world into shades of black and gray. She followed the others from the narrow passage in the wall of a ridge, and a bit more of the world came into focus.

The small ridge followed a hill that sloped upward to their left and downward to their right. Beyond the small clearing where they stood, sparse tree-shadows stood against the navy sky, but the branches looked far smaller than the trees at Braelyn. Still, this wasn't too different from the foothills on the edge of the plains. Hadn't Arlyn said there would be cities on this world? Difficult to believe in this location.

"It's late," Kai said, peering down the hill. "I doubt your friend would appreciate us calling her for a ride."

Delbin pulled a thin, rectangular device from his pocket. A phone, she thought it was called. He pressed on the side, and the glassy surface filled with light. The thin beam illuminated the frown creasing his brow. "Yeah, not at one in the morning."

"This does not look like morning," Meli said from beside Selia.

"Humans count the start of the day in the middle of the night." Delbin shrugged. "You get used to it. But hey, I have a ride-sharing app. Once we reach the end of the driveway on the other end of the ridge, I'll request pick-up."

"You don't think that'll look suspicious?" Kai asked.

Delbin smiled. "Eh, maybe. We could say the party up at the house got a little wild. It's too far away to see from the road."

Inona nudged Delbin's shoulder with her own. "You just want a chance to use Ralan's money."

"He's a rich bastard. And I'm not stealing," Delbin added when Kai frowned. "He gave me permission to hook his card to the app."

App? Card? Selia exchanged a confused grimace with Meli. "This sounds difficult."

Kai expelled a long breath. "And dangerous. We don't want to keep showing up out of nowhere with no obvious means of transportation. Even Maddy's periodic pick-ups may be causing notice."

"It's not too much of a jog to reach a few human businesses," Inona said. "I've found people willing to drive me places from there when needed."

Delbin spun to face Inona. "You hitchhiked? Ah, hell, that's not a safe way to—"

"I may not have your strength when it comes to telepathy, but I can tell when someone is dangerous. I can give them a bit of a nudge, too," Inona grumbled.

"Learn from your elders, man." Kai grinned. "You might have lived here the last hundred years, but we've been doing this type of

thing for centuries. It's best in this case. We'll find some place public, and you can take control of someone with a large vehicle. From my understanding, the cave isn't near well-travelled areas. Your app would keep a record of our unusual destination."

Delbin shook his head. "There's an official trailhead and a small campsite near the cave."

"Do humans begin such activities in the middle of the night?" Inona asked sweetly.

"Not usually for legit reasons," Delbin muttered, rubbing his neck. "All right, fine. I'll let the elderly lead the way."

Selia studied their surroundings as much as the light permitted as she and Meli followed Inona and Kai. The insects' chirps sounded a different tune, and the air carried an unusual blend of nature and… something else. A hint of something acrid, but she had no name for it. Even the energy felt different.

What little she could pull in. It was like trying to grasp something on a tall shelf. She could brush it with her fingers, but she couldn't get the leverage to pull. When Selia did finally manage a link, the flow was but a trickle. Drips from a water clock compared to a steady stream. Her fingers wrapped around the pouch of energy crystals she'd shoved in her pocket. If she had to do magic, she was going to need them, though she hoped she didn't have to waste the one containing pure Moranaian energy. That one was a last resort.

By the time they reached a road, Selia was out of breath. They'd alternated between walking and jogging, and the scouts' paces were definitely faster than hers or Meli's. More than once, she'd exchanged exhausted but resolved glances with the other woman. They might not have trained for this, but they weren't going to hold the group back.

Still, she was more than grateful for a short break.

Selia bent over for several long moments, trying to steady her breathing. She stared at the odd, smooth material of the road as she gasped in more air. A harsh scent emanated from the…rock? Shaking her head, she straightened, and only then did she notice what was on the other side. Light poured from a squat metal-and-glass building situated in a sea of more smooth stone. A variety of conveyances sat between lines all around the place.

Cars. These must be what Arlyn had called cars.

"What is the ground here?" she asked softly.

"It's artificial," Delbin explained. "This stuff is asphalt. It's a mix of small stones and pitch. Humans spread it all over the place for cars to drive on. Sometimes, you'll see concrete, which is made in a similar way to the walls of some of our houses. I think."

All along the road to the right of the building, more structures sat, little grass to be seen amidst the asphalt. Tall metal poles stretched into the sky at regular intervals, connected by a series of thin ropes, and little arms stuck out from the top with lights attached. Selia sent out a tendril of power, curious to see how the lanterns differed from mage lamps. But she retreated quickly at the intense energy surging through them, like lightning contained.

Fascinating. She might be able to work with human electricity if it was similar to lightning, but it would take some research. "Remind me to speak to you later, Delbin, about how you use magic to charge your device. There may be more compatibility than I'd thought."

"Sure," he said.

"Come on." Kai gestured toward the brightly lit building. "Let's cross the street before someone drives by."

Selia and Meli followed Inona and Delbin, Kai falling behind to guard their backs. As they hurried across the road and onto the broad expanse of asphalt, an odd sound like a buzzing whoosh

echoed off the trees. Frowning, Selia spun around, only to step back with a cry when a large conveyance—car—rushed past with such force that her hair was tossed about by the wind. Gods, those things went fast.

Without magic, too.

"We're supposed to ride in one of those?" Meli whispered.

Delbin chuckled. "You get used to it."

Selia stared at the retreating red lights, her heart pounding against her ribs. Get used to it? No. She'd ridden horses on the plains, but they couldn't approach that speed. It couldn't be safe. Were humans insane? Fear crawled up her throat and coated her mouth with bitterness. She shouldn't have come here. She wasn't an explorer like Aris.

"Selia," Inona began softly, settling her hand on Selia's shoulder. "It's a lot to get used to. Don't give yourself grief over it."

With a nod, Selia spun back toward the metal and glass building, though she wasn't so certain Inona was correct. They were all at risk if she couldn't handle this. Why shouldn't she be hard on herself? But she didn't give voice to her doubts, lest she affect their confidence, too.

"I'm ready," Selia said.

As they resumed walking, Meli gave Selia a quick smile. "She's right, you know. Shifting cultures is tough. In some ways, it was harder for me to go from Alfheim to Moranaia than it is to travel here. I get flickers of my past life sometimes, so I've seen some of these things in my head. You haven't."

Selia arched a brow. "You seemed just as worried about the car's speed as I was."

"The image in my mind wasn't moving," Meli said with a grimace. "Transportation portals are much safer and more efficient."

"You have the right of it." Selia lowered her voice. "If I can gather enough energy after we find the breech, I'll transport us back to the portal."

Kai spoke over Selia's shoulder. "It would be nice if you can manage it despite the energy limitations."

Selia shrugged. "We shall see."

She followed Delbin and Inona through a set of doors that slid open as they approached, but she was too busy blinking against the intense light of the interior to marvel over that. Once her eyes adjusted, she stumbled to a halt, stunned by the shelves full of brightly colored packages. A tall display stood directly in front of her, purple and orange bags lined up in little compartments. The bag had words, but she didn't recognize them.

Selia's brow furrowed. Lyr had used a spell to give her the English language, and he'd said the written form was included. Had there been a mistake? "What do they speak here?" she asked Kai.

"English."

She frowned. Languages did change all the time, so these words might simply be new. "I thought that was what I'd been given, but I don't understand the words on some of these items."

"Probably product names," Kai answered. "A special name intended to differentiate between similar items created by different people."

The knot in her stomach began to ease. She didn't want to consider not being able to read in a world she already didn't understand, not even for such a short mission. "Hopefully that is it. Thank you."

Selia headed over to the others where they stood beside a display filled with shelves of more colored packets. Some had pictures of oval or triangle-shaped food. Thin bread? She studied the packages

more closely for some clue, and though relief coursed through her to recognize some words, they weren't exactly helpful. *Cheesy. Crunchy. Original.*

But cheesy, crunchy, original *what?*

Meli picked up a yellow bag. "This looks familiar, but I can't remember why."

"Try it," Delbin said. "We should buy something while we wait for our friend to pick us up."

Inona crossed her arms. "What are you talki—"

"They'll kick us out if we're just loitering." Delbin flicked a meaningful glance to the left, and Selia noticed the human woman scrutinizing them from the end of the aisle as she placed supplies on another shelf. He raised his voice slightly for her benefit. "It's bad enough that we had to walk all this way to avoid Kai's dad. It's just a party."

Kai's brows rose, but a small smile pulled at his lips. "Hey, my dad is a hard ass. Barely around except when he wants to tell me what to do."

"I just wish you weren't so cheap." Delbin's eyes shone with humor. "It would've only been another twenty or thirty dollars to get a big enough car to take us all from my house."

"Why pay when you can get a free ride? Just takes a little extra effort."

Selia, Meli, and Inona exchanged amused looks. As Inona's lips twitched, Meli grabbed Selia's wrist and tugged her down another aisle. "I wonder if they think that was convincing?" Meli whispered, chuckling under her breath.

"Probably." Selia grinned. "Where are we going?"

Meli paused beside a row of glass doors and pointed at the closest one. "These bottles look like they have water in them. I don't

know about these other drinks, but it sounds like fun to try water from another world."

Selia frowned at the rows of bottles. "Will it make us sick?"

"I don't know." Meli jiggled the bag she still held. "But it can't be worse than this. Come on." She lowered her voice. "Who knows if we'll ever get another chance to try this kind of Earth stuff?"

Meli was right. If she did return with Aris and Kezari, Selia would be able to cast a transport spell back to the spot they needed—or at least, she hoped she could. Aris would be disappointed to miss the adventure, but it would be safer than trying to sneak a dragon past countless humans. Even in elven form, Kezari didn't exactly fit in, so it wouldn't be worth the risk. When would she get another opportunity like this?

Resolved, Selia yanked at the handle and ignored the blast of cold air within as she pulled a glass bottle from a shelf. But when it dented beneath her hand, she realized that it wasn't glass at all. Yet another unusual human contraption. She held the door open for Meli to grab one of her own before turning her attention to the other displays.

An unusual cabinet caught her eye. This one was glass, lit softly from within, and several shelves held rows of round, bread-like objects with various forms of frosting. She wandered closer. One of them was only lightly frosted, and except for a hole in the middle, it looked very much like the cakes her people ate during the summer solstice festival.

"I would like to try one of these," Selia said to Meli. "But I'm not sure if I can buy just one."

Delbin stepped up beside her. "You can. Here, I'll get it."

Selia watched as he picked up a thin, clear bag and a white piece of paper. After he opened the case, he grabbed a cake with the paper

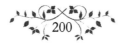

and slipped it into the sack. "It's called a doughnut," he said as he handed it over.

The small bag rustled as she wrapped her fingers around it. Selia lifted the bag and the bottle. "And what are these containers made of?" she whispered

"Plastic." Delbin's attention shifted to the window behind her. "I'll tell you about it in the car. Looks like our friend is here."

Selia glanced over her shoulder. On the other side of the window, a man stepped out of a large, boxy vehicle. He appeared human, and a quick energy scan confirmed it. "You know him?" she asked Delbin.

Delbin winked at her. "I'd say we're about to become best friends."

"Are you sure about doing this?" Selia asked, keeping her voice low. "It doesn't seem quite…fair."

He sobered. "I don't like it, but there isn't a lot of choice. We have to get to that cave. But I'll make sure the human is fairly compensated."

He left her standing there as he approached the stranger entering the main doors. The human's steps hitched and his expression went a touch slack, but those were the only signs that Delbin had taken control. Their new friend walked right up to Kai and Delbin with a smile.

"Hey, guys. Ready to go?" the human asked.

"The ladies just need to buy their snacks," Delbin said. "Then we can get going."

The man nodded. "Sure."

It only took a few moments and a swipe of Delbin's card before the group headed for the door. While the human purchased a drink, Delbin leaned in toward the group. "I've implanted memories as

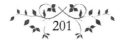

much as taken true control. I'll remove them once we get where we're going. Still, try not to say much. Less for me to deal with that way."

Inona eased closer to him, her own voice going low. "You've done a lot of work with Ralan in such a short time. It didn't seem this easy for you before."

Delbin slung his arm over Inona's shoulders. "Yep. Guess it was worth working with the arrogant ass after all."

Heat climbed into Selia's cheeks at his words, though he'd spoken them with true affection. Ralan and Delbin both needled each other like friendly competitors in a magic contest, but despite the lack of rancor, it made her uncomfortable. One didn't call the heir to the throne an arrogant ass—whether he was one or not.

The human joined the group outside the glass doors. "You guys are lucky I'm borrowing my dad's van. Climb on in, and we'll head out."

Kai hopped into one of the front seats as Delbin grabbed a handle on the side of the van and tugged. To her surprise, a portion of the vehicle slid back, leaving a large hole for them to enter. "Why don't you and Meli sit in the back? I'm probably the only one who knows how to close this door," Delbin said with a laugh.

Biting her lip, Selia hesitated for only a moment before ducking into the van. She crawled between the two inner seats and plopped down on one in the back. She gave a quick bounce as Meli settled beside her. The cushioning was adequate. Otherwise, there wasn't much to note about the unusual conveyance. Lights in the ceiling illuminated the seats and a few small panels with knobs and buttons, but the interior was overall bland. No carving or embroidery. Why not decorate something so important?

But as soon as the human placed a key into a slot and twisted, such thoughts were forgotten. Selia clutched the water bottle to her

chest and leaned back against her seat for balance when the vehicle began to move backward at an angle. A quick pause, and then the human directed the van forward with a jolt. Her heartbeat pounded in her ears as they turned onto the street and accelerated.

Delbin pulled some kind of strap over his shoulder and glanced over the seat. "Grab one of the buckles on the wall and pull the seatbelt over you. There's a small place by your hip to secure it."

Selia shifted her possessions onto the seat between her and Meli and reached for the strap beside her that matched Delbin's. It took a bit of fumbling, but she finally got it latched with a small click. "What is this for?"

Delbin smiled. "It's a safety measure. These things do go pretty fast, after all."

She gave a jerky nod and peered out the window. Her stomach immediately lurched at the sight of the trees rushing by. No wonder she had to wear a belt for safety—if this thing crashed, anyone inside would be flung gods knew where otherwise. It was foolhardy, bold... and amazing. And very, very human.

"Let's try our food," Meli said, lifting her bag from between them.

"Now?" Selia grabbed the package holding her cake. "I'm don't know. My stomach is uneasy enough."

Meli frowned. "Are you sure you aren't hungry? When did you last eat?"

"This morning, I suppose." Selia had missed the midday meal helping Aris and had been too busy after to consider food. With so much magic to perform, that could be a problem. Proper nourishment was vital to energy production. "Let's do it."

Selia pulled the round cake from its bag and stared at it. Though flattened in places from being tossed around, the cake made her

mouth water. She took a tentative sniff and was rewarded with a sweet yeasty scent that produced a yearning for home. Despite the slight sharp smell of something else, some component uniquely human, she pinched off a bite and popped it in her mouth.

It was… Selia wrinkled her nose as she tried to determine if the treat tasted pleasant. It was missing the fuller, more savory taste of the grains on Moranaia, and the sweet hit her tongue with greater intensity. As she chewed, she noticed an aftertaste, too. Brow furrowing, Selia tore off another bite. Then another. Unusual, but not unpleasant.

Meli tore her bag open, almost spilling the contents. She steadied it in her hands and lifted a piece from inside. A golden, curved oval caught the light from a passing streetlamp. Probably not bread, but what did they know? Meli studied the bit of food for a moment before taking a tentative bite.

Selia lowered her own treat at the unusual look on the other woman's face. Eyes wide, Meli worked her tongue against the roof of her mouth. Without a word, Delbin reached over the seat and grabbed the water container from between them. He did something to the top handed it over. Meli drank deep before lowering the bottle with a grimace.

"I don't know if I can eat the rest," she admitted.

Selia eyed the bag. "That bad?"

"Feel free to try one," Meli said.

Although the other woman's tone wasn't promising, Selia accepted a golden disk from the bag. Before she could second guess herself, she took a quick bite. The food crunched loudly, but that wasn't too bothersome. The intense, sharp taste that permeated her mouth? That was altogether different.

When Delbin handed her the other water bottle, Selia took a grateful sip, barely noticing the tinny flavor. "What was that?"

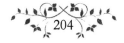

Delbin lifted the bag and then laughed. "Salt and vinegar potato chips. Plenty of humans aren't even fond of that combo, and they invented it. I wish I'd looked more closely. I would have warned you."

"Oh, certainly." With a small smile, Selia tore off a large piece of her cake and passed it to Meli. "Good thing I don't mind sharing."

The sweet dulled the remaining bitterness lingering on her tongue. But despite the unpleasantness of the snack, Selia didn't regret trying it. Eating Earth food was a small enough thing, but she couldn't help but feel brave. Exhilarated.

Perhaps she had adventure in her after all.

18

Aris stirred to awareness beneath the weighty feel of someone's regard. Although he tensed, he was able to scan with his senses before panic set in.

Iren.

Aris cracked his eyes open to see his son sitting in a chair beside the bed. Where in all the worlds had Iren found a chair? The bed had been the only furniture here when Aris had fallen asleep. He had a feeling he didn't want to know where the new addition had come from, but as a father, he also didn't have a choice.

"Did you teleport that from some hapless person's room?" he asked, then cleared his throat to try to ease some of the roughness. "I'd rather know before they come looking for it."

Far from worried, Iren grinned. "No. Well, I did teleport it, but I asked Lyr's permission first."

"You're too young to be using your power so casually."

"Yeah, probably." Iren shrugged. "But *Onaiala* makes me go too slow."

Aris sat up, shoving his hair out of his face as he studied his son. There wasn't anger in his expression, precisely, but he exuded a certain frustrated mulishness that Aris had seen in the mirror more than once. "Constraints are necessary in magic."

"Sure, but sometimes I just want to…" Iren's shoulders slumped. "I don't know how to describe it. *Onaiala* is a great teacher, but I still want to…"

"Do things your own way," Aris filled in for him. He'd felt the same often in his life. "You don't fit the steady, formal mold of your grandfather. Selia doesn't, either, but she's never had a good reason to realize it."

"Is that why you left?" Iren blurted.

"What?" Aris's head jerked back. "No. Not because of your grandfather. He never approved of me, but we reached an accord. And I didn't leave you. It was supposed to be a quick, low-risk expedition. I had no intention of being away from you for long."

Though Iren nodded, he nibbled on his lower lip for a moment before speaking again. "I thought maybe we weren't, you know, enough."

Aris's spine stiffened. "That is far from the truth. My last trip was also the first I'd taken since a couple of years before you were born, and it was only supposed to take a month, two at most. I would not have gone otherwise. Your mother knew I'd always dreamed of sailing the ocean and encouraged me."

"She wanted you to leave?" Iren said, anger lacing his voice.

"Do *not* take it that way." Aris captured his son's gaze. "I mean it. Your *onaiala* loved me for myself, not what she wanted me to be. She loved me enough to make sure I was able to fulfill a dream. I hope you find a partner like that someday, too."

After a few heartbeats, Iren nodded. "I wish we'd known Ralan and Eri then. They would have known you'd have trouble."

"Doesn't mean they would have stopped it." Aris sighed. "I'm glad I don't have to be the one to decide what information to withhold."

"Surely they would have prevented all the horrible things that woman did. You were tortured and…"

Aris froze as his son's mouth snapped closed. "You saw."

"It was an accident," Iren said in a rush. "There was so much energy coming from the training room, so I hooked in. But only for a few drips of time. I'm sorry."

His throat closed up. He might not have liked knowing that Selia and the healers had seen so much of what had happened, but his own son? Once again, Aris had failed his child. No eleven-year-old should know about torture. More than torture, if the flush on Iren's skin was any indication.

"Perhaps you should speak with Tynan," Aris whispered. "You should not have seen that."

Iren rolled his eyes. "You think I don't realize bad things happen? This kind of stuff is in my history books, you know. And I've heard some of the whispers about Kien and Allafon, whose servant I fought."

Aris's lips pinched. It was true, but… "It's altogether different when it's your father."

"I'm glad I know," Iren said. This time, the stubborn set of his son's shoulders reminded Aris of Selia. "You told me it was bad, but I didn't really get it. Now I do."

A rustling sounded from the top of the stairs, and Aris glanced up to see Tynan stride into the tower room. Perfect. The mind-healer could examine Iren for any sign of trauma. Gods, Selia would never forgive him if this mess had caused harm to their son.

Or maybe she would, but he wouldn't be able to forgive himself.

The healer smiled as he neared. "Good, you're awake."

"Where's Lial?" Aris asked.

"He will be here in a moment." Tynan paused at the foot of the bed. "I wanted to apologize for my lapse in judgement earlier."

Aris shrugged. "It worked out."

But those words didn't ease the frown on the healer's face. "Yes. However, the more I consider it, the more I am inclined to agree with Lady Selia. We should wait for her return to proceed with the secondary healing. I do not want to risk more trouble."

Iren perked up. "Trouble?"

"Oh, I'd say you've had enough of that," Aris said. Then he took a deep breath and plunged ahead. "Tynan. My son connected to the training room's shields and caught a few of my memories. Could this have caused harm?"

"Let me see."

Tynan rounded the bed and stopped at Iren's side. As he reached out a hand, Iren glared. "Do not erase anything. I am old enough to deny you permission for that."

In that moment, Iren looked far older than eleven, the resolve hardening his face that of a man. Tynan obviously agreed, for he gave a sharp nod. "I will not. But no one of any age need suffer trauma when help is available."

Aris smiled as Iren grudgingly allowed the healer to use his power on him. He'd once felt the same about having someone meddle in his mind, but he'd learned the folly of that pride. Tynan was correct. There was no reason to leave the mind unhealed. Unhappiness, stress, sadness—these were necessary parts of life, if unpleasant. But there came a point when the damage was beyond normal, a muscle torn instead of strained. Then healing was required.

Tynan's hand lowered. "He is handling it well. I believe he disconnected quickly enough to avoid the worst of it."

"See?" Iren said, crossing his arms. "I'm fine."

Relief slackened the muscles in Aris's shoulders. "I had to know."

"So are you going to tell me about the extra healing thing?" Iren asked.

Aris sighed. Clearly, his son was not one to give up. "Lial intends to reset and properly heal a couple of my bones. I'll be unconscious with the pain blocked and Tynan monitoring my mind, but they are concerned my magic will react again. Your mother had to filter the last leakage into energy crystals. But I wasn't able to be unconscious then."

Tynan's jaw tightened. "I do not want to make another error."

"And I want to get it over with," Aris snapped. "We don't know what they will find on Earth. Kezari and I may be needed at any time."

"I'll help," Iren said.

"No," Aris and Tynan said simultaneously.

Iren's eyes narrowed, and he sat up straighter in his chair as his arms dropped to his sides. "I'm not four anymore, *Onaial*. I can do this."

Aris studied his son's face. Yes, he wasn't four, but eleven was far from manhood. That said, energy transference was one of the earliest skills taught since the ability to manipulate energy was vital to all other skills. But could Iren handle raw life magic? Selia could only transfer it, but his son might have inherited—

"I can feel it," Iren blurted. "I couldn't sense much when I was younger, but over the last couple of years, I've started connecting to living things. *Onaiala* is worried about finding someone to teach me about it, but it hasn't caused any problems yet."

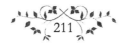

Aris's heart thumped with alarm. "Please tell me you haven't tried to use that energy."

"No," Iren answered. But he ducked his head, avoiding Aris's gaze.

"What did you do, Iren?"

His son squirmed in his seat. "There was this flower. I...tried to make it grow faster."

Worry curled through Aris. He'd tried something similar as a child, hoping to encourage the growth of a tree his mother had planted. Within days, the poor sapling had been dead, and he'd felt the loss he'd caused so deeply that he hadn't touched life magic for a solid year. His mother had found a teacher for him after that.

"Creation and destruction stand a hairsbreadth apart," Aris said softly. "A flower may be just a beautiful plant to most, but it is different for us. And that's the risk of our talent. You can let yourself merge so deeply with the life around you that it's difficult to function. You can't even walk without feeling the pain of the grass crushed beneath your feet, and no death is easy at that level. I hope you learned that lesson well."

Iren nodded, sadness beyond his years filling his eyes. "I haven't touched it since."

"I will teach you," Aris said.

Hope lightened Iren's expression, twisting into Aris's gut. Suddenly, he couldn't sit still under his son's regard. He leaped to his feet and pushed past Tynan to stare out the window. Why had he promised such a thing without stopping to consider the ramifications? The healer's work on his mind had been impressive, but there was no guarantee it would be permanent. Aris had barely been awake for half a mark, and he was making promises to his son that would take centuries to fulfill.

But few were skilled in life magic, which went beyond earth-healing and into the heartbeat of nature itself. Aris could force plants to grow or die. He could find the unique energy signature of any living creature, and if he were so inclined, he could alter the physiology of smaller animals. But the hardest to deal with was the power to kill. With enough power, he could kill even one of his own kind.

He'd extinguished more than one spark of life, a weight he would forever carry.

"I do hope you won't choose to focus on it to the exlusion of your other talents," Aris said as he stared at a group of people setting up a small table in the garden below. "Life magic can be heady. All-consuming if you let it be. I spent centuries traveling the wild places to appease it. My path is not one you should take."

Iren's footsteps sounded against the stone. "Why not? I mean, except for the last few years."

"It is a difficult thing to handle, Iren."

Like the time he'd had to kill one of the few *merk* they'd managed to find during their research trip. The great beast had stood three times his height, and it had pinned Ter against a tree with claws longer than his forearm. None of which had eased the pain of draining its life with his own mind.

"Maybe," Iren said. "But right now, I want to help you while you're being healed."

Aris turned to face his son. "No."

"This is important to me." Iren's hands curled into fists, but his downturned lips trembled as he glared. "You don't trust me."

Tynan stepped forward, one hand lifted. "Be calm, young Iren. Your father is correct."

Aris shot the healer an annoyed glance. "I am, but it has nothing to do with trust. If you have my abilities, then too much exposure to

my power could trigger yours. Awaken them further before you are ready. It's too risky."

"I thought you said you wouldn't lose control while unconscious," Iren said, lifting a brow.

Aris smiled. "Then I won't need help."

Lial's voice echoed across the room. "No, he won't. I am more than capable of cutting off pain receptors, and if Tynan monitors his mental pathways, there will be no risk. I respect your desire to help, Iren, but your aid is unnecessary."

"Yeah, sure." If Iren had been a few years younger, he no doubt would have stomped his foot the way he had as a toddler. Instead, he crossed his arms and scowled. "I'll just get out of your way."

"Iren—"

"Forget it," his son said sharply before darting toward the stairs.

Aris moved to follow, but Lial halted him with a hand to his chest. "Let him go. He's a good lad, and he'll see the sense in our words once he calms down. He only needs a bit of time."

For once, the anxiety in Aris's stomach had nothing to do with his torture. Would alone time help Iren think through the problem, or would dwelling on it make his anger worse? Aris raked his fingers against his scalp. He would have to trust the healer's assessment, for Lial likely knew Iren better than he did. That a stranger might have more understanding of his son...well, it was galling.

"You have plenty of time to rebuild your relationship," Tynan said, perhaps guessing Aris's thoughts from his expression.

"A fine start I just made."

"Parents must deny as much as indulge, as well you know." Lial pointed toward the bed. "Now go lie down. As the senior healer, I've decided to go ahead with the procedure, and I would like to get it over with."

214

Aris choked back the arguments running through his mind. They could debate parenting styles for the rest of the afternoon, but it wouldn't fix his poorly healed bones. "Fine. Then once you're finished, I'm going to find Iren."

The healer was probably right—Iren needed space. He'd certainly required time away from his own parents at that age, especially after an argument. But as Aris stretched out on the bed, he couldn't shake the feeling that he'd made a terrible mistake.

The cave's entrance was smaller than Selia had expected. Her friends had confronted Kien here, of all places? From the moment their unwitting driver had deposited them at a small roadside area and driven away, she'd been struck by the absolute peace surrounding them. Through the darkness, they'd climbed the side of the small mountain to the sounds of droning insects and chattering wildlife. Selia had scanned for turbulent energy, but she'd sensed nothing but the occasional gentle ripple. In the light of the mage globe hovering overhead, the narrow cave opening appeared almost welcoming.

But beside Selia, Inona stood as still as a stalagmite, except for her hands rubbing anxiously across her upper arms. Meli eased closer and gave the scout's shoulder a squeeze. "Do you want to stay outside?"

Inona's fingers slid to her throat before her hand dropped to her side. "Of course I want to. But I won't."

Delbin nodded, a slight smile on his lips. "Good for you, love. If anyone can conquer this, it's you."

"Thank you," she whispered.

Inona lifted her head high and marched toward the opening. Although Kai outranked her, he shifted aside and let her take the lead. He fell to the back of their group as Delbin and then Meli followed Inona. Selia gathered as much energy as she could, sending the mage light ahead as she took her place behind Meli. Blast it all, but it was tough to pull in power here. Like running honey through a finely knit sieve, possible but slow.

They wound their way through a thin tunnel that opened abruptly on a broad cavern. Fragments of stalactites lay scattered across the uneven stone floor, and a few scorch marks and one dark stain shadowed the rock in the center. The hairs on Selia's arms lifted at the remnants of the malevolent energy lingering in the space. So much for peaceful.

Inona's steps hitched and then ground to a stop. Delbin lifted his arm slightly, gesturing for the rest of them to wait, as his love stared at the dark blotch on the floor. Though her chest heaved, Inona stumbled forward until she reached the spot. Then she knelt down and brushed her fingers against the stain. Power trembled on the air, and the mark disappeared.

The scout's blood would remain here no longer.

After a few moments, Inona stood and cast an inscrutable look over her shoulder. "I don't sense any sort of rift here."

"Nor do I," Selia said after a quick scan. "Your friends were certain it's the same cave?"

Delbin's shoulder lifted. "Seemed to be sure."

"It is here."

At the harsh sound of Kai's voice, Selia turned to stare. His expression had gone slack, but his eyes burned with an emotion she couldn't quite name. Not anger, pain, or fear but some unpleasant mixture of all three. Then he shook his head and scrubbed his hands

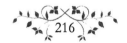

across his face. When he met her gaze, he looked like himself once more.

"Sorry." Kai's lips twisted wryly. "No matter how much Naomh tried to teach me, I never could connect to the Earth. I feel the trauma in this dimension's energy itself, but I can't get a hold on it. The schism is near. But I don't know where."

Meli lifted a small pouch from her pocket and gave it a slight shake. "That's what my runes and I are here for, remember?"

Selia glanced around the cavern. There were a few shadowed places against one wall, and the rows of stalagmites could conceal more passageways. Any number of chambers could branch off from this room. Without Meli's aid, it would take forever to find the way. Including her had been an excellent idea.

Smiling, Selia nodded at the younger woman. "We're ready when you are."

Something tickled Perim's nose as she forced her eyes open. Tall green stems fluttered in front of her face, one of them brushing her nostrils until she almost sneezed. She batted the grass away and pushed herself upright. Where was she? The last thing she clearly recalled was plunging from the water into a world of gray. She'd stumbled through endless mist, reaching for to the strands Baza had directed her to find.

How had she ended up here? She rested on an incline in the middle of a forest, but the trees were smaller than the ones she'd seen on the island. She pinched one of the blades of grass. It caught roughly against her fingers, so unlike the smooth glide of the grass at home. She'd explored most of the island, and this area was nothing like that horrible place.

Perim reached out a mental hand to replenish her energy, but instead of a deep pool of power, she found a nearly dry well. She pulled harder at the tiny trickle of energy and groaned in frustration at the lack of response. But as her mind cleared, realization set in. She might have reached Earth.

Well, she wouldn't find out if she was correct by sitting here. Perim stood and took a tentative step through the trees. If she'd reached her destination, then Aris had to be near—or would be soon. Baza had claimed that Kezari and thus Aris would be searching for a source of poisoned energy, so that was what she would look for.

She had a soulbonded to kill.

19

Selia studied Meli as she stood in the center of the cavern with her eyes closed, her cupped hands aglow with the light from her runes. When Selia looked with her other senses, she could see energy flowing up through Meli's feet and into the stones, using very little of her own magic.

Among the Ljósálfar in Alfheim, Meli had been an outcast because she had little natural capacity for energy and could not perform many spells. Foolish mages. Meli might not be able to hold a great deal of power, but she was a diviner, able to channel energy through objects like the runes. Not that the younger woman knew the extent of her ability. If Prince Corath constructed a sword with the proper enchantments, Meli could be deadly. Or with the right kind of staff… Selia had been doing a bit of research on the topic but hadn't had a chance to bring it up yet. Perhaps soon Meli would be comfortable enough around mages to consider becoming a student.

The light in Meli's hands faded to almost nothing, pulling Selia from her thoughts. Meli slipped the runes back into their pouch and tucked the pouch into her pocket. Her eyes opened, and although her gaze was distant, she was able to focus on the group waiting expectantly.

"We need to slip between a pair of stalagmites in the back left corner," Meli said softly. "But the way won't be easy. Some of the tunnels we must follow require climbing."

"You can still see the path?" Delbin asked.

Meli's lips curved upward as she nodded. "I've been practicing. Much better than wandering around like a sleep-walker, wouldn't you say?"

Behind Selia's shoulder, Kai chuckled. "Much better."

"Let's go," Meli said, waving toward the back of the cavern.

Selia hitched her bag more securely on her shoulder and followed Delbin, Inona, and Meli into a narrow passage tucked between two stalagmites, just as the other woman had seen. The path was clear for a time, but after they reached another, smaller cavern, they had to huddle close to avoid the cave formations. As far as Selia could tell, the trail ended here.

Meli pointed to a narrow shelf of rock barely visible behind a grouping of stalactites clustered on the ceiling. "We need to climb up the side of that lumpy column and behind the stalactites. A short distance along that shelf, we'll find another tunnel. We have to crawl through that before we get to another room."

Though Selia grimaced, she didn't complain. Not even when she scraped her forearm on a sharp stone as she wiggled along the narrow stone shelf. Instead, she used a precious tendril of energy to seal the wound and kept going. The sooner they reached the rift, the better.

Why did it have to be in a cave? Hopefully, they'd be able to take care of the problem today because this would be pure misery for Aris. Great gods, what if he had a meltdown in the middle of the return mission? Mind-healing was typically accompanied by weeks of therapeutic treatment, and even then, it wasn't perfect. Much could be done to return muscle and bone to their original state, but minds were too malleable.

The coming mission was at risk of failure from the beginning.

As they gathered in the next, even smaller, cavern, Meli pointed out a thin gap angled in the floor. Down. They had to slither down the passage one at a time. Selia muttered a curse as she watched Delbin try to fit into the gap, grumbling a few choice words of his own as he squeezed through. What were they going to do when it was Aris who had to try that?

Once it was her turn, Selia fought back a shiver and squared her shoulders before lowering herself in. As she eased down, balancing on one foot while searching for a hold with the other, the tunnel walls seemed to close around her. It was difficult to breathe, and she didn't even have trouble with enclosed spaces.

When she finally dropped onto the floor of the next chamber, she shifted out of the way for Kai and bent down to catch her breath. Then she straightened to study the area while they waited. The long, uneven tunnel curved like one of the corridors in Lyr's home, but the rock itself had a smoothness that suggested the cave had been formed by water, not trees. Their small mage light glinted against the tiny drips of moisture forming along one side of the ceiling in a thin line.

Kai landed beside Selia with a soft oomph. "We're close," he said. "Something is building. Both the energy and this sense of… wrongness. But I still can't pinpoint the exact location."

"It's just past the curve up ahead," Meli said absently.

Delbin tossed a glance over his shoulder. "You think Kien climbed all the way through these passages to set this up?"

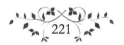

"Maybe," Selia said, trying to examine the energy flowing around them. "I get a hint of the darkness I felt up above, but not enough to know for sure."

Inona and Meli rounded the corner first, and at a sharp exclamation from the latter, Delbin sped up, Selia and Kai quickly following. At first, Selia thought Meli had cried out because of the jagged line of energy suspended in the center of the large circular cavern like red lightning frozen mid-strike. But then the figure leaning against a column of rock straightened to his full height, the arrogant tilt of his head tumbling his flaming hair across his forehead.

Selia blinked, so taken aback she couldn't even summon alarm.

Pol?

He'd been one of the people who'd traveled with Meli from Alfheim, but he'd returned there weeks ago. What was he doing here, smiling for all the world like they'd met in the gardens for tea?

"And to think you almost rejected those runes," Pol drawled.

As Inona slipped a knife from…somewhere, Selia wrapped her hand around an energy crystal in her pocket. Pol grinned, his thumbs tucked casually into a couple of loops on his Earth-style pants. Despite the appearance of the knife, his casual demeanor hadn't changed.

"Lo…I mean…" Meli lifted both hands in the air and then let them drop. "What are you doing here?"

"You know him?" Inona demanded.

Kai stepped up beside Selia. "Wait, Inona. Pol is a friend to House Dianore, or so I was told."

Pol inclined his head. "As it pleases us."

Selia had a feeling that she didn't want to know who he included in the "us."

"You left so abruptly," Meli said, "and haven't spoken to me since. Are you here to cause trouble, or do I still have your support?"

"Don't hold my absence against me, little diviner." Pol smirked. "I had a bit of a dalliance. A brandy so fine should be savored, so forgive me for not rushing back."

Meli's forehead wrinkled. "That still doesn't explain why you're *here*."

"True." Pol's face tipped up, and the crack of energy tinted his pale skin an eerie red. "You know, I'd hoped this would happen. But nothing is guaranteed."

Eyes narrowing, Meli took a step forward. "Did you make sure I reached Moranaia for this very purpose? I've spent a lot of time wondering why you helped someone so unimportant as me. At least, unimportant in the grand scheme of things."

Pol chuckled softly. "All of life is a grand scheme. However, I must remind you that I only help people I like. Voluntarily, at least."

Without warning, energy throbbed through the cavern, hitting Selia's shields so hard she stumbled. She grabbed for a stalagmite to steady herself as she reinforced her protections with help from the crystal in her hand. Meli wavered on her feet, only Pol's hand keeping her upright. Delbin tripped and fell against the side of the cave, and Kai dropped to his knees, his palms shoved against his temples. Only Inona kept her footing completely.

As quickly as it had hit, the wave of power was gone.

"Fuck," Kai muttered.

A few paces away, Inona glared at Pol. "What did you do?"

"Inona…" Meli began.

"That was no coincidence," Inona said as Delbin limped back to her side, rubbing his hip. "It was an attack."

Selia's brows rose at the hint of panic creeping into Meli's eyes. The younger woman tried to shake her head at Inona, but the scout ignored the signal. "Step away from Meli, stranger, or I will—"

Laughter rang out, and although Pol released Meli, it was only to brace his hands on his knees while he gave in to his mirth. Little sparks drifted from his hair as he chuckled, but he didn't seem to notice. And when he finally grew quiet and straightened, his lips still twitched with repressed humor.

Inona, on the other hand, tightened her grip on her knife until her knuckles whitened—the only part of her not flushed red with anger. "You should not mock me."

"Come now," Pol said. "I like you too much to exclude you."

The scout opened her mouth, but no sound emerged. Meli stepped between the two, offering Pol a smile. "She doesn't know you, of course."

"No one does." He waved his hand dismissively. "I'll spare your friend and get to the point. If you try to tap into this rift right now, you will die. All of you."

Fear slammed into Selia more effectively than the energy pulse. She'd considered doing that very thing when they'd discussed this mission, and even now, that jagged line of power beckoned. If he was telling the truth, she might have killed them all attempting to access it. But why? She hadn't intended to do anything that would widen the crack in the spell holding the rest of Earth's energy back. A probe should have been simple enough.

Kai stood, swaying slightly as he frowned at Pol. "My...father seemed certain he could connect to the fissure. I should be able to, as well."

Pol snorted. "You are not Naomh, and he's a fool if he treats you as though you are. But then, his father wasn't very bright, or he would have realized that Caolte's mother was...more than she seemed." He gestured at the walls around them. "Do you feel the energy of this place the way he believes you should? No."

Kai's eyes narrowed. "You know a great deal about my Sidhe father for one of the Ljósálfar."

"One of the Ljósálfar? Perhaps foolishness *does* run in your bloodline." Pol shook his head, a mocking tilt to his lips. "Listen, for I will say this only once. Kai will guard the strands binding Earth to the other planes, Aris and Kezari will heal the poison, and Selia will stand as guard."

Selia froze, her blood chilling at the man's words. If he was a man. For he had been long gone before Aris and Kezari had arrived, and as far as she knew, he had no reason to be aware of their names. Pol could be a seer, Selia supposed, but it didn't seem likely. The way Meli had reacted to him told a tale all its own.

"What do you mean by that?" Kai demanded.

"Just what I said." Pol glanced at each of them in turn, and when his eyes met hers, Selia froze like a *daeri* in Kezari's sight. "Bring him here tomorrow," he said, and there was no mistaking that he was talking to her.

Between one heartbeat and another, he was gone. No blur of movement or puff of smoke. If the others didn't appear as stunned as she felt, Selia would have believed his presence a dream. Whoever he was, Pol was no Ljósálfar. He was no elf at all as far as she could tell.

"Oh, this can't be good," Meli whispered. "Not if Loki is involved."

Selia's brow creased. That name sounded familiar, but she couldn't quite place it. Did anyone else besides Meli know him? Inona appeared as puzzled as Selia, Delbin's expression shifted between amused and concerned, but Kai... Kai's entire demeanor had turned stony. Was it because of the stranger's identity or the words he had said? She wasn't certain she knew him well enough to ask.

"Who is this Loki?" Inona said.

Delbin laughed, though a hint of worry lingered around his eyes. "He's the Norse trickster god."

"That's one way to put it." Meli's lips thinned, but Selia couldn't tell if it was with concern or annoyance. "In any case, where he goes, change happens. Whether it's good or bad is anyone's guess."

Wonderful. Selia stared at the rift in the center of the chamber and tried not to think too hard about what would have happened without Pol's—Loki's—warning of danger. Ignoring a random elf was one thing, but a god? No.

Now she just had to figure out how to get Aris down here without driving him insane.

Double wonderful.

Iren grabbed another pebble and ran his fingers along the smooth surface. He wanted to fling it at the nearest tree, but he couldn't bring himself to risk harming it. So instead, he skipped the stone along the stream as he had the others and watched as it sank after two hops. Not bad over moving water.

He'd wanted his father to come home for as long as he could remember, but now that he had him, nothing was going right. Iren didn't care about the torture. Well, fine, he cared, obviously. But it didn't change his opinion of his father. As much as Iren had suffered from the loss, now he knew it was nothing compared to what *Onaial* had gone through. That brought a terrible kind of comfort.

When Iren had first seen his father standing in front of the entrance to Braelyn, his heart and his hopes had soared. His mother loved him, as he did her, but she babied him. His father the

adventurer wouldn't do that. *Onaial* would see how big he'd become and encourage him to push beyond the rules. Maybe he would even find Iren worthy of training.

Iren snorted. Apparently not.

"I thought your father would pick this future strand."

At the sound of his friend's voice, Iren spun. Eri smiled at him from the garden path, tendrils of her dark hair peeking from beneath her cloak. "That bad?" he asked.

"No." Her nose wrinkled. "Really, Iren, what were you thinking? If his life energy triggered yours, it could make you lose control of your other powers. Unlike you, he doesn't have the talents of the traditional mage, too. Did you want to blow up the estate?"

Heat climbed Iren's neck. "I…no."

Her smile turned impish. "Oh, don't get upset. There are other ways you can prove yourself."

His heart pounded harder at that. If Eri suggested an alternate method, she always had a good reason. Sometimes, it was great having a seer as a friend. Well, all the time, as far as he could tell. "Like what?"

"Come on." She darted forward and grabbed his wrist in her small hand. "My parents are at the construction site today, so we can talk in my room."

Curious, he let her pull him along. This was going to be good.

20

Aris was really, really tired of waking up dazed after some procedure—or after being rendered unconscious during a fit of madness. But this time, he felt…different. He extended one arm and then the other. No sign of strain. He flexed his legs and rolled his ankles before drawing his knees up.

His breath eased out, and his body sagged into the mattress. No pain. None.

"Feeling better?"

At the sound of Lial's voice, Aris opened his eyes. The healer leaned over him with a somber expression, but he sounded calm. "Much," Aris said. "All went well?"

"It took a fair bit of time to accelerate the healing, but your bones are knit properly and should stand up well to activity." Lial shoved a damp tendril of hair aside, and it was then that Aris noticed the sheen of sweat on his brow and the lines of exhaustion bracketing his eyes. "Though if I can avoid having to break someone's body on purpose for a few centuries, I'll be well pleased."

Aris winced. "Sorry."

Lips twisting wryly, Lial straightened. "Try not to get captured and tortured again and we'll call it even."

Aris surprised himself by chuckling. He pushed upright and stretched again as the healer stepped back. When had his muscles last felt so good? For a moment, he let himself savor the feeling of wholeness. If the Myern held a running competition during the coming autumn festival, Aris could likely win it.

Then his gaze landed on Tynan on the far side of the room, almost hidden in the shadows cast by the setting sun. His body was turned away from Kezari, who sat cross-legged on the floor a few arm-lengths away. *I hope they haven't been arguing.* Kezari stared at Aris, not seeming to notice the mind-healer, but her shoulders angled a bit toward Tynan.

Aris lifted his brows. "Did I lose control of my magic? You two look somber."

"We…almost had an incident," Lial said, his nostrils flaring at the words. "But Kezari and Tynan kept it under control. I still do not understand why that segment of your brain was activated with all sensation cut off, but I am glad I followed my instinct to have a mind-healer present for the procedure."

"It is good that your spawn was not present," Kezari said. She jerked her head toward Tynan. "This one was complication enough."

The mind-healer bristled. "I did not make an error this time."

"You are a distraction," she grumbled.

Aris smiled—until their words sank in. Iren. Would his son still be upset by their earlier disagreement? He tugged his hands through his tangled hair until it was something resembling smooth. Then he leaped from the bed. Lial's lips turned down, but Aris lifted a hand before he could say anything.

"I want to check on my son." Aris shifted on the balls of his feet and sighed in satisfaction when his muscles flexed smoothly. "I don't suppose you could give me directions through the twisted maze of this place?"

Lial's eyes narrowed in thought for a moment. Then he nodded. "I sense him with Eri in her family's rooms. I'll walk with you to the base of their tower if you like."

Aris nodded. "Please."

Although the healer wasn't unfriendly, he spoke little as they descended the stairs and traversed the winding garden paths. That was fine with Aris. It was awkward enough that a virtual stranger knew the worst details of his life—inane small talk would only make it worse. A cold, damp gust of wind flowed around them, and Aris shivered, suddenly regretting not grabbing his cloak. Luckily, Lial stopped at the base of a stone tower before he could grow too chilled.

"Ralan's rooms are at the top of the stairs," the healer said.

"Thank you," Aris said, holding Lial's gaze. "For everything, I mean. Not just the escort. If you ever have need of my aid, I offer it freely. I might not be able to heal, but life energy is a powerful force."

The healer's eyebrows rose, a sign that he hadn't expected such an offer. "Let us hope I never encounter anything that requires such strength."

"Indeed," Aris said with a smile.

Then Aris turned away and strode into the tower.

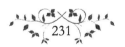

A scream ripped from Fen's throat as he jerked upright. He clawed at his heaving chest, but no physical wound marred his flesh. The pain was inside, splintering beneath his heart. Frantic, he dug his fingernails into his skin in a futile attempt at distraction.

But nothing eased the agony.

When the wave of pain finally passed, he came to slow awareness. His forehead was pressed to his upturned knees. When had he curled up? Something wet trickled down his leg and slid beneath his fingers. His face and chest felt damp, too, as though someone had dumped a bucket of water over him while he slept. The tinny but sweet smell of blood wafted around him.

What the hell?

Every muscle in his body protested when he unclenched his hands enough to straighten. He groaned as pain shot up his shoulders and down his legs, but it had to be done. The longer he stayed curled up, the stiffer he would become.

Fen rubbed at his eyes and then glanced down at his chest, only to freeze in horror. Partially dried blood coated his skin in rivulets from where his nails had dug in, the furrows barely closed. After a quick examination, he found similar marks on his legs.

The price he paid for ingesting Kien's blood, it seemed. The bastard must have sent the rending spell through his own blood link to Earth, and since Fen bore a bit of that blood within him, he'd been linked to the process. Nothing else made sense. But what had caused such unexpected pain? He'd borne the pulses of energy for over a week with only mild discomfort.

The door clicked open, and Vek strode in, only to halt as soon as he caught sight of Fen. "I hope you killed whoever did that to you."

"I'm not suicidal, so no." Fen gave a self-conscious shrug. "You took your sweet time coming in here. Pretty sure I made a lot of noise."

Vek's expression shuttered. "I was out."

Ugh. He could just imagine what his uncle had been doing—finding blood. Fen's stomach rumbled in envy, even though blood did nothing for his physical hunger. His energy was getting low enough that he was tempted to lick his own leg in search of sustenance. It wouldn't provide him any extra magic, but...

"Your fangs are out," Vek said.

"I'm fucking starving." Fen shoved himself to his feet, ignoring the agony movement brought, and rushed past his uncle into the hall. If he didn't shower soon, the smell would drive him crazy. "I've had enough. I'm going to go feed. Then I'm going to find Maddy and see if she can do something about this poison."

Vek grabbed Fen's upper arm, pulling him around. "Aren't you forgetting something? You're bound here, and feeding will only make the poison worse."

"Says who?" Fen jerked free of his uncle's grip. "I'm covered in my own goddamned blood from marks I made in mindless agony. Obviously, hunger didn't prevent that, did it? So fuck off with your patronizing shit. If it takes the last of my energy, I'm busting out of here. I'm not going to die screaming in bed."

Vek's lips pinched tight, and for a moment, Fen thought he would argue. But his uncle surprised him by nodding. "Fine. There was an energy pulse not long ago. If they're starting to hurt you, then...then I am not certain what we can do. My shield is apparently not enough. We need to go to the cave."

Fen stared at his uncle's pained expression. Vek actually appeared concerned, and that was almost worse to Fen than waking up in his own blood. His uncle typically alternated between cold arrogance, cool disdain, and exasperated annoyance. He must be consumed with worry for it to show.

"Let me shower," Fen said softly. "Then we'll head out."

Vek nodded and turned toward the living room without another word.

His uncle's easy capitulation drove Fen's fear deeper. He rubbed his hand across his aching chest and hurried into the bathroom. The answer had to be out there.

Somewhere.

The little girl opened the door before Aris reached it. Unlike the cheer she'd displayed on their last meeting, her lips curved down like a bow, and a thin line of annoyance hollowed between her eyebrows. What was her name again? Eri?

"Yes, I am Eri," she said, making a shiver trace through him. "And I am mad at you. There were eleven better strands you could have taken, you know. Now everything is going to be harder."

How…how old was she? Aris studied her young face, far too small to bear such words. She crossed her arms, staring back boldly, and even if Selia hadn't told him, he would have guessed she was a princess of Moranaia. It wasn't just her unusual golden eyes and dark black hair, traits shared by Prince Ralan and his siblings. It was the authority she carried at such a young age.

Gods help her parents.

"Perhaps I will do better next time," he said.

She grinned, a child once more. "There's a good chance of it. Come on. Iren is pouting in my room."

Aris followed her through a living area, tidy save a couple of abandoned dolls. He eyed those doubtfully. Did the prince have another child? Because Aris found it difficult to believe that a

powerful seer like Eri played with something so mundane, even at her age. Though maybe she used them to practice delivering prophecies to hapless adults.

When she pushed open the door to her bedroom, Aris's gaze went immediately to Iren. His son glared out the window into the fading light. "Guess you didn't destroy anything without me there to help," Iren said.

Eri tugged at Aris's wrist to get his attention. "I'll wait in the front room."

"Thank you, Eri."

Aris waited until the door closed behind him to approach his son. Without a word, he lowered himself into the seat next to Iren. Then he waited. They sat that way for several drips of time, both of them staring into the dusk-coated branches beyond the window.

"I'm not a baby," Iren finally said.

"No, you aren't," Aris agreed. Gods, how he'd hated being this age himself. That feeling of growing confidence twined with a lack of control over one's environment. He wouldn't repeat those years even if he could. "But you aren't an adult, either."

"I know," his son mumbled.

Aris kept his gaze on the gnarled curves of the nearest branch, unwilling to break the moment. "Iren, I loved you at your birth, and I love you now. Even if centuries passed before our next meeting, that love would hold. I am aware that you may not believe me, but it is true. And I will not risk your life for mine. Not under any circumstances. My refusal of your aid was for your sake and nothing more."

Silence descended, drawing out until he worried that he'd said the wrong thing. At the scrape of chair on stone, Aris finally dared

look at Iren, and his heart burned at the sight of the tears on his son's cheeks. He had said the wrong thing. *Miaran.* He opened his mouth to apologize, but an *oomph* slipped out instead as Iren threw his arms around his neck and squeezed.

Aris pulled his son as close as he could with the arm of the chair between them. Though tears dampened the top of his shoulder where Iren's head rested, Aris let out a small, relieved breath and hugged his son tight. And unlike before, only a hint of discomfort itched beneath his skin at the close contact. Far more than that was the joy.

"I only wanted to make you proud," Iren said.

When Iren pulled back, Aris rested his hands on his son's shoulders. "You need not do anything special for that."

Iren rolled his eyes—but some of the tension eased from his muscles. "Parents always say that kind of thing."

"They do not." Aris lifted an eyebrow. "Can you imagine your grandfather doing so?"

Iren's nose wrinkled. "Good point."

A knock sounded on the door, and after a brief pause, Eri ducked her head through the opening. A sunny smile lit her face. "You might want to get your dragon and head to Lyr's study, Lord Aris," she said. "Lady Selia will be back soon, and that's where you'll meet. I want to play tag with Iren."

"I'm too old for tag," his son grumbled.

Eri only laughed. "Not what you said yesterday."

Iren shrugged and cast his Aris an apologetic smile. "May I go play?"

"Sure."

Aris had barely given permission before the children darted out of the room, the earlier tension gone as though it had never

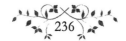

been. For a moment, he almost wished he could join them, but he'd rather go find out what Selia had discovered. Despite having a strong feeling it wouldn't be good.

21

B y the time their group stumbled through the portal, Selia was
ready to curl up in bed for a solid week. But although five
days of blissful rest might be enough to ease her aching muscles, it
wouldn't touch the turmoil of her thoughts. Stand guard, the god
named Loki had said. What did that mean? She knew little about the
dangers of Earth, and he'd claimed that tapping into the rift would
bring death.

This was a magical dilemma she might not be able to solve—and
that galled.

Dawn had been breaking on Earth, but night had fallen again
here. Traveling through the Veil helped the body shift between time
streams somewhat. Still, they'd switched from light to dark so many
times that her mind couldn't keep up. Sleepy, she trudged along with
the others down the path to the estate. At least the guards had kept
the cloaks dry by the portal, for it was cold here in comparison to
Earth's late summer.

"I am more tired than I ought to be," Kai confessed as they
rounded the front of the building. With so much festival preparation

happening in the garden, the private entrance to Lyr's study had seemed more prudent. "Especially with Inona taking part of the burden of navigating the Veil."

The female scout stifled a yawn against her hand. "Both crossings were rough."

"Probably because of the rift," Selia said, covering her own yawn.

A snort from Delbin caught her attention, but he grinned at them despite the frustrated sound. "The long hike and the caving didn't help. Some of us aren't trained scouts accustomed to hours of physical exertion."

"Please," Inona said. "I saw the type of labor you did at that carnival."

"That doesn't mean—"

Kai lifted a hand to silence Delbin as they reached the outer door to the study. "We can determine who is more drained later. I'd like to give this report and go get some sleep."

"Agreed," Meli whispered from Selia's right side.

The younger woman had gone quiet after leading them back to the main entrance of the cave. But as they entered the study, her expression brightened. Lyr straightened from his perch on the edge of his desk and rushed across the room to meet her, wrapping Meli in his arms despite the audience. Selia averted her gaze, only to connect with Aris's eyes.

Concern shadowed his face, but there was also something closed about his expression. Some aloofness they might never bridge. Exhaustion swamped Selia, weighting her muscles, as everything seemed to crash in at once. From the strangeness of Earth and the effort of doing magic there to the distance between her and Aris… it was all too much.

An abyss she wasn't certain she had the strength to cross.

"Your mate appears tired," Kezari said from her place by the window.

Aris's brows drew down. "Did something happen?"

"We weren't attacked, if that's what you're asking," Selia hedged. How could she admit her uncertainty to him when he'd faced so much already? "I'm fine."

His frown deepening, he strode over, and the rest of the room faded from awareness. Then he brushed his thumb gently across the curve of her cheekbone. "You've never made it a habit to tell me an untruth."

Selia squirmed beneath his touch, and not just because of the heat that flowed through her from the contact. "I wasn't lying. I *am* fine, and we *weren't* attacked. I'm simply tired. I transported the group from the cave back to the portal on Earth, and even with the use of two energy crystals, I'm drained."

"I know you, Selia," Aris said, his eyes narrowing. But it was true—he did know her. Well enough not to press her for more in front of others. "Perhaps you will join me in the tower once this meeting is complete?"

She swallowed an instinctive denial. She'd been bare before him in more ways than one, and she wasn't going to start hiding from him now. No matter how much she wanted to. "Certainly."

Aris stepped back, and the rest of the room returned to focus. Thankfully, the others had made an effort to ignore the exchange. Lyr and Meli leaned against the edge of his desk as she spoke to him, her hands fluttering with her excitement as she recounted her part in the mission. Kai slumped in one of the center chairs, his head tipped back and eyes closed. And Delbin and Inona stood beside Kezari. Inona's voice was too low to hear their discussion, but the dragon listened attentively.

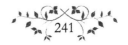

"This energy rift…" Selia began. "Perhaps I should warn you before the main discussion."

His frown returned. "Warn me about what?"

"It's deep in a cave," she blurted.

The color drained from his face, and his mouth pinched white. He gave a sharp nod, his throat bobbing as he swallowed. But although he didn't speak, panic didn't appear to consume him. He breathed in and out, the air hissing softly through his teeth, but he remained lucid. The mind-healer's work had kept him from a breakdown at least.

"Thanks," Aris whispered.

Lyr stood before she could answer, his discussion with Meli complete. "Well," he said. "I admit I didn't expect a god's involvement, but I suppose I should have. Why not at this point?"

Selia's lips twitched at that. With one crisis after another occurring lately, the Myern had clearly lost patience. "I wish he'd given more specific instructions." Selia grimaced. "What am I supposed to guard?"

"Makes as much sense as my advice," Kai muttered, not bothering to open his eyes. "He seemed to know more about my lineage than I do. Not that it helped. He implied that I can't touch earth energy the way my father can. But protecting the strands connecting dimensions? It didn't make sense."

Kezari took a few steps closer, her head tilted in curiosity. "Why would you try to touch the flow of earth? It is not your calling."

Kai jerked upright, peering at Kezari through narrowed eyes. "How would you know that?"

"My soul sings with soil and stone and my *skizik*'s with plant and animal." The dragon let out a soft huff. "I can identify one of my own kind. You do not share this link."

"Then what does my father sense in me?" Kai's fingers tightened on the arms of the chair. "He is a Sidhe lord and master of earth magic. He claims to detect the same talent in me, but..." His shoulders slumped. "What little training I've done with him has not gone well. If you have insight, I would love to hear it."

The dragon studied him, unblinking, for so long that even Selia wanted to shift restlessly. "It is believed that there are other worlds out there with their own linked dimensions," Kezari said slowly. "But for us, Earth is central. Those strands link through the heart of our home planet. The Veil."

Kai frowned. "The Veil can't be in the center of the world. That is the realm of heat and flame."

"Not the physical center." Kezari's toothy grin took on a sly cast. "You elves may use the Veil, but you do not understand it. It's the core of all linked worlds, Earth at its center. And you, Kai, guide others through the mists without understanding your potential to manipulate them. Perhaps even the Sidhe have forgotten how to identify that flavor of earth talent."

Mouth agape, Kai leaned forward. "You're saying I can alter the strands themselves?"

"The order mages made an art of it at one time."

Selia's brow wrinkled. "I know of no Moranaian mages who refer to themselves—"

"Neor," Kai said, an odd tone to his voice. "The People of Order. They were almost decimated by the poisoned energy that swept through a couple of months ago. Not to mention by the Seelie army unhappy with them for seeking our aid. But I have no connection to them. In fact, that place creeps me out."

"I cannot answer the questions you do not speak." Kezari lowered herself to a chair, and Selia hid a grin at the dragon's posture.

She sat on the edge, her toes digging into the floor as though she was trying to gain purchase on a cliff. "Even if you spoke them."

Kai let out a strangled laugh. "Wonderful."

"Seems you need to consult with Lord Naomh," Lyr said. "Last I heard, the Neorans have not returned to their previous home."

"I wouldn't, either," Kai said.

He hadn't said much about the mission he'd completed a few weeks ago, but Arlyn had let slip a few details. When Kai had gone to rescue those suffering from the energy poisoning, he'd found a massacre. Neor was a colony of the Seelie Court, and someone there had decided to eliminate the ill instead of save them. It couldn't have been a pleasant discovery.

"There is no time for that." Kezari pinned Lyr with her gaze. "I am Moranaian now, and the rift on Earth has been checked. Aris is as healed as he will be without time. We must go."

Surprisingly, it was Meli who argued. "No. Pol…Loki…said to return tomorrow."

At her words, the dragon shot to her feet. "You said we could leave once they scouted the area."

A strangled noise from Aris caught Selia's attention. He stared at Meli, his breathing a little more shallow than it had been. He'd ignored her during the rest of their discussion, but he must have turned to her instinctively when she'd spoken. Oh, blast it all. Would his healing hold well enough at the sight of the Ljósálfar woman?

His fists clenched, and his pupils dilated.

Maybe not.

Aris could have looked away. Perhaps he should have. But thought made habit, and habit made thought. As Tynan had warned, he would need to create new pathways for his mind to follow. Healing hadn't erased the old ones, but they blocked them enough for him to bypass them. So although his mind almost verged down the trail of madness, he yanked himself back from the brink.

The woman might have pale hair and a similar build, but she was not Perim.

He forced himself to study her pale face, her expression frozen into lines of alarmed concern. His tormenter had never shown either of those emotions. And this woman's eyes were light blue, not green. Instead of an arrogant posture, the Myern's bonded stood with shoulders slightly hunched. Everything about her spoke of kindness and youthful vulnerability.

The woman leaned closer to Lyr. "Perhaps I should go," she whispered.

"Do not," Aris said, though it was rude in the extreme to interject. "Please forgive my impertinence in speaking so plainly when we have not been introduced, but I do not wish for you to go. I can do this."

A slight smile lightened her face. "No need to apologize to me. My people are not so formal about strangers. Well, my previous people."

"It is I who should beg forgiveness," Lyr said with a wince. "Good thing *Laiala* is not here to see my poor manners. I should have presented you to one another immediately, especially considering the importance of this meeting."

The Myern might joke about upsetting his mother, but they all knew the real reason he hadn't offered immediate introductions—Aris's sanity. He had a feeling that if she hadn't gone on this mission,

the lady would have stayed away entirely. Considering how he'd broken down at his first sight of her, he wouldn't have blamed her.

"It is no matter," Aris said politely. "These are unusual circumstances."

Lyr inclined his head. "Even so, I will remedy the lapse now."

Aris kept his gaze on the woman, processing her full name out of habit. Once Lyr finished, Aris gave a slight bow. "It is a pleasure to meet you, Myerna Ameliar."

Color flooded her cheeks. "Ah. Just Meli, please. I still don't understand why my full given name must be included."

"A custom long ago formed, I'm afraid." Aris smiled. Yes, Meli was nothing like Perim. How could he have thought otherwise? "May blessings grace your House this day, Meli."

"Yours as well," she answered.

His muscles unclenched, his relief intense enough to make him dizzy. Not only had he looked at Meli, but he had interacted with her. Although his heartbeat still pounded a bit faster in his chest, he wasn't at risk of breaking down. A grin broke across his face, crinkling his eyes, and the woman in question frowned in confusion at his sudden humor.

Aris couldn't help it—he laughed. "Sorry, Lady Meli. I never thought I would be so happy to make it through a simple introduction."

She smiled. "I understand."

"Good. You know one another," Kezari snapped as she stepped to Aris's side. "Now we go."

Aris spun to face the anxious dragon. The skin of her right forearm was almost all scale, and a hint of steam escaped her nostrils. He settled his hand on her shoulder and squeezed, providing her the

anchor she had so often given him. "Kai and Selia need rest if they are to return with us."

He swallowed as her golden gaze pinned him. "The Earth cries. Join magic fully and you will know."

"I don't have to, Kezari," Aris said. "I can see that it is urgent. But we cannot have half of our group too exhausted to complete their tasks."

Meli took a small step forward. "It was not yet dawn when we were advised to return tomorrow, and I don't think he meant Moranaian time. A little sleep but not a full night should satisfy that."

Kezari's growl rumbled through the room, but she nodded. "No more than six marks."

"Then it is settled," Lyr said. "Go get some sleep. Kezari, Aris, Selia, and Kai, all of you return in five marks to discuss your plan."

"Of course," Aris agreed before turning to leave.

He caught Selia's eye as he strode away from Lyr, forming a mental connection with her out of habit. *"You'll still meet me in the tower?"*

She twisted her fingers together. *"Briefly. After I make sure Iren goes to bed."*

Aris couldn't quite hide his smile. *"Perfect."*

22

Selia stood at the base of the tower stairs, her fingers clenching against the smooth crystal of the doorframe. Iren was settled, and she'd taken a moment to eat a bowl of stew before heading to Aris's tower. Fatigue enveloped her shoulders like her cloak, but that wasn't stopping her from the short climb up the stairs. There was only one thing it could be.

Cowardice.

Wincing at the thought, she forced her feet to move. It was time for her and Aris to settle the issues that remained between them. Now that he was more himself, perhaps he'd decided he no longer wanted to be with her. Maybe he worried that he'd changed too much or that she wouldn't be able to accept everything that had happened. Selia sniffed at that thought. He should know she wasn't as narrow-minded as that.

She spotted Aris as soon as she rounded the last curve of the stairs. Legs and arms crossed, he leaned one shoulder against the wall a few paces away, his gaze fixed on her as she advanced. She came to a halt just out of his reach. Her heart fluttered at his inscrutable expression, but she tried her best not to reveal her nerves.

"Why didn't you tell me what was wrong earlier?" he asked softly.

Selia let out a sigh. "It is foolishness."

One corner of his mouth tipped up. "You're not given to foolishness, Selia. I don't want you to stop confiding in me when you used to tell me everything."

If only he knew.

"You've suffered so much, but you are still so ready to proceed with what needs to be done no matter the cost," she blurted, crinkling the smooth fabric of her shirt between her fingers. "And there I stood, doubting I was equal to the task on Earth. I feel ridiculous admitting such a thing."

His head tilted. "Why? You have a right to your feelings."

How could he remain so impassive? Why couldn't he see? "You. Were. Tortured," Selia said. "I could have no challenge equal to that."

Aris smiled, and she suddenly wanted to hit him. A poor impulse, considering. He unfolded his arms and pushed away from the wall, moving closer. "We can each only live our own lives in our own bodies, Selia. My past pain won't ease your current doubts."

"I don't understand how you can be so calm," she grumbled.

"You think I'm calm?" Aris grasped one of her hands in his. "I'm not. I've grown…adept at hiding my feelings."

Grief filled her at what those words implied. He had learned to do so for self-preservation. "What are you feeling, then?"

Aris lifted her palm to his chest, and the rapid thumping of his heart met the frantic pace of her own pulse. His head tipped down until their breaths mingled. "Many things. Desire. Pain. Fear. Love."

"An unusual mixture," Selia whispered. "And a sad one. Are you afraid of me now?"

His lips thinned. "Not exactly."

"What is that supposed to mean?" she asked, her fingers twitching beneath his.

"I want to be with you, but there is much…" His eyes squeezed closed. "There is a lot you don't know."

Her heart ached for him so sharply her breath caught. But perhaps she could spare him. "I saw what she did to you when I accidentally connected. If you think I would hold that against you, then you are the foolish one. You did not break our bonds of fidelity by being forced."

"Selia…"

She tugged her hand free, only to place both palms on his cheeks. Aris glanced down at her, then, and the fathomless pain held within his eyes pierced her deeply. "You *do* think I hold it against—"

"She is my soulbonded," he said, his voice stark with emotion. "My potential one, at least."

Selia's arms dropped to her sides, and she took a step back. "What?"

"I was lost at sea, barely alive when she found me." He shoved his hands through his hair, and the long strands snarled with the motion. "She took me to a cave and kept me there. When I refused to bond with her, she chained me. And…you've seen too much of the rest."

By all the gods. He'd been tortured by his soulbonded? She'd never considered that horror. "That's abhorrent."

Aris flinched and crossed his arms again. "Yes."

Oh, no. He thinks I meant—

"Not on your part," she hurried to assure him. "You can't think I would reject you because of her."

His expression hardened. Perhaps he could.

"Selia," he began, his fingers whitening where he gripped his arm. "So many believe a soubonded is the perfect mate, but the

other half of my soul is evil and twisted. Tynan claims my own soul is unmarred by such darkness. It doesn't seem possible. I should believe him, I know, but I can't. I don't see how you could, either."

She closed the distance between them and barely resisted pulling him into her arms. "I don't need to hear anything from Tynan. We've been together for more than five hundred years, Aris. You are not evil. Soulbonds might link, but they don't define. They are not always the perfect love, and we are not more or less because of them. That's why our priests can and will sever those bonds."

His lips twisted. "When you haven't faced something like this, it's easy to say such things."

"Aris." She shouldn't tell him. She had to tell him. "I met my potential soulbonded a hundred years ago."

For a moment, he simply stood there, a confused frown creasing his brow. Then he moved, so quickly his hands were gripping her shoulders before she'd registered the motion. "You *what?*"

He wasn't hurting her, but the tension in his fingers twisted something in her heart. "I know I should have told you. I wasn't trying to lie, honestly. But I didn't want you to be noble and demand our marriage be severed."

"Why?" he demanded.

Selia didn't need to ask what he meant.

"I didn't like him." She grimaced at the memory of their first meeting. "Gods, that sounds so trivial. But he was arrogant, dismissive. Nothing like your potential bonded, obviously, but I had no desire to be linked to him. He even tried to ignore my denial of the bond, insisting I accept his necklace until I threatened to find a priest of Arneen. It was…not a pleasant encounter. I knew then that soulbonds weren't always ideal, and I spent a great deal of time

attempting to figure out why my soul could join with his. It haunted me for years."

Aris released her arms and spun away. She watched him wordlessly as he paced the tower, knowing from experience that he would need a moment to work through his emotions. *Miaran,* she should have told him at the time. She'd never kept anything else from him in all their years together.

"You might not forgive me," she said as he drew to a halt an arm's length away. "But I am sorry. I…I loved you more than any soulbond. I still do. Even when I believed you dead, I had no desire for another. I don't care what the gods may have planned for my soul."

Aris scrubbed his hands across his face and then let them drop. "Aren't we a fine pair."

"I truly didn't know how to tell you." Selia's shoulders slumped. "Not without losing you."

He wrapped his fingers around her wrists and tugged. As she settled against him, he lowered his forehead to hers. "Perhaps there was a divine mistake. A confusion of souls. I wouldn't have bonded with Perim even if she'd been perfection itself. No type of link could compare with my love for you."

Selia swallowed. "I thought you'd be angrier."

"I'm upset that you didn't tell me." He brushed her lips with his, drawing out a gasp. "But I'm not in a position to judge. At least yours didn't keep you chained in a cave for almost seven years."

A choked laugh slipped free. "There is that."

"I love you, Selia," he whispered. "If you still…"

"Didn't I already say I love you? Because I do. Always." She wrapped her arms around his waist and let herself relax against him. "Kiss me."

His fingers speared through her hair as his lips descended on hers. No gentle brush this time. Selia whimpered, her hands sliding up his back to grip his shoulders as he consumed her. Their tongues tangled, dueled. Against her belly, he hardened, and a shudder rippled through his muscles. But he didn't stop.

She startled when his hands slid down her neck and headed toward her waist, his thumbs brushing the sides of her breasts along the way. Heat flared within her, an inferno she'd thought she would never feel again. A moan slipped free at the perfection of his mouth and hands. His body against hers. She wrapped one of her legs around his to bring herself closer.

He froze, panting as his lips jerked away.

"I'm sorry," she managed around her own frenzied breaths.

"I want you," Aris said, his voice rough and low. "But you'll have to let me lead. I can't…I can't bear weight on me. Or too much aggressiveness."

An image of his torture tried to flicker through, but she shoved it aside. They had a lifetime of memories to choose from—and she knew just the one. "Remember the morning we conceived Iren?"

His gaze grew heated, and his fingers gripped her bottom. "Very well. I was a bit rough, though. I don't want to hurt you. I know what that's like. I—"

Selia pressed her fingers to his lips. "Being abused doesn't make you an abuser. You didn't hurt me then, and you won't hurt me now. But this time, we'll leave off any bindings."

Aris lowered a kiss to the vee of her neck, and she felt his lips curve against her skin before he nodded. Then his tongue traced a line along her pulse as he boosted her against him, his hard length trapped between them, just where she wanted it. When he spun around and strode toward the bed, she cried out from the pleasure of the contact.

"Have any empty energy crystals?" he whispered against her flesh. "Gods, I hope you do. I'm not certain of my restraint."

She let out a breathy laugh. "Didn't think I'd be grateful for the low energy of Earth. I had to use a few crystals there, so yes. In my pocket."

His low groan was answer enough.

The sound sent a shudder down her spine, for when he truly let himself go, they created magic. Literally. Ah, how she loved making him lose control of his power! It was dangerous, especially if she had nothing to channel the overflow into, but so, so worth it.

Aris lowered her to the bed. His arm muscles flexed as he held himself above her and stared into her eyes. "With this much life magic…"

"It's probably the wrong time in my cycle." Selia tugged at a strand of his hair, bringing his face closer to hers. "But I'd welcome another child with you. Provided you stop worrying and make love to me."

He kissed her softly. Once. Twice. Then he plundered, his mouth taking hers as his hand cupped her breast. He pinched at her nipple, arrowing heat straight into her core, and she couldn't stop herself from gripping both hands in his hair. When he trembled against her, she loosened her hold until he relaxed.

Aris broke their kiss long enough to tug her strange Earth shirt over her head and toss it away. Selia worked at the clasp of her pants, barely remembering to grab the energy crystals from her pocket before helping him remove the rough fabric from her legs. He lifted away again to free himself from his own clothes until nothing remained between them but air.

Her lungs seized at the sight of his chest, pale scars marring the skin in a few new places. No need to ask where those were from. But

then her gaze landed on the image of a curled dragon painted across his left pectoral muscle. Frowning, she traced her finger along the curve of a wing. A tattoo, she realized. Not paint.

"What's this?" she whispered.

He flicked a glance down at his chest and then smiled. "You'd have to ask Kezari. It appeared when she rescued me."

"For which I'll be forever grateful." Selia slid her hand down his side, and a tendril of energy escaped his control, sending a zing through her blood. "Ready?"

"For you?" The green threading his hazel eyes brightened. "Always."

Without warning, Aris flipped her over, and that earlier zing turned to lightning. Selia lifted to her hands and knees, offering herself to him. Open and vulnerable. His hands traced the line of her back before slipping around to her breasts, and the feel of him almost made her cry out. It had been far, far too long.

He touched her entrance, then, and his groan echoed around them as his control snapped. Between one breath and the next, Aris entered her. Her breath left her in a rush, and her back arched. Not from pain, but he went motionless inside her.

"Selia," he whispered. "Did I hurt you?"

"Gods, no." She couldn't stop herself from shifting against him, and they both moaned. "If you need to stop... I hope you don't..."

"I need you," Aris said.

And then he took.

He rushed into her—his body, his magic, his mind. Her home. Her fingernails dug into the bedding as she moved with him, and her heart soared even as she shattered with pleasure that seemed to last forever. Behind her, he stiffened and cried out, and combined with the feel of his fingers caressing her skin, his release triggered another of her own.

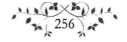

The crystals heated between her hand and the mattress as she poured the excess through by instinct. She barely noticed. Aris leaned over her, kissing a line down her spine, and she shuddered. She could have stayed like that forever. But all too soon, he withdrew.

Was he okay? Worry awoke as the pleasure faded. Then he dropped onto the bed and pulled her against his chest, nestling her close. Selia glanced over her shoulder, and some of her tension eased at the relaxed expression on his face. Sensing her regard, he cracked one eye open.

"What's wrong?" he asked.

Should she ask him? She didn't want to ruin his mood, but... "I was worried about you."

His arms tightened around her waist. "Thank you. There were times..." A sigh ruffled her hair. "I had a few rough moments, but you seemed to know what to do to ease them."

"Good," she whispered. She let her head drop and settled against him. "I suppose we'd better rest. I have a feeling your dragon is counting every drip of the clock."

Aris's low laugh echoed around her, following her into sleep.

As Selia's breathing slowed, Aris tucked his face against her shoulder and let himself bask in her presence. Unlike his beloved, he was too energized to sleep; he'd had a fair amount of that already with all the healing sessions. Perhaps, in a way, this could be counted as one of them. There'd been a few times when he'd almost had to stop, but he'd managed to steer himself away from panic. A promising sign.

Still, how long would it be before she could ride him once more? Even as his body stirred at the thought, his stomach lurched. *Clechtan.*

They'd always been adventurous and uninhibited with one another, but he couldn't offer her that freedom anymore. He might never be able to, but she appeared to love him anyway.

She'd chosen him over her soulbonded, by the gods.

His arms tightened, and he had to force himself to relax when she shifted restlessly. He'd been angry, and he still hated that she hadn't told him. But once his emotions had settled, the one that had filled him most clearly was awe. Smart, talented, beautiful Selia hadn't wanted to risk losing *him*, a reckless adventurer who hadn't had a home for centuries before her. His own parents hadn't contacted him in decades, but Selia loved him without condition.

For the first time in seven years, hope sparked and simmered. More delicate than new love, the feeling settled in his chest, warming him. It might take years, but he could heal. He would never be the same, and for once, he didn't want to be. His spirit felt more settled now. But then, being tortured on the other side of the world tended to kill a bit of that zest for adventure.

It was time he found something better to do with his talents.

Aris's hand shifted to Selia's stomach. He could sense without effort that she'd been correct—she wasn't at the right point of her cycle for them to have another child. Maybe sometime in the near future, when he was better healed, they could try. He'd felt the moment Iren's new life had begun, and he would love to experience that once more.

Family. He never wanted to lose them again.

23

The rock smoothed beneath Kezari's claw as she finished the last wall of the small hollow she'd created for herself within the cave system. She'd shifted to three different sizes to fit through the twisting tunnels, but she refused to make the entrance easy to find. Moranaian she might now be, but dragon she had always been. Some elves would not trust her as readily as the ones she'd met.

She settled on her haunches and let her claws dig in to the cool sand beneath her. She had some time, since the others required rest. Hah. A puff of smoke left her nostrils, but it was more amusement than anger. Some rested more than others, and her *skizik* was not one of those few. Not that she begrudged him his pleasure—he more than deserved it.

Kezari closed her eyes and gathered energy through her talons. The cool flow of the stone's power surged in, chilling the natural heat of her body until it neared the cave's steady temperature. Her heart slowed, and she let her senses drop away one by one. No more taste of minerals on her tongue or soft sand beneath her stomach. Only self and thought.

In that moment, she reached. Space ceased to exist. Distance was nothing. Through the thread of earth that bound them all, her consciousness flowed. Until she reached Tebzn and connected with a jolt. And in that moment before her cousin censored herself, Kezari tasted the betrayal. She might have hissed, but she paid no heed to her body. None at all.

"Why have I been named a renegade?" Kezari demanded, not bothering with a greeting.

A brief hesitation. *"You left with little warning. There is no proof of your claim that your* skizik *was held against his will or even that you have one. The fae had no clue who this Perim could be."*

"You were there. You saw my skizik. *How can you deny knowledge of Perim when she spoke to you at our last meeting?"* Kezari wanted to rend her cousin to pieces. If only she could. *"You gave your word that she would be hunted. Could you not find your own hoard? I did not believe you so inadequate that you would need to steal mine."*

"Reptile," Tebzn muttered. *"Your blood is cold to say such a thing. I am glad that the queen declared you a renegade. All this talk of Earth. Why should we care about a planet long discarded?"*

There would be no reasoning with her cousin. That, she could tell. *"You will know soon enough. Guard the young. Shield them if the wall breaks."*

"Go away, Kezari." Tebzn's tone turned mocking. *"You'll not see Earth no matter how you try to scare us. And do not contact me again."*

Her cousin severed the connection and slammed up a strong mental barrier. Kezari had no desire to try to break it, though she could. Tebzn had always been sloppy, more prepared to hunt *daeri* than practice her magic. All too many of the dragons followed the same pattern. Hunt. Bury oneself in a cave and hibernate. Mate. Hunt. Their once proud kind served little purpose now.

Kezari returned to her body with a jolt. The air steamed around her, flames licking from her mouth in time with her breath. She centered herself. Anger had no place now, and she had almost lost control more than once in front of the Moranaians already. Soon enough, she and her *skizik* would solve their problem.

Then it seemed she would have the pleasure of hunting Perim herself.

"You still look like hell."

Fen flicked a dirty look at his uncle but didn't bother to flip him off. The bastard probably wouldn't understand the gesture, and in any case, he was probably right. Fen felt like hell, so chances were good that he looked the same. He should never have taken Vek's blood. It had seemed reasonable to save time by doing so, but the rush of energy from a single sip had made Fen's chest burn as magic flooded the shard of poison near his heart. Even his breathing was shallow from the effort of hiking to the cave.

He rubbed a hand across the ache that remained. It had been pure agony to drive to the parking lot near the base of the mountain, but Vek had no clue how to operate a car. Or much of any technology designed by humans. Despite the splinter of pain digging into his chest with each step, Fen smiled. Showing his uncle how to use a television had been one of the few highlights of this mess, though they'd mock-argued the whole time. Maybe eventually, Fen could taunt him into trying video games.

Hope I'm alive to do it.

"We're almost there," Fen said, pulling a deep breath into his straining lungs.

Vek eyed him worriedly. "I can't believe you let that remark pass."

"Hard to argue with the truth." Fen paused to examine the small clearing in front of the cave entrance. Flowers waved in the wind as they soaked up the mid-morning sun, and birds chirped in the nearby trees, unconcerned with their presence. "We should have been here hours ago. I hate approaching this place in the sunlight where anyone can see."

"It took far too long for your scratches to heal," Vek said. "With my blood, they should have been gone in moments."

Another truth Fen couldn't dispute. He glanced at his uncle, who studied the clearing with his own frown of concern. Vek's face and neck had reddened with the climb despite being under the cover of trees. Hadn't anyone ever told him about sunblock? Damned Unseelie thought they knew everything, but they couldn't even keep themselves from getting a sunburn.

Vek caught him staring and scowled. "What?"

"Have you seriously not devised a spell to protect your skin from the sun?" Fen let a sneer wrinkle his nose, though he was more amused than anything. "The humans have a cream to help with that if you're not up to it."

His uncle made a dismissive gesture. "Why bother? We are never above ground."

"I hate to be the one to break it to you, but…" Fen waved his own hands at the clearing and leaned closer, lowering his voice. "We *are* above ground. There. I said it."

"Fuck off," Vek muttered before striding toward the cave's entrance.

But Fen caught a hint of affection in the insult.

He smiled again as he followed his uncle across the small meadow. He had to admit that Vek was growing on him, too. After

Fen's mother had abandoned him, he'd assumed the rest of his family didn't care. Vek's sporadic visits had seemed to confirm that, but now he couldn't help but wonder if there'd been more to his uncle's lack of attention than Fen had understood as a child. Perhaps someday he would ask.

They made their way through the short tunnel easily enough, but Vek halted just inside the cavern opening, so abruptly that Fen almost crashed into him. It didn't take long to see why. In the center of the large expanse, two men stood.

Well, shit. Not them.

One had short red hair and a ready scowl, but despite his unfriendly expression, something about him had always triggered an affinity in Fen. Not so the other. He hovered just off the floor of the cave with his shoulders back and chin tipped up, his noble aloofness a fine complement to his long pale hair. Caolte and Naomh, the Seelie nobles who'd helped Kien enact his foul plan.

Fen shifted to his uncle's side, but Vek lifted a hand in warning. "If it isn't Lord Naomh and his little brother Caolte," his uncle drawled. No affection in his tone now. "I should have expected to find you here. You Seelie love to talk about how good and honorable you are, but I've sensed your energy in this mess more than once."

Caolte stepped in front of his brother. "You should not be here."

"I've as much right as you do," Vek retorted.

"Stand down, Caolte." Naomh waited for his brother to return to his side before speaking again. "One of Kien's toys is with the Unseelie. Here to finish what that fiend started, boy?"

Fen snorted. "You're one to talk. Didn't you help create that invisibility cloak that the others used to slip into Moranaia? One of those cloaks was used in the assassination attempt on your own son. Kai, right? He seems like a nice guy."

Naomh stiffened, his hands clenching at his sides. "What did you say?"

"Kai is a nice guy. He deserves a better—"

"Before that," Naomh snapped.

"One of the half-bloods Kien sent to Moranaia was ordered by Allafon to kill Kai." Fen thought back to those terrible days in Kien's camp. He'd been so ready to escape but so helpless to figure out how. "Kien was furious about it. Of course, if any of us had known that Kai was your son, I'm sure he would have been much more pleased about the attack."

Caolte let out a low growl. "How does someone like you know of our relation to Kai?"

"When you live with a maniac, you learn how to listen to the right people." Fen met Naomh's heated gaze. "Guess you weren't aware of what happened to your son. Not close, I take it?"

Naomh lifted a hand, and a stalagmite speared up from the ground a few inches from Fen's right side. Jeez. The Seelie Sidhe had such a poor sense of humor. But Fen refused to be intimidated, especially after an infusion of energy from his powerful uncle. He flicked his fingers, and the stalagmite crumbled into dust. Unfortunately, his heart ached as though it might shatter, too. Only his years with Kien kept the pain from his expression.

Far from upset, the Sidhe lord let his hand drop and granted a slight smile. "Well done, youngling. I can see why Kien recruited you."

"What are you doing here?" Vek demanded suddenly, and Fen got the distinct impression that Naomh's praise bothered him. Which made no sense. "By all accounts, you cut ties with Kien when you discovered the scope of his plan. Are you here to prove that rumor false?"

Naomh grabbed Caolte's shoulder, halting his brother when he attempted to rush forward. The Sidhe lord studied Vek and Fen with his cool gaze before he surprised Fen by letting some of his noble veneer drop. "You know why we're here. If that wall shatters, many will die. Our people. Humans. The wave of energy won't discriminate."

"I may be able to help," Fen said.

The Sidhe's eyes narrowed. "Not in your state."

Fen's skin heated in a flush, but he refused to cave. "I had to ingest some of Kien's blood, and I was the one who connected him to Earth's energy. Not that I wanted to," he hurried to explain at Naomh's scowl. "Prince Ralan ordered it to save Maddy. A young half-Sidhe, as a matter of fact."

"Surely not from the Seelie side," Caolte said with a sneer.

Vek's hands clenched. "You iron-blasted hypocrite. You're about as much Unseelie as Seelie. But I suppose you'd rather not claim your mother with her *tainted* blood."

Not even Naomh could hold him back then. Caolte shoved past his brother and launched himself across the cavern. Vek bared his fangs as Caolte flicked a ball of flame into his palm, but Fen was too surprised to do more than stare. A Seelie lord's brother was part Unseelie? That sounded like a story he'd love to hear.

"Stop," Naomh called out.

For a moment, the other two ignored him. But there had been an unusual edge, an urgency, to his tone. Then Fen sensed it—another wave of energy coming from the rift.

"Vek," Fen warned as the dizziness hit. "We're too close. Shouldn't have…"

A surge of power. Pain.

All he could do was scream.

Aris woke with a start, Selia wrapped in his arms. *Clechtan.* He hadn't meant to fall asleep, but he'd been more exhausted than he'd thought. According to the small water clock on the wall, they still had a mark before they were supposed to meet in Lyr's study.

The hatch in the ceiling rattled and the windows shook as Kezari's wingbeats resounded above. Carefully, he disentangled himself from Selia and tucked the blanket around her as she burrowed into his pillow. It took him a moment to retrieve and don his clothes before he could head for the hatch. He cast a regretful glance at Selia, warm—and naked—in his bed and almost turned around. But he needed to talk to Kezari, and there wasn't much time before they had to go.

As he triggered the stairs to descend with his magic, Aris combed his fingers through his hair and tied it back with a strap from his pocket. Then he climbed up into the cold night. The wind whipped more snarls in his long hair almost instantly, and his clothes dampened with the thick mist. He dismissed both sensations as he edged around Kezari's large form to settle next to her foreleg.

Without comment, she lifted her wing and curled it in front of his body, blocking the worst of the weather. Her wedge-shaped head bobbed as she stared into the trees around them, and if not for the wing shielding him, he might have assumed she didn't know he was there. Something had to be bothering her.

"What is it?" he whispered as he braided his hair with a few deft motions.

One golden eye turned to face him. *"My cousin betrayed me. I have no hoard now, not even what is mine by right."*

Aris rested his cheek against her leg. "We'll rebuild it."

"It is the betrayal more than the treasures, though I'll miss those dearly." Smoke streamed from her nostrils. *"That is not the worst of it. They haven't hunted Perim."*

Bile scalded the back of his throat, but he swallowed it down. "Not good."

"I will find her when this is through," Kezari insisted.

"We will." Aris clenched his hands to still their shaking. "I cannot let her rule me."

"Mating has been good for you."

That surprised a chuckle out of him. "I suppose so."

Her head tilted. *"Why have you sought me out when you could be mating again?"*

Aris grinned. Elves weren't shy about sex, but dragons took things to a new level. "How do you know I wasn't coming up here for fresh air before waking Selia?"

"This weather is not pleasant for your form," she answered. *"Not conducive to sitting on towers."*

His humor faded. Her guess was correct—he did have a reason for coming up here. But she didn't know why. He'd grown accustomed to her presence at the back of his mind, sometimes a shadow and sometimes firmly connected. She had retreated to the farthest edges when he'd joined with Selia, granting them privacy, and she hadn't yet settled back into his thoughts.

That intrusion should have bothered him. But with each drip that passed, Aris drew closer to Kezari. She'd seen his darkest side, his deepest secrets, and accepted them without question. She shoved him beyond his limitations and into possibility. He couldn't mark the moment she'd become his friend, but she was.

For that reason, he hesitated. But there was more he needed to know despite how much he hated to request the answers. "Kezari…"

Her chest heaved at his back as she took a deep breath. *"Ask."*

"Why did you leave me in that cave for so long?"

"I thought that might be on your mind, now that you are well enough to consider it." Kezari's eye closed, and her head lowered. *"I am sorry, skizik. I should not have believed Perim's lies. I'd been hibernating, trying to connect to the Earth to find the source of my constant discomfort. It wasn't so bad then, but the changes consumed my attention. When she said you were barely an adult and needed training, I was almost…grateful."*

Though Aris flinched, he didn't interrupt.

"I spent weeks following the trails of Earth energy. Years, I suppose." Her snout tilted down until it almost brushed the roof of the tower. *"Convenient, I thought, for you to be training while I discovered the truth of what was happening. I never bothered to see you, fearing I would be pulled to bind before I knew what I was going to do. Would that I had thought of anyone besides myself."*

Aris rubbed a soothing hand along her foreleg as he processed her words. As much as he wanted to be angry, he found that he couldn't summon the emotion. Only a well of sadness for what might have been. "Your desire to save Earth belies any selfishness."

"I did not begin with thoughts of our former world, only worry about my own discomfort."

Aris sighed. "Much change begins with our own discomfort. It is what we do once we examine the source that defines us."

"You are full of wisdom, skizik," Kezari said, amusement slipping into her mental voice.

"Not really." Smiling slightly, he closed his eyes. "But I did spend hours alone on various expeditions. Do you know how much thinking you can do while tracking a newly discovered species of *daeri* across the northern planes to determine their migration patterns?"

Her soft snort sounded around them. *"New species of* daeri?*"*

He laughed at the interest in her tone. "Didn't you find time to hunt before you came back? You didn't seem grumpy enough to be hungry."

"One can never have enough daeri,*"* she grumbled in return. *"Now go back below. I hear your mate stirring. Perhaps you can ease more tension before we leave."*

Aris shook his head and chuckled at her words.

But then he complied.

24

Iren stared across the room at Eri where she perched on the edge of his bed. It was late, still several marks until morning, and they would both be in big trouble if their parents found out. He nibbled at his lower lip. Her plan had seemed so logical before he'd made up with his father. But in the quiet darkness of night, uneasiness crept into his stomach.

"Are you sure this is a good idea?"

Predictably, Eri didn't look at all worried. "We'll be seeing a lot of our rooms, but it'll be worth it."

"Your *onaial* will stop us," he argued.

"Nope." Eri grinned. "Lady Megelien said she blocked the strand. The goddess approves, so what could go wrong?"

"Ah, Eri, why did you say that?" The lump in his stomach grew. "Hasn't anyone ever told you how dangerous that phrase is?"

She swung her legs, bouncing her feet against the side of his bed with a thump. He really should know better than to listen to a six-year-old, but he couldn't help it. Eri was sweet, canny, and more persuasive than a little kid should be. She begged him with her eyes, and he did what she wanted. Of course, he usually liked her ideas. Unlike today.

"Not when I say it. We need to be there. I promise."

Great. Now her lower lip was starting to poke out. "Yeah, yeah. I already said I'd go."

"You got the cloaks?"

"Yeah." Iren slumped in his desk chair. "*Onaiala* is going to be furious. She hasn't finished working on these. They'll keep us invisible, though."

Eri slid to the floor and darted around the side of the bed. She crouched down until only her eyes peaked over the top. "You'd better get back in bed and pretend to sleep. Your parents will check on you in a few drips."

A few drips? His heart leaped, and he rushed to the bed as Eri's face disappeared over the side. Iren slipped between the covers and turned his back toward the door. He squeezed his eyes shut, but he could hear a soft rustling from Eri's location, then a muffled thump beneath the edge of the bed. The mattress shook softly for a moment before all went quiet.

Just as he evened his breathing, the door clicked open and footsteps sounded across the floor, some heavier than others. Both parents, then. Slow breath in. Slow breath out. Iren kept his muscles lax as his mother's energy neared his back. The heavier footsteps continued as his father rounded to the other side.

"I wish we could wake him," his mother whispered.

"If you prefer—"

"He'll argue to come with us." She bent low and brushed a kiss across his forehead. "But the poison makes it unsafe. I just couldn't leave without kissing him goodbye."

His father's hand rested on his shoulder for a moment, and Iren almost opened his eyes to reassure them that he would be okay. They had to be worried about this mission. And here he was, planning to add to that stress without their knowledge. As his parents trudged out the door with heavy steps, guilt twisted the lump in his stomach until he thought he'd throw up.

Eri had better be right.

Selia's boots squished into the muddy path, and she gathered her cloak around her head to block out the drizzle falling through the trees. The mountains of Moranaia gave a whole new meaning to the season of rain. Rather than the flooding downpours of her homeland, the precipitation here was a near-constant annoyance. Thank the gods that the garden paths were largely stone, or the coming festival would be a mud bath.

It was a relief to step through the portal behind Kai and Kezari. The mists swirled around the group, but despite the foggy appearance of the Veil, it didn't have the same moisture. Or maybe it wasn't as noticeable after the rain. Selia pushed the hood of her cloak back with a sigh. Ahead, Kezari's skin morphed to golden scale, and she tipped her head back, a look of ecstasy on her face. But she managed to maintain her elven form.

Aris wrapped his hand around Selia's, and she cast him a quick smile. Then Kai pulled them through with a burst of energy. Almost at once, the mists faded, and bright light had Selia squinting as they exited the portal. Steamy heat enveloped her until she released Aris in order to tug her cloak free. One by one, they tucked their cloaks into gap in the ridge wall. Then Selia waved a hand over the space, hiding the contents from view.

"Are you certain you can transport us to the cave without draining yourself?" Kai asked.

Selia nodded, her hand slipping into her pocket for an energy crystal. Her body heated at the memory of how she'd recharged some of them, and a small smile crossed her lips. "I refilled these and grabbed a few extra."

"I could fly us." Kezari rolled her shoulders as though flexing invisible wings. "The wind here feels divine."

Kai opened his mouth and then closed it again, probably uncertain how to argue with a dragon without being eaten. But Aris saved him. "That would not be safe in the human world," her husband said, resting a hand on Kezari's shoulder. "They have technology that can fire into the sky."

Kezari scowled. "I can fly higher than arrows."

"Aris is correct," Kai finally said. "Humans have created machines that fly, and some of them come equipped with weapons. I'd rather not see how you fare against them. And vice versa. We have more important things to worry about."

Selia had no clue if dragons pouted in their natural forms, but Kezari's bottom lip took a definite turn downward in this one. Even so, she waved her hand regally toward Selia. "Let us proceed, then. This skin itches. I want to shift."

Before the dragon could change her mind, Selia tightened her grip on the energy crystal and connected to the power within. With a quick tug, she spun the magic into the travel spell. A thin line the height of a person appeared and widened, and as she formed the image of her destination in her mind, it filled the gap she'd built. But the cavern on the other side wasn't empty this time.

Kai cursed. "What is my father doing there? Let's move. Now."

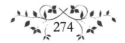

Selia held the spell firm, channeling power from the crystal straight into the gate, as Kai, Kezari, and then Aris rushed through. The small portal flickered slightly, but it steadied a moment before Selia followed. Her head spun as she was wrenched across space. Shouldn't she have had to change crystals by now? Even as she settled on the other side, she examined the spell for flaws, but it had no obvious problems. The energy didn't sputter until just before she closed the spell.

What had changed? Suspicious, she reached out for Earth's well of power and gasped. Still difficult to access, but not as much trouble as it should be. The cracks in the wall must have widened, letting more energy through.

Aris froze at her side, Kezari standing in front of them as Kai strode closer to the small group in the center of the cavern. The youngest one was on the floor, writhing, a blood elf crouched over him with fangs extended. A Sidhe man with bright red hair paced anxiously while a second Sidhe male hovered at the writhing man's feet. Kai headed straight for the second Sidhe lord, and though his hair was pale, she could see some resemblance between the two.

Must be his father.

Selia's heart lurched, and she jerked another crystal from her pocket. But her view was blocked as Kezari grew in size, her body contorting in a swirl of energy that crashed like a gale against Selia's shields. She winced and shaded her eyes until the blur of motion ended. Once finished, the dragon stood in her natural form, though a quarter of her customary size.

At a brush against her hand, Selia glanced at Aris. He'd gone deathly pale, and his chest heaved rapidly with each breath. The cave. Ignoring the others, Selia stepped in front of Aris and grabbed his face between her palms. Kezari would protect them. Aris having a breakdown could only make the situation worse.

"Stay with me, Aris."

"I'm trying." His throat bobbed. "Go help Kai. This may take a moment."

Selia brushed her lips against Aris's. "No. You can do this. Let yourself feel the cave. The life is different here, with a different rhythm. Do you sense the heartbeat? The creatures here need you."

His eyes glazed, and she feared she'd lost him.

Then green flared around his pupils as he pulled his head free from her hold.

The physical world ceased to matter.

Aris glided across the cavern floor, barely noticing Selia as he circled her to stand at Kezari's shoulder. He formed a loose link with the dragon, and the cry of stone joined the discordant song of the creatures living inside the cave. Nearer still, two lights beckoned, one of them pulsing with the darkest sliver of death.

Pressure built, ringing in his skull, and then snapped. A rough scream echoed through the chamber, but that hardly registered. His attention was on the sick energy within the light. He advanced toward it, his feet finding purchase without conscious effort. The Earth would cradle him no matter where he went.

"Don't merge too deeply, skizik."

He shrugged aside the dragon's words and kept walking.

Something tightened on his physical form, and he shook his arm to try to break free. A sharp tug, then. "Aris."

Sudden awareness washed over him at the frantic cry of his name, and he halted, blinking rapidly to clear his thoughts. The world returned to clarity. It was Selia clutching his arm, and the group he'd

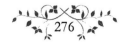

seen in the center of the cavern now stared at him, save the one stretched out on the floor. Gods. He hadn't been that pulled in by his magic since his first half-century of life.

"He is poisoned," Aris said, his voice rough to his own ears.

The blood elf hissed. "What do you know of this? If you think to harm Fen, you will have to reckon with me."

"You will not threaten one of my people, Vek." Kai stepped partially in front of Aris. "Your nephew knows me. I've spared him once already."

"I will not trust anyone who brings a dragon to undo the ancient pact." The anger Vek's expression didn't ease. "I don't care if you're the king of Moranaia. Clearly, you do not understand the intricacies of what is happening. Remove yourself, or I will remove you."

Kezari let out a warning rumble, and the air warmed with her anger.

Equally upset, the blond Sidhe lord leaned forward as though he wanted to spring. "I'll send you to your father in pieces if you threaten my son again."

"Enough!"

A crack of magic accompanied Selia's sharp command, and all three men froze. Not voluntarily. Aris couldn't hold back a slight grin at the sight of his wife marching over, not even when the red-haired Sidhe lifted a ball of flame in his palm. The stranger met Selia's eyes for a moment, and then his hand lowered, the fire winking out. But he remained tense. Ready.

Selia undoubtedly was, too.

"Caolte," Selia said, nodding her head at the Sidhe man glaring at her. "Explain what is going on here. Since all these three can do is trade threats while Fen writhes in pain."

Even Caolte looked abashed. "Naomh and I were investigating the energy rift when Fen and Vek arrived. We…might have had some

disagreement between us. Then a pulse from the rift struck, and Fen collapsed. We've been trying to determine what to do."

Beneath his feet, Aris sensed the hum of energy increasing. Slightly, but enough to give him cause for concern. "If the pulses are hurting him, you'd better get him out of here. There will be another soon."

Selia narrowed her eyes at the three men frozen in place. "I will release you, but if you begin arguing again, I make no promises."

A cool wash of power flowed around them, and her spell dissipated. She must have been feeling kind, for the slow dissolution gave the three time to regain control of their muscles. Naomh wobbled, his feet almost touching the ground before he righted himself, and Vek jumped up, glaring, but Kai tucked his hands behind his back and attempted to appear repentant. The wiser move when faced with a master mage who was thoroughly tired of one's attitude.

The blood elf snarled. "If you ever do that again, I will drain you—"

"I recommend you keep your fangs far from me," Selia said coldly. "I did not shirk my training when it comes to your kind."

Amazingly, Vek's mouth snapped closed, though anger still lined his face.

Another pulse of energy thrummed through Aris. "If you care for your friend, get him out. Now. Take him as far from here as you can manage. Once we have healed the rift, we can see what we can do for him."

"You have no intention of healing anything," Vek said. "Or at least your dragon doesn't."

Kezari's breath puffed out, filling the space with an acrid scent as her voice shoved into their heads. *The poison must be purged, but we both know that might widen the crack. I do not intend to dissolve our pact.*

However, I may not be able to control the results of what has been wrought. I didn't create this rift or the poison infusing it. I can only try to fix it."

Vek shoved his shoulders back. "Give me a bit of your blood, and I will go seal the rift."

"Impossible without trapping the poison inside," Kezari sent. Aris's blood chilled at the terrible finality in her tone. *"That's too much to risk. The sickness would only gain strength behind the shield holding back the magic, and if your fix fails, the blight would pour free all at once, killing everything it touched. Besides, the wall is permeable in places to allow for the natural ebb and flow of magic. We don't know if the poison can seep through those thin areas."*

"Fen believes he can purify the blight since he helped Kien—"

"That boy will not live beyond a few days if the poison is not purged, and well you know it." Pieces of fallen stone rattled as Kezari lumbered forward. Her golden eyes stared at Vek as though he was her prey. *"This was no accident. It was punishment. When the wall shatters, he dies if the darkness is not removed."*

Vek's jaw clenched. "I cannot heal Fen."

The floor vibrated softly, although Aris wasn't sure anyone besides himself and Kezari detected it. "He might survive until we can return to help if you go now," Aris said.

Fen let out a low moan, and his uncle knelt beside him. The Unseelie's skin was paler than the snow coating the northern mountains as he studied his nephew's face. "Or he might not."

"Caolte and I will go with you," Naomh said softly.

Vek's expression went blank. "You? Why?"

"I bear some of the same talents as the dragon and her rider," the Sidhe lord answered, no sign of concern in his tone. Only the tense, high set of his shoulders gave his agitation away. "As well as a touch of the healing gift. I may be able to help."

"But you're a Seelie lord," Vek began. "I—"

"Talk it out later," Aris said as his head began to throb with the rising energy. "Selia, can you build another portal to help them get them farther away?"

Nodding, she extended her hand, and a different, more focused power built at her direction. Vek lifted Fen into his arms, and Naomh and Caolte shifted close. Kai barely had a chance to exchange a few words with his father about contacting someone named Maddy before the unusual group slipped through the transportation spell.

Selia let the portal drop, and the four of them were alone. Just in time for the next ragged wave of power.

25

This time, Selia didn't try to shield herself from the wave. She'd been caught off guard last time, and instinct had led her to protect herself. Now she was ready. She lifted the empty crystal in her left hand, and as the pulse of energy crashed into her, she channeled it into the stone. Unlike the energy fields themselves, these waves were pure power. Infinitely useable.

"What did you do?" Aris asked after the magic waned.

Selia shrugged. "I was being practical. Don't worry, though. I filtered against the poison."

She tucked the crystal in her pocket and joined Aris and Kai in the center of the cavern. Kezari advanced, too, her slow steps rattling the ground. The dragon lifted her head over Aris, practically settling it on his shoulder as she stared at them.

"I will smooth the path to the rift," Kezari sent.

Selia expected her to grow larger, closer to her natural size, but instead, she shrank until her body was the size of Iren's. Selia's lips twitched. She had a feeling it would be a terrible idea to call a dragon cute, but…in her small form, Kezari was adorable. Her little wings flapped rapidly as she arrowed toward the tunnels they'd used to reach the energy fissure.

Aris's eyes met Selia's, and for a brief moment, they shared a grin. Then they joined Kai in following Kezari. When Aris reached for her hand, she took it, startled to feel him trembling. His expression might not show it, but he was uneasy about being in the cave. She entwined her fingers with his and gave a comforting squeeze.

Kai glanced at them over his shoulder. "I wish I'd had a chance to speak with my father about Kezari's claim. I'm not certain what I'm supposed to do to guard the strands between worlds."

Selia smiled sweetly. "Perhaps in the future you will not waste time arguing."

"You're right." Kai shrugged one shoulder. "Though I admit that I'm surprised you reprimanded a Seelie noble and an Unseelie prince so…stringently."

Her steps hitched, but she forced herself to keep moving. She hadn't been thinking about status at the time, only their useless arrogance. She might very well have caused an incident between their peoples by immobilizing those two. Talk about a breach in etiquette. But blast it, Fen had been thrashing in pain while they'd exchanged barbs.

"I wasn't considering the ramifications." She winced. "I hope I haven't created another problem."

"Don't worry about it, Selia," Kai said. "We've dealt with worse."

With a sigh, she tried to ease the concern from her expression. It must have worked, for Kai stopped sending glances her way and concentrated on his steps. Or perhaps he worried more for the low ceiling in this tunnel. The walls had grown wider and smoother thanks to the steady thrum of power directed by Kezari, but she hadn't paid much heed to height.

Selia and Aris came to a halt beside Kai inside the small room with the shelf hidden behind stalactites. After getting scratched during the climb on their first trip, Selia wasn't relishing the thought of going in again. But the dragon flew closer, and the stone shifted away from her snout like a waterfall from a shielding spell, exposing the tunnel hidden by the stalactites. Even that began to widen as Selia watched in fascination.

But they would still have to crawl.

The dragon glanced over her shoulder. *"It would take too much energy for me to widen the tunnel enough for walking. I will do my best."*

Aris shivered against her arm, but if he made a return comment to Kezari, it was private. His gaze was pinned to the shifting stone, his expression drawn and pale. How would he bear going through the tunnel, not to mention the crevice they'd have to descend later?

Before their eyes, several stalactites and stalagmites appeared to melt and flow downward into a rough set of steps. Selia blinked in disorientation as the stone heaved and shifted before settling. Gods of Arneen. She could manipulate earth a little herself but nothing on this scale. As far as she could tell, it didn't even cause the dragon strain. Kezari hovered easily, her wings flapping steadily and her talons hanging lax as she studied her work.

Not that Selia was an expert at judging a dragon's body language.

Finally, Kezari flew back to them, hovering in front of Aris. *"This is the best I can do. Connect fully with me, Aris, and I will help you. Please stand guard, Selia."*

Aris's breath hissed through his nose as he peered at Selia. "If you need to immobilize me, I will not complain."

"I will not need to," she answered, her voice ringing with more confidence than she felt. "We can get through this."

His nod was slow in coming. "I suppose we'll see if you're right."

Perim understood little of what she'd seen in this strange world so far, but power she comprehended. As she pressed against the stone wall of a small building, another wave of energy flooded her senses, blinding her for a few precious heartbeats. She was getting closer. She'd run for most of the day across a seeming island's worth of uneven, sometimes mountainous terrain, dodging unusual boxes on wheels and avoiding an endless series of strange habitations.

And humans. Like insects in summer, they swarmed everywhere.

Once her vision, and the energy, had cleared, she pushed away from the wall and started jogging once more. What a terrible, barren waste of a planet. She was no mage, but she used simple magic like any self-respecting fae. Here, it was difficult to light so much as a campfire without severe strain, except when one of those strange waves rushed through. And although there were many trees, they were much smaller. The air held an odd, chemical tang, and constant lights and noises ruined the serenity of many of the places she passed.

Who but humans could live in such a place? Even the island she hated was better.

Perim reached another road made of smooth, smelly stone. It held strange markings—white lines and yellow dashes. In some places, there were two center lines and in others, one line and a bunch of dashes. Were they magical symbols? Maps? So far, she hadn't been able to make sense of them, but if she grew desperate enough, she could capture a human for answers. Not that humans would provide much sport. She was too spoiled after Aris's resilience.

As she darted across the road, careful not to let her foot touch one of the lines—just in case—one of the rolling boxes flew around a corner. Perim yelped and jumped out of the way, barely in time to avoid being crushed. The wake from its passing shoved at her back, and a screeching sound chilled her heart.

She stumbled to a halt, glancing over her shoulder as a thin, clear panel moved downward on the box. The human inside shouted at her, but the words made as much sense as the device he controlled. Shrugging, she darted away without bothering to speak. He wouldn't understand, anyway.

Her laughter floated behind her, mingling with the human's incoherent remonstrations.

The closer Aris came to the hole in the cave wall, the harder his heart squeezed. Kezari had flown through first, and now Kai lowered himself to the floor and began to crawl through. Aris barely felt Selia's hand rubbing gently between his shoulder blades. Despite all of the mind-healer's work, this might be too much.

No. I can do this.

Aris sucked in a breath to center himself. Then he merged with Kezari. This time, he was prepared for the scope of the pain, the damage to the Earth that had almost swept him into madness when he'd accidentally connected with her before. He let it flow into him before pushing it to the back of his awareness. He sensed something deeper. More fundamental.

Suddenly, the earth beneath his feet became his blood and bone. He couldn't shape it as Kezari did, but he could become it—if he dared. A spasm passed through his body. Caves were torment and

despair. Why would he join with that? But this place was not the same location where he'd been held. The present and the future could not be judged so strongly by the past.

He let the stone speak to him. Through him. The rift in the energy field caused hurt. Each pulse a threat to a long, endless life. Minerals disturbed, water flow altered. Strangers traveling through, their bodies killing the living rock where they passed. Heedless.

Come. Please come.

Aris had crouched on his hands and knees before he realized it. He closed his eyes and crawled, shivering until the tunnel closed around him with pleased warmth. With each scuffle forward, the cave sent its welcome through him. He let it. As he followed the glow of a mage light partially blocked by Kai, some of the tension eased from his gut. He was not so broken, after all.

They emerged into a tiny chamber bristling with rock formations. Aris held out a hand for Selia and helped her to her feet. At her questioning look, he smiled. "Seems you were right."

But the crease between her brows didn't ease. "You haven't seen the next part."

Connected to Kezari as he was, he sensed her decision to shift before the others did. When the dragon's energy increased, Selia's focus transferred to Kezari. Thankfully. Aris hated seeing the worry in his wife's eyes, especially since it was warranted. He didn't know if the earth's comfort would overcome his aversion to a crevice worse than what he'd just crawled through.

In moments, Kezari stood before them in her elven form. Naked, predictably, but Aris didn't bother to mention it. Kai kept his gaze respectfully averted, no sign of discomfort on his face, and Selia let out a soft chuckle that the dragon either ignored or didn't notice. Kezari was too busy studying a narrow gap in the floor.

Without warning, bile rushed up Aris's throat and coated his tongue. That fissure looked like... *The chain shouldn't have reached the crevice, but it did. Aris's arms burned from their extended position, and the walls closed around him until he was certain there was no air. He panted. Thrashed. His back grew wet with his own blood. "Told you that you shouldn't have hit me," lilted down from above, a cheerful contrast to pure evil.*

Aris doubled over, resting his hands on his knees as he pulled in lungfuls of air. He wasn't there. He knew he wasn't there. Thanks to the healer, he could untangle himself from the memory. But nothing on Earth was going to get him through that gap without risking madness, not even the steady comfort of the cave still humming within him.

Then he heard a long, thin cry echoing from below—followed by a yelp of pain.

For one long moment, Aris's breath seized. "That sounds like Iren."

He and the others rushed toward the gap, and he plunged his senses down the tunnel.

Nothing.

But despite what his scan told him, whispers and sniffles echoed upward. With a wave, Selia sent the mage light into the darkness, but all Aris could see was the floor a couple of body lengths down.

To his right, Selia groaned. "The cloak."

Aris's brows twisted with confusion, but Kai cursed. "The one you based on Kien's design?"

Selia nodded, her lips thinning into a pale line. "Show yourself *now*, Iren," she called down into the tunnel.

After a bit of rustling, Iren's body wavered into view as the hood of his cloak dropped to his shoulders. Aris's heart lurched at the sight of the tears streaming down his son's pinched face, but an

equal amount of anger surged alongside his fear. "What were you thinking?" he found himself demanding.

Not the most pressing question, unlike *Are you hurt?* and *How did you get here?* but it was all his lips seemed willing to form.

Selia fared better, thankfully. "Are you injured?"

"I hit my knee when I fell," Iren answered, his voice quivering with fear. "And my ankle hurts. And there's blood. It's not that I wasn't thinking. I just…"

Aris went cold at the sight of the dark stain blooming on the leg of Iren's pants, and his earlier question fled his mind. Tunnel or no, he had to get down there. "We'll talk about the rest later. I'm coming down."

"Allow me, *skizik*," Kezari said. "I can widen the gap after I see to your spawn."

"I could go," Kai offered.

Selia wrapped her fingers around Aris's wrist as though she wanted to hold him back. "Or I. Though I may not have much of the healing gift, I can—"

"No." The sick taste of fear filled his mouth once more, but Aris shook his head. "I can seal the wound."

Kai made an impatient gesture. "As can I."

Aris swung his legs into the hole and pinned Kai with a level look. "No."

He might never have descended the chasm for himself or even for Earth. But by the gods, he would help his own son. Carefully, he eased down the vertical tunnel bit by bit. Memories threatened, hovering at the edges of his consciousness no matter how hard he beat them back, and his breathing came fast and shallow. Aris closed his eyes and tried to pretend he was anywhere else.

Not even the earth's comfort could ease this.

After an eternity, his feet touched solid ground. Elation weakened his muscles, but he couldn't savor it. Iren needed him, and he would not fail.

Aris had barely shifted their son out of the way before Selia dropped down beside him at the base of the fissure. Her hands shook as she rushed to the wide spot in the tunnel where Aris bent over Iren's leg. Darting around him, she sank down at her son's other side and gripped Iren's face in her palms.

"Iren—"

"I know, I know," her son said in a rush. "I wanted to prove myself. And Eri said it was important."

That explained far too much. "Where is she?" Selia asked, trying to keep her tone level.

"Here," a small voice said as the hood of another cloak was lowered.

The child's face was milk-white, but Selia couldn't summon much sympathy at the moment. "You have gone too far, Eri."

"He wasn't supposed to get hurt!" Eri's hands twisted together. "I'm not sure what happened. There was no future strand for that."

All of Selia's worry left her mouth in a rush. "I can't believe you stole these cloaks from my room to cross worlds into certain danger. It seems I will have to separate you two, at least for the foreseeable future. That's *my* future strand," she snapped.

"*Onaiala…*" Iren pleaded.

"How am I supposed to keep you safe with all of the life energy your father is about to unleash?" Selia dropped her hands before she

could squeeze his cheeks too hard. "Didn't you think of that? You can't justify this."

Eri lifted her little chin. "It was important for us to be here. I Saw it."

"And your father didn't?" Selia asked, eyebrow lifting.

"Lady Megelien—"

"Is not known to work through children at the expense of their safety." Selia studied the child's guilty expression. "I suspect there is more to this than I need to know. I'll leave that to your father."

Eri ducked her head. "Thank you, Lady Selia."

"I sealed the gash," Aris said, catching her attention. "But I can't heal the cracked bone in his ankle."

Kai crowded into the small tunnel, and Selia scooted out of his way. "If it is a small break, I can knit it a little. My healing gift is limited. Can you not do that with life magic?"

Aris shrugged. "I'm not certain. I can shift and adapt bodies, but I must have intimate knowledge of them. Unfortunately, I've never put that much study into anatomy. I'd far rather explore than modify or heal."

"Adapt bodies?" Iren asked, his eyes going round. Probably with excitement more than fear, if she knew her son. And she did. "I'll be able to do that?"

Aris's mouth tightened. "We'll see. Right now, we need to fix your ankle and then figure out how to protect you during what is to come."

"You won't need to," Eri whispered.

Usually, Selia loved the little girl, and in truth, she still did. But she wasn't particularly fond of her at the moment. One day, her overconfidence was going to get her in more trouble than she could handle. It certainly had Iren.

Here's hoping that trouble doesn't arrive today.

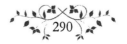

26

Selia half-expected to see the god Loki standing in front of the rift again, but the cavern was empty of all but the glowing red fissure when she and Kai led the way inside. Iren and Eri followed them in, and Selia directed the children to wait beside the tunnel opening as Aris and Kezari rounded the corner.

The dragon uttered a choked hiss and froze in her tracks, pain stark on her face as she studied the wound to Earth's energy field. "The Unseelie was a fool to consider sealing it up like this," she whispered.

Aris circled the pulsing rift, the red light painting him an eerie color. Selia tilted her head and examined it as well. More black threaded through, blocking the light, and she didn't have to be an earth mage to detect the sick hint of poison. If this was sealed within the energy field, it would sicken all who tried to use energy here, if not immediately then certainly over time.

Kien had used his death as a catalyst to turn his poison into something far deadlier than its original form. Before, he'd scattered nodes around the world, creating a framework of sickness that could be broken, if not easily. But this… This was a bomb. An explosion of this much tainted energy would kill many.

Lovely.

"Together, we can eliminate the poison," Kezari said to Aris. "But the walled off energy is going to break free. The damage is too extensive. Can you channel it while healing? Even hearing the Earth's cry, I did not expect it to be like this."

Aris frowned up at the rift. "I'll do my best. Perhaps if I channel it to Selia?"

Selia couldn't help but snort. "There aren't enough energy crystals in any world to hold this much power, and I have no ability to direct it into the living earth."

"Then I'll have to—"

"I can help," Iren blurted. He straightened from where he was leaning against the stone wall, resting his sore foot, and shoved his shoulders back. "Eri said we needed to be here, and I think this is why. I don't really know how to use the energy, but I can act as a conduit."

"No," Selia and Aris said in unison.

But Kezari peered at Iren with hope. "Your spawn might be an asset."

Aris spun to face the dragon. "Even you must admit that young should be guarded."

"What do you think will happen to him if you fail and this explodes?" Kezari asked.

A reasonable question, unfortunately. Still, Selia didn't want to concede the point. Perhaps she and Kai could escort the children to the portal first. It would cost a bit of her own reserves, but it would be worth the risk of draining herself to see Iren and Eri safe.

Before she could make the suggestion, a sputtering sound filled the cavern, and the red glow brightened—then flickered. Selia's scalp

prickled and her arm hairs stood on end at the building power, erratic and strong. The waves were getting worse. *Clechtan.* She couldn't spare the time it would take to take the children back.

"Perhaps you could test whether Iren can handle a thread of your power," Selia said to Aris before she could change her mind.

His brows rose. "You jest."

"Not about this." She swallowed hard as the rift's light flickered. "This is growing unstable. We need to fix this now if we're going to do it at all. Surely you can feel the danger."

Aris's gaze flicked briefly to the crack and then to Iren. "I would rather see the end of this world than either of you."

"If we don't act, I fear you'll see the end of all three."

Another surge swept over them, and this close to the rift, Selia strengthened her shields. The other adults appeared to do the same, but the children cried out. As the power ebbed, Iren leaned against the wall next to a frighteningly pale Eri. Selia rushed over to examine them both. Her son looked more shaken than anything, but the little girl rubbed at her head as though it hurt.

"Eri?"

"It's a lot like the other poison," the girl whispered. "The one that almost killed me before my dad took me from Earth to Moranaia a few months ago. But not quite the same."

Selia's heartbeat drummed in her ears at the solemn expression on the child's face. "You risked your life to bring Iren here."

"I probably won't die." Eri summoned a slight smile. "But I don't want to be seriously hurt, either."

Well, that was a fine choice. Put Iren in danger or risk death for little Eri, a princess of Moranaia who was likely to be the greatest seer of her generation. Maybe any generation. Iren met Selia's apprehensive gaze without flinching, more like his father than he

knew, but for a moment, all she could see was the baby the healer had first placed on her chest. She brushed an errant hair off his forehead and ran her fingers down his face to tweak his chin as she had when he was younger.

"*Onaiala*," he said with a groan.

"You're still a child, Iren," Selia said. Then she took a deep breath. "But I believe you can do this. You are a clever, fast learner. My caution with you has always been your heedlessness, not your ability. Promise to follow your father's commands, even if you don't want to."

Aris stepped up beside her, the conflict evident on his face. "Selia, I'm not certain about this."

"I'm not, either." She forced a tremulous smile. "But you saw what that surge did. Loki said my task was to protect. I'll monitor the energy and step in if necessary. I can funnel it away from Iren."

They both knew she didn't have the same capacity for life magic that Aris or even Iren had, and this would be far beyond what she'd channeled for her husband in the past. Since she wouldn't be able to direct it straight into the earth, it would build within her until she burned out like an overfilled crystal. The best she'd be able to do was force it away from them before she died.

But she would do it for Iren.

"He doesn't need to know," she sent to her husband.

Aris's jaw hardened. *"I will always know. But you are right."*

Then he focused on their son and began to describe the basics of being a conduit.

Aris settled between Kezari's shoulder blades, no saddle between him and her scales. She'd widened one end of the chamber, unwilling to take on the task ahead without being in her full natural form, and shifted while he worked with Iren. Pride swelled in Aris's chest at the memory. His son was clever, indeed. He'd almost lost control several times as he struggled to channel the life energy he was fed, but he'd picked up the skill far faster than Aris had as a child. Selia had taught him well. If they survived this, Aris could train Iren to actually use the magic instead of merely directing it back into the natural world.

To the left of the rift, Kai sat, legs crossed and eyes closed as he fumbled with his power. If Aris scanned with his own abilities, he could see a few tendrils of something whipping around the other man, but it wasn't like the earth energy he knew. Kai had nodded when asked if he was ready, so they'd just have to trust that he'd figured it out.

They'd have to trust in a lot of things.

To the right, Selia stood behind Iren, ready to take on his burden if he faltered. If any of them faltered. Aris jerked his gaze away and caught sight of Eri, still leaning against the wall on the other side of the energy rift. For a moment, he could have sworn her eyes gleamed as she returned his stare, but she blinked, and the effect was gone.

A flicker of red captured his attention. Was it his imagination, or did the lightning-like cracks hovering in the air appear...longer? Deeper? The Unseelie and the dragons had been reckless to try to wall off this much energy. How had they not considered the possibility of a breech?

Kezari shifted beneath him. *"It would have succeeded had our peoples not grown complacent. We stopped actively maintaining the wall, so it is not as strong as it once was."*

"People?" he asked, poking at her in an attempt to lighten the mood.

"This language has no better word for a civilization comprised of sentient, non-bipedal entities," Kezari answered primly. Then she relented. *"Except perhaps 'civilizations.'"*

Aris chuckled softly and patted her neck. *"We'll work on it."*

She twisted her head to look at him, and the spines around her eyes shifted in a motion he'd come to associate with raised eyebrows. *"Are we waiting on something?"*

"I'm not sure," he confessed. *"I feel like there's…"*

Eri straightened, catching his attention once more. She pulled back her shoulders and nodded her head sharply. This time there was no mistaking the gleam.

"How about now?" he asked.

Kezari bared her teeth in a dragon's grin and faced the sputtering fissure. Aris closed his eyes and let himself settle into his power. The heartbeats that had fluttered at the back of his consciousness crescendoed like the pounding of drums at a winter solstice celebration, but the creatures here weren't ceremoniously summoning the sun back to life. They were fighting to fix their world the only way they could—by lending him their strength.

Fluttering and skittering sounds filled the cave as bats shifted their wings high above and insects darted around in their holes, just out of sight. There were rats and spiders, salamanders…all manner of creatures that generally fled before any people could find them. Even as they connected with Aris, they remained out of sight, wary of so many bodies. Particularly the dragon.

He fell deeper into himself. His dryad grandmother's blood flowed strong through his veins, and he tapped into the power held within. If he strained, he could count the strand of every root

tunneling over their heads. Each tiny plant and bit of moss that grew where a hint of light reached now synched with the beat of his heart.

"What do you want me to do?" he sent to Kezari.

"I'm not certain yet."

The rustling from above increased as the bats picked up on his agitation. *"You said we could fix this."*

"We will," she answered, her mental voice placid. *"Merge. Explore. Find the discordant threads."*

Aris forced himself to relax. To let go. Kezari would not guide him wrong.

He connected fully with Kezari, and the stone around them returned to life the way it had earlier, before he'd dropped their connection to heal Iren. Rock groaned and flexed, though its physical form didn't move; even the minerals accumulating on the stalactites above his head hummed with the disturbance. The Earth held fathomless energy, but the earth was not accustomed to so much disorder, so much speedy evolution. Not here, at least, where only the occasional cave-in punctuated the steady drip of time.

Aris allowed his own power to flow into Kezari, then. She moved restlessly beneath him as the strength of it hit, but after only a moment, they managed to join their powers completely. Body and soul of the earth entwined. He basked in it for a couple of heartbeats.

Then he turned to the rift.

And he—they—knew.

A smile broke across Perim's face as she spotted the cave entrance. Finally, the source of the power. She'd had to cross two more of those strange roads and climb the side of the mountain,

but it had been worth it. She took a few wary steps closer to the cave. No sign of life. But then an energy as familiar as her own washed over her, and she froze. Aris—but not Aris. He was greater. Different. She prodded the energy carefully and recoiled before he could notice. He'd joined with the dragon.

Finally, a bit of good fortune. She could honor her oath to Baza and rid herself of the final obstacle keeping her from true freedom. Then she would recreate herself, no one the wiser. Even if the Ljósálfar rejected her, she'd survive. Here on this strange planet if necessary.

Just one thing to take care of first.

Her smile widened as she shielded herself and started walking again.

Aris probed the edges of the rift, gathering as much information as he could. This cave wasn't the origin point of the spell walling off Earth's energy, but the fissure let him examine the handiwork anyway. How many Unseelie and dragons had joined together to create this piece of spell art? There were bits of earth magic twined with the other elements and a definite hint of strands similar to the Veil. Actually—

Yes, it connected to the Veil. Suddenly, he understood what Loki had meant, and he reached out to Kai. The other elf linked immediately, though his mental voice sounded confused. *"What's going on?"*

"Look," Aris said, sharing what he saw.

Silence while Kai examined it. Then a litany of mental curses. *"And I'm supposed to keep this from getting damaged?"*

"So it seems." Aris understood the other man's fear, but now wasn't the time to indulge it. *"I know you can't link magic the same way Kezari and I can, but maintain mental contact with me as you join with the strands."*

"I've followed them most of my life, but I—"

"Figure it out now." Inside, Aris winced with his next words. *"Do you want to get stuck here if the Veil is damaged? I assume you'd like to see your child born."*

A pause. *"Harsh but accurate. You're right. I don't have a choice."*

As Kai began to explore the rift further, Aris linked with Iren. This was different yet again, for his bond with his son was of blood and energy, not of mind or magic. But this time, he didn't set up a telepathic link, and he wouldn't unless he had to. Unlike Iren, Kai could guard against any physical or emotional rebound. If there was pain, Aris would not share it with his son. Instead, he sent Iren a wave of reassurance before returning his attention to the fissure.

Small, red crackles danced along the lightning-like branches and sparked on the air. Something was about to happen, for good or ill, and Earth would not remain the same, no matter what. All he could do was try to tip the outcome in their favor.

Aris took a deep breath and loosened his awareness of his physical body. He felt more than heard Kezari's assent as they plunged into the rift and joined with it, not completely, but enough to purge the sickness marring it. His very existence thrummed with the force of the power.

Gods. So much energy. Too much—more than any person should have to handle. But he couldn't channel it through Iren and into the ground yet. All hint of poison had to be purged first. If he could manage the task.

Life. This scourge was made of death, and he would counter it with life.

He shoved against that dark stain with the essence of endless heartbeats. With the richness of fertile soil and living rock. Bit by bit, he chipped away at the poison with hope. He'd seen evil, and it did not have to win. It would not win. *Merge with life,* he offered the shattered heart of power. *Embrace it and be.*

Endless time passed, but finally the Earth heeded his call. Where poison had consumed, light poured through. But the power… His spirit ached from the strength of the magic that rushed into the spaces left in the wake of darkness, shattering through the ragged holes and deepening the cracks in the wall.

Aris channeled the magic down, toward the deepest heart of the Earth where it would merge with the existing energy field. *More than I can bear.* Grudgingly, he passed some to Iren, but his son was soon at capacity. If Aris couldn't handle it, someone else would suffer, either Iren or Selia.

No.

He doubled down, and pain shrieked through him. Body? Spirit? He didn't even know how much of it was his own. The earth trembled, and he sensed Kezari struggling to prevent the wall from shattering all at once. If they could trickle the power out slowly, in a controlled release like the floodgates of a dam, the final burst might not be too bad. Maybe.

Movement stirred on the edges of awareness. Who…? Eri and one other. That god. Loki? Bound in the magic as he was, Aris saw their glowing forms as they approached. Then they shoved their hands into the heart of the rift, and his world went white.

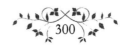

27

Selia was so focused on monitoring Iren's energy that she almost missed Loki's reappearance. He and Eri advanced on the rift, now flaring between red and white, the god holding the child's hand. Selia glanced at Kai to see if he noticed the pair, but his eyes were closed as he struggled with his own task.

What had they called Loki? The god of mischief?

"More like the god of cleaning up others' shit," Loki said, his voice echoing across the space. "Though I'll grant you I create my fair share of trouble."

Selia had no idea what to say to that. She looked between him and the child, whose focus was on the rift. "What are you doing here? With Eri?"

"Fixing things," he answered. "You know, I was once known for more than causing trouble. But call those in power on their failings one time, and you're forever the villain. I guarantee they'll never believe I did this."

He seemed to expect some response to that, but Selia didn't know what he was talking about. "I'll pass the message along."

"Tell them Lodurr still lives." He grinned. "Oh, and watch the entrance."

Before she could ask what he meant—about any of it—he and Eri plunged their hands into the ragged edges of the energy fissure. The impact of the resulting blast blinded her, and Selia threw herself around Iren as far too much power was released. All she could do was wrap her shields around them both and try to survive.

Pain flared in her side and back as she landed hard on the ground, her body cushioning Iren. Her shielding began to crumble, and she scrambled to reinforce the cracks. Then Iren linked with her, much as he did for teaching sessions, and joined his own power and protections to hers. She tried to open her eyes to check on the others but it was far too bright to see. Would any of them survive this?

Loki had said he was going to fix things, but he hadn't claimed he would spare *them*.

Kai had never linked with the strands quite like this before.

Or maybe he had on an instinctive level, as he'd always been the strongest guide at Braelyn. It was one of the reasons the previous Myern had allowed Kai to guide Lyr to Earth on his missions despite their friendship and youth. But grabbing a strand, examining it, was nothing like becoming part of it.

In this moment, joined to Earth's energy field and the very force linking the dimensions, he could create a strand to anywhere. Usually, he followed the line from Moranaia to Earth, then chose the appropriate sub-strand to the portal exit he wanted. Now he could make a direct line to anywhere.

That was far from all he could do, but right now, it was more than enough.

Locked with the rift as he was, he sensed Eri and Loki approaching. What in the…? Instinctively, he reinforced his hold on the strands. Just in time. They did something, joined in some way, and the world tipped into chaos.

Hold the strands as they are.

Kai didn't question if the words were his own or from an outside source.

Instead, he did his best to obey.

Aris might have screamed, but he was too disconnected from himself to know. He struggled against the power swamping him and tried to pull his consciousness back to his body more fully. But it was agony when he did. Muscles clenched until they spasmed, lungs heaving for air. He sucked in a deep breath.

Part of him wanted to retreat once more from the anguish. But he'd lived through worse, and he would no longer back down. *"What did they do?"* he sent to Kezari.

"They are laying the groundwork," she answered, a hint of wonder in her voice. *"A base here. A link between Earth and Moranaia. The girl bears blood of both. She is the key."*

He cracked his eyes open as the blinding light began to settle. The jagged gashes of the rift were gone, replaced by an oblong column of glowing energy. Beneath it, a stalagmite grew upward, stretching toward the light. Aris was just able to make out Eri and Loki on the other side of the new fissure.

The little girl's dark hair drifted in tendrils around her placid

face, no sign of distress in her demeanor. In contrast, Loki's hair and eyes flamed, his entire body tense as he poured himself into manipulating the energy. In Aris's magical sight, the god blazed as brightly as the rift itself. And was just as volatile.

"We should help," Kezari said.

Aris frowned. *"How?"*

"Step into the fissure, and I will show you," she answered. *"A working like this will require this kind of boundless energy."*

Kezari lifted her head, her long neck extending until her snout almost touched the rift. Aris unclenched his leg muscles from where they'd clamped around the base of her neck and forced himself to his feet. *This is madness.* But he balanced carefully between her shoulder blades and crept up the ridge of her neck toward the surging light.

Half way to the rift, Aris glanced across the chamber. Kai huddled in the same place, his skin ashen as he fought to hold onto the strands. Through their mental link, Aris caught nothing but resolve.

Selia and Iren, however, were curled up on the ground. Not moving.

Had Selia not sensed his regard and managed to meet his eyes, he would have leapt down from Kezari and cursed them all.

"We are not hurt," Selia sent. *"Whatever you are planning, do it. I love you."*

"I love you, too."

His attention shifted wholly to the rift, then, and he shivered. Stepping into this core of power was a foolish move, but it was the right one. He could better control what happened with the energy from the inside.

Aris took a deep breath, said a quick prayer, and leaped inside.

Selia's cry blended with Iren's when Aris disappeared into the column of light. What was he thinking? She'd expected him to insert a hand like Eri and Loki. But one moment, he was balanced on Kezari's snout, and the next, he was engulfed in the glow. She could barely see his body suspended in the center.

Watch the entrance.

The god's words rang through her head as though he'd just spoken them. Despite his apparent preoccupation, maybe he had. She shoved Iren behind her and spun to face the tunnel that lead into the chamber. Sure enough, a tall, thin woman stood in the dim shadows between the dark tunnel and the light cast by the rift. In her hand, a knife gleamed.

What in the world? Who would... A flickering gleam from the fissure lightened the woman's face, bringing a memory to life. But not one of Selia's. Laughing, blood dripping from a knife held high. Perim. This was Perim. What was she doing here?

Selia connected with Iren immediately. *"Get behind Kezari and stay out of sight. I mean it, Iren. That's the woman who tortured your father."*

Surprisingly, he didn't argue. But the whispered answer he gave as he darted out of view gave its own explanation why. *"I know."*

Gods, he must have picked up on Aris's memories somehow. Selia ached for Iren, for the things he must have seen were more than any child should have to deal with. Her hands clenched, that bittersweet pain morphing into anger. And the *drec* who'd caused it all wanted to do yet more harm.

Not on her watch.

Selia reached into her pocket for an energy crystal. There was enough magic swirling through the room to power an entire working group's spells, but she dared not use it. There was too much risk of unbalancing whatever the others were doing. She'd have to be careful

with any spells she used, but she had little choice. Inona might have non-magical weapons tucked in every fold of her unusual Earth clothing, but Selia was no warrior.

At least the wretched woman's scowl was pinned to Loki's back and not on Selia. But as nice as it would be for Perim to be foolish enough to attack a god, Selia wasn't relying on it. She reinforced the layers of her protective shields as she eased toward the edge of the cavern. If Perim crossed into the room, Selia might be able to sneak behind her. Unlikely, but it was something.

Quickly, she scanned the woman's shields. Good. Only a few layers designed to repel basic attacks, a standard mirror shield at the end. Selia could counter that, even the one designed to reflect magic back.

Now what would be the best spell to use? Selia ran through her mental catalogue of the most painful ways to kill. *Inverting flesh. Teleporting away a few choice organs. Transfiguring blood into water.* The first would be too grisly with Iren present. The others… She heaved an inner sigh. They might give a moment's satisfaction, but they would render her no better than Perim.

Unfortunately, the only spells she knew that would render instant death might cause Aris trouble by unbalancing the magic flowing through the room. It was no easy matter to shut down the mind or the heart of a fae, and Selia was no healer to know the best way. Most of the methods she could perform required a massive amount of energy or the type of life magic her husband wielded.

She'd have to start with incapacitation.

Suddenly, the blond woman turned a smirking glance Selia's way. "Surely you didn't believe I hadn't noticed you?"

Freezing in place, Selia gathered the spell she'd used on Vek and Kai into her hand until her fingers tingled. "How did you get here?"

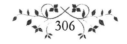

"A friend told me how to find my errant soulbonded." Perim shrugged. "What good fortune to find him so thoroughly indisposed."

"But not alone." Selia studied the woman. She was beautiful, her delicate features similar enough to Meli's that Aris's reaction to the Ljósálfar woman became clear, but Perim's eyes held a crazed glint the other's lacked. "Unlike you. You might have had an informant, but I don't believe you had a friend."

"Shut up." Perim lifted the knife and jiggled it. "Why should I care what you think when I have more important things to take care of? I can almost touch the red-haired one from here. Would you like me to begin with him? Or perhaps he isn't important enough to get Aris to come out to play."

Selia almost loosed the spell, but she hesitated. The other woman was too confident in the presence of so much power. Even with the rest of the group preoccupied, Perim was far outnumbered. She had to be hiding something, some weapon besides the knife. Perhaps a magical ability? None of Aris's memories included images of the woman doing magic, but that didn't mean she couldn't.

"You're Selia, aren't you?" Perim demanded with a sneer.

Selia lifted her brows. "What do you know of me?"

"Only what Aris whimpered or screamed when he was barely coherent."

That was more than enough. Selia cast her spell at the other woman, only to realize her mistake almost instantly. In her haste, she'd given Perim's shielding only a cursory examination—an apprentice's mistake. Her spell pierced the first couple of layers, but when it hit the third, part was absorbed and the rest rebounded.

The inner layer of Selia's own shielding held the counter for the original in case of that very thing. However, whatever piece

the shield had absorbed altered the spell enough to slice through Selia's defenses as it bounced back. It captured control of her body, inhibiting her muscles so thoroughly that only her organs were able to move.

Her heart pounded in her frozen chest as though it wanted to break free. Panic threatened, but she couldn't let it consume. She'd created this spell, and whatever that shield had done to alter it, she could erase. If she had time. Perim advanced, a wicked smile twisting her lips, and wiggled the knife again.

As the woman began to circle her, disappearing periodically from view, Selia blocked her out. Instead, she delved into the components of her spell. The bulk of the immobilization portion was there—obviously. Ah, yes. That small fragment of Selia's power, the signature left by all mages, was missing, replaced by Perim's. A tiny but crucial change.

With deft mental fingers, Selia began to unwind the pieces the kept her muscles locked. Strand by strand, she pulled the components free from the other woman's energy. Something cool slid along her cheek. She ignored it. A pinch of pain along her arm almost distracted her, but she kept her focus firm.

Finally, she dissolved the enchantment and dispelled the remnants of Perim's energy. Her muscles went lax all at once, and she stumbled as her legs almost gave out beneath her. She threw her arms out to the sides to try to regain her balance but still almost went down.

Searing agony shrieked from her shoulder, heralded by an ominous crack. From somewhere, Iren cried out her name. As Selia dropped to her knees, she could only pray he didn't try to rescue her. *Miaran,* the pain… She couldn't move her left arm without almost blacking out.

She spun, tumbling onto her bottom with a thump that drew a scream of pain from her throat. Perim stood over her with a triumphant grin. Blood dripped from the tip of her knife and plopped onto the stone beneath them. For a moment, time suspended as they stared at one another.

Selia's shirt clung to her back, and a suspicious amount of wetness soaked the upper edge of her pants. She didn't have enough healing gift to probe the depths of the injury, but she suspected it was bad. If she was going to defeat Perim, she'd have to move fast.

"Iren," she sent. *"Contact your father. Now."*

"I can blast her from back here."

"Now," Selia ordered.

She darted forward and slammed her hand against Perim's ankle. Then Selia shoved her own surprise spell straight through the woman's shields.

28

Aris would never experience life quite this way again.

He could touch any lifeform. Alter or destroy it. But first, he would have to find it. He swam in a sea of life magic, and though he could pick out individuals here and there, like a single grain of salt, retrieving anything specific would be impossible. Only Kezari anchored him, but even she struggled with her merging.

"What do you want me to do now?" he asked her.

"A gate must be created." Her thoughts quieted briefly as she considered. *"The energy that was released here is reverberating through Earth. I suspect a great deal is about to change. We need a faster connection between Earth and Moranaia than the Veil and a safe place for our people to stay once they arrive."*

Cold washed over him. *"I can't set up something like that. Selia or Kai, maybe, but—"*

"The god and the girl will handle the gate," Kezari interrupted. *"It's the fortress we must construct. Hidden. This place will require constant guard. I will build the tunnels and chambers. You find a way to give them life. We'll never have this kind of access to raw energy again."*

He followed Kezari with his mind through the layers of earth to the very top of the mountain. Meticulously, she formed tubes for air and light, doorways and stairs, hallways and rooms. And he trailed behind, cajoling plants to life where he could. Moss and vines to obscure. Flowers in the entry, along with a few small fruit-bearing trees. In one large chamber where Kezari had brought in a fair amount of natural light with a crystal set into the tube above, he coaxed forth the beginning of several crops.

As Kezari directed her attention to the original entrances to this cave system, closing them permanently, uneasiness began to invade his consciousness. He didn't need to create life where she sealed the rocks. He should return to the fortress and do more work there. But he couldn't. Something was wrong. Some discordant energy amidst the flow.

His muscles clenched. All of the sudden, he felt exposed. His body was suspended in the column of light, and he couldn't see beyond it no matter how much he squinted. Were the others safe? Selia? Iren? Another hint of that dark power brushed him, and he let out a mental cry at the sensation.

Perim.

Impossible. She was on Moranaia, hiding on the dragons' isle. Could his connection to life energy stretch that far? His throat burned, and Aris swallowed down bile. He sensed Kezari's concern, but he was too paralyzed with fear to reassure her.

Then his son's voice broke into his mind. *"Onaiala is in trouble. She's hurt. That woman is here."*

Fury and pain coalesced until Aris burned with it. The light flared around him, and he let the power build within him. *"I will do what I can."*

"There's a lot of blood. Hurry."

Blood.

Shuddering, Aris reached for Kezari. *"Selia is under attack. I must descend."*

"Not unarmed, skizik.*"*

Connected as they were, he didn't have to ask what she meant. Aris held out his hand, fingers slightly cupped, as Kezari gathered the energy and concentrated it, forming metal into blade while he grew a hilt of living wood. The column sparked green as together they fired the sword—honed it.

When it finally settled against his palm, Aris tightened his fingers around the hilt and let the cool comfort of life ease the fear coating his mouth. Perim had done her best to destroy him, but she'd failed. And he would die a thousand times before he let her kill his beloved.

Perim screamed, and Selia almost released her out of instinct at the sound. Her stomach lurched. But even as revulsion swamped her, she continued pouring the jagged energy straight into the other woman. Like lightning striking water, the charge continued into Perim until it reached the shield Selia had cast to contain it.

The knife clattered to the floor and the woman toppled. Selia slammed her body over Perim's as the energy crystal sputtered out, and her own cry sounded at the pain in her shoulder. But training had taught Selia to disconnect temporarily from her body. She ignored the agony shrieking at her mind and shifted until she straddled Perim, her knees digging into the woman's shoulders.

Perim's head lolled against the stone, and her breath came in gasps. Selia stared down at Perim's cruel but beautiful face. So much

pain caused by one person, and for what? Everyone knew you couldn't force a bond.

"Why?" Selia snapped as the woman blinked up at her.

"Escape," Perim whispered. "I didn't want to die there. I needed to control a dragon. Make it fly me free."

Selia's fingers balled into a fist. "I don't suppose you considered asking Aris and Kezari for help?"

"I will not be dependent on another. Can't count on anyone but yourself." Perim shifted beneath her. "Not even for a bond. I never would have kept him, you know. I would have killed him first."

Her vision whitened with fury, and for once, Selia didn't reach for her magic. Instead, she slammed her fist into the woman's nose with the force of seven years' worth of agony. Her cry of pain mingled with Perim's, and Selia wavered on the edge of consciousness as the wound in her shoulder tore with the motion. But it was worth it. So very worth it.

Should've teleported her gods-cursed heart to another dimension.

Selia shook out her hand and wondered if the blood was hers or Perim's. Didn't matter. The woman heaved beneath her, struggling, so Selia lifted herself up and slammed back down to knock the air from the other's lungs. Perim's breath rushed out, and she went still.

But Selia barely noticed. The light was blurring, Perim's face a swirling mass of blood and hatred. *Clechtan.* She couldn't lose consciousness now. Perim would kill her for sure and then try for Aris.

Or Iren.

Selia shoved her trembling fingers in her pocket and scrabbled for another energy crystal. She would empty herself accessing it, but it was all she had. If she died torturing someone, it would be better than letting this woman loose on the others.

Blood transmutation. That might be the easiest from her current position.

Gods forgive her soul.

As Aris shoved his body free of the rift, rock rose from below to meet his feet. He blinked to clear his vision, but his mind and spirit were still linked with the column behind him. Around the rift, Kezari was creating a framework for the portal from stone, but he was more concerned with his son. Aris could sense him nearby, but his sight kept blurring. Finally, Iren's pale face clarified as Aris descended to the floor of the cavern. His son practically vibrated with energy, life magic but other elements, too.

"I can't get a clear shot," Iren said, his voice ringing with pain. "I could do a fireball, but…"

A new kind of energy buzzed through the air, and Aris spun to face the source. Selia stooped over a prone Perim, but the surge of power obscured his physical sight after a couple of heartbeats. His beloved was about to cast a spell, and it had the taste of darkness.

"Selia!" Aris shouted.

Or he tried to. He had no clue which dimension the words rang into, and he didn't wait to find out. He hefted the glowing sword in his hand as he charged across the space between them. He might not have begun the bonding process with Perim, but stabbing her was going to hurt.

"You'll kill yourself," Perim gasped.

That voice had delivered years of cruelty, a torment beyond the physical. It had become his inner voice—but no more. He would fill the dark abyss of her influence with his own power even if he died in the process.

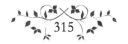

As his rage mounted, the real world became clearer. Just enough. He could see what was needed to end Perim's life. "Move back, Selia."

She shoved herself away, rolling from Perim with a cry of pain. As Perim scrambled up to her elbows, fear overcoming her usual mocking expression, Aris shoved the tip of his sword downward, straight into her heart.

Then he twisted. The blade was forged in life, but the opposite side was death. A verdict he had no qualms about delivering. He shoved his magic through the sword, the perfect conduit, until his vision went green from the glow. With another twist, he ordered the spark of life to return to the ether.

There must be no mistake. No way for her to escape death.

Aris did his best to shield himself, but the backlash was pure agony. He fell to his knees, buffeted by the storm Perim's death unleashed. His fingers tightened on the hilt of his sword, and he jerked it free. He would have no more connection to her, not even through the blade of a sword.

He sensed Kezari, then, wrapping her mind around his as she often did her wings around his body. The storm faded, and Perim's darkened spirit passed fully into the next life. He neither knew nor cared where her soul would end up. Judgement was for the gods. As he opened his eyes to focus on her lifeless face, he felt none of the satisfaction he'd dreamed of for all those years.

All that coursed through him was relief.

"Onaial?" Iren asked softly from behind him.

"I'm here," Aris said. An odd comment, but somehow fitting. "Guide me to your mother. My vision…"

Iren's hand wrapped around his arm as Aris shoved to his feet. Still bound to the rift, he tried to keep the power coursing through him from leeching over, but his son hissed out a breath and jerked

free. "Sorry, I…" Iren stuttered. "Just circle the…the body here. She's on the other side."

A shiver passed through Aris at those words. The other side. He didn't care where Perim had gone, but he certainly cared about Selia. He followed Iren around Perim's corpse. Selia wavered in and out of his sight, a dark stain pooling beneath her huddled body.

Aris knelt beside her, settling his sword to the side. He would not touch her with Perim's blood, though the blade itself might be able to aid in the healing. He didn't need it. He rested his hand on her back. Selia's chest fluttered with breath—but barely. Without thought, he reached for the power his connection to the rift granted.

He grasped life. Wholeness.

Then he directed it into Selia.

Selia forced her eyes open as the power inside her waned. For a moment, she feared she'd taken damage to her vision, for the nearly blinding light had faded to a dim glow. But the world clarified quickly, settling into Aris's glowing face.

She gasped. His skin shimmered, and his eyes blazed green as he stared at her. It had been his power filling her, returning her torn flesh to its original life. What had happened? She'd been constructing her final spell against Perim when Aris had cried out for her to stop. After that, there was only darkness.

He wasn't himself. Normally, his forehead would be creased with worry lines, and he'd be demanding she tell him how she felt. But there was a fathomless weight to his regard, a hint that he wasn't quite…alone. Or perhaps he was only more aware, more powerful. With her second sight, his link to Earth's energy glowed like the sun.

Selia reached up a hand and cupped his cheek. Ever so slightly, he leaned into her touch, and his gaze softened. "I must..." he began, his voice low and rough. "The rift."

"Go," she whispered. "But bring yourself back to me. And only you next time."

She thought his lips curved upward, but he stood and bent to pick something up before she got a good look. As he strode away, Selia gathered her energy and shifted herself to a sitting position. Her head spun, but the sensation passed quickly. Just in time to see Aris approach...an archway formed of stalactites and stalagmites? That hadn't been here before she'd passed out. A set of steps led up to the bright white of the former rift, now anchored between the stone.

What was going on?

Selia could barely make out the forms of Eri and Loki on each side of the stairs, their hands still entwined with the light beside the base of the arch. Her body trembled as she shoved herself to her feet with the aid of a stalagmite. But her gaze stayed on Aris as she rose, even after he disappeared into the gate.

"You're okay!"

At Iren's cry, she turned to her son. He rushed toward her, his arms open, but she held up her hands. "I'm covered in blood, my love."

Iren's brow furrowed. "No, you're not."

Frowning, Selia glanced down. He was right. Her clothes were smeared with dirt, and both her pants and shirt bore several small tears. But no blood. She studied the back of her right hand, but there wasn't so much as a scar to show where she'd broken her skin punching Perim. That was almost a shame. She would've loved showing that trophy off.

Selia held out her arms and sighed with contentment when Iren threw himself against her for a hug. "I guess you're right."

29

Power wavered on the air and thrummed through the floor beneath Vek's feet. The electricity was out, so a ball of mage light illuminated the unusual group gathered in his living room. His skin prickled as his gaze landed on Naomh sitting on one side of the long couch. A Seelie Sidhe lord in his living room. Unbelievable.

Caolte leaned against the window frame, the Chattanooga skyline at his back. Young Maddy knelt beside Fen's prone form on the other end of the L-shaped couch, and her girlfriend, Anna, perched beside Naomh and nibbled on the tip of her finger as she stared at Fen. A veritable party of beings Vek never would have invited into his home.

But as needs must.

He paced in front of the window and behind the couch, finally stopping to lean on the back and study his nephew. Fen was deathly pale, his moans now silent. The girl was doing some kind of scan, and the energy had Vek's teeth grinding together. Better than Naomh's attempt, though, which had released so much Sidhe magic into the air that Vek had wanted to vomit.

He'd borne that indignity, and it hadn't even helped. Naomh hadn't been able to heal the poison—he'd tried while they waited for Maddy to pick them up. Perhaps his lack of connection to the environment had altered the results. He'd refused to set foot on the ground, hovering like an idiot where anyone could come along and see.

"If Maddy's attempt fails, perhaps Naomh should try again," Vek said. "He might be able to properly ground his magic now."

Naomh sneered. "A talented mage does not need to touch the soil to connect with its power."

"To keep to this foolish pact—"

"Your kind might have chosen to forgo your word, but we of the Seelie are nobler than that."

Vek let out a snort. "You're full of something, but nobility isn't it. Why do you respect a treaty the humans barely remember?"

"We gave an oath, and—"

"You didn't give anything," Vek interrupted, leaning forward. "Your ancestors promised the human sons of Mil that you wouldn't step foot on the surface, sure. Of Ireland. You ceded *Ireland,* not fucking Chattanooga on the other side of the world. Stop hovering like an idiot whenever we go outside."

A choked noise echoed from the window. Then Caolte burst out laughing, the sound so sudden and unexpected that Vek stared. "What?"

Caolte shook his head, a grin wreathing his face. "I pointed out something similar on our last visit to this region. Perhaps he'll listen for once."

Vek's brow lowered. "Really?"

"Maybe it's my Unseelie blood, but..." Caolte waved a hand. "I think it's foolishness at this point. Besides, from the feel of the energy increasing like the tide, I'd say things are about to change."

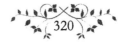

Naomh crossed his arms, his jaw clenching. Why did he cling so tightly to the old ways? Vek studied the Sidhe lord curiously. He obviously wasn't a stickler, or he wouldn't be here at all. Thousands of years before, the Sidhe had lost a war with the humans, Milesians, and sworn to remove themselves to the underhill realms a dimension away. The oldest wouldn't allow their feet to touch the surface, but they also wouldn't consider entering an Unseelie prince's living room.

Beside Fen, Maddy stirred, her eyelids fluttering open. "I can't fix it, either," she whispered.

Vek muttered a curse beneath his breath. "I don't understand. The energy fields are clear now. There was no mistaking that after the final wave."

"Maybe it wasn't connected to the rift," Maddy said with a frown. "He took Kien's blood, right? He could have done something to it before passing it along to Fen."

Silence fell. Then Anna's voice lilted across the quiet. "Water won't cure it."

Vek's attention swiveled to the half human in surprise. Her other blood had gotten stronger, augmented by the surge of energy that had swept through an hour or so before. Her features had taken on a sharper fae cast, and her aura hummed with the power of rapids and the depths of oceans. If she was anything to go by, there was going to be a problem. The magical races hadn't exactly been shy about sleeping around, so scores of humans could soon have latent fae blood surging to the forefront.

Caolte was correct—a great deal was going to change.

"We need to find a more experienced healer. One with more power." Maddy gave Naomh an apologetic glance. "No offense."

The Sidhe lord ran his fingers through his hair, his expression troubled. "None taken. You are correct to seek expert aid. My gift for healing is small."

Vek's shoulders slumped for a moment, but he forced himself to straighten as he peered at his nephew. He'd failed Fen enough over the years. That trend would not continue. "First, we'll see what happens when the others return. If they fixed the rift, they might yet heal Fen."

Of course, the geniuses had broken open the wall shielding the extra energy from Earth. They could've found another solution for the poison if he'd sealed it instead. Probably. There was no telling what damage that final wave had done across Earth. It had taken down the electricity here, and Maddy's cellphone had no signal, so they were cut off from outside news.

That release hadn't been the only consequence, either. Vek felt like he was standing in a cave, the water slowly rising from an unseen source. The life-dealer and the dragon must have channeled the bulk of the power into the natural energy field. Now the power his people had worked so hard to seal away would return to Earth, whether they were ready or not.

Here's hoping we don't all drown in it.

"It's time to disconnect, skizik. *"*

Aris floated. With each moment, the magic had become more a part of him. Did he breathe still? His body seemed a distant concept, one of billions of heartbeats forming a symphony inside of him. He could stay here and join with infinite life.

'Skizik. *"*

Something pushed at his mind. Kezari. *"What?"*

"Disconnect, or we will remain here forever."

Lightness filled him at the thought. He could exist here in this place, free from pain. Explore this nexus of life. Such purity here. Who but the gods had ever experienced it in its fullness? Even connected now, Aris's comprehension was small. But if he had endless time to wander, perhaps he could attain such understanding.

Forever.

We will remain here forever.

Kezari's words replayed in his head, a discordant note amidst the hymn of life. We. *We* will remain. Linked as they were, he'd doom Kezari, too. She'd done so much to shield him. She'd saved him. He could not reward her with a living death.

And his family waited.

The song of the rift became a dirge. Infinite loneliness. There was no life without his family. What had he been thinking? Selia and Iren were worth foregoing this power. They were everything.

With a lurch, he struggled back toward his body. He wiggled his fingers, and the sword almost dropped from his right hand. He still held it? He circled his wrists and shrugged his shoulders. A deep ache tickled in the back of his mind and then bloomed to full life as he became aware of his body, stiff and sore from the force of the power he'd wielded. He groaned, but he let himself return.

Then something wrapped around his wrist and tugged.

He stumbled down the stairs, his legs so weak that he would have crumpled if not for Loki's hold. No mistaking the man for anything but a god now. His flaming hair stood on end and his eyes blazed as he gripped Aris's shoulders to keep him from falling.

"You were not supposed to want to stay."

Aris wavered in the god's hold. "I didn't want to. Not really."

One red eyebrow rose. "Could've fooled me, elf."

"I might have gotten a bit…lost."

How could he explain what it was like to merge with such power? How he'd abandoned himself, and his will, without even realizing? But there was a serious gleam in the god's eyes that suggested that he knew. Of course, he must. Heat crept up Aris's neck at the memory of Loki standing with his hand in the rift. Yes, he knew.

Aris gave a short nod. "Thank you for your aid."

"I do hope you won't get used to it," Loki answered, though a grin lightened the words. "Time for me to go. Enjoy the gift."

Between one blink and the next, the god was gone, taking his powerful energy with him. Aris's legs crumpled immediately, too weak to hold his weight. He'd been serious about not getting used to his help, it seemed.

Footsteps pounded against the stone. "Aris?"

"I'm fine, Selia," he answered. He leaned against one of the steps as he glanced around. "Only tired. The others?"

Eri stepped into his line of sight, pale and serious but otherwise unharmed. "The god shielded me."

He peered around the frame of the new portal as Selia and Iren reached him. Kezari's side, and thankfully, her belly moved with breath. Even so, he sought her through their connection. *"Were you injured?"*

"No." Her mental voice was slow, almost a whisper, but she didn't sound distressed. *"I only need rest."*

Good. That left Kai.

Aris peered into the shadows beside the portal where the other man had been. At first, he didn't see him, but after a moment, Aris made out the elf's crumpled form. *Miaran.* His fingers tightened around the sword hilt, drawing in power from the rift-forged blade, and he stumbled to his feet. He should have monitored their link

better instead of lingering in the portal. If the other man was injured, it would be Aris's fault.

He forced himself to move, but the distance between them felt eternal. Fortunately, Selia caught sight of Kai and darted across the space far faster than Aris could currently manage. She bent over him, and her power hummed on the air as she scanned the fallen elf.

"He's alive," she said. "But in shock, I think."

Aris staggered, his hand shooting out for purchase. His palm found the side of a natural stone column, and he leaned against it to catch his breath. They needed to get Kai back to Moranaia, but there was no way Aris could carry him. If he didn't rest, he'd have to be hauled out of here, too.

"How are we going to get him to the healer?" he asked.

Selia stretched out a hand, and Kai rose silently from the cave floor. Iren rushed forward and helped his mother straighten the elf until he rested on his back in midair. Then she guided his prone form across the space, walking just behind him. Aris's brows lifted. Although her face was lined with exhaustion and sweat glistened on her skin, she didn't falter.

"It's going to be tough to get back without our guide, isn't it?" Iren followed his mother, a frown of concern focused on Kai. "And the old exit is gone."

The old exit. Aris scrubbed a hand across his face and studied the cavern. Hazily, he recalled working with Kezari to reform the mountain, but he'd been too concerned about the others to care what it looked like when he'd first emerged. The tunnel where they'd entered was gone. Instead, a staircase rose from the spot to spiral up the cavern wall.

Far above, alcoves branched into tunnels, and those led to a variety of rooms. A fortress, Kezari had said. Entranced by the

Earth's power, he hadn't given it much thought as he'd filled those rooms with the beginnings of life. But if this portal worked as he believed, the fortified outpost would be a necessity. In a few years, it would be as elaborate as any underhill home.

"I think the rift goes directly to Moranaia," Aris said. "No Veil necessary."

Iren wrinkled his nose. "You were inside it, but you don't know for sure?"

"It is difficult for a fish to analyze the water or a bird to study the air," Aris tried to explain. "For a while, I simply…was. I lost sight of what the others were doing."

A surge of light sprang from the portal, and Aris straightened in alarm. Testing the energy, he found much more available than before. Earth was absorbing all they'd poured in and dispersing it until there was almost as much magic available as on Moranaia. He pulled it in greedily as several elves marched out of the gate.

They surrounded the small platform at the top of the stairs, ringing Eri in their midst, and Aris heaved himself forward in alarm. Then he examined the uniforms they wore. Dark leather, a grayish-brown shade worn only by the *loreln*, personal bodyguards to the royal family. They'd barely come to a halt before Prince Ralan himself strode through.

"Moranai Aldiaberen i Erinalia Moreln nai Moranaia," Ralan snapped at his daughter, and Aris couldn't help but wince on her behalf. The full title was never good. "I can't believe… This was not supposed to happen for…"

Eri wrapped her arms around her father's waist and burrowed against his side. "It was time."

"Our home isn't close to finished yet, and now there's a portal entrance sitting out in the open." Although his voice rang with

exasperation, Ralan's fingers tangled carefully in Eri's hair. "How could it possibly be the right time? I'm lucky that we installed the local gate to Braelyn, or it would have taken a couple of marks to reach you."

"If I hadn't come here when I did…"

Ralan bent down and lifted Eri into his arms. "You may explain your actions in your room."

"I know, *Onaial*," she whispered.

"Let's go." Ralan's gaze flicked from Selia to Aris and back over to Kai. "All of you. Kezari will rest here and direct the guards I send through. Aris and Selia, you will need to go help Fen as best you can, but with the current state of Earth, I don't recommend transporting yourselves to the original portal. You're too unfamiliar with this world. If you come with me back to Braelyn, Delbin and Inona can guide you through."

Although the calmly spoken words were clearly an order, Aris hesitated. Leave Kezari on Earth while he traveled to Moranaia? Before he could protest, the dragon gave him a mental nudge. *"It will be a while before I can shift,* skizik. *I will be fine here. Go."*

Aris swallowed his protest. This solution made the most sense, and he *had* promised the Unseelie prince that he would try to help Fen. If Ralan had Seen the need for him to do so, then it must be important. Aris pulled in more energy and willed himself to walk forward. There would be no time to rest before their next task, so he might as well get used to being exhausted.

He clapped his hand on Iren's shoulder as he caught up. "You'll be staying in your room."

"I guessed as much." Iren rubbed at his eyes, the deep circles beneath standing out on his fair skin. "I think…I think I'm fine with that."

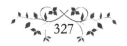

As they neared the stairs to the portal, Aris caught sight of Perim's body, abandoned near the wall of the cave. He gestured in her direction. "My captor has been brought to justice. I trust you'll see her buried?"

Ralan's nostrils flared. "I'll be certain of it."

Burial might not have been an insult to her people, but it was to his. Spirit and ash would not be released to ride the winds and merge with nature, though the worms would certainly be thankful for the feast. Provided they consumed her waste of flesh.

He turned his back on Perim, focusing on Selia as she directed Kai's still form to the waiting *loreln*. As soon as two of the guards took hold of Kai, the others filed through the portal ahead of Ralan and Eri. Then the prince and his daughter followed.

After the *loreln* and Kai were gone, Selia advanced. Aris squeezed Iren's shoulder and nudged him toward the portal. Then after one last word to Kezari, he strode through without looking back.

30

There was only a slight wrench as Selia followed the guards through the portal. She could have been crossing between estates less than a day away from one another, not passing across fathomless space. But she barely had time to marvel. As soon as she stepped through, cold rain soaked through her clothes and the light of morning had her squinting after the dimness of the cavern. It had been several marks before dawn when they'd left. Had so much time passed in that cave?

It had felt like next to nothing, yet eternal.

Selia glanced around the building site as she waited for Iren and Aris to follow her through. Only a few days had passed since construction had begun on the palace, so there was little to see. Underbrush had been cleared away and a few trees culled to make room. It appeared that Ralan had decided to use similar architecture to Braelyn, wrapping the structure around the largest of the trees, and there was already a framework at the base of one trunk.

There'd been a great deal of speculation about this new palace. Now, Selia had some idea why Ralan had ordered its creation. She spun around to face the stone arch situated in the center of the clearing as Iren emerged. It was all for this. Lyr might be in charge of diplomacy between Moranaia and the dimensions connected to Earth, but a direct gate that bypassed the Veil? All manner of problems could arise that would require quick decisions from the king, and the heir to the throne had more leeway to act in his stead.

Like setting up a colony on another planet. No small thing, that.

Aris finally shuffled through, the exhaustion on his face mirroring the heavy weight of her own body. He took her hand when he reached her side, and together they headed toward the smaller arch on the other side of the clearing. Ralan and the others had already passed through to Braelyn, although six of the *loreln* stood in clear view, guarding the area. Gods knew how many more perched in the trees.

She and Aris followed Iren through the gate and straight into chaos. The entryway of Lyr's estate was packed with people, enough that a couple of the guards stood beneath the arch next to the sacred tree. Arlyn, Lyr, and Meli gathered around Kai in the center of the room, while Ralan and Eri conferred with Cora next to the steps to the upper rooms. Several *sonal* and *loreln* waited at attention at regular intervals in case of danger.

Lial's voice cut across the noise as he tried to push through. "Out of the way."

Selia tugged Aris to get his attention and pointed toward Eradisel. He nodded, and together, they herded Iren to the side until they stood beside the trunk of the sacred tree. By the stairs, Ralan handed Eri to Cora and motioned for the *loreln* to follow him back into the portal to the new palace. Lyr commanded most of the *sonal* out of the room, leaving only two beside the gate.

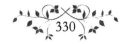

"Stop crowding," Lial said as he shoved himself between Arlyn and Lyr.

Arlyn lowered herself to her knees beside Kai's head. "He's alive. Something they did when creating the portal must have drained him. I felt him slip into unconsciousness from here."

Lial nodded. "Probably shock. Get him upstairs, and I'll heal him. Why did you put him in the middle of the floor?"

"We weren't certain how far we should move him," Lyr said.

With a quick spell, Lial levitated Kai and strode toward the stairs. "Come along, Arlyn. And anyone else who feels the need to trail me like a woebegone child over a simple case of burnout."

Despite the healer's taunting words, Lyr, Meli, and Arlyn followed close behind him. "Might as well since I can't question Ralan about what's going on. What little I heard is insanity enough," Lyr said. At the base of the stairs, Lyr glanced back toward Selia. "Come with us, Iren. I'll ensure you remain in your room while your parents meet Delbin and Inona at the gate. And I will take that invisibility cloak."

"Yes, Myern." Iren jogged over to Lyr almost eagerly, and Selia smiled at the hint of relief in her son's voice. He was brave, but he was still just a boy. One who had seen more than enough adventure. "I'll do what I'm told. I promise."

They'd all have to take advantage of *that* while they could.

Selia and Aris slumped against one another for a moment as their son disappeared up the stairs. Suddenly, they were alone, save for the two guards stationed by the now-empty arch that held the local transportation gate. Even Cora had slipped out with Eri. Now silence held sway, and Selia was loathe to break it.

How was she ever going to rebuild enough energy to cross back to Earth and save Fen? Not that she had a choice. She was exhausted, her clothes torn and dirty. Gods knew what kind of mess

her hair was—she didn't even want to touch it for fear of the tangles. But they'd promised to help the young blood elf, so help they would.

With a regretful sigh, she straightened. Aris swayed on his feet before he caught himself, and when he lifted his arms slightly for balance, the sword he held caught her eye. "Aren't you going to sheathe that?"

He scanned the blade almost absently. "There's no scabbard. I don't know where to put it."

"What about the one on your belt?" she asked, lifting a brow.

"On my…" His gaze slipped to his belt, and after a moment, he chuckled. "Well. Looks like Loki had one more bit of aid after all."

Selia studied the leather, bending down a bit to better see the engraving. A perfect replica of the rift as they'd first seen it was surrounded by a line of symbols she couldn't read. She trailed her fingers across the surface and shivered at the spark of contained power. She'd love to probe the spells embedded within, but there was no way she was messing with a god-created object without a great deal of preparation.

Shrugging, Aris twisted away enough to sheathe his sword. The life energy radiating from the blade disappeared, and with a panicked expression, he pulled it free once more. The energy around it returned to Selia's inner sight, and she smiled.

"That's a handy enchantment for when you don't want to announce the sword's power," she said.

"Yes, if a bit disconcerting." He sheathed the blade once more and took her hand. "Ready to go?"

She entwined her fingers with his. "Let's get this over with. Maybe then we can sleep."

As they trudged toward the front door, a wave of energy swept through her, a gift from the sacred tree. Selia sent a quick thanks to

Eradisel. She wasn't restored to full power, of course, but she no longer felt like she would drop over from exhaustion.

A welcome gift, indeed.

After becoming a living part of the new portal, traversing the Veil was practically tame. For once, Aris was content to shirk further adventure. The trip was short, smoother than the last, and once they emerged, he let himself pause to take in a deep breath of the Earth air. This time, the sky had gone dim with the dusk, and the shadow of the ridge behind them stretched across the small clearing.

"That's the easiest the strands have been to follow in quite a long time," Inona said. "Maybe ever."

Selia glanced at the scout. "Kai was in charge of aligning the strands when the new portal was set. He knows this route better than anyone, so I suspect it's his doing."

"Probably."

Delbin shifted from Inona's side, striding a few paces away before holding up a glowing rectangle. The young elf frowned up at the thing and turned it in all different directions. What was he doing? Finally, he gave up and rejoined the group.

"No phone signal," Delbin said, glaring down at the device.

That didn't clarify things. "Is that a problem?" Aris asked.

"It is if you want to call someone to come pick you up so you don't have to trek across town." Delbin flipped the rectangle so that Aris could see the face. Beneath a series of colored squares, an image of Delbin and Inona smiled out at him. "See? Nothing."

Aris grimaced. "You're showing me that as though I have a clue what it is."

"Ah, right. You don't know much about this world." Delbin chuckled and tucked the device in his pocket. "It's a cell phone. Imagine a communication mirror that can capture images of the world and connect to libraries full of information. Of course, there are also cat memes, but that won't mean anything to you."

Aris shook his head. Selia had told him that the younger elf had spent much of his life with humans, and it showed. It would be a good thing, too. Aris had a feeling that Delbin would become a powerful liaison between their worlds, a link they might desperately need.

"With your communication…phone inoperable, I suppose we should get moving," Aris said.

"Great," Selia muttered. "More running."

Delbin shoved his hands into his back pockets. "Gotta agree with you on that. Hey, could you teleport us near that gas station we visited earlier? It's closer to Vek's house."

Aris wasn't certain what a gas station was, but Selia appeared to understand. Her tense expression lightened as she nodded. She gestured for them to gather closer to the ridge wall, out of sight of any humans who might get near. It seemed unlikely, since the only houses he could see were a fair distance away, but no need to take a risk.

After a quick step through Selia's temporary gate, they slipped into another forest. Aris jogged behind Delbin and Inona as they rushed between trees, a smooth stone road visible to their left. Earth was a fascinating place, full of unusual buildings and strange technology. Selia pointed out the things she'd already learned about and explained their purpose as they passed.

Power lines. Cars. Fascinating, indeed.

Night had long fallen by the time they approached a house situated on the side of a mountain. Dim light shone through the

windows, and a vehicle sat unoccupied in the…driveway, he thought it was called. A few of those cars had passed by during their race here, but Delbin had been concerned by how few. The human world was busy, he'd said. The lack of life was unusual.

They rested for a moment before knocking on the door. Aris wasn't too winded, but Selia panted for air, and Delbin's face was pale and drawn. As they waited, Inona stared into the valley below with a frown on her face. Aris followed her line of sight but wasn't certain what bothered her. Moonlight gleamed on water and hinted at buildings below.

"There's no power," she said.

Delbin stepped to her side. "Damn. I was worried about that when I couldn't get a signal. The energy surge must have fried the cell towers, too, along with the entire power grid. I really, really hope that didn't spread too far."

"Why?" Aris asked. "Is this vital to humans?"

Delbin nodded. "They use electricity for everything. It's like magic contained, and all of their devices require it. I have no idea how the surge will have affected technology like phones, either. I had this one with me on Moranaia, so it isn't a good indication. But if *everything* is broken, there's going to be panic once everyone figures it out. Chaos."

They'd focused so much on saving Earth from the rift's explosion that they hadn't considered any other effects of that final energy pulse. "Wonderful."

"Maybe the others will know more," Inona said.

The door jerked open before they reached it, and the blood elf stood in the entrance, his eyes a little crazed as he glared at them. "What took you so long?"

"Nice to see you, too, Vek," Delbin quipped.

"Now is not the time. Get in here and help my nephew."

So Naomh hadn't been able to heal Fen. Aris's brow furrowed as he followed the others into the house. A pair of mage lights hovered above, highlighting the unusual dwelling, but his focus was on the young blood elf stretched out on a long, narrow bed on the other end of the room. A red-haired woman with the look of the Sidhe knelt beside him, but Aris detected no energy flowing from her.

He strode across the room, intent on the task at hand, but Naomh leapt to his feet and blocked his path. "Where is my son?"

It took Aris a moment to figure out what the Sidhe lord was asking. "Kai? Back on Moranaia. The healer seems to believe he suffers from shock after using his abilities too much."

"I should go," Naomh said, flicking a glance at Caolte.

His brother nodded. "After you."

As the pair rushed toward the door, Aris continued toward Fen, Selia falling into step beside him. The Sidhe could take care of themselves. He had more important things to worry about—like how he was going to heal the poison inside Fen without Kezari there to help him.

At that thought, her voice broke into his head. *"I have not left you, but I do not have much energy to offer."*

"I'm not certain I can do this," he confessed.

"Nor am I, but not because of your ability." Her faint mental voice was tinged with worry. *"The rift's affliction was not quite the same."*

"I suppose we'll see."

The Sidhe woman glanced up at his approach, and the freckles on her pale face stood out as she studied him. "I hope you can do more than I can. Not that I dare do much."

"I hope so, too."

Aris lowered himself to his knees beside the woman and stretched his hands out over Fen. He closed his eyes, letting himself connect to the ebb and flow of life around them. The blood elf glowed brightly, his power low but impressive, yet the dark blotch hovering near his heart hadn't waned at all. In fact, it might have increased in size.

"Aris." Selia's hand settled on his shoulder. "I have an idea."

He glanced up at her. "Oh?"

"Since Kien had hoped to return to our world, he made certain his first attempt to poison Earth's power would not touch Moranaia. So the spell is vulnerable to Moranaian energy. I helped Arlyn construct the counter." Selia pulled a stone from her pocket. Unlike her typical crystals, this one was round and milky white instead of clear. "I brought this in case it was needed."

"You know I can't use that kind of stone."

She closed her fist around it. "I'll channel the power to you in a form you can utilize."

Aris considered the plan. He wouldn't trust just anyone to perform such a task, since most mages were inexperienced with his talent, but he'd worked with Selia many times. Not quite in this way but close enough. He nodded. "We'll try it."

He let his eyes slip closed as he reached a mental hand for Selia. They joined almost seamlessly, and after he gave his assent, she began to filter energy to him. He grasped it. Tested it. The power had the rich flavor of Moranaia—ancient trees and tall mountains, fertile plains and northern glaciers. He held it close but didn't absorb it, instead letting it merge slightly with his own gift.

Then he turned it toward the poison in Fen's heart.

31

Maddy nibbled on her fingernail before she jerked it free. Stupid habit. But the tension… As the man named Aris poured energy into Fen, Maddy's own heart ached as though she bore the poison. She'd even scanned herself to make sure she hadn't picked it up.

Nope. Just nerves.

Anna scooted closer until she sat a couple of inches from Fen's feet. Unlike Maddy, she made no attempt to stop biting her nails as she watched his face. Why did Anna care so much? Sure, Fen had saved Maddy's life, but it wasn't only that. The urgency riding Maddy lined her girlfriend's face.

Maybe it was because of the growing energy. Attempting to heal Fen had been a nightmare, a struggle to balance the power rising within her like the tide. She'd almost hurt him with her capricious healing magic more times than she would ever let Vek know. She flicked a glance at the Unseelie prince and shuddered.

Yep. Better he remained oblivious.

Suddenly, Fen sucked in a sharp breath, and his body jerked. Maddy lifted up on her knees and placed her hand on his forehead, not caringif it interfered with Aris's work. But it didn't seem to. As Vek leaned over the other side of the couch, a thunderous expression on his face, Fen's eyes popped open.

"What the hell?" he asked, his gaze darting wildly around the room.

"It's okay," Maddy said.

Vek bent closer. "Calm yourself, Fen."

Fen's breathing slowed, and sense returned to his eyes as he focused on their faces. He blinked up at them in confusion. "How did I end up here?"

"You collapsed in the cave," Vek explained. "Don't you remember? We carried you back."

Sucking in a breath, Fen shoved himself upright, almost butting heads with Maddy and forcing Aris back. Fen ran his hand through his hair and swung his legs over the side of the couch. "The rift. We need to go."

"It's over," Aris said, catching Fen's attention. "We fixed it. Sort of. And best I can tell, the poison is gone from you, too."

Maddy scanned Fen for herself. The dark stain over his heart was gone. His energy levels were low but otherwise normal. But… Her brows lowered as she studied him. She didn't detect anything *wrong*, but she wasn't sure he was quite okay, either. Maybe it was her own faulty healing gift.

More likely it was his lack of energy.

Without thinking, she lifted her wrist. "You need blood."

Fen's eyes widened. He stared at her wrist with an intense, hungry look that made her squirm. And not just because she was afraid of being bitten. "I can't believe you offered," he said roughly.

She wrinkled her nose. "I can't either. You need healing, though."

"I think I'll make it," he said, but a slow smile stretched his mouth.

"He'll take from me," Vek interrupted. His cold gaze caught at her until she jerked her arm away. "Fen needs powerful *royal* blood."

Heat rushed into her cheeks at the implication, but she lifted her chin. "Fine."

Fen scowled. "Dammit, Vek—"

"I believe it is time for our guests to depart," the Unseelie prince announced. "You have my thanks for your assistance, but my nephew needs quiet to recover."

Brows lowering, Fen straightened. "You are not locking me in here again."

"Not for long," Vek conceded. "But I will see you healed."

Despite Fen's protests, Maddy was ushered outside with the others in a shorter amount of time than she would have expected. That was...abrupt. What had bothered Vek so much about Maddy offering blood? He'd been fine, if a bit peeved at having guests, before that. Perhaps he'd been offended by her inferior half-Sidhe genes, but that didn't seem right.

"Not even the Unseelie are usually that inhospitable," Inona mumbled as they approached Maddy's car.

"At least I can give you a lift back to the portal," Maddy offered. Then she counted the number of people and sighed. "In two trips, unless we want to break the law."

Delbin settled his hand on the roof of the car. "Think it'll start? We did see a few vehicles, but there are no guarantees."

"Guess we'll find out."

As Anna slid into the passenger seat, Maddy settled behind the steering wheel. Bracing herself for problems, she slid her key into the ignition and turned. Then she let out a long, relieved breath

when it sputtered to life. She lowered the window and stuck her head outside.

"Who wants to ride first?" she asked.

Aris and Selia exchanged glances before the woman spoke. "You needn't do that. I can transport us by magic since I know my destination."

Maddy's eyebrows rose. "Really?"

"The Sidhe can do such feats, as well," the woman said, a hint of confusion lining her face.

"In the underhill, maybe. There's not enough energy on…" Maddy's words trailed off as her magic stirred inside her. She stifled it again, just as she'd done while attempting to heal Fen, and chuckled uneasily. "There *wasn't* enough energy on Earth. I guess there is now."

Delbin stepped closer to the window. "You have the mirror, right? Call us if there's a problem. No telling what's going on with the electricity out."

"Yes, I do." Maddy smiled at her friend. "And I will."

The four Moranaian elves slipped away with a wave, and Maddy sat in the driveway long enough to watch the woman build a portal beside the house, out of sight of the road. Beside her, Anna gasped. "That's…"

"I know," Maddy said in awe. "I wonder if either of us could learn to do it."

Anna snorted. "You maybe. I don't even know what I am."

"We'll figure it out." As the elves disappeared, the portal winking out behind them, Maddy backed the car out of the driveway and started toward home. She reached across the console and gathered Anna's hand in hers. "I promise."

Though Lyr had sworn that Iren was in his room, Selia still peeked inside before going to her own. She relaxed to see him curled up on the bed, asleep without even getting under the covers, but then she recalled his earlier trick. Just in case, she tiptoed across the floor and did her best to remain quiet as she ducked down to look under the bed. Nothing that she could see.

Quickly, she scanned the room with her magic. No sign of the cloaks or of anyone hiding. And not only was Iren's breathing steady, but his energy was as well. She should've known to check that last time—and would have, had she not been so distracted. On the way out, she placed a charm on the door that would warn her if he left, much as she had used when he was a toddler.

Then she headed for her room. Aris had gone with Ralan through the new portal to retrieve Kezari, and then he planned to join her. For sleep—at least for now. That was all either of them would be able to do until they recovered.

Selia closed the door behind her and leaned against it, staring at the room she'd inhabited for a couple of months now. Only a few days had passed since Aris's return, but it could have been years. Her mind was jumbled from exhaustion, not to mention passing between day and night so often that not even the sun shining through the window entirely convinced her it was still afternoon. Her world had changed until the mundane seemed foreign.

The chime of her mirror distracted her from her wandering thoughts. Selia hurried to her desk and activated the link, ready to speak with whoever needed her so she could get some sleep. She smiled when Niasen's face filled the screen.

"Hello, sister," Selia said.

"Good day." Niasen returned the smile. "I hope you haven't gone to too much trouble trying to track down father."

Selia's stomach dropped as mortification rushed in. She'd forgotten. How many times had she been to Earth in the span of a day without even a thought for her missing father? Her cheeks heated. "I…no."

"He finally contacted me not long ago," Niasen said. If her sister noticed Selia's embarrassment, she was kind enough not to mention it. "He appeared a bit worn down but urged me not to worry."

Worn down? Selia's forehead wrinkled. "Do you think something happened to him?"

Niasen waved her hand. "No, nothing like that. He said there was difficulty with the energy there that caused him problems. He should be fine."

"Yes, I've heard the same." Experienced it, too, but that was a tale she wasn't sure she should share. "I am happy to hear that father contacted you."

Niasen's eyes narrowed. "Are *you* unwell, Selia?"

"Only drained," she answered honestly. "I've spent too much of my energy of late."

"Oh." Niasen's frown deepened, but she didn't push. "I'll leave you to rest, then."

Selia smiled. "Thank you. I'll contact you again soon."

"Of course."

Once her sister's image dropped from the mirror, Selia let her shoulders slump. Then she trudged over to the bed and dropped face-down across the covers. She would rest her eyes for a moment before she changed clothes. Only a moment.

Kezari's steps were slow, but she walked beside Aris into the gate at Braelyn. The shift to her elven form had been sluggish, and she'd thrown the barest covering over her body before they'd followed the prince through the portal. He'd never seen her look so tired, not even after she'd nursed him back to health after rescuing him.

They exited the front door into the late afternoon light. Her face tipped up toward the sky, and she took a deep breath. "Home."

"After you fought so hard to get to Earth, I half expected you to want to stay there," he teased.

Kezari snorted. "No. I wanted to save the planet, not live on it."

"Fair enough." Aris fell silent as they walked, but he couldn't contain the question for long. "What of our link? Once a full moon cycle has passed, I imagine you will wish to be rid of me. Our task is complete, and I can only bind you here when you could roam free."

She halted, staring at him with head tilted. "You have decided to end our bond?"

A few days before, he would have answered yes to that. Not anymore. "I do not wish to. However, I'm not certain how this works. Do you link only for a specific goal?"

"Some do. Others do not." Kezari lifted a shoulder. "I have grown to like you despite your odd ways. You are quite pleasant when you are sane, and your mate and youngling amuse me."

Aris chuckled. Leave it to Kezari to be so blunt. "Then linked we shall stay. I am considering moving from the observation tower, though, to keep a closer eye on said youngling."

"A solid plan," she said. "I believe it safe for me to sleep in my cave now. In fact, I will likely not emerge for several days while I recover."

"You deserve the rest."

Her lips curled up in an almost-elven smile. "We both do."

He wished her well, then watched as she shifted. Experienced now, he gathered his hair firmly behind his head when she lifted her wings and took off, a gale sweeping around her with the motion. A few green and brown strands still ended up across his face, but they were easy enough to push away.

He had a wife to return to—and a great deal of time to make up for.

Epilogue

Selia and Aris wound their way along the garden path, the soft sound of a flute lilting on the chilly air. She leaned into his side, and he wrapped his arm around her shoulders as they paused to watch the *omree* about to perform. Earlier, they'd cheered on Arlyn at the archery competition, and although her student had only placed fourth, Selia was proud. In a few more years, Arlyn would likely win despite her youth.

Selia had never been to such a large autumn festival, and she could now understand why many traveled from smaller estates to attend. Even Kai's half-brother Moren had joined them for a few marks that morning, a tense event since Moren hadn't met Kai's real father, Naomh, before. Kai had walked around looking confounded for a solid mark after his relatives had departed.

Iren shuffled beside them, a slight pout on his face at the proximity he was required to maintain. When the *omree's* song was over, Selia took pity on him and headed toward the tournament field for the sword-fighting competition. The renowned Kerel Liere nai Ebaia would be performing later, anyway, and Selia would far rather see her than anything else. Being at the Myern's estate while the heir to the throne was in residence had its benefits, for it was rare for Lady Kerel to stray far from the palace itself. According to rumor, she hoped to gain a permanent position as Ralan's lead *omree* once his new home was complete.

As they neared the field, they stumbled upon Ralan, Cora, and Eri. The children exchanged excited greetings and roamed over to the side to chatter. Cora smiled pleasantly, but Ralan frowned as he met Selia's gaze.

"Good day, Lady Selia," the prince said.

She exchanged a look with Aris at the stilted, formal words. "Is something wrong?" she asked.

Ralan winced, clearly growing uncomfortable. "I've been meaning to speak with you."

"But?" she asked, her heart pounding in her ears.

It was rarely a good thing when a seer wanted a word—and then delayed.

"I can't stop thinking about what happened. With the children." Was it her imagination, or had his face reddened? "That Iren encouraged Eri in this scheme makes me worry that playing with him increases her natural recklessness."

"Wait a moment." Selia stalked toward Ralan, sudden anger straightening her spine. "Are you suggesting that Iren was to blame? Eri acts on her own more often than not."

This time, there was no mistaking the prince's flush. "True. But I would expect Iren to resist her plans. He is older. I thought… Perhaps it is best that they don't spend as much time together."

"Don't be an ass," Selia snapped.

Her hand went immediately to her mouth as Aris made a choked sound beside her, but she refused to take the words back. She might

have had a similar thought about separating the children when she'd found them in the cave, but that had been in the heat of the moment. No one else would criticize her son so casually.

"Selia," Ralan began.

She didn't give him the chance to finish whatever fool thing he was about to say. "You know as well as I do that Iren wasn't to blame. I am thankful they disobeyed. Both of them. I may not want a repeat, but without their actions, that wall would have shattered before we could get Aris down the fissure. Thousands would have died from the poison."

Unexpectedly, Cora laughed. "Told you."

Ralan's shoulders slumped, and he shoved at the long fall of his black hair. "You're right. But the thought of losing her…"

The anger drained out of Selia at his stark words. "That I understand."

"Thank you." A reluctant smile crossed his lips. "Glad to see you've joined the others in insulting me. I was beginning to think you didn't like me."

"Oh, I did," she said. He lifted his brows. "I do. Your comment about Iren notwithstanding."

Ralan chuckled. "Fair enough. I'll bid you good day, Selia. Enjoy the festival."

Selia shook her head as the prince walked away, his hand around Cora's. Eri waved at Iren and darted after them, and at the sight of the girl, Selia had to admit that she didn't envy Ralan and Cora for having to keep up with her. She wouldn't allow him to insult her child, but she had sympathy aplenty.

Aris settled his hands on Selia's waist and pulled her close. Smiling, she leaned up to kiss the slight cleft in his chin. "This celebration must seem tame after everything that has happened."

He grinned. "Not after seeing you tell off a prince. I'm proud of you."

"Shut up and kiss me," Selia said.

Aris bent down and captured her lips with his. Her heart soared, and in that moment, the past fell away.

Her world was right once more.

Printed in Poland
by Amazon Fulfillment
Poland Sp. z o.o., Wrocław